AVIARY

Maria Dong

First world edition published in Great Britain and the USA in 2026
by Severn House, an imprint of Canongate Books Ltd,
14 High Street, Edinburgh EH1 1TE.

severnhouse.com

Cover and jacket design by dholmesgraphic

British Library Cataloguing-in-Publication Data
A CIP catalogue record for this title is available from the British Library.

ISBN-13: 978-1-4483-1947-3 (cased)
ISBN-13: 978-1-4483-1949-7 (paper)
ISBN-13: 978-1-4483-1948-0 (e-book)

All Severn House titles are printed on acid-free paper.

Typeset by Palimpsest Book Production Ltd., Falkirk, Stirlingshire, Scotland.
Printed and bound in Great Britain by TJ Books, Padstow, Cornwall.

The manufacturer's authorised representative in the EU for product safety is Authorised Rep Compliance Ltd, 71 Lower Baggot Street, Dublin D02 P593 Ireland (arccompliance.com)

Praise for *Liar, Dreamer, Thief*

"Mesmerizing . . . Fans of sharp, inventive fiction will be eager for Dong's next"
Publishers Weekly Starred Review

"Fascinating and psychologically complicated . . . From start to finish, this is a captivating story with dire puzzles that beg to be solved one chapter at a time"
Booklist

"[A] vertiginous debut . . . once the mystery drops into gear, increasingly bonkers twists propel the story to a cogent, poignant close. A rabbit hole worth falling down"
Kirkus Reviews

"This fast-paced, surreal tale will hook from the beginning. A perfect fit for fans of *Gone Girl* and *Girl on the Train*"
Library Journal

"Gorgeously written . . . This brilliant story is unlike anything I've ever read: provocative and unsettling, but grounded by a warm beating heart"
Ashley Winstead, national bestselling author of
This Book Will Bury Me

"A masterful work of psychological suspense"
Ava Reid, internationally bestselling author of
The Wolf and the Woodsman

About the author

Korean American author **Maria Dong** writes genre-bending suspense and is the author of *Liar, Dreamer, Thief*; *Psychopomp*; and *Aviary*. Her short fiction and essays have been published in dozens of magazines and anthologies, including *The Best American Science Fiction and Fantasy*, *Lightspeed*, *Augur*, *Nightmare*, *Khoreo*, *Fantasy*, *Apex*, and *Apparition*, and her story "In the Beginning of Me, I was a Bird" was a finalist for the Theodore Sturgeon Memorial Award.

Maria lives with her partner in southwest Michigan in a centenarian saltbox house that is almost certainly haunted, watching K-dramas and drinking Bell's beer.

www.mariadong.com

For Steve, who loved it first, and for S.E., who loved it last.
Thank you for being my candles against the dark.

There is a legend about Yu-hwa, daughter of god-king Ha-Baek and goddess of willow trees. Like all Korean legends, it has a thousand branching versions, but they all start with the god-king Hae Mo-Su, who sees Yu-hwa and her two sisters playing by the riverside, lusts after them, and formulates a plan. He builds a gorgeous palace and holds a banquet, plies them with alcohol, and blocks the exit, trapping Yu-hwa.

Ha-Baek summons his dragon chariot, rides to Hae Mo-Su's new palace, and challenges him to a duel of transformations. Ha-Baek slips into the water as a carp; Hae Mo-Su becomes an otter and catches him. Ha-Baek turns into a pheasant; Hae Mo-Su plucks him out of the sky as a hawk. In the final round, Hae Mo-Su's wolf runs down Ha-Baek's deer, and Yu-hwa's father has no choice but to concede her hand in marriage. He loads the couple into a leather bag to carry them into the heavens—but the marriage never happens, although the reason depends on your version of the story. Did Yu-hwa escape? Or did Hae Mo-Su wake up inside of the bag and change his mind before stealing Yu-hwa's hairpin and cutting his way out?

Either way, Ha-Baek sees his daughter is now damaged goods. He stretches her lips out until she can't speak and exiles her to the bottom of a pond. Eventually, she is recovered by some fishermen, who cut her lips open and take her to *their* king . . . who promptly falls in love with her and locks her away, until the day that she gives birth to the future ruler of the kingdom of Goguryeo. And it is for this, more than anything else, that she is remembered—as if her status as the mother of someone important makes up for everything that happened to her.

As a child, I used to love Yu-hwa's sacred willow tree, laden with all its meanings. The flexibility of the thin branches is associated with resilience, but willows also represent grace, vitality, protection, healing, and femininity. And to those that stood on the banks of rivers newly thawed by spring, watching as their loved ones departed in boats, they were the ultimate symbols of goodbye. But ever since learning about Yu-hwa, all I can think about is how she must have felt—her disappointment, her anguish, her resignation, her fear.

I've thought long and hard about how to tell you this story. If I gave you the truth—about me and my sister, the house and the cold and the hunger—you'd know, but you wouldn't understand. Every detail—if we labored under a tropical sun or trudged through miles of snow, if we preferred coffee or tea or yerba mate, if we spoke English or Korean or French—every detail that didn't match your own life would become another sandbag against your fear. When you felt safe enough, different enough, *exceptional* enough, you would forget.

Maybe that's the way it's supposed to be. Humanity keeps fairytales alive, even though they're designed for growing out of, for moving past. We say it's for our children, to entertain and teach and warn them, but I think we're all a little afraid that one day we'll awaken in a terrible place full of monsters, being softly enveloped by the dark.

PART I

The Body

Tyger Tyger, burning bright,
In the forests of the night;
What immortal hand or eye,
Could frame thy fearful symmetry?
'The Tyger', William Blake

ONE
Hee-Jin

In the moments before everything is set in motion, I lie on the linoleum, listening for the scrape of police footsteps. My body aches from the day's labor, but I made the mistake of reading the *Chosun Ilbo* before bed, and now I can't sleep.

I close my eyes, and the article is there. The headline is strident, branding the family as *illegal Chinese refugees*. The text weaves the dramatic tale of a woman named Kim Hyeok-Myeong, who claims she escaped from North Korea to China, where she had two children with a Chinese man. According to Chinese law, their children should be Chinese citizens—but local offices wouldn't register them for services unless their mother was arrested for illegal immigration and repatriated to North Korea, which means they didn't attend school.

Weeks ago, a sympathetic neighbor warned Hyeok-Myeong that someone noticed her children's absence and reported it to the government. Unable to bear the idea of being separated, the entire family fled to South Korea in a cramped fishing boat, laying as if in a coffin for three days, the last of their money in a broker's pocket—only to be caught by the South Korean authorities.

Now, the question is what to do with them. South Korea grants automatic citizenship to North Koreans upon arrival, even providing them with a three-month stay at a settlement support center, where they receive education, vocational training, and financial support (and where they are screened to make sure they are not infiltrators or spies). But Hyeok-Myeong has no documents to prove her identity, and she has lived in China a long time. Authorities have not been able to confirm that she really is North Korean and not Chinese, which means that to the South Korean government, her children are also Chinese—and South Korea cannot risk angering its neighbors.

The most likely scenario is that South Korea will wash its hands of the situation and deport the family back to China. China, in an attempt to remain friendly with North Korea, will deport Hyeok-Myeong—and possibly the children, too. Once they arrive in North Korea, they'll be sent to work in a forced labor camp for defectors until they die.

The trap around Hyeok-Myeong is so familiar that although I saw my mother pass, I imagine that she is alive and has written the article to play a cruel trick on me. It's hard to say if she'd do such a thing. I feel like I didn't really know her, and certainly not her past.

Most of the details I have were pieced together by Hee-Young; if my sister thinks there's something under the surface, she *poke, poke, pokes* at the skin until it bleeds. She plied our mother with alcohol, rifled through her scant belongings, tracked down old newspapers, and traveled back to the places we'd shuffled through, trying to arrange the stars of the woman into a constellation she could understand.

First is her birth in rural North Korea. We don't know if her family were farmers or hydroelectric dam engineers, if she had siblings, if they lived by the howling coast. That life ended when she was trafficked into China and sold to a man. Later, when my sister was only months old, my mother somehow smuggled the three of us into South Korea, though my first memories start with what came after: squatting in abandoned warehouses, shacks, and basement apartments. Always feeling cold, or wet, or tired, and never having enough to eat.

After the second time we moved to Seoul, around when Hee-Young mastered hopscotch, we discovered that our mother had become a sex worker. As soon as my sister was old enough, she voiced her distaste, but I understood. All work is work of the body. Sex work meant my mother could make enough for us to survive while also keeping us under her careful gaze. Sex work filled our bellies and put a roof over our heads and a hot floor under our feet—at least some of the time.

Suddenly, we had the basic ingredients for a happy life, but it was too late for my mother. Her trauma had made her short-tempered and afraid. By the light of day, she'd warn us about the police or the government, hungry wolves always ready to deport us the same way they deported the family in the *Ilbo*. But at night, when she tossed and turned, she sometimes moaned, *He is coming*, and I knew she was thinking about the man in China who had once owned her.

(Hee-Young once found an article that listed how many people in various countries would be considered slaves. She'd been so fired up, as if the world was a thing that could be fixed. And despite my dreams about escaping to a place like the United States, I know it holds half a million people in forced labor, everything from house-cleaning and child-care to traveling sales and running cruise ships.)

An aggressive noise in the alley makes my breath catch, until I place it as the slowing whine of a decelerating motorcycle. No doubt a delivery driver, looking for one of the millions of apartments just like mine in my neighborhood on the outskirts of Seoul: a single room crammed between a private English academy and a martial arts studio, a pool hall with blacked-out windows and a neon sign on top.

The motorcycle has triggered something animal in my fear, something that rejects the dark. I drag myself out of bed and fight the urge to sprint, instead taking measured steps to the switch. Light floods the room, bouncing off the peeling wallpaper, the linoleum, the glossy covers of the English-language comic books I dug out of the trash behind a rich neighborhood's international school.

But light is not enough to dispel the cold hollow in my center. I need to eat.

I push the button on the kettle and peel back the top of a plastic cup, exposing yellow noodles, wavy like permed hair. When the water's done, I pour it into the cup, fold down the lid, and warm my hands on top. The ritual steadies me. Ever since I got my current job—nightshift at a hospital laundry under another woman's identity—I've had enough money for food, but all I buy are instant noodles: cheap, filling, savory. I can't stop. I buy at least six packages a day, and after my shift, right before the sun comes up, I remember all the times my stomach has gone empty, and then I make bowl after bowl of noodles. I eat until my gut stretches, until it feels like I'll throw up—

Someone knocks at the back door.

I startle, jostling the container, but there isn't space to worry about the noodles, because the pattern of the knocks has finally entered my brain: three, then two, then one: the thump Hee-Young calls her *finisher.*

My neck tingles. Hee-Young's out of the country, and even if she wasn't, she wouldn't come *here*. The last time I saw her—six months ago?—she'd been preening with the news of her acceptance to a fancy art mentorship program in America. I begged her to forget it. They'd never let her leave South Korea without papers, much less enter America. Furious, she stomped out, slamming the door behind her. And then, a month later, I got a postcard in the mail, the stamp a small American flag, a single line scrawled on the back: *You were wrong.*

So, who just knocked? Police? My landlord? But wouldn't either have come to the front door that empties out onto the main street, instead of the back exit to the alley?

Unsure if I imagined it, I wait. The clock reads a barely perceptible five a.m., the green numbers having faded as they wait for the sun to recharge the panel on the back.

Just as I start to relax, I hear it again. Three knocks, then two—and then a long pause. The silence impales me like a butterfly on a wire.

Finally, there's a low thump.

I don't *want* to crawl up from the floor and answer it, but it's like my mother's ghost is working my nerves and muscles. I cross the linoleum, my slippers going *scuff-scuff*, and then I take a long breath and open the door.

A seated body flops over into my apartment, a woman that lands on her side. Her incredibly muscular, fatless arm is thrown over her face, casting shadows that obscure her identity, but I can make out the gaping hollow underneath her opposite clavicle and a sternum so harshly defined that it looks like a flint-knapped arrowhead. My gaze trails to her filthy hand, which ends in the worst fingernails I've ever seen—jagged and gray, like smoke trapped in a glass, and so opaque that I can't make out the bed from the tip.

I circle around her so that I can see her face. My stomach twists in revulsion. The side of her neck, her cheek, her forehead—they're all covered with inch-long spines, as if someone gutted and flattened a sea urchin and somehow melded it with her skin. Even in the washed-out light of the alley, I can see that some are tufted at the end, like paintbrushes, and they lay angling away from the center of her face like a sunflower's seeds—as if she'd slapped herself with such force that the wind of her hand descending to her cheek had knocked all the spines down, like trees away from the explosion of a bomb.

I squat to see under her arm and my breath catches at the sight of her open eyes. They're as large as 500-won coins, so grotesquely swollen and protruding, they look like they're about to pop out of her face.

But I recognize their color. My sister and I have the same eyes, dark brown that turns amber in the right light. My mother, superstitious as she was, used to say Hee-Young and I shared a soul.

This unblinking, demonic-looking body—it has my eyes.

"Hee-Young," I whisper, and then I start to cry.

TWO
Hee-Jin

I was fifteen when my mother told us about the onggi pot inside her. She lay dying, her face pale, her hair plastered to her forehead, but her gaze carved into me like a knife. "You'll need one, too."

I didn't understand. I knew what onggi were, that the clay "breathed" air in while keeping water out, a perfect environment for fermentation. I'd spied the dark earthenware jars set behind houses in rural areas, lacquered curves that glistened softly under moonlight. Pots big enough to hold a baby, or any other secret that needed keeping.

In the city—in Seoul or Busan or Daegu or any of the other places we'd traversed in our itinerant lives—cramped apartment living meant the onggi's viability as a food storage container had been eclipsed by plastic and refrigerators, though we occasionally spotted one in the windows of stores that promoted traditional, healthy foods and medicine, a throwback to more wholesome times. We rarely had electricity, much less a refrigerator. An onggi would've been useful to us, if we could've carried the massive thing.

My mother always gave the pots a sad smile whenever she saw them. I didn't know why, but I knew not to ask.

At our mother's deathbed pronouncement, Hee-Young, then thirteen, turned toward me and shook her head. "An onggi? She's delirious. No wonder she dragged us all the way out here."

I didn't agree. I understood my mother's frantic relocation. She'd elected to treat life's traumas with a combination of alcohol and drugs. And then, when her liver had failed, she'd brought us to this national park, to a shallow depression in a rock face at the base of a pristine mountain. Don't animals seek out a final resting spot when their time is coming?

Part of me wondered if she'd seen the place before, if it had perhaps provided her shelter from a rainstorm when I was still a toddler, Hee-Young a baby in her arms. If she'd liked it because it reminded her of home, despite the harshness of her life in North Korea. Don't all people grow nostalgic in their final moments?

The moist summer night had clung to us like swamp mud, the air vibrating with buzzing mosquitoes and the croaks of frogs I could hear even over her labored breathing.

She grabbed my hand, then. Squeezed it. "This life is a millstone, Hee-Jin. It will grind you into flour unless you have an onggi: a place inside to put everything you cannot bear. A place where you can breathe, protected against the weather. When this life gives you hardship, let your insides take it apart and break it down until there's nothing left."

"Mother—"

"Hush now, Hee-Jin. The Saja is coming for me."

She smiled blissfully, reaching for someone I could not see, and then she died. In that moment, I got an onggi pot of my own.

My clay pot grew until every feeling, bad or good, was sucked in with less movement than a fish's pond ripple—but now, my emotions claw into me as I drag my sister's deformed body into the apartment, fighting my attempts to shove them down and find the soft place of control I need.

As soon as we escape the frigid March air, Hee-Young's flesh feels warmer and more supple. Hope sparks in my chest that she might still be alive. I detail the favors I'll need to cash in to get a nurse to come by. Surely, the state of her eyes, nails, and skin is from drug use, although I have no idea which drug could cause this. But I can't take her to the hospital to be deported. She'd still end up dead, though far from home, worked until she collapsed in Kaechon or Pukchang camp.

When I try to take her pulse and listen to the silence where her breaths should be, she's again cold to the touch.

My hope fragments. I pass its slivers into my onggi as I close her eyes with my fingers. For a moment, it doesn't look like her lids will stretch far enough—but then they do, and suddenly, there's too much for my onggi pot to contain.

I learned a long time ago how to cry soundlessly, but a keening rises in my chest, desperate to escape. *Hee-Young, how could you?* After everything we survived—our father's absence, our mother's self-destruction, the hunger and the cold, and the constant, constant fear—you gave into your demons?

The government claims there are no drugs in South Korea, but there's plenty if you know where to look, and Hee-Young was exposed from a young age. Before our mother had escaped North Korea, she'd picked up a crystal meth habit. There, it had been offered in some places as casually as tea—a habit that started with high-ranking party officials and spread out through the populace like wildfire.

She never gave meth to Hee-Young, but after she died four years ago, Hee-Young became like a wild horse, bucking the rules that keep us safe. Two years later, at fifteen, she moved out, called herself an *artist*, and started hanging out with rich burnouts: musicians and painters whose families could afford their children's idleness. With her new creative friends came drugs, whatever she could get her hands on.

When she overdosed, they dumped her on my doorstep. On crystal meth or ecstasy, she'd be covered in sweat, her eyes filled with dark voids. On opiates, her lips would be blue, her pupils tiny needlepoints. Sometimes, she barely breathed—but she always had a pulse.

But drugs couldn't settle my sister's heart. After a lifetime of carefully following all the edicts to keep us safe, it was as if her life wasn't worth living if she wasn't *seen*. She chose an ironic, slightly vulgar pseudonym—*Pepper Queen*—and begged any storefront with a wall to exhibit her artwork, right up until her surprise announcement about the mentorship program in America with that philanthropist—*Shep-ed? Shep-ud?*

And for all I'd begged—and commanded, and threatened—her not to go, part of me had been glad. I hoped that this would be the key to her sobriety, even though I knew it wouldn't. The legacy was in her blood, and she didn't have an onggi pot like mine. She kept her feelings right at the surface.

"You stupid *idiot*," I say softly. "Your art is still up in that coffee-shop."

It was the only place I knew of that had agreed to show her pieces. I went to check it out, despite my fear of how starkly I stood out against the backdrop of Apgujeong Rodeo Street, the shining shop fronts with their seamless walls of glass, the candy-colored boutiques and cafes.

And when I saw all the little slips of pastel and jewel-toned paper, cut and folded into lifelike vistas I recognized from our itinerant childhoods?

The octagonal pavilion at the end of the Bugak Skyway, Seoul's crush of buildings below slowly falling into dusk.

The winding roads of Mount Jungmi as they cut through green hills so round and fluffy they look like sheep.

A worm's-eye view of the Milky Way, encircled by the rim of the Beotgogae Tunnel—

As my gaze trailed over her art, I smelled the exhaust of cars and buses and barges, felt the ache in my legs and the burn in my tired eyes as the three of us ventured yet again toward a place we hoped would be a safe haven.

Afterwards, my onggi failed me. I came back to this apartment and wept. For the first time, I understood art, but I was too ashamed to tell her. And now, it's too late.

She only left six months ago. It took six months to transform her from her vibrant, healthy, beautiful self . . . to this.

Had she been in Korea this whole time, doing drugs and getting sicker and sicker? But she'd sent that postcard—unless that had been a lie? If so, what was the point of the gloating note, of faking the stamp? Was it just to get back at me, because of what I'd said?

I close my eyes and, for the first time in a long time, I am so, so sorry.

THREE
Hee-Jin

It's only after Hee-Young's body is inside that I realize I don't know what to do next.

If she were anybody else—if *I* were anybody else—I'd call the police and let them know that someone had overdosed outside my apartment. Once the investigation had resolved, she'd be taken away to be cremated. There'd be a funeral with incense and a big picture of her shrouded in white flowers. A keening, hanbok-clad mother so distraught she could no longer stand, a stoic father with a mourning ribbon pinned to his chest. There'd be an update to our family register, an X to mark the deceased.

But Hee-Young and I, we are who we are. And instead of those things, I have only what I learned from my mother—that there is no such thing as *should*. That if there is a time for feelings, it's later, when the emergency has passed.

I close my eyes and name each emotion; with names, they're easier to put away. *Anger. Sadness. Grief.* Once I've identified them all, I move instead to the dangers.

In this moment, my sister's body is benign, but that's changing. Soon, colonies of bacteria will digest her intestines. Her flesh will expand, her abdomen will rupture. And when that happens, when the police follow the smell to this apartment, my sister—and me?

My life will be over. By killing herself, my sister has killed me, too.

The only way to avoid that fate is for one of us to disappear. I can get rid of her body. Or I can grab the meager savings I've stuffed into a hole in the drywall and take a night bus to Busan or Daegu. I'll spend years establishing myself the way I did here: finding the people who are safe to bribe, the places that won't look too closely at my fake ID. It will be difficult and terrifying, but if I'm lucky, I'll be able to afford noodles again.

I try to think of a better option, one that doesn't increase my risk of being discovered, but I can't. My knees give out and I compress in on myself like a collapsing bridge. I told myself I just wanted her to be safe, that the arguments and rules were me being a good sister, but Hee-Young had been like a soft, sweet plum that somehow burned for a just world, and I had hated her for it.

I approach her again, taking her in as if for the first time—her filthy hair and clothes, the corded muscles of her thin arms, the jutting protrusion of her collarbones, the spines on her face I can't begin to understand. I can almost taste her smell: sweat and vomit, chemicals and grease.

"What should I do, Hee-Young-ah? Which way is the smartest?"

No matter what I decide, she'll be found eventually. And I can't let it be like this.

FOUR
Hee-Jin

I turn the water on, let it get hot. Stage towels, shampoo, a washcloth. Eventually, I have to admit I'm just buying time.

She feels heavier and stiffer than before. As I drag her along, the rubber sole of her single shoe grinds against the floor, pulling her to one side like a shopping cart with a bad wheel. Eventually, I maneuver her back against one of the tiled walls, her naked toes pointing at the drain in the floor. Steam fills the room and collects in rivulets down the walls.

I don't want to undress her, but I do, balling up her clothes into a wet heap by the door.

I soap her body, her hair. The suds change from white to rust, exposing topography I never would've imagined: a long, deep cut only barely healed over, a constellation of scabs. I find ovoid fingerprint bruises on her forearm: one on its soft underbelly, and four on the opposite side, spanning the wadded root of the muscles that lift the fingers. Her hair comes away in clumps. On her belly and her back, I find more of the spines, though these are each as long as my finger.

Anger seizes me in a hot wave. She must've seen her body changing, must've known the drugs were having this effect. I attack the spines on her belly with a scrubbing cloth. To my surprise, one pulls slightly away from her skin.

I bite my lip, grab it with my fingertips, and tug. There is a moment of resistance, but then it slides out, leaving behind a small, red hole. After a few seconds, a bead of fluid squeezes out—not red, but milky white. *Lymph*? Some sign of infection?

Or maybe she was attacked. Could someone have stuck these spines into her like she was an art piece, and *injected* her with this fluid? Or did she do this to herself?

It takes me twenty careful minutes to pull out the rest of the spines. A few of them, the biggest ones, are different from the others, so light they feel almost hollow. One of them even crumbles apart in my hand, revealing a tuft of material like the white fluff of a dried cattail. Something to hold the fluid, perhaps, although it's completely dry.

When I'm done removing them all, her face, chest, and back are so full of holes, they look like kitchen sponges covered in a pearlescent dish soap. I hold her arms up as I move the sprayerhead up and down, trying to get all the suds and the fluid. Each time she slumps forward, I push her against the wall, but after five attempts, ten, I can feel a torrent of emotions rising inside of me: frustration, grief, fear.

It's just a doll.

The thought spreads cool relief through my veins.

My mother taught us how to do this in a suburb outside of Daegu. In the summer, the city's location in a geographic basin traps the heat of its two and a half million people, but our mother had brought us for apple season. The farmers liked her because she spoke fluent Korean, and the Thai people she worked alongside knew better than to ask questions. But that year, she'd found a small farm way outside the main city, owned by an ancient woman whose husband's passing had left her in a bind.

Her misfortune was our goldmine. My mother chopped wood, fixed doors, and tended to the vegetable patch. My sister and I picked apples and chased chickens for eggs. This was back when money was tightest, and it was the first time we'd had a room of our own, a door to shut.

Until the old woman disappeared. After a few days, we noticed a strange smell emanating from her room. Hee-Young and I snuck in and found her on the floor, her skin mottled, one hand over her chest.

Hee-Young and I didn't want to leave our warm home full of apples. Our mother had to beat us to get us moving. We took a bus from Daegu to Seoul, the two of us crying the whole time.

That was when my mother started sex work. A few days later, we rented a room, one already furnished with a square table and a mattress on the floor. We had shelter, but food was still tight, and we often complained about being hungry.

And that's when she gave us the lesson. It started by kneeling in front of the low table, our palms on the red lacquer. *The table is hot*, she said, and we laughed.

But she shook her head. *You will sit here until you feel it. Now, say it. The table is hot.*

I said it once, and then again, and still she refused to let me leave. My young hips and knees and back all ached. Over and over, I repeated it—*the table is hot, the table is hot*—until I lost all sense of time. My belly grumbled. My throat burned with thirst. We knelt past sunset, past when stars swam around in the dark each time I blinked. *The table is hot—*

And then a flame seared through my hands. I jerked them away, shocked to find my palms both stained with red. When I looked at the surface of the table, I discovered two spread-fingered smudges in the lacquer. Somehow, my sweat and the warmth of my hands had softened it, changed it into something else.

This will be the most important thing you ever learn from me, Hee-Jin. If you can control the truth, you'll always come out the winner.

She told me I could leave and get some water. Hee-Young stared daggers at me, though there'd been more than a little respect in those amber-tinged eyes.

The table is hot.

It's just a doll.

I repeat my mantra until the water runs clear, and then I shut off the sprayer and pat her down until she's dry.

FIVE
Hee-Jin

I almost dress Hee-Young in my own clothes before realizing the mistake. Can police pull my DNA off them, even freshly washed?

My mother's stern practicality echoes in my ear: *Put her in her old clothes. Don't touch anything.* But this will be the outfit my sister is cremated in. She deserves better than smelling like a rusty pail of vomit.

I scoop up her things, dump them on the tile by the drain, next to the little pile of spines, and grab the sprayer. I start with her top: a slouchy mauve sweater with fake mother of pearl buttons. Not my sister's style. She must've stolen it or recovered it from a garbage can.

I pinch a corner and hold it away from my body to spray it down. Something flutters, tickling, across my fingers: an insect. I jerk my hand, sending it flying into the wall. It lands on its back on the floor of the shower and flexes its legs weakly a few times before it stops moving. Up close, I'm not sure I've ever seen one like it before: round-bodied and dark brown, it looks like a bedbug, though it has eight legs instead of six.

Disgusting. And—

My attention is caught by a familiar blue booklet, face-down on the damp drain. It must've fallen out of her pocket when I reacted to the bug. A few inches of white paper stick out as if she marked a page.

I squat and collect the booklet; it feels thick from the paper jammed inside. On the front, two blocks of embossed gold text frame a diagram of an eagle and shield. I slowly parse my way through the English letters:

PASSPORT
United States of America

My hands shake as I lift the front cover. I freeze at a glossy photograph a bit larger than a Go-Stop card. It's my sister's face.

Our family name, *Song*, is printed in English letters at the top of the page. *Hee-Young* on the line below.

In the blank for nationality, it says, in all caps: UNITED STATES OF AMERICA.

My head swims. *There's no chance this passport is real.* Our mother kept our father secret, but there's no way either of us legally qualify for an American passport, and the father listed here—*Alex Pastukhov*—it sounds made up.

Curiously, the space next to "mother's name" is blank. And this passport is new, issued seven months ago, right before she left. My sister's birth date is wrong—June 25th, 2003—which would make her nineteen and not seventeen, sheep instead of rooster. I'm sure, because *I* was born in 2003.

On the next page are four dated stamps: leaving Korea, entering America, leaving America—and then her return to South Korea on March 22nd.

My face goes numb. Is it possible it worked? How did she find a fake good enough to fool immigration?

And March 22nd? That would mean she's been back less than a week. But the state of her body, her clothes—she looks like she's been using heavily for *months*. Would they let her on a plane like this? But why fake the stamps? Why forge documentation of a fake journey to the United States?

I start to pull out the folded paper inside the passport, but as it shifts, something brightly colored falls out and expands explosively like a popcorn kernel. I barely manage to catch it before it lands on the wet tile.

It's not until it's right side up that I make sense of the clever angles, the cuts and folds. Although my sister's one semi-exhibition was of paper-art landscapes, she started with smaller pursuits: miniature animals, like the small paper owl I now hold.

Our mother hated owls, both for what they were—powerful fliers, vicious killers, apt hunters—and for what they symbolized. With their all-seeing eyes, owls can mean wisdom or luck, or they can be messengers of the spirit realm—but the night birds are also the reincarnation of lost souls, and beacons of family strife and neglect. If your mother-in-law starves you to death, or if you attempt to rape the young goddess Jacheongbi by the side of the river, and she kills you by shoving a tree branch through your ear? Either way, you become an owl.

Despite how precious this paper bird is, I want to tear it up. It feels too ominous—but destroying it is sacrilege. It's a piece of Hee-Young, and the work is exquisite. It must've taken her weeks to carve and fold the wing feathers, the expressive face. She even engineered storing it flat, inside the pages of her passport, only calling it to life once the pressure of the cover was released.

I study it until I understand how. Then, I slip it back into the passport and pull out the piece of white paper. It's actually two stacked sheets, folded into quarters. I catch a whiff of oranges, sweet and sun warmed. They send me backwards through time until hot rays beat down on my bare shoulders and the air rings with her high-pitched giggles. Younger versions of us chase each other through green, reaching branches.

December in Jeju, picking oranges.

Hee-Young always smelled vaguely of citrus. A year ago, I would've noticed the absence of the scent on her body, although maybe it was just overpowered by the filth.

And the papers?

The first sheet is in her handwriting, columns of neat scrawls. Each grouping of random symbols and letters appears to be composed of four smaller ones, separated by slashes. I study the first: 十二/二十三/ㄱㅁ/ㅅㅎ.

The first two groupings are old-fashioned Sino-Korean numbers—*twelve* and *twenty-three*—though I don't know why she wouldn't just use "12" and "23".

The second two groups *are* Hangeul, though they're just random strings of consonant sounds, as if she'd written *G M / S H*.

Over and over, she's clumped together groups of four—two Sino-Korean number characters, two pairs of single Hangeul consonants.

After a minute, I study the other sheet. This one, too, feels random—three letter codes in English, like *ICN* and *ORD* and *PIT*, and durations (*fifteen hours, thirty minutes*) and even dates. One of which is March 28th. Today.

A shiver passes down my back as I piece everything together. I suddenly can't breathe.

It's a plane ticket. In my sister's name. To somewhere called Pittsburgh.

And it leaves in six hours.

SIX
Hee-Jin

A secret my mother taught me: there's never time to feel grief. You don't send feelings into the pot to deal with them later.

You send them there to die.

An hour after finding the passport, the bathroom has dried, the air chilling as the moist heat evaporated.

I tell myself I don't understand, but it's a lie. In some twisted way, finding a plane ticket in Hee-Young's things makes sense, because even though Hee-Young loves—

(loved)

—old folktales—the traditional ones that start with *back in the days when tigers smoked tobacco pipes* and end in just deserts, suffering, and grief—she *believed* in fairytales: the saccharine Disney stories that always begin *once upon a time.*

The question is, of course, which is right? Did I just find the key to sneaking my way into the American dream? Or am I in a folktale like Hee-Young's favorite, about a poor blind man named Shim Hakkyu?

In the story, Shim Hakkyu hears a voice from the heavens guaranteeing the Buddha will restore his sight if he offers three hundred sacks of rice at a temple as tribute, but he has no rice or money. He does, however, have a daughter, Shim Cheong, whose dead mother appears to her in a dream with instructions to go down to the harbor and find a merchant seeking a young maiden. If Shim Cheong leaves with the man, her father will get the rice he needs.

Shim Cheong obeys, only to discover that she's destined to be a sacrifice to the Dragon King of the East Sea. They dress her in bridal colors and bind her hands and feet together, and she leaps into the waves.

In this moment, holding this passport and this plane ticket, all I can think about is Shim Cheong, about how a girl and the ghost of her mother manifested three hundred sacks of rice out of thin air. Every time I look down at the leathery blue cover, every time I unfold the ticket and check the date, it feels like I've plunged into the sea.

I should just burn all of it—the passport, the ticket, the little paper owl. I'm not as superstitious as my mother was, especially toward the end, when liver disease was digesting her from the inside and the only semblance of control she had left was in clutching desperately at a few half-remembered folk traditions—but my sister didn't pass in her bed with a smile on her face. Bad luck and ghosts follow objects like these. Better to burn them and flee, maybe back to Daegu, find a spot an hour from the city picking cabbages or helping someone tend pigs.

But the ticket *could* be real. And a good passport, even a fake, could be enough to fool the authorities, to establish a new identity. It's not like Hee-Young will contest it later. In the end of some versions of Shim Cheong's story, she becomes a queen.

I'm holding a *new life* in my hand. One with a job and apartment that are both above board. One where I could learn to drive, attend school. In an emergency, I could use a credit card, the hospital, the police. I could make friends, could let someone really know me. I could get married and start a family; after a few generations, it would be as if Song Hee-Jin had never existed at all.

No more rules to keep me safe. Deep inside, I feel the pot overflow, flooding me with the aching of a womb.

There are a thousand ways for this to go wrong, to end up in a prison or a work camp—but it's also the first time I've ever seen a way out.

And if anybody can do this—why not me? Am I not my mother's daughter, with the legacy of her itinerant blood? I know how to travel light, to disappear, to start again. I know how to keep a secret.

I'll need a bag. Some clothes, the cash from the wall—though I'll need to exchange it into dollars, and not in Korea, where it could be caught on bank cameras and later linked to Hee-Young's body. I need to leave anything that could connect me to this place:

fake documents, phone, keys. And I should hurry: it's five hours until the departure time, but I've seen enough movies to know that you're supposed to be early for an international flight.

I turn, Hee-Young's body catching my eye, and the train of my ambition screeches to a halt.

Can I really leave her like this? Wet, naked, and alone, no offerings of any kind? My mother would say that Hee-Young will become a ghost.

"I don't believe in ghosts." I say it once, twice, but some part of me is still not sure—because sometimes, an inert lacquer under your palms can sear your flesh by the force of belief alone. And the last time I saw my sister, she'd been wearing a slightly rumpled linen summer suit, white like those terrible hospital sheets. I didn't have to ask to know it was stolen. Thinking of it now, it makes my skin crawl—it's too like a traditional hemp funeral shroud.

I don't know what to do for her. I've spent my whole life living quietly, living *apart*. I've never been to a funeral. I feel like planning them must be a whole career, because the grieving can't think straight—at least, I can't. All I can remember is my mother's insistence that people have to go on their final journey with three spoonfuls of rice, or they won't have anything to eat in the afterlife—an old practice that I'm not sure if people even do anymore.

But I can't pour dry rice down Hee-Young's throat. If I leave her in my bed, the landlady will find her eventually. We look enough alike that Hee-Young might get mistaken for me, but only if there's nothing suspicious to make the authorities look closer.

Can we really switch lives?

The table is hot.

And suddenly, I am in motion. I haul her body to my bed. I grab my stash of gold fifty-thousand-won notes, a black plastic bag from the GS25 mart on the corner, a few nondescript outfits: tee shirts, jersey shorts, jeans. I take Hee-Young's paper owl, retrieve her cheap tin ring with a green stone from a drawer. I don't know why I've kept it, this ring. Maybe I just wanted the reminder of when we were young, when Hee-Young didn't seem hell-bent on hating me.

I hesitate when I find the iridescent sheath we'd secretly called the *beetle dress* folded at the bottom of one of my drawers. My mother had been saving the dress for the day she had a client that wanted more than a quick lay on a mattress.

She must've known it was impossible—being that close to someone would've been dangerous for all three of us. I should've burned it long ago, but I've loved it ever since I was a little girl.

I throw the dress in my plastic bag. I wipe down everything I can to disturb fingerprints, plug in the cell phone, and leave my apartment keys on the counter. I arrange my wallet and my fake ID with the name Kwak Eun-Ah on the nightstand with a few coins, so that it looks like Hee-Young carelessly tossed everything before crawling into bed.

It's not until the cool metal of the doorknob is under my hand that my body refuses to move. It's Hee-Young: I still can't leave her like this.

Three tablespoons of rice is too much, but a single grain would go unnoticed.

I grab one out of the rice bin, cradle her head, and open her lips—

A cloudy white liquid geysers out of her throat and into my face. I double over coughing as the smell and taste hit me: sweet and complex, like a mixture of fruit and botanicals, though there's a fermented tang to it that makes my stomach clench. I scrabble backwards while wiping my eyes. Without the support of my hand, her head has fallen sideways, ear to the floor.

My heart still hammering, I get down on my knees and try to look into her mouth, but at first, I don't understand what I see: a dark disc, shimmering wetly with white fluid, something circular and clear in the center.

And then I put it together. My sister's teeth are all missing, though I see no sign of a wound or extraction. Just soft, seamless dark gums that are the same brilliant blue-black as the rest of her mouth. And down her throat, floating in the middle of all that dark, is a round object the size of a coin.

My hand trembles. I reach forward and fish out a small, hard ring, just large enough to fit on my left thumb, crusty with what looks like ink. I wash it in the sink, soaping and rubbing until bubbles form in vibrant ocean blue.

I rinse them off to reveal transparent plastic. Suspended inside the ring's hard material are wispy fibers that have been arranged into a miniature display of grass and flowers, ferns and vines, as if it was a tiny terrarium. The fibers are different sepia shades—from wheat-gold to copper-brown, some so dark they're almost black.

I feel like Hee-Young made it—but why was it in her mouth? And why were her mouth and throat so dark in the first place, as if she'd swallowed ink?

I lean back onto my heels and close my eyes. Despite all the times I've seen her after an overdose, I've never seen anything like this.

It doesn't matter, a greedy voice whispers in the back of my mind. And I feel guilty, but I can feel the clock ticking, my chance of escape slipping away.

I press the grain of rice between her lips and say a prayer for my little sister—paper artist, cat lover, shoplifter, survivor. I kiss her forehead and each of her hands, and then I step out the back door to reveal a purple morning sky.

SEVEN
Hee-Jin

I put on a mask, steal down the alley, and turn onto the main road. The air suddenly roars with morning traffic, that background hum I never notice until it grows loud enough to impede my thoughts. Dawn has broken, and it's oddly warm for late March, enough that my underarms prickle with sweat. Though the pool hall above my apartment will still be empty for several hours, students rush into the taekwondo studio for morning classes, white uniforms peeking out of bags and slung over shoulders. The English academy won't fill up until after school, the drone of their lessons drifting through our thin walls.

I keep my steps carefully nonchalant before realizing my mistake. The pace is a bit slower here in outer Siheung, past where Seoul's borders meet the massive suburb cities, but everybody still walks fast, unless they're on their phone—

My phone. I stumble, but instinct pushes me back into motion.

How could I have been so stupid? I left it behind so I couldn't be tracked—but my postage-stamp-sized T-Money card was attached to it, dangling off one corner on a small elastic band. I'll need a new one for any public transit—

I grind the heels of my palms against my eyes. This, *this* is exactly what my mother's careful rules were designed to safeguard against. A single rash moment in which I stepped out of my trusted routines, and I've opened myself up to a world of dangers.

If I'm going to take a bus, I'll need a new card, which means going into a store where I could be recorded, or being seen by a clerk that might remember me. I could hail a cab, but that means someone studying me in the rear-view mirror, and cabs are expensive enough that I've never taken one before. I might accidentally do something odd that imprints myself on the driver's memory.

It's like my brains have turned into shabu-shabu: a hotpot boiling over with worries and possible missteps. And then the storm shifts to Hee-Young, her love of tiny plastic kegs of banana milk, her claims to prefer Cass beer over Hite.

Where I'm going, there will be no banana milk, no Cass, no Hite, nothing familiar, I won't know what to do—

You can't know everything. Just make a decision. My mother's voice, so clear, it's as if her spirit speaks in my ear. The blur of the traffic around me slows back into individual cars, light glinting off hoods and windshields as a decision wobbles in my brain like the purple neon light of the pool hall. I'll buy another transit card, because I have no other choice. And then, I'll take the subway. It's fast, there's no driver, and it will take me straight to the airport, which means no asking people for directions.

As my pulse slows, I shiver at how close I was to losing my head. I forgot to push my feelings into the pot, and it turned me into a mess. If I'm going to be successful in my new life, I need to be more careful.

I enter a convenience store to buy another transit card, careful to keep my eyes away from the watchful gaze of security cameras. The cashier is a tired kid, and probably a lifer—I can tell he's from the kind of family that doesn't have the money needed to pay for private lessons or tutors. He's watching *Sweet Home* on the small television on the counter, and he doesn't glance away during the entire transaction.

I hustle to the bus stop that will take me to the subway, and a green bus pulls up almost as soon as I arrive. It's full, so I wedge myself into a gap and grab one of the overhead rings. The bus lurches forward, the driver jerkier than most, but as I clench the ring, the hair on the back of my neck stands up. I can feel someone's gaze boring into my shoulder blades.

I turn and look, but no one is watching.

The feeling passes. I stare out the window at the buildings flying by—square, blocky villas, signs for cheap student boarding rooms and luxury officetels, a porridge shop, an aesthetician. My suburb isn't like downtown Seoul, with eight lanes of traffic and skyscraper buildings. Though this particular neighborhood is a bit run-down, it's cozy enough.

A nervous chill twists in my gut. Will I miss this place, as cruel as it is?

I never thought I'd be the kind of person to get homesick. My whole childhood was spent navigating the peninsula, steady rumbles and diesel fumes in the middle of the night. Sometimes, it was because some neighbor had figured out what my mother did and run us out. Other times, my mother had seen some innocuous clue—a passerby whose glance was a bit too long, a rock by the front door that had been disturbed—and been seized with fear that the man she'd fled had found her. We were always running then, as if from some slow-moving but determined predator that could track us by scent alone.

The bus lurches, and my thoughts return to Hee-Young. Of a bus trip that brought us to that farm outside of Daegu. We were so small, my mother had hauled us each up by an arm to summit the massive steps, their non-slip edges as sharp as teeth. I banged my shins more than once, hadn't realized until we were seated that there was a thin slash of dark blood leaking out of my left leg. The nauseating fumes had smelled chemical and hot, though the rolling motion and my mother's hand on my hair had eventually lulled me to sleep.

Had there been a loudspeaker announcing stations, the way there is now, each overlay introduced with a pleasant, friendly chime? I would live in that sound if I could. Would be anywhere but—

Someone pinches my ass. There's just enough space to turn, to come face to face with the man and his leer. His hand is down at his thigh, but his intense stare confirms that the pressure I felt was his fingers.

If one of the other passengers saw what happened, they say nothing.

I shove my way down the aisle, toward the back, to take residence in front of an old woman napping on a seat, a silk-tied bundle in her lap. He follows me—tentatively at first, and then more brazenly, as if we are playing some horrible game. I close my eyes as he approaches. I want to cry out—*Pervert! Stop it, pervert!*—but I can't draw attention to myself. And it's like he knows that, like he's spotted me in the herd and realized I was the sickly one to cull.

I move a few more times before giving up. The rest of the ride, I pretend I can't feel the little nips of his hands on my ass, the hard lump against the back of my thigh.

Over and over, I repeat to myself, like a mantra: *Soon, I will be somewhere else. Soon, I won't have to hide.*

I ride the bus to the nearest subway stop, Oido station. Nervousness flutters in my breast as I descend into the earth, but I've learned my lesson. I push it into my pot.

At the bottom of the stairs, I find a map. I check my surroundings and trace my way to the airport.

The route couldn't be easier. Oido station is on the yellow Suin-Bundang commuter rail line. All that stands between me and Incheon International Airport is two transfers, and one of them at the very end of line, where everybody will be forced to disembark. I could do this in my sleep.

An hour later, I get off at Gyeyang and climb the stairs from the subway to the AREX rail ticket kiosk in preparation for the final leg of my trip. My eyes ache. In the forty minutes since transferring at Woninjae, I've sunk into exhaustion, but any attempt at nodding off just results in me startling awake with my heart pounding, barely able to breathe, the image of my sister's body floating in the forefront of my mind.

As I ascend, I'm seized by a storm of doubts. *Will this passport really be enough to fool the authorities?* I jam my hands into my pockets so nobody will see me clench them into fists. By the time I crest the top step, I have to double over and gasp, my mask fluttering against my face, my liver turned to ice.

This is crazy. You'll never make it.

The urge to flee builds in my chest. I turn back, toward the subway car I exited, the car that for some reason still has not left—

My stomach drops. Hee-Young stands in the car, framed by the open door. Her face is white, as if she's painted it with powder, and she's wearing the linen summer suit she had on when I saw her last, the day she came into my apartment waving a thick stack of acceptance papers from the mentorship program. In the middle of our screaming argument, I'd tried to snatch them out of her hand, and she'd slapped me across the face.

Now, though, there's no scowl, no flush of anger in her cheeks. Her hair is coiled around her head—*dark brown, she stopped dying it darker after our mother died, stopped trying to hide anything that made her different*—

She smiles, a toothless flash of dark blue.

After a moment, the doors to the subway car finally hiss shut, blocking her from my view and breaking whatever spell held me in my spot. Finally, finally, I find my legs and start to descend the stairs again, picking up speed as I stumble down—

But the car rumbles away, taking Hee-Young with it. When I can't see it any longer, I flee up the stairs, into one of the bathroom stalls. I rock back and forth, my arms wrapped across my chest.

I realize that I've been clutching something hard this whole time. I open my palm, exposing the reddened grooves left by my fingernails—and drifting over them, like a moon over waves, is the ring I found in Hee-Young's throat.

When did I grab it? When I shoved my hands into my pocket, before I saw her—or after, as I was dashing up the stairs?

My stomach turns. I know what my mother would say. She believed in ghosts, including the ones whose essences were tied to an object from their lives, something they valued, cherished, or hated.

I don't know what this ring meant to Hee-Young, this round trinket of resin and fibers—and I don't believe in ghosts. My vision of her was a manifestation of my guilt, my grief.

But the longer I stare at the ring, the more sinister it seems—as if it could bend light into its center, mire it in the gold-copper-black fiber flowers trapped within, so that nothing good could ever escape. Maybe the *ring* sucked the life out of Hee-Young. Maybe it's sucking the life out of me now.

This is crazy. I'm being crazy. And even if that's right—even if I'm having some sort of breakdown, even if *none* of this is happening, and I'm actually unconscious on the ground next to Hee-Young's body, the truth is this: I don't want to carry this ring. I don't want it following me into my new, free life.

I look around the stall for somewhere to stash it. I find the bin for tampons and sanitary napkins, the toilet paper roll, the purse hook. But as much as I don't want to keep the ring, I also can't toss it out like trash. I have to find somewhere to leave it, as if for safe keeping, though I never intend to come back to this place.

Maybe there are lockers upstairs. I could put it in one of those.

My emotions, good and bad, slide into the jar. The body they abandon feels stiff but functional, like a jointed wooden marionette. I exit the bathroom stall, splash water on my face and compose my hair, and then I climb the stairs to the ticket kiosk. On the other side of the room, I see a small bay of automated lockers, right next to a boxy green display booth for the station Healthcare Center, featuring a scale and blood pressure cuff.

But, despite my luck, I'm suddenly unsure. I can't rent a locker indefinitely. At some point, the locker will expire, and some poor sanitation worker will come and empty the contents.

A shudder runs down my spine. *Nobody* can ever wear Hee-Young's ring. I turn back, toward the entrance to the airport rail line, and the healthcare display catches my eye again. The booth is in the corner, wedged between the lockers and an information kiosk—but there's a small gap between its back and the wall.

I walk toward it and pretend to read the instructions for the blood pressure cuff. I look over my shoulder—though there's a woman in the information kiosk, she's helping a customer. Neither is looking at me.

My heart hammers, but I yawn, stretch my arms up, and flick my wrist to toss the ring. It drops neatly into the space between the booth and the wall. A few people turn at the sudden noise it makes when it hits the floor, but I'm already walking away.

EIGHT
Hee-Jin

The next hours are like alternating bands of light and shadow: frantic bursts of movement, followed by tense, exhausted waiting. For the cost of two gas station sandwiches, I ride the tram across the blue sea to Incheon International and, for just a moment, all my horrors fall away.

Finally, somehow, I reach the gate, which is next to a store with an English name: The Road Less Taken. Glancing in, a shiny white passport cover with pink polka dots catches my eye. I hesitate, but I buy it. Stripped of its gravitas, the passport paradoxically feels less eye-catching, easier to keep safe.

And then I sit, waiting for my turn, sure that I will be detained at any moment—but somehow, I make it onto the plane.

I almost pee myself when it takes off—the sharp, crisp transmissions bookended by static, the way the floor under me shakes, like a tropical storm. Far beneath me, Korea shrinks and turns to clouds.

A few hours after sunset, they dim all the lights except the little ones on the sides of the aisle. The day catches up with me, sliding me into sleep.

Of course, I dream about Hee-Young. I watch us play in a field that never existed, the green stone of her tin costume ring winking in the sun. And then, I'm awoken by a soft ding and the captain's announcement—in English, then in Korean—to discover that I've been crying in my sleep. When I brush the tears away, they leave an oily residue on my fingertips, one tinged with the sheen of a pearl.

"Miss?"

I look up. There's a flight attendant, handing me a form.

I guess at the answers and sign Hee-Young's name before realizing an English form probably needs an English signature, but the attendant whisks it away before I can correct it.

Next comes immigration. My heart races as one of the airport workers peeks inside my passport and points to a different line, until I'm standing in front of a gruff, uniformed white man with bags under his eyes. At the rain-like patter of his rapid questions, my fear condenses into a stone in my chest.

If listening is hard, answering is harder. Hee-Young and I never attended school, but when I was eight or nine, we snuck into a movie theater to watch an American comedy about a police officer and a criminal who worked together to protect a small boy from thugs. As soon as it started, I realized there was a white family in the row in front of us, blonde heads all lined up like dandelion puffballs. They guffawed at things that weren't funny and failed to laugh at some of the best jokes.

Later, Hee-Young and I realized the dialogue and the subtitles weren't the same and decided to learn English. We studied old textbooks and watched instructional videos in PC bangs, paying for the computer time with change stolen from our mother's purse. It became an obsession: movies, music, comic books, advertisements on YouTube. For years, if I wasn't working, consuming English media was how I spent my time, though by then, my desire had shifted from movies into something more enticing: if I learned English, then one day, I could escape to America. When I moved into my apartment, I spent hours eavesdropping on the English school's lessons through our shared wall.

It's no use wanting something you cannot have, so I dug my fantasy a deep trench and covered it with cold soil—until now, in this narrow tunnel of a room where the floors look both dirty and glistening, where every angle is hard, and every face exhausted.

Now, I remember the *wanting*.

A sick thought trickles cold ripples into my stomach: am I responsible for this? Did something I said in my last fight with Hee-Young *push* her toward her terrible end, so that I might have this opportunity?

And did she face the same dilemma that I face now? All these years, I'd been training my ear; I hadn't realized I'd also have to *speak*. Why did I never practice this? Why was it that even in my daydreams—at least, until I put them in my pot—I was silent, like a watchful ghost?

I try to answer the immigration officer's questions, but the foreign words stick in my mouth. With each noun I can't produce, each verb pattern I can't conjugate, I struggle harder, until I'm on the brink of crying.

"It's OK," he finally says, his face relaxing—not into kindness so much as resignation. "Go ahead, Miss Song. And welcome home. Your transfer is that way."

As I leave his line, my whole body unclenches like a cramp—until his words catch up with me: *Your transfer.*

I know now that I really *was* like a ghost: shocked, unable to think and feel. Otherwise, I would've slipped away there, secreted myself into Chicago like a flea, instead of boarding the next flight to Pittsburgh—but I didn't. And it wasn't until I exited and followed the crowd through the tunnel-like hallways, arrows and text sprayed all over as if we were on a busy city street, that I thought to regret that choice.

Eventually, I emerge through a final, frosted gate. I'm again in an airport, though all the signs are now only in English. Just like before, crowds bustle around like schools of multi-colored fish, clumping together at different anchor points—restaurants, charging stations, bathroom entrances—only to scatter all at once.

Shock buzzes through me, making my skin sizzle. A thousand times, I thought they'd stop me—boarding, disembarking, passport control—but I'm really here. *I made it.*

I'm in the middle of an aisle, the whirling baggage carousel in distant view, but I shut my eyes—and then I feel the prickle of being watched, the way I did in my apartment before Hee-Young's body appeared, the way I did on the bus before that pervert grabbed my ass.

The way I did before I saw Hee-Young in the subway car.

I spin, searching for her white linen suit, her toothless, blue-stained smile. I see a mother, her phone jammed between her ear and her shoulder, making absent *shush-shush* noises as her child reaches for a toy. Four teenagers with a sign covered in heart shapes and smiley faces. A businesswoman in a severe suit jacket and skirt set checking her watch—

A man is staring at me.

I only catch sight of him for a few seconds as the shoal parts. He is tall, with arresting brown eyes and sharp cheekbones, dark gray hair with patches of white. On his head is a smaller version of the mountain-like hats that cowboys wear in movies.

The crowd closes, cutting me off from his gaze, and I can finally breathe.

I soothe myself with the idea that he was looking for someone else: a business partner, a companion, the teenagers with the sign. But a moment later, the shoal parts again. He's crossed a quarter of the distance between us.

I look left and right. A small family wanders closer, tourists with trim builds and pressed, matching clothes. The children are pointing in every direction, the father snapping pictures with an expensive-looking camera. I slide forward with them.

I do this again and again, switching direction with different crowds of people as if they were buses crossing the city. I no longer see the man, but years of anxious travel with my mother take over, and I don't change my method. I slip between groups, my eyes cast downward. I let out my hair. When I pass a jacket tossed carelessly over the back of a chair, I scoop it up and swirl it over my shoulders.

The exit can't be far . . . There it is, a giant set of glass doors. This airport is so much smaller than Incheon. I clutch my passport to my chest and quicken my pace—

Someone grabs my wrist from behind. I spin like a dancer, ready to do whatever it takes to not be sent back—

"Hee-Young?"

Stunned, I don't react as the man takes stock of me. His mouth is open; his eyebrows have retreated under the brim of his cowboy hat. In one hand, he clutches a blank piece of white cardboard the size of a pizza box.

After a moment, he releases my wrist. "I'm so sorry, miss. I thought you were someone else." He bends down to scoop up my passport. I don't remember dropping it. "I'm waiting for a woman, an artist—"

His eyes dart as he studies my face. I can see him running the calculations: China has greater ethnic diversity than Korea—and on a close inspection, Hee-Young and I look like we could be mixed with some other ethnicity. Our dark brown hair is slightly wavy, though I always dye mine black. We have the same heavy eyebrows and dark brown eyes. Once she entered her rebellion phase, Hee-Young refused to attack her eyebrows like I do mine, thinning and trimming the hairs into short, clean embroidery stitches. We both have smatterings of freckles across our cheeks, though they only come out in the right light and are easy to cover with makeup, which I always do.

When we were children, everybody thought we looked the same. But I took the steps necessary to ensure that each of my features represented the national average—that if I were ever described to the authorities, there would be nothing conclusive to give me away. Hee-Young went in the opposite direction. One year, she even went blonde, a choice that stuck out in a crowd like a spotlight. Still, if you looked at us side by side, some part of you might quiver in recognition, might wonder if we were related.

My heart hammers as he hands the passport and its shiny plastic cover back to me. How close I'd come to losing the key to my future in America.

"I'm sorry," he says again. His body slumps before he turns away, revealing the other side of his cardboard sign.

WELCOME HOME, HEE-YOUNG. WE MISSED YOU!

A chill pools between my shoulder blades. He was waiting for Hee-Young. That's what he'd called me, before he grabbed my wrist.

Welcome home. I understand these words—but was this ever Hee-Young's *home*? According to the stamps in my sister's passport, she was here a week ago, possibly with this man. He might be able to tell me what happened over the last six months, why she came back—or what drove her to sink into her addiction so completely.

Even so, I'm tense, ready to put this behind me. To put Hee-Young behind me. To fade into America's fabric and forget that my life ever happened.

But then I think about seeing her in that subway car. About throwing the ring behind the healthcare booth. About what my mother would've said about either.

I can barely force out the word at his retreating back. "Stop."

Despite the chaos inside the airport, he pauses instantly, as if he'd been waiting.

"I want . . . I have a thing. To say. To you." My sentences are so stilted, I'm worried he can't thread them together—but he turns around.

His face is open but blank. Benign, yet unreadable. "I know a restaurant near here. Quieter, easier to talk." He gestures at the door. "I can drive you there."

My stomach tightens at the idea of getting into the confines of his car, despite how harmless he seems.

He chuckles softly. "I won't *kid-nap* you."

Even though I don't know the meaning of *kid-nap*, his light tone softens the anxiety in my stomach.

"We can go to one of the restaurants here, but they're all past security." He scans the room. "There's a Dunkin' Donuts on the second floor that's *ak-ses-i-bul* on our side. Does that work?"

I blink, surprised at the first loose thread in the dream a younger me had stashed away. There are Dunkin' Donuts all over Seoul. I thought everything would be different here.

Maybe it would be good to go somewhere familiar. I nod, and he turns and makes for the stairs without looking back.

NINE
Hee-Jin

The Dunkin' Donuts is just a booth near a clump of tables and chairs, as if we were in a shopping mall. Though there's a line of five customers trailing toward the seating area, most of the chairs are empty. Less people means less witnesses, but it's also easier to blend into a crowd. And this man's ridiculous cowboy hat, when I haven't seen anything in the airport more grandiose than a baseball cap—it makes me feel exposed.

As if he can hear my thoughts, he takes his hat off, revealing a crown of silver and gray, and sets it on one of the white plastic tables. "How's about I get this, seeing as how we have business to discuss?" He points to the cafe booth. "Pick out anything you like."

My stomach turns softly. Ordering is an obligation, a promise to wait as food is assembled.

Just like when he boarded the stairs, he makes for the cafe booth without looking back. I stare at his retreating form. He seems older than I thought—at least fifty, though he wears it well: the only real signs of his advancing age are his hair, the softening in his cheeks, his wrinkled knuckles, and a growing paunch that's wrestled into submission by a large belt buckle. Like a confident turtle, he walks slowly, but with an even, fluid stride, and his straight posture and low shoulders radiate a comfort with the environment.

I don't sense malice. He feels . . . innocuous. Boring, even—like the grandfathers in American sitcoms, content to mow the lawn and grouch about fishing. And still, something pricks at me, warning me to stay on my guard as I find out what his relationship is to my sister.

I circle toward the line and take a spot to his left, ever so slightly behind him. There's only one person behind the counter, a young Black woman with a soft cloud of hair peeking above and below her pink and orange visor. I've seen Black people before, but only in the districts of Seoul foreign tourists and English teachers inhabit: Itaewon, Hongdae, Gangnam.

Even as I watch the man, a small part of me imagines being *her*. Blending ice and coffee drinks, putting things in the microwave and toaster. Is my English good enough to get that job here? I wonder if she's like me, seeking invisibility all the time—or if she's proud to stand out in a crowd. With Hee-Young's passport, could I be like that?

When we reach the end of the line, the woman doesn't seem to notice us until the man turns toward me with his eyebrows raised, waiting for my order.

My stomach growls, but the strange feeling—*there's something I'm missing*—returns. I decide to play it safe. "Coffee. Please."

He nods and says something to the woman before turning back. "Why don't you sit down? You look tired." He gives me a wink.

I shuffle toward the tables. It's not until I feel the hard plane of the chair against my thighs that the warning in my stomach solidifies into something I can understand. I'd been so wrapped up in figuring out what happened to Hee-Young, in my fears about my new life, that I didn't realize how strange this situation was. If I grabbed a stranger's arm, only to realize that they weren't who I thought—and then they said they had something important to tell me? I wouldn't take them to a cafe and buy them coffee.

Explanations flit into my head like birds. *Does he think I'm about to ask him on a date? Make him a business offer?*

I tense, ready to flee, but he's already sliding down into the seat across from me, a drink in each hand. I understand, suddenly, the expression I've seen peppered on English-language chat boards: *deer in headlights*.

As if reading my mind, he says, "Now, we have something to *dis-kus*?"

Another thing I've missed clicks into place: the slow speech, the way he enunciates each sound clearly, without eliding. His sentences are short, each subject and verb carefully defined. He's used to talking to foreigners.

As he stares at me, his smile slides down and away, like eggs from a pan.

I get my feet under me. "Sorry. My mistake. I must go—"

"Wait." His face twists with concern. "What's happened? Where is Hee-Young?"

The image of her sprawled across my bed plays across the back of my eyes. "Happened?"

He nods, his eyebrows drawing together like the pucker of fabric under a seam. "Yes. You said you had something to tell me? I'm assuming it's about Hee-Young?" He cranes his neck and looks behind me, as if expecting her to pop out at any second. "Is she coming on a later flight? You know, she looks so much like you that at first, I thought you *were* her. And then, when you told me you wanted to talk, I thought, well, OK, she must have sent you, must be a cousin or a sister . . ."

He's getting harder to understand, visibly nervous, the careful declarative sentences now running together. Maybe that's why, despite all my training, I can't keep my cards hidden—or maybe it's speaking this new language, the way it makes me scatter-brained, my thoughts slow and laborious. No chance to outsmart anybody like this. Whatever the reason, I can't help the stiffness in my chest, the way my breath suddenly stops at that word: *sister*.

He misunderstands my reaction, because he stills and smiles again, but it's stretched too tight across his face. He's afraid. He hunches forward in his chair, his shoulders drifting up toward his ears. "She isn't coming back, is she?"

There's something pathetic about this old man, something that makes the news that my sister is dead try to force its way out of my throat, despite a lifetime of keeping secrets. "No."

His face sinks. "I thought . . ." He sighs and straightens his shoulders. "Well, that's it. I told her when she left that if she didn't return, it could ruin us. I never thought she'd do this to us, despite—"

There's another word, one I don't quite catch, though it sounds like *Hae-Rin*—a common enough Korean name—but I don't have time to wonder about what it could mean, because the rest of his sentence suddenly organizes itself in my mind. Hee-Young let this mysterious man down in some way, and it surprised him. For a moment, I am almost comforted—there are a lot of things I never thought my sister would do, but in the end, she did them all.

That's what I'm thinking when he says the words that wrest me back to this moment—to this cafe and his wrinkled knuckles and the hiss of the espresso machine, the fluttering blast of the too-cold air conditioner: "—without her, the money is gone."

The room sinks into the onggi pot like debris below the waves, leaving only that word, *money*. Is that why Hee-Young left? Did he give her a loan that she exchanged for drugs and an early death?

Could there be more money she stashed away before she reached my door?

My guts churn; only the foolhardy refuse to leave the dead alone. And in another universe, that's what I do: I thank him and get up from the table, and everything that happens after disintegrates like seafoam. Maybe then, I would soon have found myself in a cafe, an orange and pink visor on my head.

But in this world, I open my mouth, and I say, "Money?" And then he looks at me, his eyes narrowing, and I know I've been weighed against some great test and failed.

"Yes. What do you know about the program?"

I don't like this change of subject, but I'm willing to humor him to get what I want. "It is for . . . *men-tor-ship*." I stumble over the word.

He nods, the light dancing in his silver hair. "Right. The—" (and here is a word I don't understand, one that doesn't even sound like English) "—program lifts up the underserved." His voice has taken on a canned, tinny quality, as if he's reciting from a pamphlet. "We find promising young artists that've just graduated high school. Artists from *im-pov-er-isht* backgrounds from all over the world—places where it would be hard for a young female artist to succeed without resources, like areas of significant *gee-oh-po-li-ti-cal* conflict or with low class *mo-bi-li-ty*."

He nods as if I understand, but I have only the vaguest impression of what some of these words mean. It feels like I'm listening to subway announcements over the roar of an approaching car. I miss part of what comes next.

"—and then we bring them to our facility to mentor them in our unique style of artistic expression. Once their mentorship is complete, we connect them with our network—other artists, agents, critics, art buyers. Everyone that makes it through the program eventually has a fulfilling and *loo-cra-tiv* artistic career, should they choose."

As he speaks, his voice fills with pride. It shifts the pressure of the air, makes me unsure of myself again. Maybe he rightfully interprets my silence for confusion, because he sighs and strokes his chin. "It's like . . . Do you know *Hey-ri*?"

He pronounces it well, but even so, the Korean word's as unexpected as an indoor breeze. "Heyri? The art . . ." I bite my lip, frustrated. I don't know the word for *valley*. "Yes, I know Heyri."

Hee-Young used to dream about living in Paju City's Heyri Art Valley—a planned settlement that started not long before I was born, populated by artists. For her eleventh birthday, my mother gave us just enough money to take the bus from Hapjeong station and spend the day wandering through themed buildings: the Magazine building; the Chocolate Design Gallery; The Step, which features extensive depictions of Dalki, a red-headed cartoon character.

Our mother didn't come with us. It was only later I realized there probably hadn't been enough money for a third ticket.

He pulls out his phone, taps through some windows, and he pushes it toward me: a web page emblazoned with *About the Petite Sea House Program* on a banner. I blink at the name—I know how to pronounce these words, *Petite* and *Sea*, and although they sound somewhat like the name he'd used for the program, they didn't quite match. I scroll through the pictures: an old-looking white house with what looks like a massive fantastical glass seashell on top, shots of manicured gardens and flowers.

"It's like Heyri, where we live, though just a few buildings. We get money from the government, in *grants*, and from a private *foundation*. The rest, we get it from *patrons*: people that buy our art to support all the good things we do." He sinks down into his chair. "We got a special donation from a patron, *Mels Gae-Rin*."

"Gae-Rin?" I say the name out loud without meaning to. *That* was the word that sounded like *Hae-Rin*. It could still be a Korean name, although an exceedingly rare one.

"Yes," he says, and then, as if he can tell that I'm trying to make sense of the name, he spells it: *G-A-R-I-N*. But then his eyes search mine, beseeching. "The donation was to establish a scholarship for a North Korean person, and Hee-Young applied and was accepted."

"North Korean?" I mirror the words, my ears ringing. There's no way Hee-Young would've given away our heritage so freely, not when we'd worked so hard to keep it secret. *Right?*

He pauses. "Your—" his gaze alights on me "—*sister* was very special. Shy, yet bubbly, and so talented. Everybody's favorite."

Maybe it's because I'm forced to rely on context and tone, but the lie in his voice strikes me, as certain as a hammer between the eyes. *Someone* didn't like Hee-Young, though I can't tell who.

A thrill wriggles under my skin. I've spent my life trying *not* to occupy space in people's minds, but Hee-Young took the risk of talking to people, of letting herself be known, and everybody adored her. This time, I have to work hard to put my feelings in the jar—the soft glee that Hee-Young had her detractors, the guilt and horror when I'm reminded she's dead. I almost miss the man saying, "—but then she left to see your mother."

I'm not sure I heard right. "Mother?"

He squints at me, suspicion clouding his eyes. "Yes—she said your mother was very sick. Something about her liver?"

I nod, though my mind is racing. Why lie about this?

"When she went back to Korea, it left us with a big problem. You see, one of the reasons the patrons give us money is that they enjoy visiting our facility—our house. They like having dinner with the artists, watching as they create. It makes them feel special and important."

I cannot fathom this, this giving away of money so someone can stand there and say: *Yes, I did this.* But I nod.

"And Mr. Garin will be visiting again soon. If he sees that we took his money and Hee-Jin's not there—he's going to want it back. And we already spent it. We desperately had to get the roof repaired. Mr. Garin—he's not a good man, but he's not *evil*. But Hee-Young must've heard the rumors about him and gotten scared off." His eyes widen. "Or maybe he scared her off on *purpose*. He *had* to know we wouldn't have time to get another artist. It takes months to do the papers. We got lucky with Hee-Young because of her passport."

Scared Hee-Young off?

I test the idea, feeling its edges disappear as it slots into place.

It's hard to imagine her leaving her dreams behind when she'd been so close. It could explain the relapse, the way I found her on my doorstep. Had Mr. Garin discovered her passport wasn't real and blackmailed her?

Inside my mind, the light shifts. This man, he just said *because of her passport*. Had he not been the one to procure it for her like I'd assumed?

Every answer brings a flood of new questions. "Why did . . . Mr. Garin . . . scare Hee-Young?"

The man's face goes tight and gray. "He knows we've been having some money problems lately, ever since . . ." He averts his gaze. "The girls we help, they're not from stable backgrounds: war, *gen-o-side*, *fa-min*, poverty. They come into this program with trauma. We do our best to provide structure and make the Petite Sea House a safe place—but some are too far gone."

He closes his eyes. "About seven months ago, a girl, *Pri-yan-ka*, killed herself. Took some pills we didn't know she had and overdosed. After that, a lot of our patrons stopped their donations. Our foundation started wondering if our project had *run its course* and we should shut it down. And Mr. Garin—he's a patron, but he's also on the foundation's board—I think he's using this tragedy as an excuse to take over the program. We had to sign a contract after Hee-Young arrived to get that money. The terms are *ironclad*. If we can't repay it?" He shrugs. "Garin will take over, and he's either going to change everything or end the program altogether. Either way, it'd be a terrible thing." Animosity smolders in the depths of his eyes. "He didn't have the votes before. But if we can't produce Hee-Young or repay the debt?" He sinks back into his chair again as his question lingers.

I'm listening, but I'm still thinking about the girl that died seven months ago. *Suicide*. A question unspools sleek coils through my head: is it possible that Hee-Young's death wasn't just the consequence of her addiction? Did she kill herself on purpose with a terrible drug, one that bulged her eyes and made spines sprout across her skin?

If so, why? The threat of Mr. Garin? Losing her shot at success? After everything we've both suffered, I want to dismiss both explanations, but I can't. It's only since I found Hee-Young's ticket that I've imagined leaving my life behind as something tangible.

At the thought of it being taken away now, the despair that fills me is so profound, I can't form a single word.

I realize he's staring off into space. His right hand is in a loose fist on the table, and he's nervously rubbing his thumb down the length of his pointer finger, from tip to knuckle and back.

Finally, he looks at me. "I need Hee-Young. All of us do. Or the program as we know it is over. You've got to convince her to come back."

I don't care about his program. I care about how and why Hee-Young died, though not as much as I care about my own survival. "Hee-Young not coming," I say, but it's not enough. He may seem defeated now, but he's also desperate. He might get on a plane and try to find her himself, might somehow discover that I used her fake passport to come here. He could ruin my new life in America. I close my eyes, but I force myself to say the word: "Dead."

At first, he doesn't react—no sinking into his chair, no quiver of his jaw—until he swallows, his Adam's apple sliding up and down. "Then, are you her closest relative? I need to deliver her things. I'm tempted to keep her *stai-pend* money, though it's not nearly enough to pay off what we owe Garin—but that wouldn't be fair. She was always free to leave, even if it would destroy us."

There's that word again, as cold and slick as a snake, as unyielding as stone. "Money?"

He nods uncomfortably. "Yes. When we initially set up the program, we had a hard time with recruitment. The trauma of these artists makes them *sus-pi-shus*, and even when someone came, they often dropped out early. So, we established a reward. Each month an artist stays at the Petite Sea House, they receive two thousand dollars. After a year, they get a bonus twenty-four thousand dollars. It's led to a significant improvement, though graduation rates still aren't where I'd like them to be."

He rubs his thumb down his finger again. "Hee-Young is owed a month—so that's two-thousand dollars. But if she's really . . . *passed*, then the person she named as her *ben-i-fish-ae-ry* can receive the money: her mother."

My insides are at war. Why name a dead person to claim your money—unless you wanted to make sure *nobody* could have it? "Two thousand . . ."

"It's about, um, two million won. Does that sound right?"

Large numbers are different in Korean and English, but once I convert the units, it strangles me with greed. Two million won? And she was getting that *every month*? A barely middle-class income—but a king's ransom for me.

And then I think about the end-of-year payment. It feels like a ghost takes over me, settling into my bones, shaping my lips to form words I didn't anticipate. I can feel my sister beside me, her girlish laugh echoing in my ears.

"You need Hee-Young," I carefully pronounce. My heart is hammering again, a *doo-goon, doo-goon* that shakes the room around me with every beat, but I can smell the desperation on him. "So Mr. Garin doesn't close your Heyri."

His expression changes—not quite anything so audacious as hope, but an openness that gives me the courage to continue.

"I can . . . be Hee-Young."

He shakes his head, not understanding. "What?"

I open Hee-Young's passport and point at her name, then the picture, then at myself. We aren't identical: Hee-Young has always been thinner, the cant of her lips more expressive, her face more open. Here, the difference is even more pronounced—the lighter shade of her hair, the density of her eyebrows.

But at a rough glance? It was good enough to get me onto the plane and into the country. "I can be Hee-Young, at your Heyri. You pay me Hee-Young's money." Still, my heart is hammering.

The change is slow, like cave water gradually eating away at stone. He tenses his jaw, drops his shoulders. Somewhere, in the back of his mind, he's surely thinking about her death, wondering why I have her passport. But I was right: he is desperate. "It wouldn't fool the girls," he finally mutters. "They know her too well. But we could tell them . . ." He rubs his jaw. "We could say it was Garin's idea, some kind of performance art. That way, they'll play along, and they won't be scared. I don't want them to worry about their own futures or what's going to happen to the house."

He closes his eyes for a moment, thinking. "The other patrons won't be hard to trick, I think—barely any of them have talked to Hee-Young. And Garin—well, I'm not sure how well they know each other. Until now, I thought they'd only spoken at the patron dinners. Some polite conversations. But he had to scare her off somehow. I just can't believe she'd abandon us unless she really had to."

I can believe it, but I don't voice that thought.

"Still, it could work," he finally says, his tone raspy. "But, are you an artist?"

I bite the inside of my cheek. I want to lie, but this man will find out. And when he does, there could be punishment. I shake my head.

He looks tired. Massages his temples with his fingertips. "We can work around that. We can . . ." He glances around the room, but it's clear he doesn't see it. "We'll tell Garin you've decided to explore a new medium. Abstract sculpture to, er, *in-cor-po-rate* and *re-in-ter-pret* folk art. You'll have to learn quickly, though—Garin has a sharp eye."

I don't understand that last sentence. I *do* understand his relieved smile, and the sudden fall in his expression. "It's dangerous," he says. "Living as another person. It has to be more than *pretend*. You have to *be* Hee-Young. No mistakes. Do you understand?"

It feels like someone's wrapped a hand around my throat. It's one thing to grab her passport and take her plane ticket, her residence, her job—but this is so much more audacious. How far can I push things before she really does become an angry ghost?

And yet, isn't this what I'd intended? I was lucky that the customs officers, the flight attendants, everybody called me Miss Song. But my plan all along had been to use her documents in my new American life. Surely I didn't think nobody would ever call me her name?

It's the safest way, really. This is just the first step along a path I'd already decided to tread.

The table is hot.

My name is Hee-Young.

"Yes, I understand." It should be enough, but it isn't. I know what's coming, the terrible thing he's about to ask me, because I can see it written on his face, reflected in his dark eyes.

"I'm sorry, but I need to know you can do it. You have to say it."

A mist prickles in my eyes. "I am Hee—"

"No." He shakes his head. "Not in English. In your own language."

No, no, no. Not this. "Please," I beg, but his face hardens, and I understand then, that this is the price of becoming my sister.

I close my eyes and steel myself. Our intertwined lives flash in my mind, only this time, after every memory, the screen turns dark, as if burning that moment away.

Buying a chalky chocolate popsicle with a coin we found in the street, passing it back and forth until the top fell off. I ate that bit, and it tasted like dirt, and I resented Hee-Young for that, even though she'd offered to be the one to eat it, even though it'd been my choice. *Black.*

Shoving her next to a cooking fire my mother had rigged out of a tuna tin and a broken piece of concrete. Hee-Young had flipped over backwards and then stood, no awareness on her face of the long slab of skin that had burned off her leg, knife clean. When my mother saw what we'd done, she'd laid down on the ground and cried, and only then had Hee-Young felt the pain. *Black.*

The time we were living in that crappy apartment in Ansan and she found the roof access door propped open. We climbed the stairs and lay on the roof with our eyes closed, pretending the wash of the city lights was an endless sky of stars. We'd been bathed in smells: the exhaust and hot-concrete scents of the city, the drying laundry line behind us, and over it all had been her orange scent, like something wild and magical.

Black.

When there's nothing else, I lick my dry lips. "I'm Hee-Young," I say in words he cannot understand, and this time, it's like I've killed her myself.

PART II

The House

In what distant deeps or skies.
Burnt the fire of thine eyes?
On what wings dare he aspire?
What the hand, dare seize the fire?
'The Tyger', William Blake

TEN
Callie

When it happens, I'm pouring tea in the old servant's kitchen, concentrating on making sure the stream of water doesn't stray outside the cup's rim, as if I was a small child and not a thirty-five-year-old woman. I can tell from the rust-colored stain's speedy leach that the water's too hot, and the tea will be bitter—

A vivid flash of white. Then comes darkness, a sliver of the moon thinner than a fingernail. Though everything's shaking, I can tell I'm on my back, can feel the pressure of hands behind my shoulders and hips, holding me up. I try to concentrate on the dark triangular patches that must be tall trees, the scattering of stars between them—

I hear my own remembered voice: *Lisa*. It's wrong to say my daughter's name, but I can't remember why—

And then the servant's kitchen is back. The teacup overflows with boiling water, and the motherly part of me asserts itself—*Don't splash Lisa; Where is Lisa?*

I carefully set the pot down, the lid rattling, and scan the room.

I see the facilitator first, a white-suited, handsome young man that nervously eyes the soft undulations of the ceiling as it responds to the change in my pulse. I take in the stainless-steel stove, the antique china cabinet, the fleur-de-lis wallpaper, as if the servant's kitchen of the Petite Sea House is descended from French royalty and not western Pennsylvania steel barons—and finally, I spot my little girl, curled up by the window and staring out at the pines past the side garden, entranced by some bird or squirrel. She hasn't noticed my mistake.

My heart unclenches, and the ceiling responds in turn, settling back into its normal flat plane like bread deflating. By now, caramel-colored water drips off the table. The facilitator doesn't move to help me; he's well-trained despite his newness. Or maybe he isn't new, and I just don't remember his face after seeing so many come and go.

This was my second vision in a week. They scare me, but I haven't told anybody—not even Shep, not even though the flashes feel like they hold clues to what happened in my car accident five years ago.

At the thought of having that veil lifted, I want to fall to my knees weeping—but there's also a sick pit in my stomach, a mistrust of this boon that has deigned to arrive at such a crucial time. It was just last week, after Hee-Young's departure, that I first thought about leaving the Petite Sea House for good. Am I really getting the missing pieces of my memory back now?

In the eighties, *thousands* of people thought they'd recovered childhood memories of ritual satanic abuse. Thirty city buses' worth of people, all certain they'd experienced blood-drinking, cannibalism, bestiality, incest, and child sacrifice. Their accounts were so convincingly relayed that their psychiatrists ran screaming to the FBI. Allegations were leveled against over a hundred preschools, including one McMartin preschool, which went to trial and was eventually convicted of a more mundane but equally horrific kind of abuse.

The demonic allegations were false, but for the McMartin children, bedposts rattling and being touched inappropriately by people they should've been able to trust, maybe rewriting history was the right thing to do.

Maybe I'm rewriting it now.

Like Rumpelstiltskin. Like Hee-Young and her little book of fairytales—

Lisa turns and sees me standing over the table, rag in hand, as the last of the water drips onto the floor. She pats her belly, her symbol for hungry, and I nod and turn, grateful to have something to do, as if my voiceless little girl can shield me from the chill.

She can't, though. Even through the click of the starter, the *whoompf* of the gas catching flame, I hear Hee-Young's fingers turning pages. Hee-Young's soft, thickly accented voice trying to wrap its way around the German and French names. I tried to learn Korean from her, one awkward word at a time, but found it incomprehensible.

I miss her. I hope she comes back soon.

Lisa tugs at the corner of my dress and points at the pan.

There's a light smoke coming off the cast iron, filling the air with a burnt metallic smell. I pour oil in and push it around with a spatula before realizing I've done things out of order again, heated the pan before prepping the food.

I turn the knob. The flame goes out, but I'm suddenly tired. "I know you're hungry. Just give me a moment." I sit in one of the velvet-backed chairs and rest my eyes. Despite Lisa and the quiet presence of the facilitator, a soft loneliness pervades me.

I've always been lonely. It's strange naming the ache that's followed me, waxing and waning and sometimes hidden, as inexorable as a shadow. It's painted on the bright Victorian walls of my childhood home in the Mexican War Streets neighborhood of Pittsburgh's Central Northside, where I mutely trailed my mother through the high-ceilinged rooms, blind to her swatting me away like a fly. It followed me to college, where my friends pretended they didn't see me at career events and forgot to invite me to the frat parties that spanned from Oakland to Bloomfield to Shadyside.

I knew why they avoided me. I, too, was exhausted by my constant need to be closer—as if knowing them well enough could keep them from turning away from me. But it didn't, just like it didn't stop coworkers from declining my dinner invitations or lovers from forgetting to return my calls.

My relationships were like cheap sweaters, quickly unraveling into scraps. After college, I only had one friend, Cassie, who somehow seemed to be immune to my destructive powers.

And then, at twenty-seven, I was helping Cassie with wedding catering to pick up extra cash, and I tripped while rounding a table. My tray went flying, the canapés that had once covered its surface soaring in formation like a flock of geese. When they returned to earth, it was in a pelting hailstorm that left oily stains on the gunmetal-gray suit of the forty-ish man in front of me.

I'm so sorry, I said, my breath tight in my chest.

It's nothing, he answered, his gaze meeting mine. For the first time, I knew the magnetic alchemy that is being truly seen.

I waited, mute, as he took my hand, hauled me to my feet, and excused himself for the restroom. That night, when I finally changed out of my sweaty white button-down, I found a sharp-edged business card tucked into my front pocket: *Olympian Wealth*

Management, a cell number below. On the bottom, in minuscule capital letters, was a single line: TRUSTWORTHY. DISCREET. LUXURY.

And there it was, my reprieve from loneliness. Even then, I almost didn't call—no, that took my life standing on end. But Shep had proved I could rely on him when I needed him most, and everything that came after:

The lavish, whirlwind wedding full of strangers whose outfits cost more than I made in a year;

The soft manipulations, the clashes, the fights that grew so venomous I couldn't tell right from wrong;

(The drinking)

The accident that changed everything, leaving my daughter mute and me with only a patchwork ability to form new memories;

The conversion of my husband's constant work travels into a devotion to philanthropy as he scooped up worldly young women to keep this place running—

Those were all my fault. No, they were the fault of that empty, angry, lonely, broken part of me, that part of me that couldn't bear that I would never fully please my husband. That loving me stemmed from the novelty of being with someone whose world didn't include boarding schools and alphanumeric financial investments and golf and white gloves and sumptuous, understated wealth.

Novelty can't sustain a marriage, especially not one to a broken person. So, I asked for a divorce. I knew it would hurt less if I was the one in control, that separation was a kindness I was granting him. Even then, it hurt when he said yes.

And still, I didn't understand. Not fully, not until Hee-Young, some tenuous connection despite our vast differences that made me feel like I'd walked into an old attic and seen the accumulation of all my junk with fresh eyes. Finally, I knew the full shape of my loneliness and that my time in this house had come to an end.

Can I handle leaving? The thought turns my gut—but I've gotten better, despite my incident with the pan and the tea. I realized my mistake, didn't I? Turned off the burner and started over without breaking down.

I had a coworker that worked in a dry-cleaner's in high school. She said that most of the day people left her alone, giving her plenty of time to do her homework. If Lisa and I move into an apartment in one of the towns outside of Pittsburgh—Cranberry, or maybe Beaver—maybe I can sit there between customers and let my brain recuperate, let all the thoughts that skitter away from me when I'm stressed slowly coalesce. Or maybe I can't, and my firing will be a valuable learning opportunity, a sign that I've got to try something else.

The point is, I'm finally starting to see that there's a way forward, for me and Lisa both. I just have to figure out a way to tell Shep—

The telephone's muffled ring makes me realize I've just been standing still. It's the higher pitched one, a special line that only Shep calls on and only I answer. Urgent business. I hope nothing's wrong.

I lift the cast-iron pan and put it back, out of Lisa's reach. "Wait here with the nice man," I say, and then I leave to answer it.

ELEVEN
Callie

I run through the hallways, across the lobby, and up to my room, the trill of Shep's direct line crescendoing as I draw closer. The special phone has only ever rung a handful of times, and although it's never been anything bad, it makes me nervous. It's like he knows I've been thinking about leaving.

I pull the base and the ivory-handled receiver from the alcove cut into the hallway wall. I couldn't have been exerting myself *too* hard, as the house is still, but before I lift the handset, I steady my breathing and compose myself. "Hello?"

"Hello, darling," Shep drawls. "I need you to do me a *favor*."

And even though we haven't been husband and wife—legally or in any other sense—for years, the way he stretches that final word out . . . I have to push back, hard, against the longing threatening to unfurl inside of me, drown it in ice water and the memory of my sins, but it'll be waiting for me later. "Sure, Shep. What is it?"

"There's going to be a welcoming tonight. I'd like you to run it."

I glance around the room, but the bell for studio time rang fifteen minutes ago and the girls are all in the greenhouse—and even if they weren't, it's not like they'd be able to eavesdrop from inside their rooms. "A new arrival? But, Shep, there's only six beds, and they're all spoken for—"

"She's going to stay in Hee-Young's room."

"Hee-Young isn't—"

"She's not coming back."

A lump forms in my throat. "Her mother isn't doing well?"

"Evidently," says Shepherd. He sounds frustrated, which I don't understand, but he moves on. "I think you'll find our new girl interesting. She's Hee-Young's friend. They've worked out a performance piece."

I can tell he doesn't want me to say anything of substance, so instead, I squeeze the handset and wait for more details. "A performance piece?"

"Yes. She's going to live Hee-Young's life. She's going to *be* Hee-Young, and we're all going to play along."

There's a little bit of a growl in his voice—defensiveness, maybe. He must've already guessed how I'd react to the idea. I don't like performance art, but even if I did, I like Hee-Young more, and I *don't* like the idea of someone replacing her. "What about Mels?" I say, a bit desperately. I can tell from the silence on the line that it was a mistake.

"Garin's signed off on it. In fact, it was his idea," he says, with more gruffness than the question merited.

I wish I knew what had come between Shep and his old childhood friend—or why Garin insists on attending Patrons' Night every week despite the animosity crackling between the two of them—or maybe I'm imagining that. I seem to be imagining so many things of late. "If she's pretending to be Hee-Young, she doesn't *need* an initiation. Hee-Young's already had one."

His exasperated sigh is almost, but not quite, a scoff. "The initiation's important. It gets them into the right headspace—for some of these girls, it's the first step to becoming what they were always meant to be. You can just say that we're doing it as a way to welcome Hee-Young back after being gone for so long."

"She's only been gone for a week."

A long pause. "This one's special, Calleigh. I don't want to entrust her first experience of us to anyone else. It has to be you. You're the founder, the inspiration, the center of it all. Hell—this house doesn't work without you. You know that. *Please.*"

My mouth falls open. It's not Shep's way to beg. And though he's wrong about my role here, a meagre glow of pride courses warm in my abdomen and flushes my face like bourbon, but it's not enough to stop me from voicing my fear. "Shep, I haven't done one of these since . . ."

I can't bring myself to finish the sentence, but he knows how long it's been. Since we were freshly married and the reserves in his bank accounts were still profoundly deep. Relieved of the pressure of providing for myself and haunted by mistakes I couldn't share with anyone, I'd returned to the love of my youth—art—and eventually come up with the program that would become the Petite Sea House—even if that's not the name I would've chosen.

After the crash five years ago, though, nothing lasted. Shep's already frequent work trips became near-constant travel as he attempted to build back the capital he'd spent on my and Lisa's medical bills. My love for art died, our marriage crumbled. The program should've died, too, but Shep had refused to let it. Even in the beginning, when I was still in the hospital, he'd been hard at work, forming a new board, finding grants and patrons, redecorating the house inside and out to pique interest and establish its artistic legacy.

The Petite Sea House stopped being my dream some time ago. None of those women that so inspired me are here anymore. Now, I'm surrounded by girls that act like I'm the maid—and not a very good one.

But Shep doesn't agree. To him, I am still *important.*

"OK," I say quietly. "I'll pack up her things and get the room ready. And the drinks—"

"Will be in the same place as always," he says, and then he hangs up. Dazed, I stare at the receiver, as if it will somehow confirm this was all just my imagination.

Pride is so unfamiliar to me these days that I feel like I've swallowed a lightning bug, one that blinks, blinks, *blinks* in my guts as I float to the greenhouse to talk to the girls. The glass is in sight before I remember Shep's description—*this one is special*—and I stop, right there in the garden, almost trampling on an early spring flower.

He's never asked me to do something like this. For the last five years, except for mentoring the girls and the expectations of Patrons' Night, he's been content to let the mentees decide who runs things, as long as they follow the program's rules. *Why* is this artist so special?

Hee-Young was special, too. I often caught him watching her—paternally, I thought. Though I have no claim on him anymore and it's none of my business, cold trickles down my spine.

Then comes the guilt: twice as strong, twice as swift. Shep's a good man. He's never acted untoward with any of the girls. He supported me and Lisa after the accident without complaint, even after I divorced him.

My discomfort with the artists is jealousy—over their youth; that their whole world is still wide open. Until Hee-Young showed up, I'd started to feel like a corpse—not even forty, and somehow so decrepit that my just-shy-of-fifty-year-old husband no longer looked at me with anything more than pity and fatherly concern, as if I were just a pet.

I'd give anything to change that. Shep's a drug like no other—but there's no undoing the past.

My breath seizes. I want to head back to my daughter's room, dismiss the facilitator watching her, and spend the day crawling on the floor, having tea parties and pretending to be animals. Making up for the time I lost after the accident.

But Shep said *please*. It's the least I could do, after everything he's done for me.

I get moving again, more slowly, but forward momentum all the same. From this angle, the girls are fractured into cubist shapes by the textured glass. A few are bent over their workstations, their whole bodies tense with urgent concentration, while others bob and sway as if to music. They create with paint and charcoal, canvas and ink. Hee-Young was the only paper artist we've ever had—and she was the best out of all of them, the most original, turning the ordinary into magic.

I push the door open and step into the small hallway that connects to the studios. The sun's rays through the glass concentrates the lavender-almond scent of the shampoo we all use. Shep espouses that certain odors trigger creativity, going so far as to pipe various scents into the girls' bedrooms at night, although I'm not sure if he believes it, or if it's the same myth-making that led him to turn the entire house into an art installation.

The greenhouse used to hold plants, back when the Petite was a stuffy steel baron's manor, but Shep thought the natural light would be perfect for creating art. I tried to explain that light was not enough—that painting and sculpture require regulating moisture and heat, that cramming six artists together to stare at each other wasn't ideal, but there's no reasoning with him once an idea sinks its teeth in.

Over the years, the girls made it work. Shep was smart enough to section the greenhouse into six individual rooms, three on each side of the hallway—though *room* is an overly kind word, given that they're partitioned from each other by wooden white half-walls tall enough to block the sights, but not the sounds, of your neighbors.

Except for the white half-walls, everything else is glass. Walking down the central connecting hallway, the effect is like spying into a row of snow globes. Instead of glitter or acrylic trees, each space contains a girl, a series of canvases, a smattering of plants, and a bench and shelves for supplies and tools. At the very back of each room, like a portal to another world, is the frosted glass of the greenhouse's exterior.

I clear my throat. "Excuse me."

They filter toward the doors to hear me better—all save Ksenia, who's absorbed in a particularly flamboyant brush stroke. I sometimes wonder what matters more to her—the art, or the performance of making it. She's one of the best, though when she arrived, her talent was so raw as to be unnoticeable by any but the keenest eye.

Then again, they're all like that at first.

"Ksenia, can I have your attention, please?"

Finally, she turns around and exits her studio.

Five girls from five different walks of life. When I see them lined up like this, all wearing white sweatsuits as if they've just finished a series of spa treatments, I can't help but think about how youth makes us all the same: giant, wet eyes; thick, glossy hair; poreless skin that glows from the room's humidity. "There's a new artist coming tonight, and I'm going to be running the ceremony."

The girls exchange glances. The tallest, Eliana—from Bolivia, I think, although I admit I haven't talked as much to this batch as some of the previous ones—gazes resolutely at her feet.

It's Heta that reacts first: cheeks turning pink, jaw tightening. "You don't have to. I handled the last one fine. You should *rest*, Calleigh."

Anger pops hot behind my left eye. Both of my hands suddenly spasm, the way they used to when I went too long with a chisel. I hate the way she pronounced my name—it should sound the same whether it's *Callie* or *Calleigh*, but when she speaks, I can hear all the extra letters Shep insisted I stick on there when we got married, letters I've since come to regret.

"Maybe I don't *have* to," I say, keeping my voice level. I'm glad we're here, and not inside the house, where my irritation might manifest itself as a banging shutter or a trembling stair tread. "But Shep asked *me* to do it, so I will."

Her mouth falls open, but to her credit, she shuts it quickly. Behind her, Ksenia smiles like the cat that got into the cream and brushes some hair back from her forehead, flashing me a view of the blob of bright-red paint on her sleeve.

The headache builds behind my eye. I know *why* Shepherd insisted on the matching outfits, on freeing the girls from fashion decisions and markers of the outside world, but there's no way a passel of artists can keep them spotless all the time—

They're all staring at me. I don't know how long I've been standing here.

I clear my throat and nod once. "Also, this one is going to be doing some performance art. She's going to pretend to be Hee-Young, and everybody is going to pretend that's exactly who she is. Now, I'll see you after dinner. You know the drill. Wear a clean outfit, and for the love of God, be *nice*. This one is special."

"Dresses?" Heta sounds joyful, which is such a sharp contrast to the shudder in my guts. I've always hated the formal costumes.

I shake my head. "Let's save those for Patrons' Night. Don't want them getting dirty." I stalk away before they can ask anything else. None of them will brave following me—not until the next bell, when they're due back inside.

For the second time in an hour, I'm glad for the house's strict schedule.

TWELVE
Hee-Jin

Once I agree to impersonate Hee-Young, the rest of the conversation passes by like a dream. I drink lukewarm coffee and try to concentrate on the man's words, to not fade into the soft murmur of the crowd and the grumbling of the milk steamer.

He names himself: Shepherd. He says the women in the mentorship program are his sheep and he laughs. Finally, we leave for his car.

He raises an eyebrow at my luggage, the single black plastic bag from the convenience store, but he's polite or desperate enough not to ask. When I add that to my other observations of him—the way he opens my car door, the way his white-suited driver opens his—I start to get a picture: old money, or perhaps a government official. Somebody to whom it's important to keep up appearances.

Quickly, we leave the signs of civilization behind. I discover that this new place, *Pennsylvania*, doesn't look that different from Korea. The same late-March weather: that floundering, tepid warmth that consistently slips back into winter's bitter cold. The same trees—shaggy pines and naked oaks just starting to bud.

Before my flight landed, I'd envisioned several Americas—Florida's palm-lined streets, picturesque western deserts, fields of waving yellow corn from the country's national anthem. But for some reason, though I knew that mountains were not Korea's alone, it never occurred to me they'd be America's, too.

Is that why an uncanny worry presses in my gut, resolutely resisting my attempts to put it in the onggi? Or have I missed something? If so, I don't think it's Shepherd: every time I look at his goofy ears and the graying hair peeking over his headrest, he feels old and soft.

Maybe it's just the way the car climbs and sinks, climbs and sinks, my ears popping and my stomach swirling.

"We'll be there soon." Shepherd's been talking this entire trip, a flowing monologue about the program. The good work they do "boosting women of color"—I hear this a few times before I realize it means "helping people who aren't white." The opportunities afforded their most talented graduates—he calls them that, *graduates*.

It makes me uneasy. A job I can understand and agreed to, but the closest I've ever come to a school is eavesdropping on the muffled lessons of the Best American English Academy through my walls.

I don't speak at all. Neither he nor the silent driver seem to notice.

We pass a small village: rows of tall, square sister-houses with pointy roofs of overlapping gray shingles, their sides covered in four-squares of wood-framed windows. Each house's red-brick chimney ornaments it like a hairpin.

Seeing them all together, the overwhelming impression is of angles—the straight lines of the walls, the diagonals that form the roofs. They lack the curving elegance of traditional Korean hanok or the futuristic lines of Seoul skyscrapers; in fact, they look more like children's drawings than real houses.

Shepherd's voice jolts me out of my reverie. "This part of western Pennsylvania was important for . . ." He pauses to select easier vocabulary. "Making metal. Steel. For over a hundred years, everybody that lived here, that's what they did. But then it fell apart. By the eighties, this whole town was abandoned." He glances out the window. "There are lots of little towns like this one."

I survey the dilapidated buildings and try not to shiver. In Seoul, land's too expensive to abandon. Everything's perpetually made anew. I'd walk down a familiar street for the first time in a month and discover a cafe that was now a gym, an appliance store converted into a daycare.

I'd dreamed of New York City, of California, of the desert—but these houses that've been empty longer than I've been alive, this must be America, too.

The road narrows and becomes curvy, pressing me against the car's walls with each long turn. We ascend a hill so steep my eardrums tingle, but then we crest, and everything is below us.

There was only a moment to catch details. I'll forever wonder if I remember right the long descent of the road into a deep valley before climbing up to a second, smaller hill. It's thick with green trees, except at the top, where it's adorned with the building from the website Shepherd showed me.

The house resembles a theme park attraction—white walls, manicured gardens, and a surprisingly flat roof—but it's what's *on top* of it that makes me doubt my eyes: a huge, glistening sculpture, the one from the pamphlet, made of shining white glass. I'd thought it was something abstract, or maybe a conch shell, but now I can see that it's meant to be a human heart, supported from beneath by curving metal legs that arc to the ground like ribs.

The car's nose dips down as we descend, the house disappearing from sight.

Near the base of the second hill, we turn onto a narrow dirt road that leads up toward the house. Although the white building is cloaked by pine trees, I can feel it glistening in the distance.

"Keep an eye out for the trains," Shepherd says. "My family collects them."

Before I can figure out what he means, I spot a sign hanging down over our path. It's near enough that I can parse about half of the words: *garden, artist, petite, sea.*

THE PETITE SEA HOUSE
LOCOMOTIVE GARDEN
& ARTISTS' ABODE

I don't notice the gate until we've passed through it. Nestled in the trees is an eight-foot-tall iron fence, overgrown with vines. On either side of the gate, the glistening eyes of two cameras peek between the leaves.

The angle of the road steepens abruptly. My breath catches as my right periphery fills with a rusty assortment of haphazardly stacked cubes and cylinders, nothing like the silver snakes that course their way down Korea's middle. From the ferns gripping its base, the train's been here a while.

We pass five more trains: black, red, forest green. One's so pristine, it looks like the track just disappeared from under it, but they're mostly falling apart. The worst is a dark red, rusted monster with vines climbing the angled grille and prying into the cracked glass of the windshield.

After the trains is a tall stone bridge that tucks so tightly into the tree-trunks, it feels like it grew from the forest. Underneath is a long, dark tunnel with a bright pinpoint in its center. Once inside, damp pervades even through the walls of the car—but I'm transfixed by the exit, where a sliver of the house glows, luminous, as if sharpened by the dark.

Coming out of that tunnel, it's like being born.

"Here we are," Shepherd says chipperly, his voice softly undercut by the crunch of gravel under the tires. "Welcome to the house."

THIRTEEN
Callie

I promised myself I wouldn't wait for the new arrival like a junior on prom night—but after studio time ends and the girls return to their rooms, I tuck myself into Lisa's window in the servant's kitchen and stare nervously through the glass. My anxiety isn't strong enough to trigger the house's animatronics, although part of that may be the tipple I had to steel my nerves, which required bearing a facilitator's silent judgment as he stalked off to fetch a bottle.

I've even crammed myself into one of Shep's dreadful costumes. My mother, Ximena, would've hated it, not for its lack of authenticity, but for the same reason she hated our old neighborhood, which had been named in honor of veterans returning from the Mexican–American War. Ximena was a third-generation American and the daughter of two Texan transplants that died young, and her goal was to obliterate any hint we didn't fit in with my father's people and their legacy of Polish whiteness.

Now, I have as much in common with Mexico as this dress does. Shep encouraged me to connect to *my culture*, but it's a hard thing to do, alone, in one of the whitest metro areas in the country.

I spot something moving in the shadows through the tunnel. My heart stops—is it Shep's car?

I can run a welcoming ceremony. I've done it before—

An unkind voice in my mind interrupts: *Have you?* And I'm suddenly not sure—as if my whole life was déjà vu. Nothing ever feels real in this house, partially because of the way Shep *transfigured* it. He couldn't have known, though, what it'd meant to me. We'd had a whirlwind courtship—four weeks of lavish dinners, shopping trips, and jetting off to Europe. Not enough time to extinguish the doubts that whispered as I floated down the aisle—especially not given why I'd first dialed the number on his business card, face cold and fingers trembling.

But then—*then*—came the house. When Shep first crept over the gravel driveway in his understated Bentley and I glimpsed the false columns, the lavish plasterwork reliefs, the elaborate carved accents around each window—fauns and angels, clumps of grapes, as if someone had taken an old English cottage and blown it up to elephantine proportions, dropped in Jacobean Revival and Richardsonian Romanesque—my heart sang as bright as the sun in the afternoon's last hour.

I can't explain it. It wasn't different from the other mansions put up in and around Pittsburgh during the Golden Age by the titans of industry: Lovejoy, Mellon, Heinz, Carnegie, Frick, Westinghouse, and yes, Shep's great-*(great?)*-grandparents. But there was something about the blend of old-world stateliness and utter American excess, the way nothing matched. I loved it desperately.

But then came my accident. Then came Shep's idea, to turn the house itself into an art installation to help my mentorship program succeed. He butchered it, tearing apart the façade, ripping out its guts, adding new girders, organs, bones. Hiding clever machinery in the first-floor ceiling, the windows, the roof. Even the house's manicured hedges and lush gardens can't save it. Now, everything always smells slightly of hot metal and glass because of the massive sculpture on top. When it's windy, sometimes the scent gets swept away, leaving behind snatches of manure or petrichor—but when the air is dead, there's nothing to mask that this place is a monument to my worst self—or at least, the worst self of the woman I was before I met Shep: Calida Nowak.

Calida wasn't all bad. An absent father and a cruel mother had molded her into someone kind and clever, someone who fervently believed she could glimpse the shape of the butterfly growing within a chrysalis. But she was also tempestuous, nervous, and impulsive, and when Shep—wiser, wealthy, assured, *connected* Shep—saved her from a mistake that could've sent her to jail for the rest of her life?

(I'm so happy you called. I didn't think I'd hear from you—)
(I need your help—)

That Calida married him. And then she turned into a seething mass of resentment for all the things she now couldn't have. She couldn't even hold onto her own name: Callie, at first, in the company of friends, and then one day, Calleigh on all the documents that mattered.

But, as Calida, she'd also constructed the house in miniature, although she hadn't known what it would become.

Thinking of it, I can feel the tools under my hands, can smell the cloying-burnt scent of the maple out of which I'd carved the mold. My palms had blistered after hours of gripping the chisels, carefully preserving the veins of wood that would become inlays in the metal, tight ridges of vines like the whorls of a giant's fingers.

When I was finally happy with it, I preheated the mold to drive off any moisture, lit a whacking fire, and poured thrifted treasures into a cast-iron ladle: a small figurine of a dog, three replica coins, a tarnished, empty locket. I watched them melt into a pool, certain that pewter had been the right choice: a metal discovered during the Bronze Age, made from tin and copper, antimony and lead. Used for damn near everything, then cast aside.

People are like that, I'd thought, my hand shaking as I took the ladle in my glove and poured a silver river into the mold's hollow. While it cooled, I blew the glass bulb into the shape of a human heart, the colors changing before my eyes.

And then when both pieces, box and topper, were done, I wired the interior of the glass so that it would spin like a ballerina, and then I opened the lid and whispered inside all my secrets, all the things I hated and regretted.

I should've known that my bile was too heavy for something so small and fragile. A week before I crashed my car, before the accident that set Shep on the Petite like a crazed house flipper, that turned our daughter quiet and strange, that turned me—

I press my lips together so hard I can feel the circular burn of my teeth. The walls on either side swell toward me, like lungs inflating, as I envision our fight. It was over something stupid—Lisa, I think, the styling of her hair. But it was really about the fact that before I found the strength to tell Shep I didn't want children, this daughter had somehow emerged from me, like the changeling creature of a spell.

He'd said something two-faced. Sweet but cutting. Something like *Don't trouble your pretty head* or *I don't expect someone like you to understand.*

The world went white. And then I turned and saw the box—all of my ugliness and bile, hidden inside silver and glass.

Do you see this, Shep? This is proof of what you've done to me. I was a different woman when I made this, the kind that could still make art. What am I now?

And then I hurled it against the wall and stormed out. I'd been so drunk and angry, unable to see how Shep's paternalism always kept me safe.

When I woke up the next morning, all the evidence of our fight had disappeared. It's the last thing from that period I remember clearly. After that, my memories start to fade, until there's only a black space, nothing to fill it but what Shep has told me:

Two weeks later, I crashed the car, scrambling my brain and Lisa's speech. Nobody knows where I was going, if the accident had happened midday or in the dead of night, because hours had gone by before Shep realized I hadn't come home. Hours more for him to find me mired on a gravel-covered runaway ramp, the kind semis use to stop in emergencies. This one hadn't been maintained, and I'd gone crashing through five-foot-high brush for yards before plowing into a tree-trunk.

According to him, I was just sitting there, lights off, engine off, staring through the windshield. By then, Lisa was unconscious from the swelling in her brain—but she, young thing, bounced back quickly.

Then came the hospital. Then came doctors and visiting hours and inpatient rehab—and still, still, there's none of this in my mind but the vaguest of shapes and colors. Everything is as buried as the scents outside the house.

And then there's a sharpening: the drive home from the hospital. Shep, soft-voiced—for Shep sorry is Shep at his most gallant, and by then, he'd become used to speaking endlessly to his absent wife. He explained that the house was all that was left, that everything else—the summer home in Vermont, the winter estate in Georgia, the groves of grapes in California—was gone. Some of it he'd sold to pay for my treatment. Some was after he'd stopped returning client calls and they'd pulled their money from his management while he stood at my bedside.

But the bulk of it went into this. Into turning this place into a true artist's house; into creating the foundation that would support me and our daughter forever; into *trying to give me my dream—*

I hadn't managed to say anything yet. It was my first conscious moment in six months, and my mind was one of those sheet-metal propellers that spins when the wind blows: I'd been in an accident, but Lisa was fine, and Shep's money was gone, and there was a *foundation—*

And then we emerged from the tunnel, and there it was, my pewter hate-box made monstrously large, the glass bulb of a heart now an infernal anatomical model towering over the entire structure. A constant reminder of my worst self, for everyone to see.

Do you like it? He'd been gripping the steering wheel so tightly his fingers had blanched. *The base isn't pewter, obviously—not very practical—so I went with white. I want to keep your dream alive, Calleigh. Now, no matter what happens, your work will continue to inspire generations of artists. The insides have changed, too, although it's not so obvious at first glance. I've installed motors, speakers, gears—the house will react to you now, as long as you're wearing this proximity key. Well, the ground floor, at least. I thought it would be best to keep the spectacle out of the bedrooms.*

He gently looped the string holding the pendant-shaped key around my neck. Glued by six months of disuse, my tongue was stuck to the roof of my mouth, but words flew to the front of my mind like birds:

First: *There's a reason they don't make bells out of pewter.* Then: *That wasn't yours, and you knew it, and you did this anyway.* I meant to say: *I'm your pet now, aren't I, just like you always wanted.*

But instead, I said: *Thank you.* I exited the car to his cries of joy, and when we crossed the threshold, I wasn't Calida anymore, and I wasn't Calleigh, either.

I was just Callie, and that wasn't anyone that mattered.

FOURTEEN
Hee-Jin

When Shepherd stops the car, I wonder how my sister felt as she waited in this same spot. I know it isn't like this, sick with the memory of tossing her filament-filled resin ring behind the healthcare booth, a void in my stomach that begs me to stuff it full of noodles and let their sedating pleasure wash over me.

The driver gets out and opens our doors. We exit, and he slides back into the car and drives away, and I realize Shep never said a word to him. This isn't new to me, people being treated as furniture. I'm just usually part of the furniture.

Shepherd gestures at the house. "What do you think?"

I don't know what to say. Though wide, the house isn't as towering as it had first felt—not even as tall the apartment building where we lived in Ansan, with its many flights of stairs to the roof. It's maybe four stories, except that the frosted glass heart suspended above distorts all perspective. And there's something almost childish about the giant sculpture, its obvious attempt to shock the viewer.

It's like Crystal Island. Hee-Young begged me to take her to the ice theme park shortly after our mother died and we returned to Seoul. *The money is no big deal. I have a coupon, ninety percent off. Think about it, Hee-Jin: a sparkling wonderland.*

But when we reached the front of the massive line, Hee-Young couldn't find the coupon. As she pretended to scramble through her pockets, I realized it'd never existed.

By then, the ticket sellers were staring, along with the people in line. Every second gave them more reason to remember our faces.

Finally, I broke down and paid the fee, the taste of meals we'd almost eaten souring in my mouth.

As soon as we were through the door, she sped ahead. Her excitement was catching—she was only fourteen, then—but after we entered the first tent, my heart fell. Crystal Island was just an exhibition hall, the walls covered with tacky black fabric overlaid by Christmas lights that climbed up to festoon the ceiling. The sculptures were barely our height: cartoon penguins, Disney characters, and sled dogs, all dyed the nauseating shades of children's candy.

Something cold prickles near my liver, as if all my secrets are trying to get out. "It's a very nice house," I say to Shepherd. This close, it looks old, though it's hard to tell when every shingle, board, and piece of trim are painted white. On some of the surfaces, I detect a mother-of-pearl sheen.

In one of the windows to the far left, a curtain shivers, and then Hee-Young looks out. My heart stops.

Shepherd clears his throat. "Hee-Young?"

Hearing that name, so close to seeing her face—for a moment, I forget where I am. But Shepherd is almost at the door. And the window is now empty, the curtain undisturbed.

He turns and raises an eyebrow. "Are you coming?"

A frenetic jangling comes over my muscles, my limbs. I bolt down the gravel driveway and the scene in front of me changes, small glimpses of the house's interior—pops of color, square paintings no doubt created by the young artists studying here—revealing themselves through the front windows.

With a theatrical groan, the door opens to reveal a short, dark-haired woman that doesn't come close to filling the entryway's massive confines.

Already breathing hard, I stumble to a stop at Shepherd's side and try to make sense of her. She's like a candy counter, like those pastel ice sculptures: everything so jumbled and colorful, it's hard to know where to start. She's missing one earring, and there's a trembling line of eyeliner on only one eye. Her hair is piled on top of her head, adorned with a crown of red plastic flowers.

But I'm drawn to her dress. It's more costume than garment, the kind of thing that hisses when you pull it on like branches in the wind. The top part is black and sleeveless, the off-the-shoulder collar lined with a four-inch-wide band of embroidered flowers. The pleated skirt has three tiers, like a cake, each a different color: fire red, emerald green, and snow white—though there's a stain like a maroon thumbprint on the white band of her skirt.

I realize, too late, where I've seen a dress like this before: on the sign for a Mexican restaurant in Itaewon. I don't know what to make of that.

After a moment, her eyes widen and her lips tremble, and before I can stop her, she's embracing me. "Hee-Young! Shepherd said you weren't coming—" And then she freezes and takes a step back, as if she's felt the difference between me and my sister by the contours of my body alone. "I'm so sorry," she says, her voice trembling. "You look so much like her. I just thought—"

"Are you drunk?" asks Shepherd, and I sense something stretching between them like the baking heat of an angry midsummer night. I can't tell if it's love or hatred, just that it has teeth.

"No," she says coldly, stepping to the side to permit us to enter. "Come in."

As I cross the threshold, her gaze tracks me closely, as if trying to find something hidden beneath my features.

I step in to a massive foyer. The orientation of the many colorful paintings and statues feels random, as if they were scattered without intention on the white, asymmetrically sculpted walls. Interspersed between them are floating schools of circular mirrors.

My view of the looming cathedral ceiling is bisected by two narrow, railed platforms that span the width of the room: thirty-foot-long green catwalks shaped like vines. Tracing down their lengths, I'm surprised to discover that I was almost right: there are three floors, though the second and third floors are both split into two banister-lined, lofted halves. Each of the halves is connected to its mate by one of the vine-platforms, the access to which is likely by a winding spiral staircase that leads both up to them and down into the floor.

Shepherd waves his arm, encompassing the entire room. "Do you like it? The vine entry was not part of the original design for the house, but I think it fits in swimmingly."

His voice musters my reeling senses. The milieu washes over me, scents and distant sounds: somewhere to my left, where the ceiling suddenly drops as the second floor imposes its dominion over that wing, people are eating. Mostly women, from the patters of conversation between the clinks of silverware.

"Well," says the woman. "Why don't you come and sit down—"

"I need to change," says Shepherd, glancing up at one of the odd landings. "I'll come down as soon as I'm ready. You can start our meal without me."

The woman pinches her lips together hard enough to turn them gray, and something rumbles in the ceiling above me—mechanical, like an engine firing up, like gears turning. Again, I feel that tension crackling between them, and again, I don't know its shape.

"OK. But I have to talk to you about something important. After the ceremony, maybe?"

Shepherd nods before turning away to ascend the stairs. I watch him circle round and round, all the way to the third floor, like a small orbiting planet.

It's only once he's out of view that the woman turns to me. "Well," she says, smoothing her hair around the crown of flowers. "I know I'm supposed to pretend you're Hee-Young, but I thought I should introduce myself, at least. My name is *Ca-lee*, and it's my pleasure to welcome you to the Petite Sea House." Her posture is no longer so straight: the strange energy that galvanized her in Shepherd's presence is gone.

I smile cautiously. "Thank you."

She rubs her finger against her thumb, just like Shepherd did in the airport cafe. "Normally, I start with a tour, but since dinner is on the table, do you mind if we eat first? I can have a *fa-sil-i-tae-tor* take your . . . bag to your room."

All I understand is *eat*—the smells have gotten stronger, as if they're condensing around me: the caramelized sulfur of fried onions and garlic. "Thank you."

A man steps forward and takes my bag. Ca-lee points down the left hallway. "The dining room is at the end. I need to check on my daughter, and then I'll meet you there."

Before I can protest, she's descending the staircase, a slow melting into the ground that mirrors Shepherd's earlier rise. Being abandoned makes me nervous, but I can taste the air—the tang of salt, the complex sweetness of starch—and the void flares to life in my stomach, insistent and painful.

It makes me frantic, like I could burst out crying at any moment. If I can just fill my stomach, I'll be able to shove those feelings back where they belong.

FIFTEEN
Hee-Jin

By the time I spy the open door at the end of the hallway, I can make out distinct voices, but the snatches of conversation don't prepare me for the four young women in matching white sweatsuits, all seated on one side of the massive table. There's a white platter in front of each girl, heaped high with a steaming bounty: mashed potatoes and corn and salad. Fat slices of bread, finger bowls of fruit. Portions of fish larger than my hand, slathered with a cream sauce—at this, my mind and stomach go to war. I don't normally eat animal products, but I'm so desperately hungry, I could run down a pig and bury myself in its flesh.

They freeze as soon as they see me, mouths open, forks suspended in the air. The long-limbed blonde girl on the far left has a striking, angular face that would fit right into a fantasy movie about a Scandinavian winter queen. Her cheeks redden, as if she is embarrassed for me. "Oh my god," she says, breaking their silence as if it were a curse. "You really look just like her. I'm Heta. H-E-T-A."

"I'm Sumi," says the third girl. She's dark, maybe South Asian, with full lips and glossy black hair.

"Sarah," says the last girl. I think she might be Middle Eastern; it's clear from the gleam in her gentle eyes that she finds this whole thing amusing.

"Eliana," whispers the second, her hand in front of her mouth. She has brown skin and close-cropped curly hair, but she puts her hand down too quickly, and I glimpse a bad tooth.

There are two seats to Eliana's right. Both are empty, but the one nearest her has a plate in front of it. I rejoice—until I see the hole in the potatoes, the half-eaten fish. My stomach roils in frustration.

"You can sit there." Heta points to the final, empty, plateless seat. "A *fa-sil-i-tae-tor* will bring your plate."

I echo the strange word. "*Fa-sil—*"

Heta spells the word for me. "*Facilitator.* It means someone who makes things easier."

As if on cue, a white-suited man steps through a door on the opposite side of the room, his arms bowed under a heavy platter that he places in front of me before retreating.

"I'll never get used to that," Sumi says dryly. "Men waiting on us hand and foot, and all without *talking*." She laughs, and the honest pleasure in her voice makes it easier to cross the room and take my seat. "So, what happens now? We were told to act like you were Hee-Young, but that feels so strange. Do we have to?"

"Have to," I repeat, nervousness twisting my gut. "For Garin." These girls could all tell immediately I wasn't Hee-Young; I wonder if Garin will be the same.

The girls exchange glances.

"Why's that?" asks Sumi, her eyes narrowing.

I don't know how to answer her, so I just shrug helplessly. I debate explaining that Hee-Young was my sister. If they find out later, they'll think me strange for not mentioning it—but something tells me I should ask Shepherd for permission first, that he would've told me if that was part of the story.

"I thought Garin was *Hee-Young's* patron," says Sumi, before shaking her head. "Other Hee-Young, I mean. Unless—are you his, too?"

I don't understand the phrasing, but I don't have a chance to ponder it before Heta reaches out as if to pat my hand. She stops, midair, and withdraws her hand. "It's OK. Listen. Being here and becoming—" she stumbles for her next words— "a better version of yourself requires *sacrifice*. The schedule is demanding, the work mentally and emotionally *tak-sing*—er, difficult," she corrects, seeing my confusion, "and you have to spill out parts you'd like to keep secret. So, when it's just us, we choose how much we want to tell each other."

I don't understand all of it, but a hot snake thrashes deep inside my onggi pot. She's wrong if she thinks this place and its *work* will extract my private thoughts. I have my onggi. I will not be made vulnerable.

The expressions around the room are stony, and something

tells me that Heta's position as their leader and speaker was self-granted—and that I should be careful of her.

"God, you've twisted her all up." Sumi tilts her head towards Eliana, who hasn't spoken since introducing herself. "Some people are just shy. Oh, I know—let's play a game!"

"Yes, *let's*," says Heta, a bit too loudly. She's clearly set on reclaiming her spot as artist-in-charge. "Something to get to know each other better. How about 'Never Have I Ever' or 'Two Truths and A Lie'?" She winks at me. On Sarah, or even shy Eliana, it might've been playful—but Heta's intensity makes it feel like a command, like I'll be in trouble if I don't count myself in on the secret. "Do you know how to play?"

"I'm tired of those games." Eliana's interjection is so soft, her small hand muffling her voice. "Hee-Young, is there something *you'd* like to play?"

An idea comes to me, but the girls seem surprised that Eliana's spoken, and I don't want to make Heta angry by challenging the hierarchy any further.

I shrug and look at the ground before I respond. "Can we play 'Image Game'?" I'm dying to see if the false deference is working, but I don't look up.

"OK," Heta finally says. "What are the rules?"

Image Game is played in bars all over South Korea whenever there's a large enough group to make it interesting—which is why I've never participated. But the rules are simple: when it's your turn, you make a general descriptive statement, like *most likely to throw up in a cab after drinking*, or *has the most disorganized closet*. Everybody points to their vote, and the person with the most votes has to take a drink.

"It's a . . . alcohol game," I say, suddenly doubting my choice. I'd wanted something that would reveal the girls' dynamics—but without a buzz smoothing over rough edges, it's possible someone might feel slighted by the group's accusations, and they might blame me.

"Alcohol's no problem. It's your welcoming—er, re-welcoming—tonight," says Heta, smiling wide. "We can start the party early." She claps her hands. "A bottle of . . . what do your people drink?"

Your people. If only she knew how complicated that phrase was. "For games? Soju. Or beer."

She wrinkles her nose. "Let's have champagne," she says lightly, and instantly the door opens, another white-suited *facilitator* sweeping into the room. He bears a platter with six champagne flutes, a sweating golden bottle on ice in the middle. I swallow as he places a glass in front of each of us, leaving one in front of the empty chair.

"OK," Heta says. "I'll go first. Let's all point on three, and the winner asks the next question. Who here—" her eyes dance theatrically around the room— "talks while a movie is on? One, two—"

On three, all fingers point to Sumi. Her mouth opens in mock outrage before she happily brings her glass to her lips, making everyone dissolve into laughter. "Fine, fine," she says, rolling her eyes. "Who—" she smirks as her gaze falls on Sarah— "has ruined her sister's date by pouring a handful of salt in the *tannour* dough—"

"Not fair!" cries Sarah. She turns toward me, her eyes sparkling. "Is it?"

I freeze. I'm not used to being part of someone else's joke.

"Drink!" Sumi laughs and brings her own glass to Sarah's lips. Sarah smiles and takes a sip, but it's Heta that my eyes are drawn to—she doesn't seem to care for whatever's kindling between the two women.

One by one, just as I'd hoped, the girls choose each other, my presence a seeming afterthought. I squirrel down half of my meal—break apart the moist fish with my tongue, suck down the sweet bits of fruit—while observing their interactions. It strikes me, suddenly, that an outside observer wouldn't know these women had been selected for their passion and skill as artists. They look like any group of giggling girls.

Most likely to be married first? Eliana, who just laughs shyly into her hand.

Most likely to be rich one day? A tie between Sumi and Heta, who decides she'll take another turn.

The person that likes to sleep in the most? Sarah.

Fastest runner? Sarah again, the girls all giggling as her own question comes back to her. I can't tell if her choice was deliberate: the champagne looks sweet and cool.

Sorts their laundry? Heta.

The most likely spy?

At Heta's question, glances circle around the room. After a moment, they all turn to point at me, making me choke on a spoonful of fish. "I am . . . spy?"

Sumi laughs. "You're the only one we don't know."

I nod, relieved.

"It's your turn," says Heta.

I should've prepared a question in advance, but I'd been distracted by the food and enjoying my position as a fly on the wall. I've eavesdropped on this game enough times to know that, by now, everybody starts asking about the seedier side of life—sex, crimes, embarrassing things like shitting your pants—but none of the others have brought the conversation there, which means I shouldn't, either. I need something that paints me in a positive light.

It takes me a moment to conjugate the verbs. "Who . . . likes being here the best?"

The shift is immediate. The girls power down as if they've run out of battery, their smiles melting off their faces. I've made a terrible mistake—

"Heta does," says a voice by the entrance.

And then I am unmade. There's an angel in the doorway, so lovely that at first I can't take in the whole sight of her. Instead, my eyes bounce from part to part, as if her inner nature could be revealed in the soft curve of her jaw or the delicate lengths of her fingers, which are each capped with dark pink polish—but though her features are beautiful, they're not uncommonly so. You could find the same in any Seoul subway stop, bank, or gas station. They don't explain why the sight of her makes my mouth dry and my insides hot.

Maybe it's the way she crosses through the room. She does not *stride* or *float*. She walks comfortably, naturally, reminding me that we are all made of muscle and bone, of ligament and cartilage and skin.

Or maybe it's the way the girls in the room have changed in her presence, stiffening, the game forgotten.

"Where have you been?" asks Heta, her tone sharp. "Painting your nails? You're lucky Ca-lee and Shepherd are so late for dinner. If they'd come—"

"What if, *what if*. What if you sucked up less to Shepherd all the time?"

Heta gasps, but the new girl doesn't seem to notice as she takes the seat next to me and smiles. It's close-mouthed, pleasant without being overly friendly. "Hello, I'm Ksenia." She spells it before picking up her fork.

I'm vaguely disappointed this will be the entirety of our interaction for right now—*Hello, I'm Ksenia*—but then she scoops the tines into the mound of potatoes on the corner of *my* plate.

I was saving those. Of all the foods the facilitator brought, mashed potatoes are the most similar to the instant noodles I crave, the most likely to tamp down the nervous energy of this meal. I should be upset, but instead I watch, riveted, as she barely opens her lips, inserts the fork upside down, and scrapes off the white fluffy mass with her bottom teeth.

And just like that, I'm not hungry. All I can think about is how long it's been since I've been touched, since I've *wanted* someone to touch me. I need to know what she sounds like when she laughs, what noises she makes when she sleeps. The taste of her mouth, of her tears.

I want so badly that I can't speak, so badly I feel like folding over in my chair. And yet, I understand my own illness—I know that if I prick the skin of my obsession and suck the blood that wells to the surface, that it will taste only of my own grief.

If only I cared, things might've turned out differently.

The game forgotten, the girls fall into side conversations about art and the way the house groans at night.

Ksenia eats another bite of potatoes, and then another. When they're gone, I slide my plate to her and watch as she breaks the fillet into slivers. I can feel each movement of her fork, as if it were me being carved away.

SIXTEEN
Hee-Jin

It's as if Ksenia is an explorer, cutting a path through the jungle of isolation that once cloaked the room. The next expedition to arrive is a pair of facilitators that sweeps away empty plates, wipes down the table, and straightens silverware.

Then enters our hostess: face flushed, eyes glassy, more disheveled than before—she's been drinking heavily. The conversation fades, but a few minutes later, Shepherd edges into the room with the slow, even steps I noticed in the airport. The late hour has revealed his age in the slight bow of his back and the stiff turns of his head. He takes the seat opposite Ca-lee, which makes me realize how strange our arrangement is, the six of us girls—Ksenia, Eliana, Sarah, Sumi, Heta, and me—all squeezed on one side of the table with our backs to the wall, our host and hostess at opposite ends.

The facilitators multiply until there are eight men whirling around us. Despite the lucky number, my stomach turns. They remind me of Jeoseung Saja: mythological beings that guide newly departed souls to the afterlife. They're usually depicted wearing long black robes from the Joseon Dynasty, a wide-brimmed gat on their heads—though my mother once told me that was wrong.

They wear white, she'd said, her face grim. *The color of death.*

Jeoseung Saja are relentless; completely devoted to Yeomna, the god of the underworld, they can't be bribed or otherwise thwarted from taking the ghost they've come to reap. They're also supposed to appear en masse where lots of deaths will occur—battles, natural disasters, hospitals—to wait for their spiritual cargo.

Maybe my mother was right, I think, her final blissful smile cemented in my mind. Though I don't know if I believe in a religious afterlife, I'll never forget her last moments as she reached for someone I couldn't see.

Did Hee-Young do the same? Was a Saja standing on my doorstep, ready to claim her? I try to shove the feelings into my pot, but the silence of the table presses in on me, and between that and the strange, stiff faces of the girls, the ghoulish sameness of the facilitators, I'm suddenly reminded of the tale of the two brother woodcutters. The first happened upon a goblin feast. Appetite stimulated, he bit into a ginkgo nut, startling them so badly with the sound that he was able to take their magic club and become a rich man. The second, envious woodcutter tried to do the same, but the goblins were wise to the sound and caught and tortured him.

I wonder: *Which one am I?*

The facilitators continue until the table bursts with carnivorous excess: a roast chicken, a rack of lamb. Small round potatoes almost afloat in butter, long noodles swirled with shrimp, slabs of bread bubbling with browned cheese. Their combined smells fill the room, and despite how much I've eaten, my stomach roars to life, but then I catch Shepherd's gaze. His expression is smoothly blank—and yet, the mist of desire over my eyes disperses. I'm suddenly not hungry for food or even Ksenia's attention.

This meal isn't for us. I don't know how I know, but I do.

I back away in my mind, float above to observe: Sarah and Sumi surreptitiously hold hands under the table. Ca-lee is riveted to Shepherd, her full wineglass forgotten, and again, I feel that odd tension between them, so palpable I'm tempted to reach out and tug on it, to see if the two of them bow inwards like snow-weighted trees.

The facilitators fall into a line on the side of the room. Shepherd points at the one remaining space on the table, a bay in the middle of the islands of food. The facilitator nearest the door disappears to fetch a platter of six martini glasses, each filled with a bright green, slightly cloudy liquid. He sets it in the open space.

Heta picks the platter up, giving me a moment to recognize how strange this ritual is—*why not just bring us the glasses?*—before passing it to her right. I watch, fascinated, as she drains her drink.

"Hee-Young. We're so glad to have you back again. I trust you're settling in well after your trip?"

I look up, startled, but I should've guessed we'd leap right into the pretending. "Yes," I say hesitantly. Something about his benign form keeps making my gaze float away from him, like oil on cold soup. Around me, the girls are exchanging glances again.

"I expect you to work hard in the studio tomorrow, so that you have something to impress Garin."

I nod, though my heart is racing. A day is not enough time to convincingly fake being an artist. I suddenly recall our conversation in the airport, Shepherd's statement that Garin had done something to scare Hee-Young away. Something big enough to make her give up her dream. Something that launched her off the cliff of her addiction so completely that in only a week, she'd become like a walking corpse.

What happens if he doesn't believe I'm her? I try to smile, but my face is stiff, and I can't hold Shepherd's gaze. I glance around the room as heat fills my cheeks.

Heta and Ca-lee are both staring at me. Eliana's attention is on her lap, and Sarah and Sumi only have eyes for each other.

But Ksenia? I'm shocked to see that she's got another plate and is eating exactly the same as before, her dark pink nails dancing through the air as she delicately spears a noodle and twirls it around her fork. She senses me watching and looks up before glancing at Shepherd. Her eyes darken.

She turns to me. "You must be excited," she says between swallows, "to visit the *saiko-mantee-yum* again."

"Ksenia." Shepherd's low voice is a warning.

"*Hee-Young.*" She stresses the word so intensely, it's clear she's teasing one or both of us. "Did you forget?" She puts down her fork and picks up my hand. My heart hammers as she folds it into a fist, unpeels one of my fingers, and uses it to draw along the tablecloth, spelling each letter: *p-s-y-c-h-o-m-a-n-t-e-u-m*.

After she drops my hand, I slowly slide it under the table, trying not to think about everyone's stares, even as my mind turns over this odd word, *psychomanteum*. Like *psycho museum*—not very promising.

She grins. "Maybe you'll see a *ghost* again—"

"That's *enough*," interrupts Shepherd, his face contorting—but then he turns toward me, and the rage is gone. A trick of the light? "This house has been in my family for generations, ever since it was first designed by Frederick J. Osterling, though each new owner has of course updated it to suit their tastes."

He spreads his hands wide. "Old houses are noisy. Foundations settle, wood shrinks and expands, animals create nests in the attic. Sometimes, people seek out supernatural explanations—which is why, when my grandparents took over, they installed a room they *thought* would allow you to see ghosts. It's nothing more than mirrors and the power of suggestion." Maybe he *is* upset, despite his bland face—I suddenly realize that he's broken the charade of pretending that I'm Hee-Young.

In the corner of my vision, Heta presses her fork into the table as if testing its hardness.

He ignores her. "We reserve it for special occasions, like a welcoming ceremony. It's big enough to fit everyone and has comfortable furnishings, which you'll need to relax, so the ceremony can do its magic, unblocking your energy and letting your sister-artists in so you can better work together." He hands me the final glass from the platter Heta passed earlier. "Now, drink up, Hee-Young. It'll help you relax."

I'm put off by the fluid's green glow, like light through an emerald, but I take a sip. It's sweet—until a bitter, medicinal undercurrent takes me by surprise, making me grimace. There's something familiar about the taste, though I can't quite place it.

Laughter erupts around the room, Shepherd laughing hardest. "Sorry, it's hard to mask the herbs. By the way—" For the first time all night, he looks directly at Ca-lee. Instantly, her posture straightens, as if she's touched a live wire.

"Eliana has unfortunately confirmed she'll be leaving us to deal with some family issues. We're going to bundle her leaving ceremony with Hee-Young's re-welcoming."

When he doesn't clarify, I look at the girls, but their attention is on Eliana, who stares into her glass.

SEVENTEEN
Hee-Jin

An hour later, I'm either high or the most drunk I've ever been.

It starts as a percussive buzzing at the union of my neck and my skull, then a long, rolling wave through my chest and abdomen. I grab onto the table, only to discover that my fork is still in my hand, though my mouth is dry and I haven't eaten since the table was reset for Shepherd's meal.

It's as if my onggi pot shatters, all the fear I've ever stuffed into it suddenly roaring out like a wind of evil spirits. What drug have they given me? Is it the one that transformed Hee-Young's body, shriveling her up, covering her with ugly black spines? *They're trying to kill me.*

I stand, intent on running—but then I find that I'm still seated, that I haven't moved at all. And if I'm going to escape, I've got to be careful. Everyone here knows I'm not my sister—but they know *her*. If they discovered that she was dead, or that I was here *on her passport*? One call, and I could get picked up by the American authorities, deported back to Korea—or worse.

For the first time, I understand how dangerous my situation has become.

"It's beginning." Heta's imperious voice sounds like it's resonating from inside my ear. "We should get her into the psychomanteum before it's hard for her to walk."

"Yes, I *know* that." It's Ca-lee. She's no longer at the end of the table—instead, she and Heta are holding onto my wrists and guiding me up from my seat.

Once I'm standing, Ca-lee turns me by the shoulders so that we're face to face. This close, I can make out a smattering of freckles across her cheeks, though they fade each time I blink, only to reappear seconds later. She whispers the next part: "Listen. Sometimes, this can be scary. No matter what happens, you need to remember that *you* are in control, and that we are all here to help."

I don't believe her. I don't *feel* in control. And it sounds like she's slurring her words.

"Say it," she says, her fingers pumping once around my upper arms. I imagine a giant boa constrictor, its coils squeezing. "Say: *I'm the one in control.*"

"I'm the one in control," I repeat—and suddenly, I am. It's just like asserting any other truth, like *Hee-Young is dead* or *The table is hot.*

"OK." Still holding onto my arms, she guides me into the hallway like I'm an errant shopping cart—and for a moment, I remember Hee-Young, her dragging leg and missing shoe on the way to the shower—only it's no longer a hallway. It still *looks* like a hallway, but there's some part of me that's sure it's a train tunnel, that any moment, one of the hulking metal behemoths will come hurtling up the mountain and smash through the wall on the opposite side of the building, and we'll only have a few precious seconds before it slams into us as the room floods with smoke and the whistle pierces the air—

I'm in control, I think, and the hallway is a hallway again. I hold onto its shape, its size, the sounds of the girls around me as we proceed into the house's other wing. I try to ignore the fact that I taste something sulfuric, like coal smoke—that for a moment, I saw the glint of the overhead lights bouncing off the rivets around the train's great body.

In the right wing, there are only three doors that branch off from the hallway. They guide me into the first.

I'm not sure if what I'm seeing is even real, but blinking hard and telling myself I'm in control doesn't change the result. It reminds me of a swamp, dark and glistening, soft balls of gas floating at different heights over the water. I count seven dark red boats—no, they're daybed couches with low, padded backs—and in the middle of the room is what looks like a piece of rigging: a flat platform, suspended from a chain that loops over a pulley in the ceiling before dropping down to a hook in the floor.

And then I blink, and it really *is* a swamp, the platform's chain tossed over a fat tree branch. I can smell moisture and algae, can hear the chirrups of crickets and the *gaegul-gaegul* of frogs into the night. My throat tightens, tears sliding out the corners of my eyes. It's beautiful, but it's also so close to the national park my mother dragged us into, the vista that surrounded us as she lay dying.

I'm in control, I think, and the feelings drop away, as surely as if I'd put them into my onggi pot. Already, it's hard to hold onto the panic I felt earlier, hard to separate it from the buzz in my limbs. Instead, another emotion is buoying its way up through my center, though I can't name it yet.

Ca-lee wades through the water and plunges her hands under the surface. She stands, the end of the chain in hand, and slowly lowers the platform. It floats like a lotus leaf. "Heta, will you hold this?"

Heta eyes her coolly for a moment, but then she sloshes through the water and takes the chain in her hands.

"All right," says Ca-lee. "Now, this will be strange, but I promise you you'll be safe. You just have to trust us."

I try to protest, but my tongue has grown, bigger and bigger, until it's crushed in the confines of my mouth. Another wave pulses through my body, heavy with the sensation of falling.

"Go get on the platform."

The water parts as I step forward, my body wobbling as if I'm on a beam. Ksenia comes to my rescue, looping her arm through mine. A gentle warmth floods me, like the press of a spring morning on snow, the soft draw of a recently occupied spot on the bed that has not yet cooled. I want to lean into it. I want to be *inside* it.

At her urging, I kick off my shoes and let her lead me onto the platform. It's wood, polished completely smooth. I'm seized by the idea of taking off my clothes and rolling on it, feeling it like grass.

"You have to sit down," she says, interrupting. I sit, a bit too hard, but the girls are already swarming around me. Each carries something: pillows, a blanket, a sheet. Sarah has a soft, sheer scarf that she ties around my eyes. I can see through it, but it's like looking through a frosted window, light catching in the fibers.

They lay me down with the pillows and tuck the blanket around me. Then, I hear the rattling chorus of the chains as the women all haul in concert, until finally I'm borne aloft and swaying. I can tell from my gauzy vision of the ceiling that it's drawing closer. I raise my arms to push it away—but I just hit empty air.

"You have to trust us." Ca-lee's voice sounds like it's coming from all directions at once. "I want you to take several slow, deep breaths, and as you do, think back to being a child, to your very first memory."

Tension tugs at my muscles, prickles through my flesh. Of all the things I don't want these women to know about, my childhood tops the list.

"Don't worry. You're safe." Ca-lee's voice is warm and drips like honey. Through the scarf, I watch as her words scatter clouds of fireflies across the swamp, and they signal and signal, waiting for someone who'll never come. "Your first memory. Just try."

It happens *without* trying. An unwinding, creaking and painful, in the very center of me.

I'm hiding in a bedroom closet, wrapped in my mother's beetle dress as if it were a baby blanket. I can smell dust, the chalky-wet scent of drywall that's been soaked by leaks and left to dry out. The floor is heated. It's pleasant, but I'm hungry.

"No," my mother says. I want to whimper, because I don't like "no", but then she keeps talking. "He's found me. I don't know how. He's a monster, Eun-Jin. I'm leaving tonight." A pause. "Thank you. That will help us a lot. I don't know where—maybe south, toward the coast. Somewhere that Russian bastard can't blend in."

There's a soft beep. "Thank you," she says, her voice softer. "For letting me use your phone."

And then it's gone, and I'm weeping, and I don't know why.

My tears make it impossible to see, but I feel the platform start to spin. I turn my head, trying to find a dry spot to peek through. I can just make out the girls as they grab the edges of the platform with their fingers.

"Think on your very first memory, and let us in." Ca-lee's voice again. I realize this moment directly follows the last time she spoke, that the memory of my mother passed in the blink of an eye. "Imagine us there. Let us be one with you, inside you. We *love* you, Hee-Young."

And then the room fills with an echo—*We love you, Hee-Young*—and it's like I'm bathed in a bright, rich glow.

We love you, Hee-Young.

Not once in my life has anyone directed this word at me: *love*. It plunges into my body and shatters me with its vibrations as if I were made of glass. A euphoria pours through me, so extreme that I almost cry out with the beauty and anguish of it. I can't take it anymore, can't take being unable to see the faces of the first people to offer me this gift.

I tear the scarf off my eyes. I'm spinning so fast that it's hard to make them out, but I need to see these women that have cracked me open so I could love them back, and so I focus hard with each revolution, engraving this perfect moment into my memory—and it's as if the world obeys my desires. The motion of the platform slows to half its speed, then a quarter, and then suddenly, it's barely moving at all.

But it's not only the world around me affected by this spell. Every muscle in my body twitches in slow motion; even my eyes seem riveted to the platform. My gaze drags across the women, snagging on their details like a paintbrush. I see Eliana, first just her scrunched eyes, then her jaw, tight with the effort of turning—but then my view expands out to her head, which is as bald as a plucked hen, and her open mouth, which has no teeth, just like Hee-Young's did. A thought crosses my brain, as slow and effortful as a worm through rice syrup, as distantly felt as if shouted from down a long hallway: *I should be afraid.*

But the brilliant, chemical joy that has filled me refuses to let me go, and so it is with the utmost love that I thank Eliana and move my gaze to Heta. She, at least, has all her teeth, except they *can't* be her teeth, because her canines are long and sharp like a cat's. My eyes, though, are drawn down, to a red slash that blooms across the width of her throat. From the open wound spills dozens of tiny red flowers; they cover her chest and legs, they pool invitingly on the floor, begging me to lie in them and roll in their scent.

Next are Sumi and Sarah. I register them almost as one unit, because they are—Sumi is speared bloodlessly through the chest by a giant, curling piece of iron that looks like a fishhook, and attached to its end is a length of chain. I drag my gaze across it, to Sarah, who is likewise speared, but then I remember Ksenia—

Ksenia. Her name makes my heart clench with love. *Ksenia.*

I find her, though I hardly recognize her. Every exposed inch of her skin is covered with spines, the same as Hee-Young had, though these are longer, and they glow with shifting patterns, as if under a blacklight. It feels like she meets my gaze, like the spines all suddenly go erect in warning—but I blink, and she disappears.

In fact, they're all gone—all of the girls, every soul except Ca-lee, who stands in the middle of the room. She looks more alive than she did hours ago, her hair frozen in a wild, windswept configuration, her face gleaming with sweat. Vines, hundreds of them, spring out from her chest like petals bursting forth from a bud. They run the length of the room and beyond, climbing the walls, pushing their way into the air shaft, the door.

But I blink, and Ca-lee is gone, too. All that is left is a new girl, neither sweating with effort nor giddy with drink. Her flesh is pale, her hair loose, and she wears the same white pantsuit as she did in that train car, the doors closing around her.

Hee-Young. It's like her name in my mind breaks the spell, and I'm suddenly spinning again, so fast the room is blurring together. She's speaking, though, her toothless mouth forming a silent, repeating pattern that I catch with each revolution.

Finally, the movements of her lips coalesce into something my brain can understand, something that ends with the word *window.*

And then the room fills with a bright flash of white light. When my eyes adjust, I'm no longer spinning, and my sister is gone.

I hear my name. *Hee-Young? Hee-Young?* And just as I realize that there's something wrong with that—something wonderfully wrong with this whole world—everything fades to black.

EIGHTEEN
Callie

It's annoying, dealing with the girls when they're drunk or high. To my surprise, Eliana's the worst—no doubt because of those family circumstances Shep mentioned. She started to weep shortly after the ceremony was complete, and the moment where the drinks finally carried her off into sleep was a blessed one.

I used to feel uncomfortable about the drugs, what with some of them being only eighteen, but that's still an adult, old enough to leave their countries behind. And it's not like it's for *fun*. One ingredient in the concoction for welcoming ceremonies is a tiny dose of lysergic acid.

It breaks people free from old patterns of thinking. Shepherd's voice, from when he first explained it three years ago. It'd been winter. That's what I remember the most, the way the softly falling snow mirrored the house's white walls. I couldn't focus on anything else, because if I looked away from the window, I saw the girls projected on those walls, acting as they had earlier that evening: stroking each other's faces, staring at things that weren't there.

You drugged them?

They consented, he'd said archly, his fingers curling into fists. *I explained the ceremony and offered them the chance to opt out. And Dr. Pepperdine carefully calibrated the dosages. These girls, they have so much trauma. LSD can help them challenge maladaptive beliefs and try out new perspectives. And an experience like this will cement them as a group. I would've explained it to you, but you're not involved with the program anymore.*

Other unsaid accusations hung in the air between us, but my guilt had taken control by then. Of course, he'd asked their permission. How could I accuse him of something so terrible?

It's amazing how quickly we accept the once uncomfortable. Now, I'm just annoyed by the inconvenience of caring for them as if they were children—I had to carry Eliana slung over my shoulder, praying the entire time I didn't drop her and leave her with *another* bad tooth. Especially since the facilitators aren't permitted on the girls' floor after the evening meal is finished. Though they're well trained and carefully vetted, it's best not to create opportunities for temptation.

Once the girls are safely tucked in, anxiety twists my guts. It's time to tell Shepherd I'll be leaving.

I calm myself before ascending the stairs to the main floor—I've asked Shep again and again to turn off the house's practical effects once the sun goes down, but he never does, and I don't want the ceiling jiggling or the windows randomly slamming and betraying my feelings.

Up one flight to the Patrons' floor, then another flight, my breath coming harder. It strikes me that I used to be afraid of the stairs. At the span of Shepherd's terrible, surrealist abomination of a vine gallery yawning white and gaping below me, my body would go into spasms. I wonder what's changed; something tells me it was meeting Hee-Young.

At first, she'd been like a cat I once adopted. Both had spent months doing anything they could to avoid me. I'd enter a room, and if Hee-Young couldn't find an excuse to leave, she'd float behind a piece of furniture.

She also got thinner as the weeks went on. It wasn't uncommon for girls to suddenly lose weight—the rigor of the program got to them all eventually, though some had more physical manifestations than others: skin rashes, chewed up nails, hair falling out—but I worried that it wasn't just the stress of artistic perfectionism. The patrons could be domineering, and some cohorts of girls didn't get along to the point of bullying each other. No matter the reason, Hee-Young's already slight frame needed food, and she was determined to avoid it.

Two months after she arrived, I slipped into her room to let her know dinner was ready and to encourage her to eat—and caught her hunched over an illustrated volume of fairytales from the library, her lips barely moving as she traced her finger along the text. She was too engrossed to notice my approach, despite how loud those rooms are, magnifying every sound until it seems like they're originating from inside your own skull.

"Hello," I finally said.

Hee-Young dropped the book and it hit the floor like a gunshot. I fetched it and tried to hand it back, but she shied away as if it would burn her.

"It's OK. Nobody's mad if you borrow from the library." I could feel her desire for the book, like a root struggling to break through the soil. "I won't tell. It can be our secret." I slipped it under the corner of her blanket as proof.

She must've liked that, because she uncoiled her limbs from her body and retrieved the book. "Secret. Not tell anyone." After a moment, she opened it and pointed at one of the painted interior leaves. "How can you say this?"

The design was too busy to make sense of upside down, so I slid onto the bed next to her. "Ah. *Rumpelstiltskin*."

She repeated after me, her accent breaking it into eight syllables: *Rum-pu-lu-su-til-tu-su-kin*. "This word?"

I glanced down at the line.

> *A year after, she brought a beautiful child into the world, and she never gave a thought to the manikin. But suddenly he came into her room, and said, "Now give me what you promised."*

She'd bitten her lip, and something dark had tugged at my heart. Shep spent all the time between appointments with his few remaining clients searching the world for new artists, this bevy of barely-adults that were never ugly or old, that always seemed haunted by their art and looked just a bit too helpless. I understood that candidate selection was up to the board and patrons, that the mission of the program was to work with young artists just starting their careers—but still, Hee-Young's teeth upon her lip, so flush with youthful vulnerability, stuck in my chest like an arrow. If she already knew which words she needed help with, she'd been pondering this story for some time. "*Manikin* can mean a big doll, the kind for making clothes. But it also means a very little man."

She smiled, and in that moment, something shifted in my heart. My eyes stung with sudden tears as I took the book from her. "Once upon a time, there was a poor miller, who boasted to the entire village that his daughter could spin straw into gold—"

Like a bat startled from an attic, it happened—a sudden flood of memory, the reclamation of something lost. At first, it was just the sticky-wet heat of midsummer in one of Pitt's insufferably ancient buildings. The wooden seat cut into the backs of my thighs; I couldn't touch the floor unless I slid to the edge, but I hated sitting that way, the message it telegraphed, and so I always leaned forward, toes behind and en pointe like a dancer's.

The class was about stories. I can hear the professor's nasal drone: that *rumpelstiltskin* was German for "little rattle stilt," a reference to goblins called popharts that run around your home, shaking things and tapping on posts, though it must've been nice to have such a pat explanation that didn't involve your own mental illness.

But then we learned that when the goblin asked, "*What will you give me, if I spin this flax into gold for you?*", it was likely an allegory referring to sex, and the child Rumpelstiltskin would try to claim was his own. The story was a parable about loose women, but the Grimm brothers purified tales by adding violence and subtracting sex, chopping off hands to avoid being "touched by the devil".

That day, I learned that in life, your choices are to either die at the king's hand or fuck a terrible, post-rattling goblin in secret. And if you fucked the goblin, it would go away, but the entire kingdom would always know what you'd done.

When that memory broke, I was in the room again, sitting on the edge of Hee-Young's bed and gasping. Her gaze darted over my face, and I was so embarrassed, I ran away without saying anything else.

But the next day, she didn't avoid me. Instead, she sought me out, always with that little book under her arm. Over and over, I read it to her and tried not to think about the things women do when we have no other choice.

Until one day, when she set the book down beside her, and softly said, "The *man-i-kin* tears himself apart." After that, she never asked me to read it again.

I realize that I'm standing at the top of the stairs, on the upper of the two strips of vine-shaped landings. To my sides are the banisters, rendered almost useless by the way they snake to follow the platform's borders.

The anxiety returns. My heart pounds and pounds, my body refusing to let go of the feeling of falling, the terror growing even as I turn towards Shep's room on the third floor and edge closer to my new life. One where I work at a dry-cleaner's, where Lisa goes to public school and the Christmas flowers are all red and not white.

When I reach his door, the ceiling is trembling above me, but I muster up all my courage and knock.

NINETEEN
Callie

Shep's answer is immediate: "Enter!"

I push the door open. As always, the layout strikes me as odd: a sitting room, the door to Shep's bedroom in the back. Every time I see that door, it grows until it fills my whole mind: is the knob cool to the touch, or surprisingly warm? Is the bedroom behind still painted a stately gray? Has he kept our old bed?

The door didn't exist before my accident. Shep has redesigned this room's floorplan, just like every other room in the house. Below grade was a basement, a place to keep wine cool and store tools. He sectioned it off into small bedrooms to give the artists more privacy. The bedroom we once shared on the first floor he cut in half, converting the unused portion into storage.

And Shep's apartment? This half of the third floor had been one contiguous room. Golden light spilled through the floor-to-ceiling windows every afternoon, and I loved to bask in it while imagining his ancestors using the room as a leisure space—a warm conservatory in the winter for a small jungle of exotic plants, or enjoying some light reading against a warbling gramophone.

By the time he brought me home from the hospital, he'd already finished all the renovations and moved himself up here, but I still had a nurse that helped me to the bathroom, plugged the holes in my memory, and made sure I took an entire pharmacopoeia of medications around the clock. I stayed in the remnants of our old bedroom on the first floor, secretly wounded by our separation.

It could've been the beginning of the end, though I think that came after, me walled off by my grief, him sick of the fact that his wife had been replaced by a *patient*. Or maybe it came before, when I hurled my jewelry box against the wall. Maybe the renovations had been a desperate attempt to keep us together all along, his version of a "relationship-rescue baby".

Six months later, I'd healed enough to make it up the stairs, but there was no longer any reason for me to see the place where he slept.

"Calleigh? Are you all right?"

I'm horrified to discover I have been staring at the door to his bedroom. I clear my throat and turn away, rub the numb spot on my sternum, nerve damage from the accident. Nervousness flickers in my gut as I remember why I came here. "Yes, sorry. It's late, and I'm tired."

He's holding his phone, his elbow bent. He was reading—perhaps something appropriate to his station, like the *Wall Street Journal* or the *Times*, though it could be a recipe for adobo, or an article about local precipitation patterns. During the years we were together, his phone was always a revelation, though he hated my snooping and frequently left red herrings to wind me up: a browser open to a dating site, a search history full of strange pornography.

He sets his phone down and pats the chair next to him.

I don't want to sit where I won't be able to see his face. I slide into the chair across from him.

"So?" A smile tugs up the right side of his mouth. Of all his expressions, this lopsided grin has always been my favorite.

Although he no longer sees me as a woman, the sudden ache in my core tells me my body still recognizes him for a man. I've been in denial. I'm not over Shep. Maybe I never will be. "I think that it might be time for me to, well, not leave the nest, exactly—"

"I've been waiting for this." The leather groans as he leans back. "Hoping, even. I mean, don't get me wrong. I love having you here. Having my *family* together, but I understand your need for independence."

I notice that odd stress—*family*—but then his words sink in. Relief breaks over me like a blissful summer storm. I'd fretted so much, and he'd dispatched my fear as easily as Rumpelstiltskin's secret name foils the pophart.

His kindness shouldn't have been a surprise. Hasn't Shep taken care of me and provided for me—not just during our marriage, but after? He's had his quirks and preferences, sure, but he's never denied me something I *really* wanted—not even the divorce. How could I have made him into a monster?

He lounges artfully against the back of his chair, like the centerpiece for an installation in that horrible gallery room downstairs. "Do you need help getting started? Some money?"

My shame deepens. Ten years we were married, and several years of cohabitation after that, and a month's rent is all my funds. And what kind of job can I get when I can't pour tea without making a mess or go to the grocery store without an escort?

No, no, that's not true anymore. I can do this.

I visualize working in a dry-cleaner's. A soft chemical scent, not unlike when my mother straightened my hair with a box of L'Oréal while I sat on the toilet lid. A long, undulating row of clothing bags as it swings, snakelike, around the room. *Picking up? Do you have your ticket? Thank you.*

I have to try.

I open my eyes, and the room swims back into focus: the leather armchairs, the antique wood and glass coffee table, the shelves packed with books and trinkets. "Thank you. That's very generous."

He waves his hand, dismissing the compliment. "And when does our bold Calleigh feel she'll be leaving us? I need to make arrangements for the artists."

I feel a blush of pride. If it's work to replace me, then what I did here had to have *some* value. "Maybe two months, if that's amenable? I need to do some exploring, maybe go down to the city—"

His face tightens. "You're going to drive?"

A darkness looms in front of my eyes—the stars above, the pressure of hands beneath me—

Stop. That's not real.

But what *I* did was. What I did to our *daughter* was. "Of course not," I say, my voice steadier than I feel. "I should've been clear—I'll need a driver. Sorry." I smile to put us both at ease.

He relaxes back against the chair, but his eyes look tired. I want to know if he's lonely, if he's ever regretted the divorce—though neither are mine to wonder. "No, *I'm* sorry," he says, his voice heavy. "I shouldn't have assumed, but I just worry."

"Yes, of course." I nod, glad he's not angry, desperate to show him I've thought things through. "It's fine. This is . . ."

Scary. Odd. Ironic.

"*Awk*-ward," he sing-songs, drawing out the first syllable. And then he smiles his half-smile again, my cue.

It's a trained response. I chuckle: small, dry bursts with hardly any sound. They slowly grow until my brain catches up and drops the appropriate hormones into my bloodstream. Then, it becomes a true laugh.

Shep's eyes widen. Before long, we're both doubled over: bellies sore, faces aching, tears swimming in our eyes.

What else can we do when life has dealt us such a shitty hand? And it cheers me to see him like this. He likes to seem clever, to entertain. I'm happy to be that person for him again, even for just a moment.

Once the laughter dies down, I take a deep breath. "Don't worry. I won't go far. Just stretch my wings a bit and remember I'm alive. And Lisa—"

There's a change in pressure, like the sudden sealing of a hermetic room. It unbalances me, leaves me stumbling. "She . . . could use . . ."

I realize I don't know much about Lisa's friends, her routines. It's only in the last few months I've been consistently able to track time: to know what day it was, what I'd done yesterday, what I'd be doing tomorrow.

When it comes to Lisa, I'm more of a stranger than a mother. The thought twists like a roach caught in a kitchen light. It's only with a supreme effort that I manage to stomp it out.

Shep stares at me, debating his approach. "Calleigh." He reaches gently for my hand. "I don't want to come between you and your freedom. But Lisa—"

He's always been able to read my moods, my private thoughts. That's one of the things that kept us fighting, before the accident: the feeling that I had no part left that was mine and mine alone.

But maybe it goes both ways, because I know what he's going to say. My stomach sinks, down past the chair, the floors beneath.

"Lisa can't go with you. Not after what happened."

I wrench my hand away from his. "Shep! You can't be serious. That was years ago! Even you wouldn't do this—she's my *daughter*—"

"And mine!" His roar bursts so fiercely I ricochet backward, my shoulders slamming into my seat. I hear a series of bangs, somewhere deep below us, before remembering that no, I'm upstairs, out of the range of the house's sensors.

He takes a breath and sinks into himself. His voice turns gentle again, pleading. "Calleigh, you must have known—"

"She needs her mother—"

"—that you *can't* be trusted with her alone."

I sag into the chair, recollecting myself. I want to say, *You're wrong*, or, *I have the right*, but the argument that ekes out is far weaker. "I'm getting better. I remember everything, all the time now. I catch it when I make mistakes—" No, no, why did I bring up *mistakes*? "And I'm learning to do things for myself again—"

"Callie, *it wasn't the first time*."

My remaining resolve sloughs apart like a sandcastle. "*That* doesn't count. It was different," I say, because there's no point pretending I don't know what he's talking about.

The accident that I can't remember. The one that took my ability to form new memories for years—that took Lisa's voice. That was my *second* accident.

The first was before we got married, back when I still catered with Cassie.

I shudder as my mind sinks to the places I so rarely tread.

Me, waking up from being passed out behind the wheel of my Cavalier, no memory of how I'd gotten there, the contents of my purse emptied onto the dash.

Me, glancing through the cracked windshield to spy the soft, pale underside of a right forearm, slung over its owner's face.

I drag myself out of my car as the terrible realization filters into my consciousness: *my life is over*. No more catering with my best friend, no more girls' nights full of surprisingly un-shitty boxed wine, no more listening to the Smashing Pumpkins on my headphones while crying fat tears over my last disastrous date and wishing I had anybody to talk to besides the always-popular-with-men Cassie.

Once the police find out what I've done, I'll spend the rest of my life behind bars. All for one tiny mistake.

And then I see, nestled in the hailstorm on my dash, the small white business card for *Olympian Wealth Management*, forgotten since that chance encounter with Shep at the party I catered.

I reach for it, the tremble in my hands dissipating as my fingers find its sharp corners. When I pick it up, my thumbnail points like an arrow to that simple tagline on the bottom, a mandate as if from heaven: TRUSTWORTHY. DISCREET. LUXURY.

Anybody I dialed—Cassie, my estranged mother—would ask what I'd done and call the police, sure as rain and no chance for anything else. Shep, though, was an unknown.

I made the call.

And then Shep came, and instead of being marched to jail, I strode down the aisle in a spectacularly expensive mermaid dress flown in from Milan.

I will owe him forever, but knowing that won't make the ache that's taken permanent residence in my chest fade—not like wine does. It won't change the way I sometimes wake up in the dead of night certain I'm not alone, that the ghost of the man I killed is watching me. The way I sometimes wonder what it would be like to climb to the top of the house's glass heart sculpture and swan-dive into the green earth below.

Am I a terrible person, a murderer? Yes, and yes. But that doesn't mean I deserve a life behind bars.

"You're still drinking," he says, reading my mind again, hammering a nail in my coffin. "Even after both accidents, after what happened to Lisa. And I've never judged you or tried to control you."

His soft voice makes it worse. I can't argue with him when he's almost whispering.

"Think about it, Calleigh. *Really* think about it. What are the chances that a person has two mysterious car accidents, both of them under the influence, both of them with such tragic consequences—and then has no memory of either?" He shakes his head. "I . . . *care* . . . for you, but I need to keep our daughter safe."

I wish I'd never stepped into this room. I wish I'd just kept on floating through these halls like a ghost, sweeping and dusting and holding Lisa's hand. *Lisa—thank God Lisa's not here to hear this . . .*

"Shep," I utter, my voice hoarse. "There's got to be a way to undo the past."

He lifts his face until he's looking me dead in the eyes, and for a moment, it's like he's not a man at all, but instead something cold and inert, like that flash of pale forearm on the road. "Tell me you remember either of those nights. That you remember the accidents, or at least getting behind the wheel—"

"Stop!" My vision swims with a sudden image, like the rolling flicker of an old-fashioned projector: the upturned sky, dark and covered with stars, the jostling bouncing, I think I can hear a man's laugh—*Is this real? Is this real?*

"Calleigh—"

The second accident, or the first? Am I imagining broken glass—or is that just the stars?

A flash of pain, like wrenching on a loose tooth. "Shep, just *stop*! You've made your point!"

He stands. I know what he's going to do, can feel him moving closer the same way that Jonah must've felt the jaws of the whale closing around him. I fight even as his arms encircle me, even as my ears fill with the rapid thudding of a pulse, though his or mine, I can't tell. "Don't—"

"It's OK, Calleigh. It's OK."

His warm and rumbling voice calls forth a need in my traitorous body, as if I'm dry earth and *he's* brought the flood. My defenses collapse, and I am left so raw, so open—

Before he can say anything else, my body is moving, arms and legs and waist and lungs, all of my parts and pieces desperately striving to take me away from this room, away from this place, away from this man who could be so cruel as to tell me the truth, so cruel as to make me remember what it feels like to be in his embrace.

"Calleigh!"

I won't turn around and look, because I won't be made a pillar of salt, I won't be turned to stone.

"Calleigh!"

But I am down the stairs. I am out the door. I smell the gardens, the earth, the petrichor, and I run into its embrace.

TWENTY
Callie

I cry like a little girl. That's one thing the nursery rhymes get wrong. Little girls aren't sugar and spice; they're the *rage* of taking your first trembling steps toward autonomy, only to spy the diamond-hard edges of the cage around you. The clothes you aren't allowed to wear, the expletives you can't say, the raises you'll never get, the people you're not allowed to fuck.

I thought I'd outgrow that rage at some point, but nothing's changed. Shep always gets his way. It's the quality that helped me most in the beginning, and though I hate it now, I can't help but feel a rueful admiration for his inflexibility, for the way he had let me think, just for a moment, that I'd won.

When I run out of tears, I'm left with a quiet void. For the first time in years, I observe the small, shriveled thing I've become, dried out like a discarded apple core.

I close my eyes and turn my face toward the night sky. I imagine the sun reaching its apogee, rays so hot they scorch the backs of my eyelids before burning me away, but my thoughts soon return to Shep.

He doesn't think I can be trusted with my own child.

What kind of mother was I, before the accident? I know I wasn't like my father, who abandoned us, his obligation downgraded to the house he let us live in and the child support checks he dutifully sent every month. Or like my mother, so cold and self-hating that young me felt like a piece of grocery-store chicken, pumped full of bleach and shrink-wrapped in plastic, a sheet of foam underneath so no one could catch me bleeding.

But doubts still cut sharp paths to the surface: the way Lisa pops in and out of my sphere under no control of mine, as if she was a fairy and not a little girl. I don't know her friends at school or what she's studying. I would blame the injury that left her mute, but she communicates her wants well enough, and I'm always forgetting where she is and sending myself into a panic—

I don't even know where she is right now.

I repeat the mantra, as if thinking it hard enough will make it true: Lisa is inside. Lisa is asleep in her room. She's protected here, where she can run as wild as the heroine of one of her jungle storybooks, full of airships and princesses and intrigue. She's safe, her needs well accommodated for, because of Shep.

Shep, who provides for her schooling, arranges her schedule, consults with her doctors, and dutifully tracks her growth and milestones. All of it, without me.

As if called by my thoughts, I hear the barely audible shuffle of house-slippers on gravel crunching behind me. The crickets and frogs know Shep's here, and they hold their sounds for him as the air blooms with mint. In his desire to find me, he's traipsed right through the early sprouts in the herb garden.

"I'm sorry," he finally says, his voice soft and rumbling, and I wonder how I ever thought I'd fallen out of love with him. Maybe I just realized there was no way he could still love *me*, that asking for the divorce and pretending was easier than all this.

"Don't be sorry." My voice is weak and hoarse, vocal cords scraped rough. "You're right, you know. I couldn't manage her on my own—"

"Maybe I'm wrong."

My heart lifts, buoyed up on the swell of a wave.

"But I have to be certain."

I sink as fast as I rose. "Of course." The words are so bitter, I can feel the shape of them in my mouth, a choking thickness like a fat beetle.

And then it comes to me, like the quiet rise of a released balloon: *What if I can convince him I'm getting better?* I shut my eyes, finding strength. "I'm starting to remember things."

Behind me, a cricket finally chirps. A tree casts an answering rustle into the breeze. I know these things because it's as if I'm suddenly in one of the girls' bedrooms, every sound so breathtakingly loud.

"Callie, that's great," he says, his voice full of forced cheer. He doesn't believe me. "May I ask what kind of things?"

A warning light blinks orange in the back of my mind: I've overplayed my hand. I don't even know if these flashes I've been getting are real. If I describe the night scene, give him the wrong details, that would just be more evidence against me.

And even though all those things are true, the fear I feel—it's something more instinctual, a deep pit in my stomach, one without a reason or name. "I'm not really sure," I finally say, trying to make my voice light, but I just sound manic. "Just little flashes, here and there."

"Of?"

Connections broker rapidly in my mind, shaking my resolve. After all, Shep found me behind the wheel on that gravel runaway road. Who, then, were the men I remember carrying me, and where were they carrying me *to*?

EMTs? It would make sense, but something about the feeling of their hands on my body—they don't strike me as medical professionals. And I don't remember any lights or other signs of an ambulance.

"It's not much," I add, too belatedly for comfort. "Just little flashes, but it makes me hopeful. With some time and effort, I think I could put together some of the pieces."

A pause. I know speaking now gives up some of my power, but I have to fill the silence. "I've been getting better in other ways, too. My working memory is improving. I've got a clearer sense of time. My problem solving, my ability to remember the steps for a task—it's all been stronger, lately."

His face is so blank, it fills me with a chill. But then he says, "Maybe we could compromise," and it's as if the earth shifts underneath my feet. Did he know my thoughts about his rigidity before he came out here? Or is he changing, just as I am?

A sudden flush of desire roots me to the bench. I want to pour myself over him in a flood of fingers and lips, to show him with my body all the things I cannot say.

"I know the doctors weren't very helpful in the past and you didn't like the way the medicines made you feel—but it's possible your brain needed a chance to heal. Maybe we could have a doctor come in and re-evaluate you, and if he agrees, I'll scout out places and set you up somewhere. You wouldn't have to stay there permanently, but it would be good to have you close by, in case you need something, and I can send some facilitators to assist you until you've got all your routines in order."

I'm trying to keep up, but I've been pinned to the spot with a sudden memory of a drawling southern voice, a white coat, a smile too wide to be real. "Not Pepperdine."

He doesn't react.

I swallow. He hasn't mentioned our daughter yet. "And Lisa?"

"If everything goes well, we could start sending Lisa over in degrees—a few visits, and then some overnights. Maybe we can just ease into it—in fact, I'm sure we can." And then he adds, so softly I can barely hear it, "You were always headstrong, Calleigh. Always able to do anything you set your mind to."

Should I be insulted by this *compromise* he's offering? The idea of having Shep's helpers and Shep's money and Shep's doctors all flitting around me, tucking and lifting and keeping me afloat, like the little birds in Cinderella—maybe, as horrifying and oppressive as that image is, maybe it also makes me feel so much safer that I want to fall to my knees and weep.

And though there was no evidence of it in the gruffness of his voice as he called me *headstrong*—in my memory of it, I can suddenly sense something underneath. A tenderness, maybe.

There was a reason I married Shep all those years ago—and it wasn't just the shock of what I'd done, the relief of his macabre rescue. He's always been like this, able to take a thorny problem and split it into concrete, emotionless steps. Compared to the chaos always raging inside of me, it had felt both superhuman and unknowable.

And I'd been lonely—but I could've been a better wife. I could've held my tongue, learned to stop seeing bad intent in every opaque gesture, every turn of phrase. If I'd done that, my accident could've brought us closer together, instead of driving us apart. Is it possible my memory loss *isn't* because of the accident, but because I don't want to confront the ways I tore apart our marriage?

It hits me, what I've done. How close we came to another future, one where Shep and I passed long hours on the porch of a place that wasn't a carnival attraction, sipping sun tea while he read the *New York Times*. For the first time in years, I don't want to leave.

"Just think about it," he says, oblivious to the storm tossing inside of me.

Gravel crunches as he turns away. I can feel the thread between us growing taut, threatening to break. "Shep?"

The crunching stops.

"Do you still—" My throat closes up. I can't finish the sentence, can't bring myself to learn this final, terrible truth. "Never mind."

A long pause, electric. I suddenly catch birdsong, the birds singing for him the way they never sing for me.

"Always," he says, voice tight.

I can't bring myself to look up, to find out if what I heard is really there. I try to make words, but nothing will come out.

And then he's gone, as if he'd never been in the garden at all.

PART III

The Patrons

And what shoulder, & what art,
Could twist the sinews of thy heart?
And when thy heart began to beat,
What dread hand? & what dread feet?

'The Tyger', William Blake

TWENTY-ONE
Hee-Jin

Soft fingers of dawn light prod me into consciousness. For a moment, I'm a child again, back with Hee-Young on that apple farm—a place so bountiful and safe that for a few months, my mother had soft words for us and slept through the night.

But the scene that greets me when I open my eyes—a lamp brightening overhead to expose white ceiling and white walls, like an endless sheet of snow—sends the world spinning. I feel crushed by a gravity that shouldn't be possible on earth.

I stumble out of bed, spy the bathroom in the back of the cramped quarters, and lurch forward, tripping over something unseen. As soon as I reach the toilet, my stomach empties, a wave of red foam and bile that I manage to spray into the bowl. Vaguely, I'm aware that I'm wearing a white sweatsuit, like the girls wore during that first meal. I don't remember putting it on.

I heave again, my retching impossibly loud. Between explosions, I time-travel through disconnected snatches of last night. What happened after the ceremony? I vaguely remember lying flat on a bed, something soft being tucked around me. Next is waking up in a dark so severe, small artifacts danced in front of my eyes. I tried to sit up, and it was like the sheets had turned to mud, and I sank farther each time I moved. And then I heard something—a hiss of white noise, like the churn of ocean waves—and all the hair on my arms stood on end. I turned sideways, blinking rapidly, hoping the dark would lighten just enough for me to get a sense of this space, and all the while, the room grew colder and colder.

And then came dreams, strange dark ones. Dreams about laying flat on my back with my mouth open as flowers dripped their sweet nectar between my lips. Dreams about a mosquito plunging a long proboscis into my arm. Dreams about Hee-Young, her teeth falling out and her skin erupting into spines—and for the first time, a new suspicion snakes its way out of my onggi pot, no longer content with coiling in the dark.

I was drugged last night against my will. What if Hee-Young was, too. Drugged—or *poisoned*?

In my desperation to escape this place, I never considered that there could be more to Hee-Young's death than her addiction. And if I do leave, I might be throwing away the only chance I'll ever have to find out.

But if they'd do it to Hee-Young, they'd do it to me, too.

"Here," says a voice, making me jump.

As I retch again, someone pulls my hair into a makeshift ponytail, tugging on my scalp. I panic, but they're gripping my hair too hard for me to turn.

A wad of toilet paper wings toward the center of my vision like a butterfly. "Take this," says a voice I suddenly place: last night's late-arriving angel. Ksenia.

I watch, mortified, as she leans forward and flushes the toilet. It fills the cramped bathroom with a roar. My hearing is off, the nerves raked over until each drip of water, each scuffle of her shoe is painfully loud, and yet there's also a muffled white hum in the background.

"I thought you might need some help." She's whispering, her lips barely parting as the breathy rasps float out from between her teeth, but I can hear her perfectly. "The stuff they give you makes you so sick the next day. And Ca-lee said she'll be here soon to talk to you. Do you think you're . . . done?"

My stomach's still unsettled, but the urgency is gone. I nod carefully, my world wobbling with the movement.

"OK." She grabs my upper arm, pink fingernails flashing. The warmth of her hand somehow penetrates the thick fleece of my sweatshirt. Her fingertips dig into my skin, the pressure exquisite.

She guides me to the bed. It's the room's sole furniture, save a large white armoire and a white chest of drawers. In fact, the only color in view comes from a vertical triptych of two-foot-by-two-foot paintings on the wall opposite the bed: three square pieces depicting folkloric forest scenes of cabins in different seasons.

I get another flash of last night—*window.* Part of what I'd hallucinated Hee-Young mouthing, no doubt from the drugs in that green drink.

"No windows." My voice comes out creaky—and incredibly loud. I blink, startled, but Ksenia makes a dismissive wave in front of her face.

"The rooms are soundproofed," she whispers, cocking her head to one side. "It's supposed to connect us with our innermost thoughts and feelings, the outside reflecting the inside. This whole place is crazy like that—everything white, not allowing clocks. They say it's so there's nothing to keep your creativity from following the paths it needs to go down."

She swallows. I'm shocked to find I can hear it—the soft, guttural closure of her throat, the resumption of her breath. I can hear my own heartbeat, the rush of blood through my body. Experimentally, I rub my hand against my thigh. It rasps like sandpaper.

"Personally, I think it's a load of *bull-shit*." She's doing me the favor of speaking slowly, inserting spaces between clauses to give me time to process. "After some time in our rooms, anything else feels like a reward."

"Last night was . . . very dark."

"The lights are automated. Keeps us . . . on schedule. I think Eliana had—" Her brow furrows. "Wait here."

I'm tempted to follow her, but she moves swiftly, as if the previous night's drinks were sugar water. Halfway across the room, she turns back. "Before I forget: be careful around Ca-lee. She's a terrible drunk and not all there. And—"

She glances over her shoulder at the door, as if it will sense she's being uncharitable and open under its own steam. For the first time, I notice its odd design—painted white, with a lip that seals all the way around, and no visible knob. "Watch what you say to people. Personally, I wouldn't trust *anybody*."

She turns to leave, but this conversation is one of the first chances I've had to try to get information without a group overhearing. "What about . . . Garin?"

She stops, her back to me. "What about him?"

"What . . . is he like? No, what *does* he like?"

"He *liked* Hee-Young," she says, and then she's gone.

My breath is tight in my chest. *Liking* her implies that he *knew* her more than from glances across a dinner table. If so, is it really possible to fool him?

If not, then why would Shepherd agree to this plan in the first place?

A shiver courses down my back. After a moment, I crawl out of bed and try the door, almost sure that I will find it locked, but it swings open with the slightest pressure. When I let go, it closes itself.

I crawl back into bed before Ksenia can return and find me playing with the door.

I don't know how long passes—a few minutes? An hour? Although I slept like a dead thing, it wasn't restorative—no doubt due to the green drink—and my eyes burn too much to keep them open.

With them closed, it doesn't matter that the room is stark and windowless. The bed is far softer than anything I've ever slept on before. In its grasp, I feel a touch of the euphoria that filled me last night on the platform.

Before long, my thoughts coalesce around Ksenia. I'm embarrassed that I threw up in front of her, but it's not enough to make me push the nervous tingle in my stomach down into my onggi pot.

I don't usually allow myself to fantasize. Wanting things makes you vulnerable.

But I break my own rule and imagine us at a small underground bar in Hongdae—I rarely found myself in that neighborhood, but when I did, I couldn't help but peer down the bar's stairs, trying to catch a glimpse of young Koreans and expats sipping Jamaican beer while a projector threw silent videos of surfers against the wall—

My eyes snap open. In that moment, two things happen at once: the first is that I remember my bag, which had supposedly been delivered to somewhere in this room. But even before I finish that thought, I hear the door grind away from the frame, the soft whoosh of air being disturbed. My heart thumps hard as I roll over, trying to think of what to say, but the new arrival isn't Ksenia.

"Good morning," Ca-lee murmurs.

With the door open, everything sounds normal again. I watch it swing shut with more than a little regret.

She pauses as she crosses the room, sniffing air that must be rancid with vomit, and sits on the very far edge of the bed without making eye contact. She looks wrung out. "Did you sleep well?"

I nod politely, but Ksenia's cryptic warning about Ca-lee—*she's a terrible drunk, she's not all there*—rings in my head. I don't know what it means to be not "all there," but from the way the buttons in Ca-lee's collar again don't match, the unevenness in her makeup, I can guess. She's exchanged the costume from yesterday for another like it, although this one is mostly red with white accents.

"Excellent. Well, let me explain what's on the *dock-et*. I know I'm supposed to just *pretend* you're Hee-Young, but I think Shepherd will forgive me if we drop the façade for a few hours this morning. Otherwise, you'll be wandering around with no idea what's going on."

I wait patiently as she runs me through a quick orientation. Many of the words escape me, but I'm too nervous to interrupt for clarification.

I understand enough, though. At the Petite Sea House, we wake up when the lights come on. There's thirty minutes to get ready before breakfast, though breakfast is always delayed on days after a welcoming ceremony. Meals are eaten together, always in the same room at the same time, except that there's no time here, because it's "insignificant" and "*ar-b-it-tra-ry*." Instead, life in the house is organized by a series of—I don't catch these words, though they sound like *echo stick excuse*.

After breakfast, there is "studio time" until lunch, then more "studio time," and then dinner. Some evenings we have free. Others, there are group activities designed to expose us to our inner artists.

I don't point out that I have no inner artist.

"Tonight, there's no activity, of course—Fridays are usually the patron dinner. So, you'll want to wear one of the outfits in the left-hand side of the closet and try to be on your best behavior—without our patrons, there would be no scholarship fund, no program at all. Also, we need to go over some ground rules. The basics all apply—no violence, don't be an asshole—but there are a few more . . . particulars. I'm assuming Shep told you about cell phones, doors, all that?"

It takes me a moment to understand that "Shep" is short for "Shepherd." I shake my head.

She bites her lip. "OK, well, the first thing is your cell phone. We don't allow—"

"I didn't bring this. A phone." I try not to think about my phone next to Hee-Young's rotting body, the screen flashing as my old boss texts threats about the punishment for missing my shifts.

Her eyebrows go up. "Well, what about a computer? Or a tablet or—"

"No."

"I see." She sighs. "Well, the other major point is the windows and doors. The windows don't open, for security reasons, except—" And here there was a long string of words, something about the walls and *practical effects* and *bi-oh-met-ric*. "The doors don't lock except in emergencies, and only I have the key."

The hair goes up on the back of my neck. Korea has programs for the homeless, but we stayed clear of those—we didn't want anyone figuring out the circumstances of our citizenship. After our mother died, Hee-Young and I usually split up. Between her easy laugh and her silver tongue, she could always find a couch or a floor to sleep on, usually some artist or musician she'd been following around, trying to get them to notice her.

I wasn't so lucky—or so careless. If I had the money, I grabbed a shower and a mat in a twenty-four-hour sauna, though between the snoring and worrying about my things being stolen, it was hard to sleep. When I was broke, I slept in the subway to get out of the weather, either Seoul Station or Myeongdong. The police at those stations usually looked the other way as long as we were tidy and out before the first trains came.

Locks aren't infallible—but when I finally moved into my apartment, when I could fall asleep without anybody taking my things or touching me in ways I didn't want—I wept harder than when my mother died.

And now, I was in this glittering place of white and glass, and I didn't have a door that locked anymore.

"—so I'll meet you in the studio for your tour once I finish my errands. Does that sound good?"

Ca-lee's been speaking this whole time. I don't really know

what she said. Something about . . . laundry? Leaving it on the floor, I think. "Yes."

"Great. Well, you'd better get ready, or you're going to be late for breakfast. And don't forget your passport."

She pats my knee as if encouraging a small child and leaves the room. As she departs, I notice the slump to her shoulders, the way her feet drag ever so slightly across the floor. Exhaustion, maybe.

Why did she tell me not to forget my passport? Unease snakes through my belly as I look around the room, searching for the black garbage bag that had my things—and then I see it tucked into a shadow at the foot of the armoire. I quickly retrieve it and pry the plastic open.

I breathe out a sigh of relief as I take inventory. There's my passport, and Hee-Young's tin ring with a green stone. I find the paper owl, the cryptic sheet with her handwriting—

And then something clicks into place, and I stop. I re-examine the first line to confirm my newly forming theory:

十二/二十三/ㄱㅁ/ㅅㅎ.

Translated into English, it would be something like:

12 / 23 / GM / SH

I scan the rest of the list, and it's the same pattern, again and again. Two numbers, the first between one and twelve, the second between one and thirty-one. A date, then.

And the letters? Some pairs repeat more than once, usually combined with the same other pair, but not always—the translated NH pairs with GM, but also PS and CB.

I turn it over and over in my mind, but nothing quite fits. And enough time has passed that if I don't hurry, I'll be late for breakfast. I tuck everything back in the bag, slide it under my bed, and return to the bathroom.

TWENTY-TWO
Hee-Jin

Getting ready is hard when you don't know where anything is. In the bathroom, I find a small pyramid of white washcloths and towels, but no toiletries except a clear, lavender-scented soap in a square porcelain dispenser. I wash my mouth out, grimacing at the soap's bitterness. When I gargle, it stings like fire, but at least I no longer taste vomit.

I almost don't bathe, given Ca-lee's admonitions against lateness and the time I spent trying to decode the note, but I feel disgusting.

I've only seen full western-style bathtubs in the movies. When I turn the knob, the water pours out of the bottom spigot. I resign myself to hunching under it, until I discover that turning a thumb-sized, leaf-shaped handle on the wall drives the water up into the wide showerhead.

I soap my hair, my body. The heat and the pressure are heavenly, and for a moment, I'm not here in this gigantic tub. Instead, I'm eight years old and squatting on a tile floor in hard rubber shower slippers. My mother scrubs my back with a green exfoliating mitt until my dead skin sheds like a snake's, polishing me to reveal fresh lobster-pink underneath.

Hee-Jin-Ah. When you're all clean like this, you're worth more than gold. Now, let's rinse you off. It's Hee-Young's turn—

My eyes snap open at a sudden flash of pain. I stop lathering myself to discover a sore spot on my left arm, right in the crook of my elbow. I rinse away the suds to reveal a small dot, like a pinprick, that aches when I poke at it. An insect bite, maybe. For a moment, my dream flashes again across the backs of my eyelids: a giant mosquito with a long, unfurling proboscis.

The bite feels like it's in the same spot as in my dream. Could I really have been bitten—maybe by one of the insects I saw on Hee-Young's body? Or is it something worse—like the very beginning of one of those little black spines?

In front of me, something knocks. My eyes widen as the knocks repeat: three knocks, then two.

Soap stings my eyes. I hold my breath.

But instead of my sister's *finisher*, the pipe groans and rattles, a quirk of the plumbing. Still, between the bite (?) on my arm and the reminder of my sister, I'm too unsettled to enjoy the shower anymore. And the room doesn't lock; anybody could walk in at any time. I finish rinsing while staring at the bathroom door, wrap myself with a blanket-sized towel, and check the wardrobe for fresh clothes. In the left side hangs five of the white sweatsuits. Peeking out from behind them, though, is a bright burst of deep purple.

I shuffle past the sweatsuits, revealing an ornate silk outfit that looks like a hanbok—a traditional Korean dress with short-jacket, though there's no tie around the collar, the skirt is too form fitting, and the top and bottom have matching fabric, which isn't typical of hanbok. I mash the sweatsuits to the other end of the pole to get a better look. The garment is just a single piece—and there's a long sash belt looped over the hanger and tucked inside the collar.

It isn't a hanbok. It's a *kimono*.

Japanese, I think, though it's my mom's voice that angrily spits the word.

Like most Koreans of a certain age, my mother hated the Japanese for the annexation of her peninsula. For thirty-five years, they ruled with an iron fist, intent on destroying the Korean spirit and culture. They forbade our language, replaced our names with Japanese ones, and burned historical documents and non-approved texts. They razed part of Gyeongbokgung Palace, a five-hundred-year-old symbol of the Joseon Dynasty, and turned the rest into a tourist attraction for Japanese visitors.

And then there was the forced migration. Over five million Koreans were conscripted or kidnapped to work in Japan and its colonies: potters, laborers, soldiers, and *comfort women*—sex slaves, many as young as eleven years old.

Hundreds of thousands died. Others were given no way to return, becoming stateless—whether officially or because of a lack of documents.

My hand shakes as I reach for the garment's collar. I pull it forward on the rack in slow motion, afraid of what I'll find behind.

Red with white blossoms. Pink, orange, and purple bands like a sunset. Black with gold vines.

Although the feelings of young Koreans toward the Japanese have softened—we watch Japanese dramas, eat their food, listen to their music—I know there's no way Hee-Young chose a kimono for herself to wear. Not here, and not when it surely brought up questions about belonging and statelessness.

And I'm supposed to wear one of these outfits tonight.

Inside my chest, there's a hot twist, like wringing out a steaming rag. This feels like a betrayal—but Garin is *expecting* the costume. I shouldn't give him a reason to suspect Hee-Young has become someone else.

I hear my mother's voice—*the table is hot*—and her strength gives me what I need. I pour my disgust into the pot. A coolness fills my center.

I'll be ready, when it's time. I slide the sweatsuits back into place, but as I do, a puff of orange-scented air makes my stomach sink. I open the right door of the wardrobe, seeking its source. The rack on this side holds identical white nightgowns. In the closet's bottom is a folded pile of clothes that I recognize as Hee-Young's.

A lump forms in my throat, one I can't seem to swallow. I should've guessed Shepherd would put me in her room—but I didn't. My hands shake as I pull out the top garment, a tiny tee shirt with a graphic of a sandwich, cut into two triangles. *I'll always be half without you* circles the image in the rounded, blocky font they sometimes use in comic books. I can tell Hee-Jin folded it, because she always folded her shirts in perfect thirds, the collar and the hem hidden behind a padded square of middle, as if she was displaying them to sell.

I back up and sink against the bed. She stole this shirt from a department store a year ago. She'd been staying with me then—she'd almost overdosed with her new *friends*, and, desperate to avoid the authorities, they'd dumped her on me out of fear. Her breathing had been shallow, her pupils astronomically small. I guessed she'd been doing painkillers. I watched her overnight as she recovered: her lips, once blue-gray, turning pink again, her breaths growing deeper and steadier.

The next day, she told me she wanted to go shopping. I couldn't believe it, but she was out the door before I could stop her. She dashed into an All For Kids, popped the shirt into her bag, and carried on, nose in the air, and nobody thought to question her. No matter what we did, people always assumed she belonged in a way they never did for me.

When we got home, she squeezed into the shirt and danced around the apartment. For a moment, my memory is so vivid, a projection of her pirouettes like a ballerina over the stark white room.

Underneath the shirt are other familiar items: a pair of cuffed shorts, some folded white socks. A sundress of soft, crumply fabric that doesn't fold so much as pool. These things had all been dear to her. She wouldn't have left them behind, unless she was coming back—or unless she *had* to.

Grief squeezes my chest, claws at my throat as I pull the pile to my face and inhale my sister's sweet citrusy scent. When I can't smell her anymore, I push it all back into the closet, doing my best to fix the shirt so that it's folded the way she left it—but then I notice the corner of a folded piece of paper that's wriggled out from beneath the heap.

I pull it out and unfold it, revealing text that's artfully scattered across the space:

My effervescent
astrological queen
I give you my secrets
as you shine
dark and light
two sides of a moon.
Can something so inhuman
Still have a heart?

A poem? The way the words dance up and down, sitting on imaginary waves—it's Hee-Young's handwriting, I'm sure of it. But I can't tell if she copied it from somewhere or came up with it herself, though I don't think I ever saw Hee-Young write a poem.

If it *is* Hee-Young's creation, then what, or who, is it about? Before I can ponder it, the room fills with a long, ringing tone that stretches out over several seconds—it reminds me of the mystic syllable Buddhists sing in meditation: *om*.

After a moment, I realize it's coming from the wall with the paintings, though it's hard to be certain with the way this room distorts sounds. It dies away before I get close enough to investigate.

It must be one of the *echo stick cues*—the way this place tells time.

Which means I'm now late for breakfast.

I fold up the paper and tuck it back into the clothing pile, but if the poem and the bell-like tone have shown me anything, it's that this room holds secrets.

TWENTY-THREE
Hee-Jin

Five minutes after the bell-tone sounds in my room, I finish wringing my hair out and throw on one of the white sweat-suit sets. My stomach's turned into an engine, roaring with explosive ferocity and seemingly no awareness of me vomiting in the toilet only minutes before.

I run up the stairs, grateful my scant memories of last night are enough to find my way. As I pass through the main floor, my eyes dart between the paintings, the windows, desperately drinking up all of the colors. I pass a white-suited facilitator standing silent guard in the hallway, and despite my discomfort at being watched, the blue in his eyes gives me a thrill. I understand why they'd take this away, the thirst you suddenly develop for color when there is none.

When I reach the dining room, I hold my breath. From the animated chatter of the girls inside, I can tell Ca-lee and Shepherd aren't there.

I slide through the doorway toward one of the white velvet seats. It's again four girls watching me as I approach, although now it's Eliana that's missing. When I see their faces, I feel a soft echo of the joy that filled me during the ceremony on the platform—so much beauty, I couldn't tell it from anguish. *We love you, Hee-Young.*

It's not real, I tell myself. The truth, even if I wish it wasn't.

"Hello," I say, taking my seat. Almost instantly, another facilitator rushes in, a heavy plate in his hands. It's drowning in animal products: fried eggs, sausage, bacon—but just like last night, seeing it all laid end to end and glistening makes my stomach clench with hunger.

At least there's the bread: two thick slabs, just barely toasted and hugging a small bowl of strawberry jam.

It hurts to turn away from the rest of the plate, but I spread three huge spoonfuls of jam onto the first slice of toast, hoping the indulgence will satisfy the ache in my belly.

"On a diet?" Ksenia makes a wry face. "Shouldn't have so much sugar."

I want to tell her the truth—want to tell her everything about me. But this feeling that I know her, that I've always known her—that's a lie, too.

When I don't answer, she rolls her eyes and sighs. "Hee-Young would've eaten it." She cuts one of her eggs in two, a sunburst of yolk erupting from the center to drip onto the white plate.

"Hee-Young was *thinner*," says Sumi, a bite to her words, but then she looks at me bashfully. "It's a lie, anyways. She didn't eat much." She turns back to Ksenia. "And we should probably stop talking *about* Hee-Young, since we're supposed to be pretending—" She wiggles a hand in my direction.

"I refuse," says Ksenia, filling me with alarm.

"You . . . *have* to," I beg. "Maybe . . . not now. But . . . for Garin."

Sumi tilts her head at me appraisingly, making her black braids catch the light. "I thought he was your *patron*. Or . . ." Her eyes widen. "Does he *not know*?"

Panic closes my throat as I glance around the room. The girls all look stunned: mouths open, eyes wide. All except Ksenia.

"It is Garin's idea . . ." I say, repeating the strategy Shep came up with at the Dunkin' Donuts. I'm mortified to discover my voice is trembling. "To pretend."

"We really are all the same to them," Sumi says cryptically, but then Heta clears her throat.

"Let's all calm down," she says, quietly but imperiously. "Hee-Young's just returned. Perhaps she's *forgotten* the way things work around here. And if that's what Garin wants from her, then we should help her. We don't need her running out of here the same way Eliana—"

"That wasn't our fault," snaps Sumi, eyes glittering as she stares daggers at Heta. The tension between Ksenia and Sumi was the normal friction between any two girls, a sudden gust of wind that's already died away. But between Sumi and Heta? I get the feeling it's been brewing for a while. "It was her choice to leave. You saw how she was. She couldn't handle it."

Handle what? I wonder, but Ksenia lays her hand on mine, making me dizzy. I put down my toast.

Heta doesn't bother to acknowledge Sumi's response. "Hee-Young," she says primly, "what do you remember about *patronage*?"

"What would *you* know about it?" mutters Ksenia.

Heta's jaw stiffens, but she waits quietly for my reply.

It's hard to speak. "Shepherd says—*said*," I correct myself, "they pay. For artists . . ." I trail off as the flaw in my understanding suddenly makes itself known. At Dunkin' Donuts, he'd described the situation as if the patrons operated as a charity, donating to the facility to experience the art and support all the artists at the same time.

But previously, Sumi and the others had called Garin *Hee-Young's* patron. I hadn't thought much about it—assumed that this had been a reference, maybe, to the grant that Shepherd had mentioned, the one that had provided the funds to create Hee-Young's position in the program.

But Sumi had also asked me: *Are you his, too?*

I look around the room, trying to understand. When I get to Ksenia, I see her as if for the first time. I notice that her irises don't match perfectly—though they both look black, one feels slightly warmer, an almost imperceptible amount of brown mixed in.

"Hee-Young," Heta says slowly. "Maybe you remember, but when you first got here, you didn't have a patron." It takes me a panicked second to realize that she's playing along again, talking to me as if I'm actually my sister, newly returned to the facility. "And then you went to the dinners, and then you made art, and you danced in the *ae-bi-ae-ri*—"

I shake my head at the strange word, but she continues without stopping: "And eventually, someone noticed you. Mels Garin. And he became your patron."

I swallow. The timeline doesn't line up, exactly, with what Shepherd told me—no, with what I *understood* of what he'd said—but it had been so much English at once that the words had started to crash into each other like waves. Maybe Garin's donation of the funds and his becoming Hee-Young's patron were two separate things, and I'd just connected them myself. "What . . . is patron?" I finally ask.

"Someone to give you a *future*," Heta says breathily. "Money, and a new, better place to live. Contacts with local artists and organizations to help you find a *koo-shy* job. A comfortable living as an artist."

I look around the room again, puzzled by the different expressions. Ksenia's face is stony; Sumi and Sarah look sad. "And Garin . . . he choose . . . Hee-Young?"

Behind me, Sumi and Sarah nod. "That's where . . . we thought she went," Sarah says softly, and I realize it's the first time she's spoken since I sat down. I have trouble parsing her accent: thick, heavy *r* sounds that dig deep in her throat, vowels that shift into places I don't expect. "But then Shepherd told us she went to . . . visit her mother. Is—is she OK?"

And for a moment, despite everything, between the fear and the exhaustion and the sudden ball of grief in my throat, I almost tell them. But then I catch something unexpected—Ksenia, glancing up at a spot near the ceiling, then furtively away. There's a shadow there, embedded where the crown molding meets the top of the wall. It almost looks like it could be a small hole.

Or a camera.

I tear my gaze away from the ceiling. "Yes," I say carefully. "Hee-Young . . . is . . . happy." I need to change the subject. "What . . . is Garin like?"

"Mels?" Sarah giggles. At first, I think she misunderstood my question, but Sumi shoots daggers at Sarah with her eyes and mumbles something under her breath. Then *both* of them start giggling.

Sumi purses her lips. "What Sarah *means* to say is that Garin is *sort-of*-handsome, educated, rich. Retired, but he had some kind of job in government, I think. Good manners, too. Compared to the other patrons, you could do worse—and you're lucky. You've just arrived, and you've already been chosen. Chosen in *advance*, even."

"Did they . . . know each other well?"

Sumi's mouth flattens into a thin line. "Hard to say. I imagine each of them would give you a different answer to that question."

I get the feeling that I'm missing something important. Heta clears her throat again. "Hee-Young, Garin is an *adequate* patron—"

Sumi's good cheer dissipates as she squints at Heta. "What do *you* know?" she says, echoing Ksenia's muttered remark from earlier.

"*Sumi.*" It's a single word, the first harsh one I've heard come out of Sarah since I met her—but Sumi falls silent.

"I don't think we need to talk about that." Heta's gotten much quieter, her tone so light it's almost juvenile, but it makes my stomach turn.

Last year, I started taking a new way home from work that was fifteen minutes longer but saved three thousand won in bus fare. One of the transfers was next to a girls' high school. I'd stand waiting for my next bus, my breath turning to frost, and watch them milling around before the first bell as they tried out curse words and snuck cigarettes. Without boys to observe them, most of them didn't use aegyo: acting cute and childish, with a baby voice.

Except for one, Binna. She barely ever spoke—but when she did, it was in a voice like this, soft and sweet and far too high. And she was the meanest bully of them all: grabbing girls by the hair, slapping them across the face, and organizing entire shunning campaigns as if she were exiling disgraced Joseon Dynasty nobles.

If any of the other girls noticed the danger in Heta's soft reply, they give no sign.

Sarah smiles at me again. "I think Garin . . . seems nice . . . though his name is . . . maybe silly. *Garin*, I mean—I never . . . heard name like this? And *Mels*. So strange."

"Russian," Ksenia says, leaning back in her chair. She shuts her eyes. "Garin could maybe be something else, maybe Spanish—though it's in a play by a Tolstoy. Not *the* Tolstoy—a relation. But Mels, it's . . ." Her brow furrows as she searches for a word, which surprises me. Her English is second only to Heta's, who feels to my untrained ear like a native speaker.

As everyone waits for her to finish, I glance around the room, studying faces. They're rapt: either this information is truly interesting, or *any* information about Garin is interesting.

"It's an *invented* name," Ksenia says finally. It's clear from the dissatisfaction on her face that she couldn't find the word she sought. "His father was committed to, *nu*, old revolutionary ideals.

It was a common practice to combine the names of leaders together. *Mels* means *Marx-Engels-Lenin-Stalin*."

On that last name, *Stalin*, she narrows her eyes. And her expression makes a bell ring in the back of my mind, something that itches like a wet shirt, though I can't remember why.

"How do you know this?" asks Sumi, one eyebrow raised. "I thought your patron was Nichols—"

"We've talked, Garin and I." She turns her face toward her plate again, and I get the feeling the discussion is over.

TWENTY-FOUR
Hee-Jin

From that moment on, the conversation vacillates wildly between topics I have no knowledge of and can't begin to approach in English: politics, the historical significance of great master painters, world events, economics.

I feel a gulf growing between us, wider every second, but I don't mind—it gives me time to turn Ksenia's cryptic statement about Garin—*we've talked*—around in my head. Is there a forbidden relationship between them that would explain the girls' long silence—or some seedy behavior Sarah didn't want to mention? But Ksenia seems to know things about Garin that no one else does, which means that she might be able to help me fool him tonight, if only I could get her alone and explain. And I need to speak with Shepherd, because it's starting to feel like tricking Garin will be impossible.

When my attention returns to the room, a creeping feeling edges down my shoulders, like cold seeping under a coat collar.

At first, I can't put my finger on it. I have to turn the room in my mind, side to side, listen to their birdlike chittering, examine the too-erect postures they sit in. And then it hits me: there's something *performative* about this conversation, something that feels stilted and academic—and entirely dishonest.

I've cut through the neighborhoods circling Ewha Womans University enough to know that while smart people talk about smart things, they also discuss the more personal, the emotional, the crass: ways to tell if a romantic partner is *really* interested or just after sex, how to get out from under your parents' thumbs, scoring a good deal on an excellent knockoff handbag. It's possible the women that inhabit this place are an entirely different breed, but I find that hard to believe.

Is this because of Ksenia's words about Garin? Some almost

superstitious way of shielding themselves from something distasteful? If not, for whose benefit is this show?

The only potential clue I find is Heta's repeated comments on the luxury of having this meal without Ca-lee's "watchful eye." Sumi and Sarah nod and agree, but it's perfunctory—and afterwards, there's the barest turn of heads between them, as if they were about to seek out the other's gaze but thought better of it.

Before I can worry at this further, the bell-tone rings. The girls rise like a troupe of musicians being called to take a bow. Seeing them move together, the differences in hair and skin tones turn into window dressing, highlighting their contoured cheekbones and sharp jawlines. I notice that except for Ksenia, their plates are still mostly untouched.

And then Ca-lee appears. *The tour.* I'd forgotten all about it.

"Let's go." Her smile is fake, but I still get a glimpse of another woman, one that almost reminds me of Hee-Young. "We can start with the rest of this floor. Then we'll do the third floor, and we'll finish up in the gardens, as they're on the way to the studio."

There was no mention of the second floor. Do Americans number them differently?

We step out of the dining room and turn right. She waves at a small sitting room and explains that the furniture is from the 1940s, before doubling back and taking us past the dining room, into the final room of this wing: a small kitchen with a door in the side.

"This is the servant's kitchen," she says.

I nod, but she isn't paying attention to me. Instead, she peers out the window, her body tense, the way cats are before they pounce. "Wait here."

She pulls a necklace out from underneath her shirt. On the end is a thick silver coin as big as a walnut, with the image of the house on the front. She holds it up to the back door, and then a lock turns, *kak!*

I almost follow her out before remembering her instructions to stay. Just as I'm starting to wonder what's taking her so long, she reappears.

"Sorry." She smooths her hair back and straightens her robes. "I thought I saw Lisa out there, but it was nothing."

She holds the key up to the door again—*kak!*—and proceeds

with the tour of the left wing, pointing out a bathroom, a study, and a library not much larger than a broom closet. It's packed neatly with books, organized by size. Ca-lee scans the shelves with an earnest expression. "We lost a book a while back. I keep hoping someone will return it, although—" She glances at me, before looking away. "The reader may have taken it with her on the plane."

We move back to the foyer. She points down the hallway to the right wing. "We'll head that way to get to the studio, but there's not much there you haven't seen. You know the psychomanteum. My bedroom is also down at the end, as is Lisa's, though she usually just sleeps with me. If you have an emergency, you can come find me, but ring the doorbell, as knocking won't work for obvious reasons."

She waves a hand at the staircase. "Now, let's go up. It's easier to, *em*, appreciate the gallery in the foyer that way. Did you bring your passport with you?"

My pulse jumps. I'd forgotten that instruction in her deluge of information this morning. "No, but . . . why bring?"

She looks irritated by my question. "Shepherd needs it for some forms."

I can't give it to her. If she flips it open, she'll see that it's Hee-Young's. "I already . . . did forms," I say a bit desperately. "Ask Shepherd." Surely, he'll be able to run interference for me.

There's a long pause. The air turns so chilly, I can almost see my breath hanging in it. "I just spoke to him this morning," she finally says. "He needs your passport for travel *re-im-burs-ment*. If you don't trust me with it—"

I understand too late how she's interpreted the situation. "No, I—"

"Go get it, and you can put it under Shepherd's door yourself. I won't even touch it."

I feel a spike of guilt, but pushing back now might raise even more suspicion, so I obey, running down the twisting stairs to the bedrooms. For a moment, I'm not sure which door is mine, but then I find it and retrieve the booklet with its polka-dotted cover.

I dash back up the stairs. I'm wheezing, but she pivots and marches straight up the circling staircase, rattling off information with each step, as if trying to drive away any attempt to talk about the tension of the previous moment. "This house was built by Shepherd's great-grandfather, who was heavily involved in steel production. He got the design from his friend—" She pauses on the staircase and turns back to look at me. "It's Garin, your patron. Their families go back quite a ways. The two of them even went to boarding school together. Garin's people are all well connected, like royalty: *byoo-row-crats*, politicians, a few movie producers. One of his ancestors spent time in the tropics—I think the Philippines—and he showed pictures of the house to Shepherd's great-grandfather. He loved the high ceilings, which are admittedly *ar-ki-tek-tya-lee* impressive, although they're not really suited to this climate."

She turns and proceeds up the stairs. "It's dreadful in the winter. All the heat goes straight up, and Shep's modifications didn't help—I'm sure his room and the engine room are the only warm places in the whole house. And the bedrooms—they say that being below surface grade makes you warmer, but I don't believe it. Though with me being on the main floor, I wouldn't benefit, anyways."

Engine room? Surface grade? None of these words are new to me, but the way she's combined them together, they don't make sense, though I imagine the latter probably means *underground*—down the stairs, into those cramped, windowless bedrooms.

"Oh, I forgot! There's a phone up by my room on the first floor, in an alcove in the wall. It doesn't call anybody except for a few specific numbers, but I think it'll probably dial 911."

I make a note of the emergency number, but my mind is drifting. There's something about her constant speech: it's like a wall of smoke that descends over the room, obscuring everything—but then it disperses, and I pick up from her the frantic energy of someone desperate for a paycheck, although she obviously doesn't have any such issue here.

It's exhausting to listen to.

Ca-lee pauses halfway up, on the first vine landing, but makes no move to tread down it. "This second floor is off-limits. Patrons only. You need a key."

I should be looking down as we summit, observing the gallery, but my entire focus is wired to the landing slowly growing in the top-right corner, the lofted half-floor that I know holds Shepherd's room. It's surrounded by a banister just taller than my waist—someone could push me off to my death, but it would take effort.

And there it is, Shepherd's door. Closed. I glance at Ca-lee, nervous, but she ignores me and gives a perfunctory knock. "Looks like he's out. Go ahead. Slip it under the door." She jiggles the doorknob. "Locked. It'll be safe until he's done."

It suddenly occurs to me that I have no idea what he could possibly need with it. Hee-Young was here before—surely he got all the information for any forms then? Unless he needs the stamp from my most recent entry into the USA? Or maybe this is his way of making sure I hold up my end of the bargain.

"We don't have all day," she says exasperatedly. "And it's safer in *there* than it is in your room. Honestly, most of the girls just *ask* Shep to hold their passports."

Because the rooms don't lock. I glance up at her, trying to get a read on her—but she's not looking at me at all. Instead, she stares at the door, almost as if she's trying to see through it.

I don't know what her strange behavior means, but she's right that it might be safer in there than in my room. There's clearly tension between the girls . . .

She moves faster than I thought possible, snatching it right from my hand, but the paper owl tucked inside falls out, exploding to its full size and startling us both.

"That's pretty," she says, her voice quaking. "Where did you get it?" Her tone is light, but it's forced. Even in my rage at her grabbing the passport, I realize how stupid I've been—Hee-Young likely made it here, and it's possible she even *showed* it to Ca-lee at some point.

"Hee-Young," I say carefully. "Present. For—going away."

My passport is on the ground. I reach down to grab it, but she kicks it under the door. "Sorry," she says. "Shep's orders."

TWENTY-FIVE
Hee-Jin

Once my passport is inside Shepherd's room, Ca-lee turns in the opposite direction and proceeds back over the skinny, vine-shaped platform. On this side is the lofted left half of the third floor, its landing surrounded by an identical banister. I follow her to the door, but she doesn't go in.

"This place is very special." Her cheeks are pinker than I remember, probably from exertion. "The engine room. It leads to the *Ae-vee-ae-ree*."

I wrestle with the strange word. Out of all the English letters, I've found Vs especially troublesome to pronounce. No matter how many times I try, I can't seem to roll my bottom lip from beneath my top teeth at the right speed to smoothly execute the sound.

She winks and spells it for me. "A place for birds." And then she taps her pendant necklace against the door. Another loud *kak* echoes, just like the one in the servant's kitchen. She pushes the door in and turns on the light.

The room is dominated by the guts of massive machines—gears, springs, cables, a huge series of steel motors, though it's not like any engine room I've ever seen. The machines are all curvaceous and wet-looking, as if they were carved from flesh that weeps through a thin coating of metal. And they're all so still and silent, packed tightly together for an eerie sleep. The only walkable space left in the room is a narrow strip that terminates against the back wall, from which a small, airy staircase of dark brown metal pierces the ceiling through an oval opening. It looks like an old-fashioned fire escape, meant to collapse and extend.

"It's up there," she says, pointing to the opening. And then comes another one of her rehearsed scripts, one I only partially understand. "It's not original to the house, of course. And I know it looks like glass, but it's a polymer—stronger, and far lighter.

Even with all the modifications, it weighs so much that the entire building had to be reinforced with carbon-fiber steel girders."

My mind works desperately each time she pauses for a breath. She'd said *it looks like glass*, but I don't see anything that looks like glass in this room, only the dark shine of the machines.

"All right," she says, doubling back. "We should look at the gardens next."

We descend and go out through a door at the end of the right wing, this one requiring no key. Once we're outside, Ca-lee falls into an easy monologue, one she's obviously given many times. Her voice fades into a buzz as I take in the plants: early flowers, dried-up stems, and a huge number of dancing willow trees that make me think of their goddess, Yu-hwa, disgraced by her failed engagement and abandoned by her father. Half-buried near one's base is something thin and white, like a hairpin. It's oddly familiar, though I can't place it—not until I dig a finger into the soft loam and reveal a small spine, the skull at the end the size of a chestnut. I gasp and fall back while rubbing my hand on my sweatpants.

"Oh!" Ca-lee squats, entranced. "I think this was Eliana's *geh-nee-pik*. See the teeth?" At my confused expression, she clarifies. "A pet. Like a big mouse." And then she mimes with her hand, a wiggling motion like a small animal.

She must mean "guinea pig." The words are almost the same in Korean.

"It disappeared right after she arrived. She always blamed the others—she and Ksenia almost came to blows over it. But it must've been out here the whole time." She *jjeut-jjeut*s to herself in disapproval, and then she covers it back up, shoving the dirt with her finger. "No wonder this plant bloomed early. Well-fed."

Her morbid statement makes me recall Ksenia's warning—that Ca-lee's not all there—but then I realize I might recognize the plant, the huge bunches of spear-like, dark-green leaves. When Hee-Young and I were much younger, before we moved to Seoul, our mother used to treat our illnesses with herbs. She would've preferred medicine, but without papers, we couldn't use the national health insurance, and we didn't have the money to pay for it ourselves.

So instead, she walked through the woods with a plastic bag, snipping stems and pulling moss off trees. We were always worried she'd misidentify something and poison us. Other herbs she grew in her garden, though they always died eventually from neglect. But there was one, michigwangipul, she gave to us for pain, especially when our lungs hurt from bad air and damp living conditions. I remember it was bitter, and that it made me sleepy, and that we should never ingest it without preparing it properly or being careful of the dose; too much of the *madman's plant* made people and cows alike rave like they'd been possessed.

"All right," Ca-lee says. "This way." She turns and forges ahead.

Before I follow her, I grab a leaf and pop the very tip in my mouth. It tastes exactly as I remember.

Ca-lee and I hook left, behind the house. A structure materializes in the near distance: a small glass greenhouse, the panes frosted so that the image through them is blurry, like smearing lotion on a glass.

"You can take yourself from here." She gestures at the building, but her eyes flit back in the direction from which we came. "Just ask Heta to show you to your station. I'll check on you soon."

She doesn't wait for an answer before she leaves. I walk across the yard, my heart starting to beat faster, but long before I reach the door, it swings open, and Ksenia steps out.

"I thought you'd be by," she says. "I've been waiting for you."

The thought gives me an entertaining shiver—and then I remember where I am, how I got here, and I feel like a ship dashed to pieces on the rocks.

She steps forward until she's close enough for me to see the pores of her nose. My heart accelerates as she takes my hand, but only for a moment; by the time I register the flush of heat, the fireworks of shock, she's let go.

But she's left me a gift in my palm: a flat piece of long, thin plastic, a drawing of a flashlight on the front. Where the bulb would be, there's a small LED embedded in the end. At the other end, instead of a battery cap, is a thin circle stamped with the words, PRESS ME.

I squeeze, and the LED winks on. My fingers brush a hard edge on the flashlight's back—a magnet.

"It was Eliana's," she murmurs. "I was going to bring it to you, but then I saw Ca-lee go into your room. Hide it, though. There's no rule against it, but you still don't want to get caught with it."

She holds the door open for me to step inside.

TWENTY-SIX
Hee-Jin

Ksenia's gift is so thoughtful, it's not until I'm inside the greenhouse hallway and staring at the glass doors labeled one through six that I remember *why* I am in this room: I have to make *art*. Something that will convince Garin that I am, in fact, an artist.

Fear buries me like an avalanche. I feel like one of the giant hospital washing machines, gallons and gallons of water tumbling through white sheets. I don't know what staved it off for so long: grief, desire, or just the way the last few days have been engineered to overwhelm me in any way they can. Following conversations around me is hard enough; there wasn't time for anything else.

I close my eyes, trying to remember what Shepherd said at Dunkin' Donuts. Trying to hear it over the soft hiss of the machines, the cheerful yet tired voice of the pink-visored woman behind the counter.

Something about sculpture. Sculpture and . . . folk art.

I don't know anything about Korean art, much less folk art—but that was the point, right? However much I know, Garin knows less.

Something oily wraps long tendrils around my guts. If I *don't* fool Garin, Shepherd will have no use for me. Not only will I not get my money, he could have me deported. And with that will go any chance of figuring out what happened to my sister.

"Your studio is next to mine, *Hee-Young*." Ksenia points at one of the rooms, which is labeled with a big number one. "I think Shepherd left something for you there."

"Left . . . something?"

She nods. "A box. Looked heavy."

I'm so grateful and relieved, my voice quivers. "Thank you." I realize, suddenly, that a part of my brain feared that Shepherd had just abandoned me, despite his sob story and our agreement.

All the time we spent in the initiation ceremony, on Ca-lee's tour—that's all time that I could've spent rehearsing for the dinner, and I can't understand why he's just let me float aimlessly through this place.

Unless . . . is it possible we're being watched, and he's afraid of being observed speaking with me? The white-suited facilitators are *everywhere*, and it's impossible to keep only loyal words in that many mouths. What about the girls? Could one of *them* be colluding with Garin?

Ksenia raises an eyebrow. "Aren't you going to, you know, look at it?"

"Yes. Sorry."

I follow her as far as her room, which is labelled two, and then she waves me toward number one. As I slide in the door, I pass the room directly across from mine, six, and see Heta immersed in opening small tubes of paint and setting out brushes.

I swallow hard as I inventory the space. The white wall to the left is just a bit taller than me, barely covering half the distance between the floor and ceiling. It's lined with plants: hanging in baskets, pots interspersed between easels. To my right is a bookshelf heavily laden with an assortment of supplies that I allow myself the briefest moment to examine: silvery tubes of various sizes. Paintbrushes, some as thin as a few eyelashes banded together, others with clumps of bristles as fat as my thumb. Small cylinders like crayons, rectangles of what looks like sidewalk chalk. Tall, fat bottles of black and blue ink, with and without droppers. Blocks of wood and chisels, small thin tubes of what look like glass, a fist-sized chunk of beeswax.

Straight back, by the frosted-glass outer wall, is some kind of workbench with a tall stool, a large cardboard box on top. I rush toward it, dig my hands in, and extract a short note:

I'll come talk to you later. Make something, and in the meantime, memorize this guest list. It's in seat order from left to right.

Hans Smallet (Smal-let): Software mogul. Like Pepperdine, he's only just started attending and has not selected someone to sponsor.

Julius Pepperdine: Doctor, older, Southern. First time at the patron dinner. Do not act like you know him. He isn't eligible to fully sponsor someone yet, but he's joining us to see if he likes it.

Mels Garin: Retired, currently an advisor for a senator. As far as I know, never talked about work or anything of substance with Hee-Young.

Margarete (Mar-ga-reet) Jones: Late 40s, will be the only woman there. Actress, director, philanthropist. She tends to be very curious about the artists. She also has a sixth sense for picking up on lies, so I would try to answer any questions she asks you honestly, if you can do it without giving yourself away. If she does get suspicious, I think I can convince her to keep quiet. Sarah's patron.

Buster Carlson: Corporation owner, works in media and publishing. You shouldn't have anything to worry about with him—he's Sumi's patron, and very attentive to her.

All that's left in the box is a stack of bricks of clay wrapped in cellophane, their colors varying from a gray that's almost white to a deep red, labels stamped with words like *modeling* and *terra cotta* and *polymer* and *low fire*.

There's no mention of Ksenia's patron, *Nik-ols*. And his notes about Garin are so barebones, they're almost useless—no physical description or mention of his personality, his likes and dislikes. And Shepherd was supposed to have been investigating how Garin scared Hee-Young off—but maybe he didn't want to leave details in a note where they could be found by any of the girls.

He could've at least given me a hint as to what to make, though, or how to go about it. Maybe I could ask one of the girls for help? I peek out the door to see if any of them look open to being interrupted, but there's a woman standing in the hallway, turned away. It's Ca-lee.

I don't want to be subject to another strange, time-wasting conversation, so I back away from the door before she can see me and return to the workbench. I select a brick the size of a block of tofu with a friendly picture of a bear and the word *modeling* on the label. I try to tear apart the plastic, but when that fails, I grab a scalpel-like tool from a wooden cup on the workbench and stab it a few times. When I grab the edges of the package and pull, the plastic stretches on either side of the perforations, turning opaque and milky white.

I slide the clay onto the table. *Art.* I will myself to channel Hee-Young, the way she could find inspiration in every falling leaf, every bend of a road.

It would be easiest to just copy something, though most of the traditional figure sculptures I've seen are made of wood or metal. But what would make it *folk* art? Should I use a Buddhist or Confucian symbol, or an animal like a tiger or a magpie . . .?

My eyes suddenly sting with frustration. I glance over in Ksenia's direction despite the wall blocking my view, and then I swallow hard and push my feelings back down. I say a silent thanks to my mother, who taught me to survive anything. Even this.

Maybe I should try to do some kind of vessel. Korea has long been famous for its ceramics. While I was at the hospital laundry, venturing into public areas was strongly discouraged—but one day, an electronic lock malfunctioned. Until they fixed it, we had to cut through a lobby to get to work.

On the second day, a newsreel on the lobby television caught my interest. I stopped and watched the perfectly pressed anchor present a recent archaeological find in Japan: a number of artifacts dating to the late 1500s and early 1600s, including clothes and tools used by Korean potters that had been captured during Japanese invasions.

"Many people outside Korea don't know about the major influence Koreans had on Japanese pottery. A number of famous Japanese porcelain styles, like Arita, Satsuma, and Hagi, were all developed by kidnapped Korean potters. And giant advances in Japanese pottery-making were due to the enslavement of Koreans during the Imjin War."

I couldn't walk away, even though I was late and the anchor was telling me things I already knew. One of the only revelations Hee-Young extracted from our mother was the knowledge that somewhere deep in our lineage was a woman left behind after the capture of her ceramic-making husband.

Working this clay should be in my blood, but the lump in front of me doesn't agree. It just sits, cold and unfeeling, waxy and wet, the same texture and color as dead fish meat.

Except for the pictures I doodled as a child on paper street-food cones, I've never tried to create *anything*. I've never even cooked a novel dish or picked out clothes with the intent of expressing my personality, like Hee-Young's sandwich tee shirt or the old canvas shoes she dug out of a dumpster and dipped in purple dye. Before I got on that plane, my focus was on one singular goal: achieving some measure of stability, of safety. There was no time for anything else.

I never should have come here. Maybe, if I broke into Shepherd's room for my passport and ran away now, I could get far enough to find somewhere to hide before my absence was discovered—but then what? I don't have any money. I barely speak English. If Shepherd reports me to the authorities, Hee-Young's passport will be worse than not having one at all.

Leaving now would throw away any chance of a new life. And all of the clues she left behind—cryptic notes of dates and letters and poems, papercraft and resin rings—would amount to nothing. All my questions about what happened to her—if anything did—would never be answered.

Frustrated, I dig my fingertips into the block, squeezing until my pointer fingernail presses into the pad of my thumb, as if my inspiration is hidden somewhere inside this piece of clay. When that proves fruitless, I smash my fist into it, making the table shake. It hurts, but in a good way.

"I'm not familiar with that technique." Ca-lee's voice.

I spin, blocking her view. I don't know how to explain what she just saw, but her eyes are unfocused, almost glassy, and when she steps close, I smell the sweet tang of wine. "I see that you've picked modeling clay—is that for your pre-work and getting the *pro-por-shuns*?"

Sweat breaks out along my back as she steps around me. Her brow furrows as she draws closer, and then she peels the clay off the table, leaving behind a wet stain.

I didn't know clay could stain.

She turns to the bookcase and retrieves a green mat with white markings on it—a grid, I think. For measuring. "This will keep you from ruining the table." She drops it on the bench. "I'm going to check on the other girls, and then I'll stop by again." She reaches over and pats me on the hand so gently, I'm not quite sure if I imagine the touch, or if she just hovers her palm above my skin, sending down a soft wave of heat. "Can I give you some advice?"

She doesn't wait for me to understand, much less to answer.

"The best art is the kind that scares you. Dig deep. Let out your worst fears. Only then can you be free of them."

I almost laugh, but what good would that do?

After she leaves, I hold my breath, trying to calm myself—and then I hear her voice from Ksenia's room on the other side of the half-wall. Ksenia had warned me not to trust Ca-lee—and yet I felt no malice in her, though she was drunk and strange. As for her advice? I'm afraid of so many things, I don't even know where to start.

When I resume my spot at the table, something catches my eye—a clear bit of plastic, sticking out from underneath one of the flowerpots. I lever the heavy pot to one side, just enough to slide out a baggie. Sprinkled inside is what looks like a small bundle of threads, but when I bring it to the light, I realize they're human hair—and from the different shades, it's from dozens of different heads, everything from blondest blonde to deep auburn to darkest black.

This was Hee-Young's studio before, wasn't it? What could she possibly have been doing with this?

I stuff it into my pocket for later, adding it to my endless list of clues.

TWENTY-SEVEN
Hee-Jin

Ca-lee checks on me twice more. Her words for what she calls *my work* are kind. Which means she must be delusional, seeing things in my battered lump of clay that don't exist.

As soon as the bell-tone rings for lunch, I bolt toward my room to hide the bag of hair and study the guest list Shepherd gave me, but I barely make it into the outer garden before someone calls my name. "Hee-Young, wait!"

Ksenia. Anybody else, I might've pretended not to hear. I turn and drink in the sight of her. There's a startling economy to the movement of her limbs, no artifice to her stride. She's probably walked the same since she was a little girl, never once debating the space she takes up. "Where are you headed so fast?"

I lick my bottom lip before remembering she can see me. Though I hadn't meant anything lascivious, the shame is immediate. "I just—I don't feel so well. I'm going . . . to lie down."

Ksenia nods slowly—not agreeing, just acknowledging she heard me. "If you can bear it, I think you should just come to lunch."

She inclines her head at the other girls filtering out of the studio door. They nod back as they pass, though Heta's expression is suspicious, and Sumi and Sarah mostly have eyes for each other. Once they're all safely out of earshot, Ksenia murmurs, "Eliana didn't leave because of family problems. We should stick together."

"Why did . . . she leave?"

Ksenia shakes her head, apparently unwilling to reveal more—but then she takes my hand, and a throbbing warmth spreads down my arm and through my chest, my abdomen. When she strides toward the house, I've no choice but to follow.

"I don't want to be alone right now." She mutters the words

almost directly in my ear, and I slow down, just for the thrill of feeling her pull me forward.

At lunch, both Ca-lee and Shepherd are again missing. From the way the girls remark on it, this is atypical. Between glances at my copy of the guest list, I look at Ksenia, but she isn't paying attention to me. Instead, her gaze is trained on a decorative centerpiece in the middle of the table: a whitewashed wooden bowl which someone has filled with small clay beads, into which plunge the stems of a handful of baby's breath.

At first, I think she's concentrating on the stems, the little pop of green, so vivid against the stark white of the table. But then, out of the corner of my eye, I watch as she furtively grabs a few of the beads and palms them. After another glance to make sure nobody is watching, she takes one and pops it into her mouth like a mint.

Fascinated, I wait for her to spit it out—but then her eyes close and her throat bobs, and I realize she's swallowed it.

She eats three more beads like this before the bell-tone rings. I grab one on the way out of the room, but from every examination I can make of it—weight, smell, taste—it's just a piece of dry clay.

TWENTY-EIGHT
Callie

After I drop Hee-Young off at the greenhouse, I check on Lisa. She's napping peacefully, almost too beautiful to be real, but I see from the window that Shep's car is gone again, leaving a restless jitter in my chest.

I make myself a cup of herbal tea in the servant's kitchen. The sun burnishes the room as Shep's earlier single-word reply—*always*—rotates in my mind.

If only I'd been brave enough to finish the sentence. *Do you still* is no more than a vessel heading, a compass direction, a line on which an infinite number of points reside. Like: *Do you still remember our first anniversary, where we flew to Krakow and I discovered that some places really look like enchanted kingdoms, and we sipped black tea out of tiny cups and made fumbling castles out of snow?*

A flood of images fills my mind. Mornings curled up on the settee, the roasted smell of his coffee clinging to the air like mist. The almost imperceptible sliding of the linen sheets as he crept into bed to make love. He was never too tired. I always burned with envy seeing that: the soft, easy aging of a man that's never sacrificed body and mind to make rent.

I wrap my hands around the cup. There's a kiss of warmth left in the ceramic, a memory of the tea. Could our love be like that?

Maybe there's a way to find out. My pendant's keyed to his apartment in case of emergencies. It won't give me access to his bedroom, but something in his sitting room might reveal how he feels about me—or if he's really moved on. And now's the best time to sneak in: the girls are in the studio, the facilitators crowded in the kitchen to prepare lunch.

I creep into the hall, the faint scents of chamomile and vanilla following me out. Cooking echoes from the main kitchen—chopping and sizzling, the dull ring of plates and pans hitting counter tops. The wings of the house are so claustrophobic compared to the high-ceilinged entry hall, but for once, I appreciate the intimacy of the space.

When I get to the main staircase, I spot a movement behind me, but it's just a reflection of my dress: the walls, no doubt responding to my accelerating pulse, have started to shudder, making the mirrors dance. I climb the stairs to his room and try the knob, my heart slamming in my chest, and then I hold my pendant up against where the electronic receiver should be. The answering click is so soft, it feels imaginary.

I push my way into the room, step over Hee-Young's passport, close the door behind me, and hold my pendant up again. This time, though, there's no click.

My heart sinks. I can't re-lock it. I'm committed to whatever happens, now.

A soft glow filters through the windows as I try to get the feel of the room. It doesn't seem like anything's changed since my visit last night. Everything's perfectly arranged on the shelves on either side of his bedroom door. The chairs and the coffee table and the little cabinet in which he keeps the alcohol are all angled *just so*. Shep would notice if I shifted them even an inch.

A bitter poison slides down my throat. I've always found it impossible to leave an imprint on any space we shared. I'd choose a new rug or swap a painting, and the help would put everything back. When I complained, Shep would deny he told them to—or that anything had changed.

This silent war made me furious: furnishings disappearing, curtains suddenly re-materializing as if I'd never thrown them out. It felt like they were all colluding to erase me. I should feel affronted, then, by this residence my ex-husband has created—unreachable, if we're willing to respect his privacy—but I'm just sad he's hidden himself away.

If I was a good, kind, loving woman, I'd leave the door to his bedroom alone, but it feels like I'm teleporting to it. I try the handle—locked—and only then do I take a breath. From the keyhole, it seems this door requires a physical key.

Where would he hide it? The Shep I knew was a practical man that hated to be troubled by small things like losing the remote or hiding presents. He'd keep the key somewhere easy and accessible.

I beeline for the display shelves. My mind readily supplies the stories of the curios: the watch his father gave him when he turned sixteen, the candlesticks his ba-ba's mother had somehow saved from revolution.

I don't find it on the first shelf, the second, or the third. On the fourth, just as my heart is sinking, something glints from inside a handkerchief-covered basket. I pull back the cloth, and my eyes suddenly mist.

The pewter jewelry box I made. The shattered heart is missing, all traces of glass swept away—but Shep kept the base.

It's heavier than I remember, as if our secrets have filled it to bursting, but when I flip open the lid, its edges gleaming in the low light, there's nothing inside, save a single key.

I put the box back on the shelf. In the moment before my fingers leave its familiar surface, I imagine I feel a note of warmth.

And then I break into my ex-husband's bedroom.

TWENTY-NINE
Callie

After years in this house, I've found foreign country. The beams that float through Shep's sitting area don't dare to penetrate his room, and stepping in feels like pushing myself out of an airlock into the void of space. When I close the door behind me, the sound goes, too, leaving me directionless and reeling. I hastily flip on the light.

The changes he's made astound me. The bare, once-gray walls are now a dark red so lurid it turns my stomach. Lining both sides of the massive bed are bookshelves stuffed with curios, the only recognizable one a small glass bowl of beads. The air has an odd astringent smell, like fresh paint. I peel the heavy drapes back, and my heart breaks: he's blacked out the windows.

I don't know what silent pain these awful walls hold, but Shep—who demands nothing but the finest in all things, who taught me about the importance of wine vintage and what it means to summer somewhere—my Shep would never do a thing like this.

I feel myself sinking. I barely make it to the mattress before my legs go out. The sheets rustle oddly, too stiff, as if even soft bedding was a pleasure he felt he didn't deserve.

It happens before I realize it—the shift in angle, the disorientation. One moment, I am sitting up. The next, I am lying full-length, my head on his pillows, as if I were in a coffin—

I catch a scent and stiffen: I know this smell. I've tasted it many times as I leaned over Hee-Young, helping her with that nursery book, imagined her slathering on orange-scented lotion before realizing it was just her natural essence—*though Hee-Young's replacement also has a bit of that smell, doesn't she?*

But the implications of this scent, here, in this bed, they're just not possible. Shep wouldn't take advantage of someone young enough to be his daughter, and Hee-Young's been gone for weeks—

And then I see it: a long hair, too pin-straight and too dark to be mine.

Everything comes crashing down on me. Women cycle through this place. Surely, he hasn't slept with all of them—but five, ten? Did he tell them it would be necessary for their residence here? Or was it something that just happened—all these passionate, artistic, confused young women, attracted to the scent of old money, the hint of foreign power?

My cheeks are suddenly on fire. These girls—were they watching me haunt the halls? Did they gossip about me, about Lisa and the accident, about my drinking?

The most disgusting and awful truth is that the ball of rage and hurt inside of me is already cooling. I've committed too many crimes of my own. I *deserve* his infidelity.

Even now, I want to embrace him.

I extract myself from his bed. The bowl of clay beads on his shelf catches my eye, the one piece of this room I recognize, though it's far fuller than I remember. There are bowls like it all over the house, but this one is somehow special. Right after we got married, he installed it in our bedroom, calling it *the only art I know how to do.*

I give the room a final look, trying to memorize this snapshot of my ex-husband's pain—and that's when I notice it on the back wall: a vertical crack so slim it nearly disappears when I change the angle of my approach. It could be an imperfection in the plaster, a seam—but I see it and think *door* and *secret compartment*, and I advance, ready to try to pry it open.

But then the bell-tone rings. It ends in a slight crackle, some faulty connection in the room speakers.

Studio time is over. The girls are on their way back.

I rush out, barely remembering to lock the bedroom door behind me. The door to his quarters I can't relock, and I have no choice but to leave it before dashing down the stairs.

THIRTY
Hee-Jin

After watching Ksenia eat beads and furtively studying the roster under the table, it's almost a relief to return to the studio.

Before long, my right hand is so tired, I can barely close it into a fist, but in between brief sessions of quizzing myself on the roster, I discover that there's a strange, meditative quality to my attempts to create something, like doing laundry or cleaning the apartment. Somehow, the part of me that *wants* all the time goes quiet. If all art is like this, I understand why Hee-Young wouldn't give it up—although trying to make a career of it is another matter.

It's almost a surprise when the next bell-tone rings. I back away from the bench, interlock and stretch my fingers. There's a shape to the lump in front of me, clear signs of something starting to emerge. *Maybe Ca-lee was right.*

"Interesting." Before I can react to Shepherd's voice behind me, he steps in closer. "Wait here a moment."

And then he backs into the hallway, but he holds the door open—so I can hear the conversation? Or so he can keep blocking the doorway with his body? "Go ahead, everyone. Get washed up."

Their footsteps bounce off the glass as they shuffle out. Then it's just the two of us: me with my back to the bench, him in front of the only exit. He's holding a shoebox-sized, cloth-wrapped bundle.

As if he senses my discomfort, he slides sideways, toward the half-wall to my left, and points behind me. "You've done a good job. Certainly *looks* like it could be some kind of folk art—at least an *in-tre-pre-ta-shun*."

My glance back at the clay is reflexive, but in that moment, the lines come together in a new way, and I realize what my subconscious has made. It's small, the sides not nearly smooth enough—but it's the rough shape of an onggi pot.

I twitch, wanting to smash it down with my fist. *Not in front of Shepherd.*

"I thought we should talk before tonight. Make sure we're on the same page—"

Behind him, a reflection moves. Shepherd must notice me tense, because he stops and peeks his head out the door. "Heta, dear. What are you still doing in here?"

She emerges, blonde hair glowing in the sunlight. "I just . . ." She glances at me, and I can tell she wishes I wasn't here. "I wanted to ask you. I wasn't sure why you had Ca-lee do Hee-Young's, er, second ceremony, when I've done all the ones for the last year. Did I mess up in some way?" Her pitch has risen until it's wheedling, but I remember her at breakfast, the baby-voice of the school bully.

He laughs, a full, robust sound that ricochets off the glass. "No, of course not! I just think it would be good for Ca-lee to be more involved—"

"Why?" A pause. "You're not married anymore."

My chest tenses. A divorce would explain the odd tension between Shepherd and Ca-lee—but not why she still lives here.

"It doesn't matter," Shepherd says softly. "We all have responsibilities. Like you—shouldn't you be getting ready for the patron dinner?"

She pouts but turns away. When I'm sure she's out of earshot, I pull out the list. "I . . . studied it. But . . ." I don't know how to phrase my objections: that the girls' gossip has impressed upon me that Garin knew Hee-Young better than Shepherd thought, that we should've realized her frame was slimmer than mine, that fooling him might be impossible.

But he seems to sense my anxiety. "Don't worry. First of all, Garin is going to be nice and drunk for the patron dinner. He always is. And second, I doubt he'll recognize you, given your new *commitment* to folk art." He hands me the bundle.

I take it and unfold the cloth to reveal two wooden masks, face-down. When I unstack and turn them over, though, my blood goes cold. They're both tal: wooden masks used in traditional ritual dances. Tal all have specific characteristics representing the archetypical role of the character assigned to them. The first mask is gaski—a bride, with closed lips, no ears, and one eyehole positioned as if looking down, all to reflect the advice that used to be given to newlywed daughters: when it came to the imperfections of your husband, you should turn a blind eye, be deaf, and say nothing for three years.

The other mask is also female, with red, rouged lips that are barely open and a cheerful smile. I recognize it as Bune, the "flirty woman", who is usually portrayed as an entertainer and concubine to scholars and other members of the elite class.

I swallow, not understanding what he wants from me. "I should . . . wear this?"

His eyes flick from left to right as his gaze searches my face. "Why? Is there something wrong?"

"Where . . . did you find?" I wave at the masks.

He sighs, exasperated. "I sent a facilitator out and told him to find me some masks that look like Korean folk art. What does it matter?" He picks them back up off the workbench and shoves them at me with both hands. "Dinner is in less than an hour. You have to get ready. Just choose one."

My throat closes up. Tal are not just masks. They're powerful cultural objects of religious and historical significance, and the choice between them feels heavy with omen. Ancient brides were treated as property—virgins who often had their eyelids glued shut on their wedding day so they couldn't see the much older strangers they were being forced to marry. But unlike the concubine, they were upheld as icons of purity, a representation of society functioning in harmony and as it should—as long as the opinion of the bride wasn't considered.

Either way, it feels cheap and wrong to wear one at the dinner to hide my identity, especially when I remember the rest of the outfit. "I don't . . . with *kimono*—"

"The clothes are part of the image. Non-*ne-go-sha-bul*." At the furrow in my brow, he clarifies. "You *have* to wear them. The patrons insist, and Garin will be suspicious if you don't."

My stomach sinks. I want to argue, but something tells me he won't care about the atrocities of Japanese occupation. After another moment—one where I see Hee-Young's body, abandoned on my bed—I pick the mask of the concubine.

Shepherd glances at the glass behind him at something I can't see. "Get washed up and dressed. Make sure you're not late." And then he leaves.

After a moment, I slip into the hallway and scan the glass, but whatever caught his attention is gone.

When I finally get back to my room, I intend to rest just long enough to cool down after the brisk walk from the greenhouse, but once I sit on the bed, I'm too dizzy to stand. Anxiety? Or could the white noise bouncing around inside my head be exhaustion, the weariness of being immersed in English from the moment I woke up? I'm almost grateful for the way this room blocks the sounds from the outside world, eerie or not.

And even though I don't have much time, I close my eyes, flop backward, and sink into the soft mattress's embrace. It feels like I'm floating—and then I *am* floating, back on that spinning platform in the mirror-filled psycho . . . *psychomanteum*, the room transformed into a night swamp by my addled mind. I can see the girls grabbing the edge, their brows creasing and jaws tightening with the effort of turning me—and then my sister's face, appearing and disappearing with each revolution, mouthing a sentence over and over.

Something *window. Find the window? There are no windows?* Or maybe it was just my imagination and not a real sentence at all.

I've had so little time in her room, and most of that has been drugged and in pitch darkness. Shepherd said there was an hour before the patron dinner—which means I might have enough time to look for clues.

I open my eyes and slide off the bed. Since I can't lock my door, I need to be careful.

I check behind the sink and in each crevice of the shelves. I go through the armoire again, shaking out every article of clothing and checking for hidden seams. The only new discovery is both strange and innocuous—a long gray and white feather, about the size and shape of a duck's quill. When I run my fingers over the edge, the fibers don't lock together as they should. It's fake.

Under the mattress, I find a square children's book. I flip through it, looking for hidden messages in the margins, codes of circled letters, but the only trace of Hee-Young's touch is a pressed flower that marks the page for a story called *Rumpelstiltskin*. It sounds like a nonsense word. I try to scan it, but the language is strange.

But then the triptych of paintings catches my eye. I crawl out of bed and study them closely for the first time, moving top to bottom: a small cabin in some forest, passing through the seasons. There's a square red chimney on its roof, like the ones I saw over and over as we drove through that abandoned village, but the position varies with each painting. I realize the three images are from different views.

The top-most is of the front of the cabin, a dark-red door in the exact middle of the wall. Surrounding the building is a lush tapestry of bright, green leaves that have a pleasant texture when I run my fingers over them, though on closer examination, a number of them are actually cleverly disguised frogs.

The second picture turns the cabin ninety degrees to the left. The leaves have changed to a riot of oranges and reds, and in the bottom-right corner, a fox disappears against the splendor of a carmine shrub. I don't like foxes. They're supposed to be shape-shifting swindlers, seducers, and murderers—and symbols of forbidden love.

I pull the painting down and flip it over. The frame is extra deep, like a shadowbox, and there's a white card slightly larger than a postage stamp tucked into the bottom right.

The name on the card isn't Hee-Young's. It reads: *Retreat in Fall, Kitty Pachenko, 1945.*

I replace the painting, but I feel like I'm teetering on the edge of a realization. I squat to inspect the final picture. Of the three, it's the least eye-catching: a snowy night scene in a palette of muted grays, browns, and blues. In the painted window, I can just make out the barest reflection of the moon in one of the panes, a smudge in another—

I bring my face closer. The smudge almost looks like an owl flying toward the glass.

Could that be what Hee-Young had been saying? Something about *the owl in the window*?

My stomach tightens. I grab the painting, but it's stuck. I brace myself and haul on it. Its right side suddenly swings out like the door of a safe, revealing an open hollow. The uncovered space is about two feet deep, with sheet-metal sides and a grate across the entire bottom, the holes too large to catch rice. Sitting on the grate is a small padlock, the shackle open, and a flat file the size of a dinner knife.

I hold my breath as I kneel and pull the objects out. It's cold over the grate, air seeping in from somewhere else. I shuffle the lock and file into my right hand before sticking my head in and peering down, but I can't see past the grate. I plant my left hand for balance and turn to look up.

It's some sort of shaft—for ventilation, I'd guess, though I can't tell how far it goes. After a few feet, it fades into dark.

It makes sense—the rooms have a lip around the door and no windows, but the temperature is always comfortable. Even being set into the ground—what had Ca-lee said? *Below grade?*—they'd need some kind of HVAC system for extreme weather, some way to exchange the air. That must've been the hiss that I'd heard the first night, the one that sounded like the ocean.

I pull my head out and check the painting-door. There are small slits in the sides, meaning my room was never fully sealed. On the bottom of the frame is a metal ring that exactly matches one on the wall—and from the size of the holes, I guess they're for the padlock.

I thought the lock's shackle was just open, but it's been filed through, the cut surface polished and shining. Hee-Young did this, I'm sure. *But why?*

My stomach turns to stone. The shaft would be the perfect place to hide things . . . things that might still be there. I could only see up a few feet, but there's no telling how high it actually goes. I need a light—

Of course.

I pull the flashlight magnet from my pocket and squeeze the button at the end. The LED twinkles on. This time, I can see about six feet before the shaft sharply bends toward the center of the house, out of my view.

I can just spy something peeking over the edge of the bend. Something round and metallic, like a showerhead.

I try to press in closer, but my shoulders don't *quite* fit, my position and the bulky sweatshirt both working against me. I slide out, strip it off, and put the end of the flashlight in my mouth. When I clamp my teeth, the light blinks on. *Good enough.*

I lie on my back and wriggle in again. My shoulders clear the opening, but the shaft's walls pin my arms to my sides. I wedge myself in farther, pushing hard with my legs. My lungs burn, demanding oxygen, but I can't open my mouth without dropping the light, and the rasps of my breath through my nose echo in the tinny shaft.

Once I'm in as far as my elbows, I can't move anymore. I'm too big—but just by a centimeter.

My sister could fit, I bet. Especially the flesh and bone version of her that was on my doorstep. She could hide something up on the ledge formed where the shaft bends toward the house, and Shepherd, the facilitators, and everybody else that outweighed her could never reach it.

What if the Hee-Young I saw while spinning on that platform was more than just fear and drugs?

Cold prickles my neck, my sweating back. I suddenly don't want to be in here anymore, pinned like a butterfly and blind.

I straighten my legs and let myself slide down. I have to press my heels into the ground and bend my legs as hard as I can to pull myself out, my hamstrings burning with the effort. Finally, I'm out of the claustrophobic press of the shaft, though my damp skin is covered in black streaks of dirt. For the first time, I notice that the air out here smells different—stale, like paint.

Before I can think of what to do next, the bell-tone rings for dinner. If I don't show up on time, someone will come to check on me. Hee-Young's little book and flower are still on the bed—and I need to get this shaft closed.

My legs wobble as I stagger to my feet. I throw the file and the padlock back in the shaft, but the pressed flower flutters through my fingers and haphazardly glides to the ground. Something about the change in angle brokers connections in my mind, and I recognize its shape for the first time, despite its flatness and the yellowing of its colors. It's a michigwangipul—the same plant as the one in the garden, the one my mother used to grow.

So Hee-Young recognized it, too. She'd plucked it and saved it on purpose—but why? Nostalgia for a time when we still maintained some sliver of innocence, despite our hardships?

It doesn't fit, but I can't think of another reason. I jam it into the book and slide it into the shaft, adding the flashlight and the bag of hair I recovered from the studio for good measure. A moment after I close the painting, the door to my room opens.

"You're going to be late for dinner." Heta's wearing the most ridiculous dress I've ever seen: cobalt blue, with poofy white sleeves and a yellow panel like a half-apron on the front of the skirt. On her head perches a fluffy white assembly that resembles a folded towel.

She reminds me of advertisements about butter, the milkmaids, but with an attempt to add sex appeal: the skirt only reaches halfway down her thigh, and the white sleeves are some diaphanous material that doesn't hide the lines of her arm.

My cheeks burn as she looks me up and down. I'm filthy, covered in sweat, and shirtless. I have no problem with nudity, but I don't like feeling exposed in front of Heta. "Sorry I'm late, I—"

She shakes her head as if to clear it. "We've got to get you cleaned up." She grabs one of my hands and pulls, and I scramble onto my feet. "There isn't time for you to shower. Go wash your face and brush your teeth—"

"No toothbrush."

She curls her lip at me in disgust, but she leads me into the bathroom and pulls open the mirror. Behind it is a small, recessed cabinet, bare of everything except a toothbrush and toothpaste, still in their packaging. She opens both, puts the paste on the brush, and hands it to me, as if I am a small child.

"Hurry," says Heta. I'm not sure if the tension in her voice is irritation or fear, but I'm suddenly aware of the way her gaze keeps flicking backward, toward the door, as if she expects another to join us.

I rinse my mouth out and quickly bathe myself in the sink. Heta towels me off and spins me to the wardrobe. She yanks out the first kimono—

"The black one," I say, my heart hammering. If I have to wear one, I don't want it to be something eye-catching, like deep purple, bright red, or gold.

She sighs, but she grabs it and snaps it as if she's about to hang washing on a line. And then she becomes a flurry of activity—pushing my arms forward, smoothing my hair back. She's even brought some sort of product for my hair that adds temporary highlights. It feels like a violation, having her hands all over me, but I bear it.

When she pushes forward a small bag of makeup, though, I shake my head.

"I'll do it like Hee-Young's," she says, and then she follows my glance toward the mask on my bed. "Oh. Smart."

When we're finished, I glance at the mirror and my stomach rolls. Like hanbok, kimono are modest garments, but the interpretation in front of me is the Asian sister of Heta's sexy milkmaid outfit—tight, short, and sleek. The dress's thin fabric clings to my form, and the collar opening is deep enough to show cleavage. The sash-belt, which usually covers the whole stomach, is only a few inches wide and pulled tight to accentuate the shape of my breasts. Even the typically loose sleeves hug my arms before billowing open at the ends.

Worse, though, is the skirt. Longer than Heta's, but with a slit running up the side that lands at the top of my thigh. I'll have to move carefully if I don't want to expose myself.

But nothing is worse than the mask. Staring at my reflection, it's hard to breathe. "No."

"It's just a costume," says Heta, though her voice is less gruff. "The patrons like the feeling of . . . *aw-then-ti-si-ty.*"

I don't need the definition of the word to know I hate it.

THIRTY-ONE
Hee-Jin

Though only a few minutes have passed since the bell-tone, we're alone when Heta drags me into the hallway, pulling me forward like a child with a wagon. I toddle on tiny steps, trying to prevent my leg from sticking through the slit.

But just outside the dining-room door, she pulls me in close enough to catch the lavender scent of her soap and murmurs into my ear. "You need to be careful of Ksenia. She's going to betray you. The only thing she cares about is herself."

Before I can react, she shoves me forward into the room. Instantly, the odd seating arrangement—all the mentees on one side of the table—finally makes sense, because the chairs opposite our normal spaces are full: four men and one woman with their backs to us, all dressed lavishly. *The patrons.*

Heta sits down swiftly, leaving only the newcomer across from my normal seat unpaired. He hasn't looked up yet, which gives me a moment to study him. His gunmetal suit jacket is draped across the back of his chair, which makes it easy to see that inside the wine-colored button-up shirt, his shoulders are broad, the cut of his torso V-shaped. His silver-gray hair is so neatly buzzed, it looks military.

I swallow. This must be Mels Garin. And he doesn't look drunk to me.

And I am Hee-Young, I think. *The table is hot.*

I edge my way around the table and take my seat, to Ksenia's right.

Garin is mid-sip, something yellow and bubbly in a goblet-style glass. He's pushed his sleeve up to his elbow, revealing a forearm of ropy muscle, though I imagine he's never seen hard labor.

He notices me. His eyes widen and the blood rapidly drains from his face. But then his gaze snaps toward Shepherd, and I see something like fury in his eyes.

Is it because he's spotted that I'm not Hee-Young already—even though that should've been impossible with the mask? Or is this because he thinks I *am* her, and he is sure he frightened her off?

"Good," Shepherd says. "You're all here."

"Sorry we're late," says Heta, her voice high and silky. "*Hee-Young* had a little trouble getting ready."

My stomach tenses at her prod, but I keep my face neutral.

Shepherd narrows his eyes, as if calculating, but then he paints on a smile that stretches from ear to ear and turns to address the patrons. "Now, most of you have been here before—save our new arrival, Dr. Julius Pepperdine." He waves at the man sitting across from Ksenia.

Pepperdine wears a white suit with a chunky silver necklace and leather boots with sharp toes. On the table in front of his plate is a large cowboy hat, just like the one Shepherd had in the airport.

"It's a pleasure." When Pepperdine addresses the rest of the patrons, he places a hand over his heart, as if accepting an award. "Excited to finally *be* here, after all my years of service."

Shepherd chuckles as if it's a joke. Garin doesn't react, which gives me time to observe Ksenia coolly bring her fork to her mouth between my anxious glances at him. Her costume is a loose, light-blue dress of almost see-through fabric, though it's wrapped tight to her torso by a leather vest that reminds me of the garment of a nomadic people—Mongolia, or maybe Eastern Europe, though I don't know much about either. She also wears a strange hat: dark-blue velvet with an upturned brim, a long thin point at its apex that points behind her like the tail of some fanciful bird.

I check on Garin again, but I can tell from the way his torso is twisted away that he's avoiding me on purpose.

I glance at the other girls, hoping one of them will save me. Sarah is sitting across from Margarete Jones. Her gaze is riveted to her patron, and her costume turns my stomach: a bra covered in jingling coins and a wide matching belt that dangles over a skirt of pink tulle strips. Sumi is muttering something across the table to her patron, Carlson. Her costume, a cropped shirt and skirt set in a bright orange shade, is the only one that resembles real clothing. Although the shirt doesn't cover her midriff, she's wrapped one side of her body, from shoulder to foot, in a dark-pink cloth—I think it's called a *sari*—and the bright colors suit her.

As the minutes pass, dishes are taken away, new ones brought in. Facilitators float like bees to refill wineglasses. I take stock of Smallet and Buster Carlson. Smallet has a squirrel face: small-mouthed with a receding jaw, eyes set too far apart. Unlike the others, he's dressed casually, in a plain white tee shirt and jeans, and when he speaks, his accent sends his *R*s deep into his throat. Carlson is a large, portly man whose shoulders strain the seams of his jacket. He only talks to Sumi, muttering things into her ear that I can't make out.

Shepherd dominates the conversation—and, it seems, Garin's attention, which must've been part of his plan all along to keep Garin's focus off me. For his part, Garin doesn't speak a single word.

I think the other patrons are noticing, too. As I glance around the room, I'm suddenly aware of how uncomfortable they look: brows furrowed, shifting in their seats. But then Pepperdine laughs, a booming sound that fills the room, and I catch both Jones and Smallet give him dirty glances. Even Carlson looks like he's trying to melt into his chair. Maybe they just don't like Pepperdine.

This time, when I look up, I catch Garin observing me, but he looks away quickly.

Ksenia leans over to me and whispers, her breath hot in my ear. "You should eat something. Hee-Young would." I turn and look, but I have no appetite, and the sight of the main course actually makes me feel sick: platters of small fowl roasted on beds of carrots and round potatoes the size of a toddler's fist.

For a moment, I think of algamja: peeled baby potatoes fried in vegetable oil until golden brown, eaten with a toothpick. I liked mine with sugar; my sister always rolled hers in salt.

And the memory of those potatoes is so heavenly that despite the precarity of my situation, my stomach growls. I have to mentally steady my hand as I take bread and a handful of leafy green salad, before looking back up at Ksenia. She is just barely squinting at me, her expression thoughtful.

"How was your trip?"

I realize too late that the woman, Jones, is speaking to me. "Good," I say, trying to make my voice sound like Hee-Young's—but

I don't know what she sounded like when she spoke English, just that my English was better than hers.

"How's your mother?" Jones reaches over and touches my hand lightly, invitingly—but across the table, Sarah's face goes flat. Is she jealous?

Shepherd told me not to lie to Jones—but I can't exactly tell her that my mother is dead. "Good," I say again.

"I forgot to ask you last time—what is your mother's name, anyway?" Her tone is too light. It makes me think of Heta and her baby-voice, the danger softness can hide. "I hear Koreans don't usually use their parents' names, is that right? They just call them, *our mother*, *our father*, things like that?"

I nod carefully. I'm not sure what she's getting at.

"But family names, that's the more interesting part, isn't it? I mean, so many *Kim, Lee, Paks*—but your family name is different, isn't it?"

"Song. It is . . . common."

"That's your father's family name, is it?"

There's a strange gleam in her eye, one that makes sweat break out on my back and warns me not to answer any more of this woman's questions. Maybe I should pretend to be sick? I look over at Shepherd for help.

He clears his throat and jumps in. "Hee-Young! I was so excited to hear about how your trip *re-vit-a-laized* your interest in folk art. Your mask is so cute! You mentioned you were trying out a new medium?"

I nod. "Sculpture," I try to say, though it's clear from the confused looks around the table nobody understands me, so I mime with my hands in the air.

A few people laugh as if they'd just heard a punchline. Smallet, though, turns his squirrelly face to Shepherd. "I thought you said they all speak excellent English?"

My cheeks burn.

"Hee-Young is a special case—"

"That's not Hee-Young," Garin snaps. His voice is surprising—rich and melodic, so at odds with the horror I feel in this moment. I plummet into a deep abyss, one with Hee-Young's ghost at the bottom, but Garin doesn't seem to notice. "What did you—"

"I'd like to see you prove it," growls Shepherd, and the malice in it—so different from the anxious old man at the Dunkin' Donuts—makes me wonder if my fear of Garin has been misplaced all along.

Garin doesn't answer, but his fist squeezes so tightly around his fork that his knuckles are blanching, his forearm trembling.

At my sides, the girls stiffen. Across from me, patrons raise their eyebrows, interested in the potentially explosive dynamic between the two men. I'm suddenly aware of the stifling temperature of the room, of the sweat beading down my spine and soaking into the tight dress.

I plunge deep into my onggi pot and try to focus. I need to think of some way to convince Garin that I really am Hee-Young, but how can I do that when I don't even know how he figured it out?

As if he can hear my thoughts, he suddenly stands, his chair skidding noisily behind him. The table falls silent. "You're a bastard, Shep," he growls. "Do you really think I don't know what you're doing—"

"Let's talk after," Shepherd says, seemingly oblivious to the tension in the room.

Garin turns, and I'm filled with the certainty that he's going to look at me, that he will see into my very soul. I know it, just like I know my name is Song Hee-Jin and my sister's is Song Hee-Young and my mother's is Song Eun-Ja—

And then he does. He stares right at me, rage plain on his face, and it's every terrible thing I thought it would be. But then he turns to Jones, and although I have no way of knowing what's being telegraphed between them, I can feel it's something dangerous.

"I'm going for a walk and a smoke," he says, his voice now perfectly calm. "Come find me when you're ready to talk."

And then he's gone.

THIRTY-TWO
Hee-Jin

It occurs to me that I need to find Garin and throw myself at his mercy. But the moment I gather my strength and try to stand, Shepherd gives me a hard stare and the tiniest shake of his head. Frightened, I collapse back into my seat—but a moment later, hope blossoms in my chest. I'd been too stunned before to consider Shepherd's response to Garin: *I'd like to see you prove it.*

I feel like I did on the closet floor, eavesdropping on my mother, overhearing secrets I couldn't fathom and didn't understand. Had Shepherd known all along that Garin would realize I wasn't Hee-Young? If so, why have me and the girls pretend? Why provide me with a mask? Did Shepherd have a backup plan, in case this one didn't work?

After all, I am here, with Hee-Young's passport. If Ksenia and Heta and all the others were willing to lie and say I really *was* Hee-Young, if Garin doesn't find out about the body in my apartment—*if, if, if*—how long do we need to stymy him before there's no chance of him ousting Shepherd from the facility, before I can get Hee-Young's money and disappear from this place, and the truth of my identity can't be questioned?

Do I have time, still, to find out what happened to Hee-Young?

What follows next feels impossible. Despite Garin's outburst, despite the revelation that I've failed in my task to impersonate my sister—that my life could be *over*—the dinner continues. Patrons drink and eat with varying degrees of interest. Shepherd cracks jokes I don't understand that send Pepperdine guffawing. And Jones—Jones is the worst, because she does not see Garin's departure as a reason to stop interrogating me.

Her questions are all deeply personal, and I don't know how much Hee-Young told her before, or if I'm still supposed to be maintaining the fiction that I am my sister to the other patrons. And after the strange look that passed between her and Garin, I'm not going to tell her anything else about me, which means I'll have to be both vague and careful—all while translating everything into English.

The task consumes all my brainpower. I honestly don't know much about North Korea, but Jones probably doesn't, either. I pick out a drama I liked to watch whenever I could—*Flower-Swallow*, which is a term used for homeless North Korean refugees, for the way they've flit, searching for food and shelter—and use the character's life as a frame. At least, this way, my lies will be more consistent.

What was your favorite activity as a child?

I liked to fly kites—

How many siblings do you have?

One.

What was it like, living under Dear Leader?

I pretend I don't understand what she means.

Finally, though, she wears down. From the glassy look in her eye, the champagne has caught up with her. Her silence gives me a blessed moment to observe the room.

I'm surprised to find a new arrival in the once-empty seat at the foot of the table: Ca-lee. I don't know when she got here, though it must've been after Garin left. There's something strange in her expression, almost like a snarl, and she's staring daggers at Pepperdine and his cowboy hat.

Do they know each other? No—Shepherd said it was Pepperdine's first visit. Maybe Ca-lee just hates his laugh, like everybody else.

Like Jones, the other patrons look half-drunk, but in good spirits. Every so often, one of them filters out of the room for the bathroom or a cigarette. Unlike Garin, they always return, but I see the signs of a party coming to an end.

As for the girls, we're a pathetic bunch. Sarah stares gloomily at her plate. Sumi stares longingly at Sarah whenever her patron, Carlson, isn't paying attention. Ksenia's face is completely unreadable, and Heta—Heta's had so much to drink, she's already fallen asleep at the table. Without the tension of command on her face, she looks almost innocent.

Smallet watches her, as if trying to find some secret hidden in her hat. Then he yawns and stretches. "I'd like to turn in," he says, again launching that *r* into the back of his throat.

Rumbles of agreement circle. The patrons stand—not at once, but taking turns—and exit the room. And then Ca-lee goes, and then Shepherd. I think there's a moment as he passes where he almost but doesn't quite look at me.

The girls don't move until ten minutes after everyone has left. Only then does Sarah go to shake Heta awake, and they wordlessly file out into the hallway, a somber procession making its way to the bedrooms underground.

Any moment now, the final bell-tone will sound, after which all the lights will turn off at once—and still, I have no idea what just happened, if the dinner went well or poorly or what any of it means. I watch the girls enter their rooms, but none of them acknowledge my presence in any way. Finally, it's just me in the hallway.

I push open my door. There's an envelope at my feet.

For a moment, I am relieved—*Shepherd's returned my passport*—but then I bend down and pick it up. The envelope is too thin, and far too light.

I turn it over. There's a three-word note written on the back in an elegant, scrawling font I've never learned: cursive. I struggle for a moment, trying to make it out. I think it says: *Dangerous. Be careful.*

My skin crawls as I open it. Inside is a folded piece of paper with some printed text: the top half of a newspaper article from this morning's *Chosun Ilbo*. I skim the headline:

> *—dead body of a teenage girl found in apartment near Siheung under mysterious circumstances—*

I dash back into the hallway, looking left and right, as if the person who dropped this off will revisit the scene of the crime—but of course, there's no one. I re-enter the soundproofed confines of my room before hiding in the bathroom. I sit in front of the door to block it and try to breathe.

A teenage girl was found dead in an apartment near Siheung under suspicious circumstances following a call by a motorcycle delivery driver, who claimed to have seen it on the stoop outside. When police questioned the neighbors, one stated he had not seen the girl leave or enter the building in several days, leading to a welfare check that exposed the body. Authorities have identified the body as one Song Hee-Jin, an undocumented immigrant from China that may have been of North Korean ancestry. Police have launched an investigation into the woman's death, encouraging citizens to call—

And then the article stops, the rest of the text cut off. I almost cry out at the suddenness of its end.

I sit quietly in the room for several seconds. How did the police find my real name? Even my landlord and the woman who lent me her identity to do her job at the hospital laundry both knew me as Kwak Eun-Ah. The documents I left say Eun-Ah on them.

And more importantly: who slipped this article into my room? People roam through this place: Shepherd, Ca-lee, all the other patrons that left and returned—and the parade of facilitators that watch us all the time, trying to anticipate and meet our needs. Heta and I were the last ones to dinner, which means none of the other girls could have deposited the article before joining us—but one of them could've slipped out while Jones was questioning me. I was so distracted, I hadn't even seen Ca-lee come in. And all the patrons went to their rooms before we did.

Jones never left during dinner—but could her fascination with my past be explained by the fact that she already knew who I was? *Was she trying to catch me in a trap?*

The truth is that anyone could've done it. And now that they have, I don't know why, or what they were telling me to be careful of.

I flip it over, trying to find some clue in the paper, the ink, in the way the flap of the envelope was tucked in—and then a soft chime rings through the room, and all the lights go out.

THIRTY-THREE
Callie

From the lunch bell-tone—the girls returning from studio time, me bolting out of Shep's room—I've felt his attention on me, like the twitching bristles of a bobbit worm. It doesn't matter that *I* can't see *him*; in the same way the birds always sense if he's home, I know he's figured out I trespassed into his space and is pondering what to do with me.

It doesn't stop me from my new compulsion. Whenever I almost manage to immerse myself in the smallest activity, I picture the long, dark hair in Shep's bed, and I'm shaken by the knowledge, heavy as iron, sharp enough to cut bone: *Hee-Young was up there.* The woman I thought of as my friend, the one I read the same children's story to, over and over. Each time, it makes me so heartsick, I dump Lisa on a facilitator and find an excuse to walk down the main hall.

That's how I pass the afternoon. Cruising the foyer, peering up past the vine platforms to Shepherd's door—the proverbial watched pot—and waiting for him to burst out with murder in his eyes, or worse, disgust on his face. I know he finds me pathetic, but now, I've given him proof.

If only my key *locked* that outer door. There's no point in letting me open and not close—except to catch me in the act. In an effort to not give away my feelings, I've put the traitorous key in my pocket, but I forget and reach for it over and over again, my fingers grazing the sternum I can't feel as they grasp the empty air.

Hours later, the bell-tone rings again. Sometimes they remind me of a singing bowl—but this one sounds like a death knell, one that confronts me with the *real* horror of the evening: despite the disgust and pain in my heart, I have to attend the patron dinner. I have to sit in front of those blow-hard, stuck-up, born-rich, power-hungry know-it-alls and pretend my world isn't tearing apart. I have to display myself to the *girls*, those bright pretty things with their clear, attentive stares.

One of them must've known he was sleeping with Hee-Young, and still, they'd all sat with me at the table every day, had let me babble in the greenhouse about their artistic choices and ask questions about contrast and mood and fifth and sixth lines.

It's disgusting. *Disgusting.* But of all the duties that Shep has assigned me since he took over the Petite, the patron dinner is one I can't miss. Not if there's any chance of having an open conversation, of getting him to admit the truth.

Still, it's hard. So hard, I can't seem to get moving. It takes me twenty minutes to don my outfit, these ridiculous, appropriative *interpretations* of traditional clothing I've never hated more. At one point, I looked them up, learned the names of the pieces in my closet. They're mash-ups of styles from all over Mexico and even Central America, as if the peoples of the different states were interchangeable: the enagua skirts, sleeveless huipil tunics, and lace resplendor headdresses of the Tehuana, mixed with the high-collared blouses of Jalisco, the embroidered collars and gala skirts of Tabasco's chontales, the Spanish influences from Campeche.

My mother's people might have originally been from one of these places. Or maybe we were native *Tejanos*, Mexicans that became Americans in 1845, when the border suddenly crossed over *us*.

Finally, though, I'm moving. I try not to think about this morning, when I imagined what it might be like to stay here and find my way in a new iteration of the familiar instead of abandoning it to work in a dry-cleaner's.

Now, as I near the dining room, the only thing I can imagine is fleeing. A moment later, the door bangs open, and I almost collide with the man storming out.

I know Garin sees me, but he just pushes past. I turn to the open doorway, looking for an answer—and then I see *him*, and all thoughts of Garin are forgotten.

Pepperdine.

It's as if the patrons, the girls, the white-suited facilitators—all of them cease to be real. Instead, there is only me and this man that resides in the spaces I can't fully remember, this man whose *huh-yuge* hat and *huh-yuge* accent has shown up in my nightmares more times than I can count. And all the walls I've erected, the lies I've told myself to make everything better—they go winging off to flap around the chandeliers like bats. Soon, they'll return—but not yet.

Above me, the windows rattle, threatening to start their infernal, flapping dance. Apparently, the biometric sensors work even when the key is in my pocket. I don't want to be embarrassed by Shep's stupid house-tricks here at the patron dinner, not after the utter humiliation of learning about Shep's tryst. I squeeze the emotions inside of me until something *breaks*—

He was never here, says Shep, a memory I am not willing to place—

And then I float across the floor, my feet never touching. There is no room, no girls, no Pepperdine. There is no first car accident with a dead man, no night years later where Shep found me on the runaway road, crashed through the brush, Lisa rattled mute in the backseat. And there are *definitely* no nights with Pepperdine in my hospital room, talk of him administering his *medicines*.

I once told Shep the lapses in my memory were Pepperdine's fault. That most of the time, I didn't remember him coming at all—I only knew he'd been here because of the *white noise* and what came after. I'd close my eyes to sleep and there would be a frosty static like a television screen, and then I'd wake up flat on my back—sometimes in the hospital bed, sometimes in my room—and it'd be hours or even days later.

You've just had an episode, Shep would always say. That's what he called them. Episodes. *You went crazy—throwing things and screaming. And then you just . . . checked out.*

He was referring to what Pepperdine later explained was *sudden catatonia*. The first part, the flurry of manic activity—agitated, combative, delirious—that was *excited* catatonia. And then, then came *akinetic catatonia*, the part where I turned into a corpse: lying with a thousand-yard stare, not responding when people spoke to me.

It's remarkable—that's exactly the word Pepperdine had used, *remarkable*, as if I was one of Pavlov's dogs and not a human being. *Usually, if you hold someone's hand up and let go, they'll move it so they don't hit themselves in the face. That's how we know they're* mah-ling-ah-rin', *you understand? They're fakin'.*

But you—you just let it land, ker-splat! And then he laughed, that terrible laugh, that laugh he's making now as he sits at *my* table, eating *my* food, and for the first time in my life, just for a moment, I knew what it was like to want to *hurt* someone. To *kill* someone.

But then I heard Shep's voice: *It can't be Pepperdine's treatments, Calleigh. Some of these times you don't remember, I never called him. He was never here.*

And that was even more horrible, because it meant those times I awoke after the white static, nauseated, my head and neck and my entire body down to my womb aching, no memory of everything—those weren't coming from Pepperdine and his medicines and his experiments with my goddamn head.

They were coming from *me*.

THIRTY-FOUR
Callie

Dinner is long enough that, one by one, the inner walls that have saved me for so long stop fluttering by the ceiling and return to their roost in my head.

I concentrate on making Pepperdine small. *He's just a man, Callie.* Little by little, he retreats, his horrible laugh getting softer, his *huh-yuuuuuge*s getting shorter. Little by little, he ceases to matter, because he's in my past.

Just like the rest of this place. Yes, even Shep. For a moment, I'd let my heart grow weak, let his cryptic statement—*Do you still? Always*—make me believe he still loved me. For once, Pepperdine proved to be the medicine I needed, shredding the fantasy away.

That's what I tell myself through the rest of dinner, the long walk to my room on the first floor. The facilitators have already put Lisa to bed, and there's nothing to do but crawl in and lie down.

But as soon as I do, all the work I did to make Pepperdine smaller unravels. He's *here*. Not in the hospital, not making a quick house call—he's spending the next few nights in my *home*.

What if the sleep I slip into is full of white static? What if I wake up not remembering the dinner or his presence, just a body that aches all over, inside and out, and a horrible hole in my mind?

I can't breathe. I can't think. And I can't lie here any longer in the dark.

I could check. The thought is soft and terrible, and as soon as I think it, I know I will. *I can just go crack his door and listen. Make sure he's really asleep. He can't hurt me if he's asleep.*

And then I'm tiptoeing into the hallway. I didn't even grab the flashlight stashed under my bed, not when it would let—

(Pepperdine, Pepperdine, Pepperdine, my heart beats, each convulsion as brittle as shattered glass)

—someone else see *me.*

I creep down the hallway onto a quiet main floor, not a facilitator in sight. Everything is dark, but not *quite* the pitch black I've grown used to.

Which means that somewhere, there's a bulb burning, lightening everything a shade. And God forgive me, I think I know where.

I steal out to the lobby. As I approach, the mirrors gleam softly, moving with my own shadowed reflection.

There it is, on the third floor: a crack of light under Shepherd's door.

He's likely meeting with one of the patrons—Garin, probably. Could it have something to do with the way he stormed out of the dining room? The next iteration in their swiftly devolving relationship?

I really don't understand it, this tension. From what Shep's told me, they were bosom buddies their entire lives—same boarding school, same college, rotating in the same circles of friends—but six months ago, something changed. Garin stopped coming to most of the patron dinners. When he did show up, Shep sometimes refused to let him in the gate. I kept thinking I'd never see him again—but then he'd be there, like he was tonight, almost running me over on his way out of the dining room.

It's not my business. I turn around guiltily, as if even my thoughts are akin to eavesdropping. But halfway to my room, I stop cold: it might not be Garin up there. It might be Pepperdine.

And then I'm *racing* back down the hall as quietly as I can. It's only once I start climbing the stairs that I'm able to get hold of myself and use a normal stride.

My nerves are stretched tight as guitar strings, threatening to snap with each groan of the metal under me. Despite gritting my teeth, my limbs shake, and with that comes an awareness of my dry mouth, my scratching throat. A drink would cool the heat burning through me, yes it would, but I don't stop.

Finally, I'm on the platform to the third floor. I don't look down as I cross. Once I'm safely on the landing, I hold my breath and sidle up to his room.

"Yes, I know about that. *I* called *them.*" Shep's hard to make out, especially when I don't dare touch the door, not when the soft sliding of my dress on the wood might alert them to my presence.

"Regardless, you know what I want." Garin's voice.

"Not a problem, of course." Shep's tone is light—honest or mocking, I can't tell. "But doesn't pleasure come *before* business?"

"I'm not in the mood tonight."

"Take a look before you decide."

Light footsteps recede away from me. And then there's a wet thump like dropping a cantaloupe—*tonk!*

Then everything's so silent, I can't help myself—I push my ear against the door, its surface cool on my skin. Now, there are sounds again. The rubbing groan of furniture sliding across the floor. A long scraping, like a knife being sharpened—and then a loud click. This one I know for sure: it's a door opening.

Someone moans, high and protracted, like the call of a conch shell. Muffled, as if into a pillow, too feminine to be Garin.

A soft expletive: "Fffffuck."

I've heard Shep swear like that a thousand times, but not lately, because *that* "Fuck" with the *F* that seems to go on forever, that's the one he used to make when entering me.

"You think you can fuck around with me? Let's find out what you—" And then a word that could be *know*, save that it would make no sense. I wrack my brain, trying to guess at what I'd misheard—but then the woman moans again. Before she finishes, there's a click, and then it's silent.

I have to restrain myself from beating down the door. I know what's happened, can tell it to myself blow by blow like it's one of the stories in Hee-Young's stupid book. *They were in the sitting room, and then they moved into the bedroom, and a moment later, a woman moaned, and then Shep swore in pleasure, and they shut the bedroom door behind them.*

My heartbeat slows. My muscles go slack, despite the storm in my chest. *I thought it was just Hee-Young, but she's gone, and he and Garin are sleeping with another one of these girls.*

My knees feel weak. Somehow, I don't take off running. Instead, I turn, as stiff and unnatural as if I were made of wood, and retreat down the stairs. The girls' faces tumble through my mind with each circle around the center banister, the view changing like one of those open elevator cars in old hotels.

Which one? I would've thought Heta, who clearly wants my place—but in someone that young, it could just be a mistaken eagerness to please. Sarah, maybe, so much quieter than Sumi, though Sumi's loud, brassy laugh could so easily be a cover.

What if that wasn't Hee-Young's hair that I found after all? What if I'd just imagined the smell of oranges?

From the strand's color, the hair would have to be Sumi's, Ksenia's, or *new* Hee-Young's.

I need to know. I *need* to know. But I can't go back up there. I don't *want* to catch them in the act, same as I don't want Shep to see me like this—not when I have no real claim to him, not when Pepperdine and his numbing medications are so close.

Hysteria, I think. *A state of ungovernable emotional excess.* Not so different from *excited catatonia*. No matter how betrayed I feel, how angry I am, I won't let Shep see me like this.

Which means there's only one way to find out who's up there. And it's as if my feet have thought through all of this before my brain, because I realize I'm standing at the very bottom of the staircase, the girls' rooms waiting for me in the dark.

THIRTY-FIVE
Hee-Jin

I clutch the cryptic note—*Dangerous. Be careful*—in the dark bathroom, unsure what to do. I don't feel safe in this house, but the newspaper article confirms I can't go back. The police gave Hee-Young's body my *real name*. They've found some thread to pull at. If there are cameras—and there are cameras everywhere in Korea—they'll unearth me exiting my apartment and boarding the bus. With my transit card's signature, they can follow me all the way to the plane.

The American authorities could be looking for me already.

A terrible pressure crushes my pounding chest, making it impossible to inflate my lungs, making me see stars.

I'm having a heart attack. I open my mouth to scream, but it's just a strangled rasp, as if I've been punched in the stomach. I double over, my hands clenched around the toilet rim, suddenly aware that I'm crying—*sobbing* incoherently, and I don't know when that started.

I reach deep for my onggi, but a wall has sprung up between us, one of the whitewashed ribbons of stone that surround castle complexes. There's nothing more than a throbbing emptiness where my pot should be, no way to push these feelings away.

The hunger rises in me. I need to devour noodles until my stomach stretches painfully, until I vomit—and then I can fill it again, and again, and again, the only thing left in my world that makes sense.

"Hee-Young?" A voice in the dark. I freeze, but I can't stop crying, and in this soundproofed room, each snuffle is gunshot loud. "Hee-Young? Are you in here?"

It's Ksenia—Ksenia, who Heta told me not to trust. Ksenia, who I yearn for—who makes it so I can't trust *myself*.

I need to stay silent, but in this moment, I'm so afraid and alone.

A soft knock on the bathroom door. "Hee-Young, are you OK?"

I don't mean to answer, but I do: a sob at hearing a name that should only ever be said in the whispers used for the dead.

A moment later, a soft crack of light opens behind me. I blink as it turns into Ksenia in a long white nightgown, one of those flat refrigerator flashlights in her hand. In the shadows cast by its thin beam, her face looks both terrible and beautiful, the hollows of her cheeks and neck so deep she looks like a caricature, but her eyes catch the light like little fires.

She studies me for a long moment. Then she kneels and wraps her arms around me, and despite my suspicion, despite my fear, I don't know how to do anything but break.

THIRTY-SIX

Hee-Jin

Later, I'll think back on Ksenia's embrace, the way her flashlight barely pierced the gloom in my cramped bathroom, and I'll feel shame. I was like a moss-covered limb blown down by a storm wind: soft, rotting wood, so easy to tear apart.

But in that moment, the shock comes first. For years, I've spent every breath of my existence futilely striving to become a shadow: untouchable, without needs or desires. And then Ksenia takes me in her arms, and I suddenly swell into three dimensions, brimming with weight and substance. I am real again, and it *hurts.*

Still, I'll die if she lets go. I don't care if *she* slipped the article under my door, or if Heta's warning is true and Ksenia only cares about herself and will betray me, or if she was the one that drove Hee-Young from this place. For once, the unending hunger inside of me is sated, and I'm nothing more than a collection of cells and fluid that somehow draws breath.

And I'm so, *so* tired.

"I need to put the light down." Ksenia speaks so softly. My heart crumples with the tenderness of it. "These batteries burn out quick, and there's no more of these flashlights. Let's go sit on the bed."

I don't want to move—not when it brings me into the bedroom, its unlocked door under which slip threatening notes—but I let her guide me. She releases the button, plunging us again into that perfect dark.

Dark can feel safe and cloaking, or empty and cold. Now, it's just full of her presence.

Her breaths sound crystalline, razor sharp. I sense her movements before I feel them, every shift of her legs on the mattress, each turn of her head.

"Crying like that, it makes me think you're having a breakdown. What happened? Do you finally regret coming here?"

I almost laugh. Do I regret it?

The truth is that I'm not sure. When I think about why I agreed to come in Hee-Young's place, my motivations are a complicated, sticky mass, each desire impossible to separate from the others. I wanted money. I wanted to be free of the fear of being discovered and sent back to China or North Korea. I wanted to act out a childhood dream. I wanted to know what had happened to my sister.

Except now, here, my heart stripped bare in the dark, I know that's not completely true, is it? There were a thousand things I could've done while still in Korea to find out more. I was both devastated and *excited* to leave her body behind in my bed, to know that she'd *never again* show up on my doorstep requiring care, that her art projects and wild behavior could no longer threaten my safety.

But if safety was all I wanted, I wouldn't have followed her footsteps back here, to this place. Was that for love, then? Or maybe just guilt?

After a lifetime of sliding my feelings into the pot, I shouldn't be surprised to discover that they're now strangers to me.

"It happens to all of us." Ksenia rubs small circles on my shoulder blades, making me ache. "The regretting. Although it doesn't feel like you came for the art."

It's as if a bone snaps in my chest, the jagged ends finally free of the constant pressure of being bent into shape. "I came . . . for money. Hee-Young's money," I say. It's true, and it's not true, and both are horrible things.

The hand stills. I sense the twitching of her waiting muscles, like electric sparks in the dark. "You mean Garin's money?"

I shake my head. "The . . ." It takes me a moment to find the strange word. "Stipend."

"What stipend?"

"The money . . . for staying. Every month."

The sheets rustle as she slides away. My nerves scream, wanting more of her touch, but I don't move. I knew this comfort wasn't for people like me.

"Oh, Hee-Young," she says, her voice heavier than my jangling nerves, but then I hear her push it *down*, down, into a pot like mine. "You don't know what this place is, do you? Shepherd . . .

runs a kind of *service*. He finds girls that are *trapped*—by poverty, war, a bad government. They have to be from situations where they feel like . . . like dying is preferable to living that way, because it's important they're *desperate*."

Desperate. My limbs are going dead, and small lights like jellyfish have started to dance in front of my eyes.

"That's why Shepherd picks artists, I think. We want things so badly. We're willing to suffer for what we want—but desperate isn't enough. We also need to be beautiful and smart and speak amazing English. An *accent* is OK, but the patrons want intelligent conversations—the feeling they've rescued someone *worthwhile*. And we should be young—but not *too* young. Old enough that they can fake our papers to say we're of legal age. Do you understand? Legal?"

She waits for me to answer, but the numbness is getting worse, traveling down my back, up my ribs. I hold myself perfectly still even in my thoughts, because I know where this is going. If I move the tiniest bit, I'll shatter and shatter, and there'll be nothing of me left.

"Once he finds you, he offers you the *deal*. You come and work for him. You be whatever the patrons want—a lover, a girlfriend, a wife, *whatever* they want—and in exchange, Ca-lee and Shepherd teach you about art. And once you've made him enough money, he'll let the patron have you. You will be their pet, but you'll be rich and cared for, with the connections and education you need to have an artistic career. But there's no stipend. There's no money, other than what the patron agrees to give you once they take you with them. Do you understand?"

It's as if the soundproofing has stretched into my skull and muffled my brain. In this perfect quiet, I can hear each neuron firing, each thread being stitched in the fabric of my life.

I see my mother. A woman whose ancestors were ravaged by colonization and war. A woman who was trafficked into China and managed to slip into South Korea—but who could never outrun her nightmares and addictions. She chose sex work for the good of her children, but she was never so audacious, I think, as to hope for something better for them. Too practical, right until she gave me my own onggi pot. Right until the end.

I should be something—shocked? afraid? sad?—but I know

exactly what we are, we girls in this house of stone and glass. Did Hee-Young hide the truth about this place from me because she was ashamed?

If so, she shouldn't have been. While she was reading fairytales, I studied history, because history is the mother that teaches us all things. I could've told her about the gisaeng—the painted women of ancient Korea, courtesans that entertained rich men with music and conversation, dance and poetry. During the Goryeo Dynasty, they were revered as paragons of culture, able to become royal concubines and achieve a measure of nobility. Later, during the Joseon Dynasty, they represented the lowest caste of society and were considered the property of the state. The impoverished sold their daughters to gisaeng schools, and disgraced women whose male family members had committed crimes were punished with a life of gisaeng servitude.

And yet, the gisaeng always had comfortable clothes, shelter, and food. At a time when women were expected—and legally mandated—to bend their body, mind, and speech until they were chaste and pious servants whose entire world was their husband, gisaeng lived in a different universe. They traveled and socialized freely. They studied medicine and etiquette and the textile arts, philosophy and history. They didn't worry about the chilgeojiak—the seven sins that led to divorce, like talkativeness, disobedience toward in-laws, or an inability to bear a son. Instead, gisaeng survived on their wits, beauty, and intelligence, which made them stimulating companions for the men who had imposed the rules for women in the first place.

My sister chose to become a gisaeng. Maybe I should feel something about it, but *feelings* won't change it, just like they won't bring my sister back.

"Say something, Hee-Young."

This place, this twist of fate, it is what it is. I have to concentrate on *my* survival. On the *future*. "And . . . if we don't want . . . we can leave?"

"Yes, but you can't just walk out the front door. Shepherd's clients are rich enough to be above the law, but that doesn't mean they take stupid risks. There are guards and a gate to make sure of that."

I close my eyes and try to remember—and yes, there was a

gate, the black iron menace at the bottom of the hill. "Does he . . . have your passport, too?"

She nods. "Another security measure, so we don't try to run away. You can ask to leave, though, and he'll fly you back to where he found you, but you'll have nothing to show for your time here. It's too much for some. A few have committed suicide, but that's rare. Like I said, he picks us carefully. Sarah is from Syria. They're embroiled in a terrible civil war—hospitals and schools and all basic services destroyed, constant violence and bombings. The situation has improved over the last few years, but her whole family was killed. She doesn't want to go back."

Thinking of soft-voiced Sarah, my heart aches. "And Sumi?"

"She's Bangladeshi. She responded to an agency ad for a housecleaner in the *Yoo-Ae-Ee*. The agency paid for her ticket—but when she arrived, they assaulted her and kept her as a slave." She clears her throat. "I think, maybe, Shepherd bought her from them, but I'm not sure. She doesn't talk about it."

It makes sense that these women would choose being gisaeng. I want to ask Ksenia about herself, but it feels too personal—like requesting she strip naked in front of me. "If you . . . don't leave?"

"Like I said. After you earn enough, you go with your patron, although it's understood you'll help Shepherd, from time to time—find other girls who are desperate and hungry for a better life. Speaking of—" Her hand rests on my wrist again, making the jellyfish lights in front of my eyes pulse bright. "I stopped by Sarah's room. I thought she might be upset because Jones seemed so interested in you at dinner. Although we're brought with specific patrons in mind, every once in a while one will become interested in someone else, and then they'll switch. But she said she doesn't care if Jones switches, because she's cruel. So that's something to be careful of."

After what Sarah has been through, a cruelty big enough to make her risk her own comfort to warn me gives me a shudder. Is this why she and Sumi have bonded so tightly: though they're from different places, they share the same history of fear and violence? "Do you think Sumi and Sarah are . . . in love?"

Ksenia flicks the light on, pointing it right at me. I blink despite its weak beam, blinded by the change. It goes out again. "Sorry.

I just needed to know if you were being serious. What do you mean, exactly? What do you think love is?"

A stirring in the pot. "I don't know."

She exhales, soft, as if she's just puffed on a cigarette. "*I* think love is what you do to help someone *else* survive." The back of my neck tingles with the truth of her statement, one my mother would've agreed with. "But it also needs trust. Which means I don't think anybody here *can* love, not really. Being broken makes you selfish and a liar. Sarah's a people-pleaser, Sumi's always angry, Ca-lee drinks like a fish. You can't trust people like that, even if you feel something for them."

I shouldn't say what comes to mind next, but if we're all broken, then Ksenia is, too. "Heta says not to trust *you*."

She snorts. "You should trust Heta least of all." The bed creaks as she rolls over, though I can't tell into what position. The jellyfish lights vanished when she turned the flashlight on, but little by little, they reappear. "Do you remember when we played that game? The image one? And everyone said you were the spy?"

I nod, but she can't see me. "Yes."

"Well, we were *lying*. If there's a spy, it's Heta. Out of all the girls I've met here, she's the only one I don't understand. Her family situation was lousy—some abuse there, I think—but she comes from money. She's got a Swedish passport, everything she needs, but she doesn't *want* to go back."

I find that hard to believe. "Why not?"

"I think it's Shepherd. She's in love with him, or she *thinks* she is."

Finally, I find the courage to ask what I wanted before. "And you? Where are you from?"

Ksenia sighs. "Kazakhstan. My family is Russian, but I wasn't born there. Actually," the mattress groans, "my ancestors are Korean, like yours. We're Koryo-saram—Koreans that moved to Vladivostok a century ago. Within two generations, my family had become part of the fabric—ranking members in the party, going to important dinners, working and living their lives. And then Stalin deported them all to Central Asia and left them to starve. Most of them did."

Koryo-saram. They're Korean words, but Ksenia's usage rings strange and archaic to my ears—now, we call those like her the

Goryeo-in. She has boiled away the pain of most of their struggle, the forced exile on trains that took a month to cross the country, without food or water, in bitter cold. So many people died: their bodies dumped, their souls left to wander the tracks. Even now, they call them the *ghost trains*.

This, then, is why Ksenia's features look so familiar. And if she's Goryeo-in, there's a bond between us. Although she might not personally know what it means to be stateless, she must've heard the stories of her ancestors.

Tears sting at the corners of my eyes. "I'm sorry," I say in Korean. "I'm sorry this happened to your family."

"I don't speak Korean," she says, matter-of-factly. "The Soviets banned the language. Maybe my parents could've taught me, but they died when I was young. I got sent to live with my aunt, and—"

She removes her touch from my skin. I turn, desperate enough to grab for her arm, but my hands come up empty.

Ksenia chuckles darkly. "If I have any luck, it's in being beautiful—and if I have any misfortune, it's the same. My aunt married me off to a man in *Al-ma-ty* three times my age, a high-ranking police chief. He raped me every night and beat me every morning. Finally, I broke the lock on one of the windows, climbed out, and ran.

"The only money I had is what I found in his underwear drawer—just enough for a train to *Kok-she-tau*. As soon as I arrived, I looked for a place to hide, because I knew that he'd turn the whole country upside down. I was fifteen-hundred kilometers away, but he had power, money, and the combined police forces of all of Kazakhstan at his disposal. It was only a matter of time."

She sniffs. I can't tell if she's crying.

"My second day there, I got caught in the rain. A beautiful woman passing me in the street decided to take pity on me. She took me to a cafe and bought me tea. I remember raising it to my lips and thinking it was—how can I call it? Like the touch of frost, but pleasant, like when you're too hot from a sweat in the *ban-ya*, and you step outside into the winter air and there's that sudden, welcome chill. And she asked me if I liked art. If I thought I could learn to paint. If I wanted to go far, far away. I said yes, and she told me to meet her back at the cafe the same time a week later. I spent the week hiding as best I could, but *Kok-she-tau* is not that big of a city. I saw police, prying eyes everywhere. I lived in fear every second."

And just like before, I know what she's going to say next.

"And when I returned to the cafe, she was there, and so was Shepherd. He made me the offer, and I agreed."

"And then you were here," I say.

The bed creaks, and then her hand finds my arm again. It skates up to my shoulder before coming to rest. She pulls at the ends of my hair, making my scalp twinge. "And then I was here. It's not so bad. Yes, there's the sex, but the other parts—the talking, the performance in the Aviary, the art—*that's* why they really come. They're rich; they need to feel like they're receiving something nobody else can provide."

I can't tell if she believes it.

"I'm sorry you didn't know what this place is, but you can go back if you really want. And you don't have to decide right away. They won't touch you, not for weeks or sometimes months. Shepherd makes sure of that. It's part of what makes you so valuable. They have to visit several times, and pay, and pay, and pay, and each time, Shepherd lets them get a little bit closer."

She sighs, hot breath on my neck. My skin lights up, nerves all singing so loud I almost can't hear what she says next.

"*That's* what they want, really. They're rich and powerful, and they could have anything in the world—except here, in this place, where Shepherd makes them earn you. They like that. But it means you have time to decide."

I shut my eyes and take a deep breath. My heart slams in my chest, so loud I'm sure she can hear it, so loud I want to press on my breastbone until it crushes in, just to keep it quiet. "Garin . . . picked Hee-Young, yes? They were close?"

I can tell from the shifting of the sheets that she's lying down again. "Garin spent a lot of time here. It seemed like he really liked her. Ca-lee told us that he'd offered to pay everything she owed, all at once, so that she could leave with him."

My breath catches painfully in my throat as I wait for her to continue.

"But I guess she didn't want that. Or maybe he changed his

mind, that Russian bastard. But she went to go visit her mother, and now she's happy somewhere, drinking bubble tea."

"She's not," I say, more harshly than I meant. Hee-Young must've told Ksenia she loved bubble tea, the kind with fruit jelly at the bottom—

That Russian bastard. Ksenia's turn of phrase bounces down a long hallway in my mind. I've heard something like it before—like it, but different. *Where?*

That Russian bastard—

And then I have it. On the welcoming ceremony platform, the dream-swamp spinning below me, the girls' faces contorting as they pushed and pulled. After the drugs and the vision of Hee-Young, her open mouth saying *window*, I'd somehow forgotten the memory of me on the closet floor, wrapped in the beetle dress. *He's found me. I don't know how. He's a monster, Eun-Jin . . . maybe South, toward the coast. Somewhere that Russian bastard won't be able to blend in.*

But having made this connection, I'm not sure what it could mean. I'm not even sure if my memory of my mother was real. There's no way that Hee-Young's relationship with Garin has anything to do with the man our mother fled, is there?

It has to be a coincidence—

"Hee-Young? Do you hear that?"

At first, I think the snake-like hiss is part of my memory, but no, it's coming from the wall behind us.

The little flashlight flicks on, now stunningly bright. On Ksenia's face is an expression of utter fear. "*No.*" Her low moan covers me in goosebumps. "Not now."

She springs across the room, the plastic magnet held out as if to cleave the air—but then she lets go of the button. Before I can ask why, she cracks the door, and a sliver of bouncing light enters the room.

She shuts the door. "I'm too late." Her voice trembles as she clicks the flashlight back on. "There's someone at the end of the hall. Hee-Young, you have to hide me. I can't get found here."

I don't understand what's happening—but her fear's as heavy as a wet coil of rope. I glance around for hiding places—*the closet, the bathroom?*—and then I see the paintings.

I cross the room and open the bottom of the triptych, revealing the shaft. As the door swings open, it feels like the hiss gets louder—but it's hard to tell here, in this room where sound refuses to obey the laws I remember.

Ksenia stares at me, dumbfounded, but a hardness comes over her—fear, determination, there's not enough light to see which—and she dashes across the room and plunges herself headfirst into the shaft. "Help me," she whispers, dangling the light below.

I lean down and grab her legs, push them with all my might while she kicks. After a moment, all I can see of her is the very bottom of her nightgown, the tops of her slippers. In the glare of her flashlight, her ankles look like the shadowed trunks of birch trees. "I'm in," she whispers urgently. "Close it."

I shut the painting-door. For a moment, light leaks out from the corners, but then it disappears.

"Now get in bed and pretend to be asleep," she says, her voice muffled by the shaft.

I still have no idea what's happening, but I stumble back into bed and pull the quilt over my body. I instantly feel warmer. I realize I'm shivering violently.

I lie there in the dark, my breath rasping. I can just barely hear Ksenia's own exhalations, rendered tinny by the shaft.

A minute passes. Then another. I realize the room is steadily growing colder, and there's an odd smell—bitter and herbal, like a gin drink, but then it turns sweet. The jellyfish lights dance in front of my eyes again, the nerves firing from a lack of stimulation, trying to draw patterns and washes of color in the dark. At first, it's fragmented patches, sliding sideways each time I blink, but then the patches knit together into almost recognizable forms, like one of those inkblot tests in old movies about psychiatrists.

They all draw toward the center and converge. Recognition chimes in the back of my mind—*it looks like a face.* As the eyes form, two bright orange globes the size of softballs, so large for their orbits that they bulge like a rotting stomach, I whisper Ksenia's name, but she doesn't answer. The face grows a large protrusion below it, a tentacle of white smoke that quickly fattens into a body, even as a gaping hole of mouth opens below the eyes. And then comes sharpness—a sharp beak, sharp talons, just like the owl in the paintings. Long spikes that cover half of the ghost's visible face, as if I never squatted next to her in my bathroom and pulled them all out, one by one, leaving a patchwork of bloody perforations behind on her skin.

Hee-Young's face. I can see that now. The room fills with the smell of summer oranges, even as it grows cold.

From the wall in front of me comes a deafening bang. Behind me, the hiss falls away, subsumed by the ringing in my ears. It doesn't matter—hiss or no hiss, I can sense the malignancy of Hee-Young's ghost as it seeps into this room. Her too-white flesh glows brightly as she floats forward, blinding me with her righteous anger, her *han*—

I throw myself down on my knees, my hands held up, begging for my life.

"Please, Hee-Young-ah," I say, the words running together like water. *"I'm so sorry. Please don't do this. Please don't do this—"*

"Hee-Young?"

The form dims and coalesces. Where my sister's ghost once clearly stood is now only Ca-lee, a bright flashlight clutched in one hand.

"I'm so sorry," she whispers, her voice shaking. "I was sure it was you." The beam dances around the room as she speaks, jittering with each tremor from her body, casting shadows across her face.

Ksenia and the others had mentioned Ca-lee's eccentricity, but in this moment, she looks dangerously unstable, and I don't have a weapon near me. I feel like saying anything could set her off, so I don't speak.

Or maybe I'm quiet because I'm not sure if it's really her, or if this is some cruel trick of the ghost I was so certain of only seconds ago—if, at my first movement, she'll spring screaming across the room and bash my brains in with the flashlight.

Behind her, doors open in the hallway. Ca-lee looks back with the flashlight, holding the pose like a deer about to be taken by a hunter. She turns, the beam tracing across my wall before landing on my face and whiting out my view like a snowstorm.

"Hee-Young," she murmurs, no longer content to whisper. Somehow, it's more ghostly still. "Do you know where Ksenia is?"

I shake my head. After a moment, the door shuts, and everything is perfectly silent.

PART IV

The Display

What the hammer? what the chain,
In what furnace was thy brain?
What the anvil? what dread grasp.
Dare its deadly terrors clasp?
'The Tyger', William Blake

THIRTY-SEVEN
Hee-Jin

I don't immediately free Ksenia from the shaft. No matter how hard I will myself to *just sit up*, my muscles refuse to respond, and I lie there as if dead. With every second, I'm more certain the figure in the doorway was Ca-lee—and yet, I can't shake the feeling that before I heard Hee-Young's name from Ca-lee's lips, I saw my sister's ghost.

I don't believe in ghosts. The thought feels like a lie. All I know about them is from dramas and what my mother's told me, like the idea they're tied to an object of great emotional significance. But everything that was Hee-Young's is in Korea, save some clothes and the tin ring she liked when we were kids. And really, *I'm* the one that cared about that ring, that memory of my sister, young and unbroken.

I try again, and this time, I manage to wiggle my toes and curl the fingers of my left hand into a fist. With a great heave, I roll onto my side, then my forearms, though my entire body shakes as I try to push myself into a seated position. "Ksenia?"

The only answer is the soft rhythm of her breathing, echoing from inside the metal walls of the shaft.

I slide off the bed. I feel submerged in the darkness, like it's gone down my throat and permeated every part of me. *I could drown like this.* By the time my fingers brush the wall, the frame of one of the paintings, only the knowledge that Ksenia might start screaming at any moment keeps me pressing on.

"Ksenia? Can you hear me? You can come out now." I work my way down to the bottom painting and pull the door open. A cold breeze leaks out of the shaft. I reach down and wrap my hand around an ankle, give her a little shake.

After a moment, she starts to slide down, down, her feet traveling forward through the opening as she sinks. I grab for her, and my hand closes around the warm, curved planes of fingers. Her hand's poking through the opening.

I take it and pull, but I can feel resistance—as if she's just flopped forward in the shaft, her upper body blocking her movement.

Prickles travel up my spine. *Don't panic. She probably fainted*, I think, but I'm already picturing Hee-Young, the glowing of her flesh, the malignant thickening of the air around her as she hovered in the doorway.

I back up, running my hands down Ksenia's legs until I find her ankles. On the left one, I feel a small protuberance, like a large mole—but then it crumbles under my fingers like a dry leaf.

I shudder and let go of that side, switching both hands to her other ankle instead, and then I drag her backwards while pushing away thoughts of dried-up spiders and disintegrating flesh.

Finally, it feels like she's out. I run my hands up her sides to confirm, only this time, I brush something hard and sharp-edged—the flashlight magnet. She's still clutching it in one fist.

I squeeze her hand in mine, and the light flashes on.

Ksenia lays on her back, staring up at the ceiling—but when her gaze meets mine, she smiles ear to ear, the light drawing dark shadows in the crevices of her face. "*Heeeee—Young*," she says slowly, her voice light and airy. And then, to my shock, she giggles, turning her face from side to side, and I can make out places on her cheeks where the shadows don't move—small bruises, I think, or some other kind of mark.

I bend toward her, but she laughs and pulls her fist away from my grasp. The light goes out as she thumps her hand on the floor, soft raps as if against a door, checking if someone's home—

Three knocks.

Two knocks.

But just like before, the banging of the plumbing—the *finisher* never comes. Instead, she starts to whistle, a quavering, up-and-down series of notes that's more noise than tune, and I back away, unsure of what to do. The part of me that holds my mother's voice—the part that's always kept me safe—screams that the worst possible outcome is Ksenia being found here, like this.

Or maybe she's had a seizure, I think, and my gratitude for a rational explanation is like sunlight flooding into the room.

Wouldn't something neurological explain her crazed fear, her need to hide—and then her stupor, her giggles and radiant smile, the knocking of her hand? All at once, I'm not sure *how many* knocks I heard, or if there had really been a pause.

I'm afraid to leave this room when wild-faced Ca-lee roams the halls, but Ksenia needs medical attention. I take her flashlight and crack the door open.

"Wait," Ksenia says, her voice still high and girlish.

My heart is in my throat, but I stop.

"I found something on the ledge up there."

I click the flashlight back on to see she's holding her hand out toward me, as if in supplication. Nestled in the valleys of her palm is an imugi—a six-inch-long juvenile dragon, folded out of paper.

I hold my breath as I take it from her. From the clever details, I can tell it's Hee-Young's work. She even included a yeouiju—a mystical orb that, if caught on its fall from heaven, could grant the python-like imugi the ability to become a full-fledged dragon.

This yeouiju looks like a marble, though it's unevenly shaped and painted blue. Although dragons are usually depicted with the yeouiju in their claws, Hee-Young folded the paper of the imugi's mouth to support the ball without losing it.

I'm stunned. Of all the things to hide—why this? "Was there . . . more?"

She giggles and shakes her head. The movement is sloppy, making her head roll on her neck, as if she was warming up to exercise. When she's still again, I examine the bruises on her face. Some are swollen, like little bumps—like moles. I wonder if she's had some kind of allergic reaction to something in the shaft.

"There wasn't anything else on the ledge—although it kind of looks like there's a door up there."

My stomach drops. "Door?"

"Like a maintenance hatch or something in the ceiling. I couldn't reach it—it's in deeper, toward the rest of the house."

A *door*. It seems almost elementary—of course a place like the Petite Sea House has secret passages—but that certainty is just followed by more questions.

Where does it lead? Did Hee-Young know it was there?

She yawns then, her tongue stretching and glistening in the

harsh glare of the flashlight magnet. "I need to get back to my room before someone finds me. I'll come back tomorrow night, though." Ksenia bends forward and kisses me on the forehead, a gesture so tender that my chest tears apart with longing.

"Delicious." She slides her lips to my temple. Despite the oddness of the situation, I stop myself from reaching for her as she works her way down—to the apple of my cheek, the corner just outside of my lips—but she leaves, laughing, before she reaches my mouth.

THIRTY-EIGHT
Callie

So, it's Ksenia, then, that Shep's sleeping with. I checked her room again after Hee-Young's, and her bed was still empty.

I should be angry, or maybe even relieved, but there's just shame. Shame I let the accident drive us apart instead of pulling us together. Shame my husband had to resort to *this* to satisfy his most basic needs—

(Or maybe this was Garin. I never trusted that man. Maybe Garin dragged him into this, somehow, took advantage of him when he was at his most vulnerable—)

But most of all, shame I missed the signs. That I have no idea how long this has been going on, that I thought even for a moment I could stay here under this roof when I was just a sick, sad joke.

Lisa is snoring softly when I make it back to my room. She's always been a heavy sleeper, thank god, though it's been so much worse since the accident. So many nights, I've sat by her bedside, sure she's dead—only for her chest to suddenly expand with the violence of a deploying airbag, bringing me to tears each time.

For once, though, I'm glad. She doesn't hear me uncork the bottle and pour myself a glass of red wine—not the first glass, nor the second. It's only once I empty the bottle that I feel myself start to relax.

Shep's . . . *needs* are terrible, but I've survived terrible things. I was changed from a girl to a woman the night I ran someone over with my car. I see the poetic justice of it being another accident that took my life away from me. It's so honestly goddamn funny, I have to clap my hand to my mouth to contain my laughter.

Warmth spreads through my belly. I can survive this. I can still leave. Shep can't stop me from taking Lisa, not if he can't find us. I'll find some cabin in Idaho, some rural farm in Tennessee—

Those are just fantasies, though. The dreams you have when you're young and don't understand that you have to live with the repercussions of your actions. If I want to leave and have the chance that Lisa can come with me, that Shep won't just use his money and influence to have me committed or put in jail—I've got to do things right. I've got to show I'm willing to try things his way, to go with his plan.

So, I will. First thing in the morning, I'll let him know about my intentions—and whatever it is he wants me to do to buy my freedom, I'll do it.

I don't sleep, but as I make my way up to Shep's room at the crack of dawn, I feel lighter than I have in years. I left the key in my room, and it feels like I've turned off a spotlight that's followed me nonstop for the last decade. The panic I always feel climbing these stairs is still there—after all, I'm only *hoping* that he's alone, that his companion went back to her room once their dirty deeds were done—but it's faint and distant, like a shadow glimpsed behind sheer curtains, the window locked up tight.

Love is wonderful, sure, but nothing buoys someone up like having finally made a difficult decision.

I press the button to notify him he has a visitor. *It's time*, I rehearse to myself. *I'm ready to leave. I'm ready to move forward with my life.*

When he opens the door, I take a step back. Dark bags well under each of his eyes, and the skin on his face is sagging and puffy. *When did he start looking so old?*

But then he smiles. It's like dropping change into one of those automatic coin-sorters, his disassembled features all incrementally sliding back to their proper places, until the man revealed is radiant. Almost God-touched. "Good morning, Calleigh. To what do I owe this pleasure?"

"I need to talk to you." My throat is the Sahara. "If you have a minute, I mean."

He nods and pulls open the door. Inside, the room is the same. I expected books strewn on the floor, vases shattered, clear evidence of his passionate tryst—but everything's exactly as I remember it. I have a sudden mental image of his belongings flying back to their proper places on his shelves as if by some storybook spell.

We take seats around the small coffee table. "I'm ready," I say, just like I practiced, but to my mortification, my lip quivers and my eyes well up with tears. I wipe them quickly, trying to look nonchalant.

"Callie—what is it?"

I tell myself his dalliances are none of my business—that I can't do anything to jeopardize leaving in Shep's good graces—but the words force themselves out. "I *know*," I say, my voice cracking.

His face turns stormy. "Know *what*?"

I shake my head, as if negating what I'm about to say could in some way lessen the damage. "About the girls. About Ksenia—I came up yesterday to . . . talk to you about leaving." I'm grateful the excuse fills itself in so quickly. "And I heard you two last night. It's OK, Shep. It's none of my business. I lost claim to you a long time ago."

His eyes search my face. For once, he's the one that turns away first. "You . . . know."

I'm relieved he doesn't insult my intelligence by playing dumb. "We're not married anymore, so I guess it's not *infidelity*—it's none of my business, but all the same, I thought I should tell you that I found out."

He nods. I can just glimpse the edge of his expression: composed, carefully neutral. "And what told you it was Ksenia?"

The return of the shame is sudden. I stare at my hands. "I checked their rooms. I didn't mean to; it just happened. I thought it was Hee-Young, but she was in her room—"

"And Ksenia wasn't," he says flatly.

"I'm so sorry." This time, I don't try to stop the tears. "I don't know what I was thinking. It was such a crazy violation of your privacy, the girls' privacy. I just—" I turn away from him and cover my face. My nose is snotting up like I'm some teenager, making it hard to breathe.

I hear shuffling, but I can't make myself turn back, can't bear to see his judgment. But then he takes my shoulders and rotates me gently, before handing me a glass of water he's somehow magicked from the liquor cabinet. "Drink."

I take a sip. It's warm, but my breathing slows some.

"Is that better?"

I nod tentatively.

"I wanted to make sure you could hear me. *Really* hear me."

He takes a deep breath. And then, "Listen, Calleigh. You have nothing to be sorry for."

I turn my face away, not wanting to hear his lies, but he takes my chin and guides it to the soft invitation of his dark eyes. "Everything that happened between us—it's my fault, too. Almost losing you, it was terrifying and excruciating. When you came back, you were so delicate. I could tell that if I pushed you at all . . ." He traces down my jawline with his thumb, a well-worn movement I'd somehow forgotten.

The gesture spikes me with desire, until I remember last night, and then I feel sick again. "That's my fault, not yours. I shouldn't have been drinking and driving—but I swear, Shep, I don't know how that happened. All I had at that party was water."

That's all I remember, but that doesn't mean that's all there was. Halfway through the dinner, my memories grew thin and hazy. I could've forgotten the drinking. I don't even recall leaving.

"Yes, I've been thinking about that a lot, lately."

My heart goes still. "Shep?"

"You're beautiful, Calleigh. Beautiful enough that I can imagine someone slipping something into your drink so they could have you for a few hours—especially if it meant stabbing me in the back."

The warmth I felt at that word—*beautiful*—turns to ice as his implication takes shape in my mind. "You think—you think I was *drugged*?"

"Maybe. I don't know. It would explain why you can't remember. Why you were so out of it when I found you. I thought it was just the trauma of the accident—"

He doesn't finish, but I hear the end of the sentence, all the same. *But I could've been wrong.* "Why didn't you tell me this before?"

"When you came and said you were getting better—" He closes his eyes. "I think some part of me was still hoping that the accident wasn't your fault, and that hope kept me from touching *my* memories of that night. As if probing them might reveal something I was afraid of, and then all that hope would be gone."

His shoulders rise and sink. In any other moment, it would be too much, the drama almost comical. "But then you came to me and told me you wanted to leave, and it was like I was back there again. That whole week, we'd been fighting, and then you threw the pewter box—"

It's strange to feel embarrassed now, but I still blush. "I'm sorry—"

He doesn't seem to hear me. "And then you at the party, that silver dress you wore. You inside of that car, your head lolling. I thought you were just drunk, and the brain injury . . ." He bites his lip again. "But no matter how many times I turned it over, I didn't remember *you* drinking, either. I started to wonder if something else had happened."

I clasp my hands together, chilled. Shep's always been a little paranoid, but the idea that somebody would use me—would *rape* me, just to hurt him—it seems impossible. And it's hard to think when I feel like I'm being tossed about in a storm, bathed in his confessions and compliments, revelations I hadn't dared to dream of—where were these frank declarations all those years we were together? Was he really so terrified of losing me that he let me push him away?

I run through my fragmented recollections of that night, trying to find faces. So many are Shepherd's clients, people I barely know. The only person I can remember clearly is Mels, and though I don't love the man, I can't imagine he poses any threat—

Except it was *him* with Shep last night. And I know Shep as well as anybody *can* know him. He would never do something like that on his own.

How much influence does Mels Garin have over my husband, really?

His brow furrows. He drops his face into his hands. "I've been so awful to you."

"No, Shep—"

"A bad provider, a bad husband, and now a cheat. No wonder you were so unhappy."

In the back of my mind, I hear that soft, high moan again, that call like a conch-shell. My gaze trails toward the bedroom door, the place I'm not allowed to enter—but then I rip myself away from it. I can even hear the break, the bright *zip* of tearing a sheet in half.

"Shep, *no*. None of that is true. You were so much more than

I deserved. What you spent in medical bills alone—selling off your properties so I'd get the best care, hiring staff to wait on me hand and foot—how can you say that? Even now, you take such good care of me, such good care of Lisa—"

"Then why do you want to leave me?" His voice trembles. He raises his face, and I'm shocked to find that it's covered in tears.

Before I can stop myself, I reach out and touch one, breaking its tension, and it glides down my finger.

He grabs my hand, his grip so tight my wrist twinges in pain.

"Shep?"

"Think about it, Calleigh." He still doesn't let go. My wrist throbs in little beats, his pulse or mine, I can't tell. "I'm distinguished and educated. I'm wealthy—maybe not as wealthy as I was, but wealthy enough. I could've easily found a new wife—some beautiful divorcee or widow, or even some frivolous thing half your age. But I didn't."

"Shep." I try to withdraw my hand, making my wrist lance with pain, but he doesn't let go.

"Why haven't I found someone else, Calleigh? Why do I waste my time bedding stupid, petulant girls when there's the pinnacle of womanhood roaming my halls, haunting me like my very own personal ghost?"

"Shep, you're *hurting* me—"

My hand snaps back toward me as if my arm was made of elastic. "Oh god, Calleigh—I'm so sorry. I don't know what came over me. You just . . . you make me so crazy."

In that moment, I float outside of my body. There's a feeling, an energy in the room I suddenly recognize, and it's not until I close my eyes that I know what it reminds me of.

When I first moved in with Cassie, we had a balcony we couldn't access. The wooden platform was rotting and broken in several pieces, so the management company had nailed boards over the door. One night after a bad shift and a bottle of wine, I went nuts—*didn't I deserve nice things, like a balcony? Who cared if it was shabby?*—and pulled all the nails out with a little claw hammer.

The balcony door was dusty from neglect, but as I slid it open, in spilled the air of the city, the warmth of the departed day still rising off the pavement in wisps of sad heat. I slipped outside, onto the rotting platform. Even as it groaned, threatening to give way under me, I finally felt free.

I feel like I'm on that balcony now.

I realize for the first time what Shep and I had, and what we didn't—that though I loved him desperately, I never trusted him.

But what is trust, really? I had no trust in that balcony, and I did it anyway. No matter what Shep does or doesn't do, I'll always be that girl, listening to the wood creak under me, daring it to break.

"I'm still in love with you." I say it calmly, as if there isn't a circlet of bruises slowly forming around my wrist. As if neither one of us is in tears.

He bows his head and leans forward until his forehead touches my stomach. One long breath, then two—and then sobs overtake him, long, wracking movements that shake us both. He reaches for me, for my hips, and pulls me into his lap.

And then his lips are on mine.

They are hungry lips. Expert and searching, made strong by the years we spent together, honed sharp by the ones apart, even as we sat in the same rooms and breathed the same air. His touch is like fire, and my skin buzzes with anticipation and want. I melt into him, into this man I once gave myself to, this man that I'll give myself to again, as many times as he wants, as long as he'll have me. He bites my nipples through my shirt, a pain so exquisite I grab his hair and pull, and the noise he makes, it's the rumble of an animal—

And suddenly I'm not in his lap. I'm in the air, my legs wrapped around his waist as he stands. In one fluid motion, he undoes his pants and pulls up my hem.

I'm not ready, I think, but it's a lie. I need him more than I've needed anything in my entire life. There's only a moment of resistance as he pushes into me—just a moment of tension, like biting into an apple.

"F-f-f-uck." The word threatens to drag me up from the depths—but he's inside me, now. He's moving, and I'm his, and everything I have ever worried about, every care I've ever had, is gone, because my husband is once again mine.

THIRTY-NINE
Hee-Jin

There's a little door up there. Like a hatch.

Between Ca-lee's volatile surprise visit and Ksenia's terrified flight into the shaft—and her giggling, flirtatious behavior after—I spend hours lying rigid in the dark before I give up and crawl into the bathroom, my flashlight magnet in hand. It's only once the door is shut and I'm curled up in the tub that I feel like I can breathe.

This place is getting to me. Making me attached to Ksenia and behave in ways I normally wouldn't. Making me doubt my reality and see Hee-Young's ghost. I can't think of anything more dangerous—and I definitely can't run the risk of being sent back, not when the wheels of bureaucracy are already turning to connect me with Hee-Young's death.

But I'm so exhausted, it hurts to breathe. I have no money or transportation, and we're in the middle of an unfamiliar nowhere. I don't even know what day it is. I need to recover my passport, get my bearings, and come up with a plan. There might even be something in Hee-Young's shaft that could help.

And if it takes longer than I think? Could I sleep with a man like Garin, or one of the other patrons, just to stay safe? Try to entertain them with *sparkling* conversation and my shitty "folk-art pottery," hanging on for as long as I have to?

The table is hot.

The calm that steals over me is like the sun finally setting, like a great beast lumbering down for the night. *I am my mother's daughter. I could do anything to survive.*

And as that certainty spreads cool comfort through my limbs, I drift off. It's not sleep, exactly. Instead, the tub seems to enfold me, swaddling me like a baby.

I don't know how long I stay like that. One moment, I float in that perfect darkness. The next, all the lights are on, and Heta is standing in front of me, biting her lip, her brow lifted.

"I called out a few times," she says. Not *What are you doing in here?* Or *Are you OK?* And because Ksenia has given me the framework to understand this place for what it is, I realize I'm probably not the first girl to seek out the safety of the cloistered bathroom, the solid walls of the tub. She grins. "You sleep like a dead thing." Her gaze flicks down to my hand, to my flashlight magnet.

I shove it behind my back, but she doesn't remark on it. "You're late for breakfast. They sent me to get you."

"Sorry." Just like last night, I'm not hungry, but I force myself to crawl out of the bathtub.

Heta looks away as I maneuver over the rim. "You know, it was strange, what happened last night. I think Ca-lee is going crazy."

I know she's watching me, even turned away. "Strange," I echo.

"And Ksenia—she wasn't in her room. You've been spending a lot of time together, haven't you?"

"She is kind. To me." It's a lie. She's not kind—but even if I had the words, I wouldn't tell her about my desperate need for the unknowable woman who seems resolute on confusing and scaring me.

She turns back and leans in, drops her voice. "Do you remember the first morning you were here? When she was late for breakfast?"

My stomach turns. I don't want to hear what Heta has to say. "Maybe she slept in the tub."

Heta ignores the joke. "She was up *there*. With Shepherd. *Alone*."

She lifts her brows meaningfully, as if her intonation wasn't enough for me to understand her implication: Ksenia is *consorting with the enemy*.

But if Ksenia told the truth, and Heta's in love with Shepherd—she wouldn't think of him as an enemy.

Before I can compose an answer, she flips her hair at me. "You should get cleaned up. Do you want me to walk with you?"

A coldness sinks into my belly. Last night, Ksenia told me to hate Heta—because one spy turns us *all* into spies. But by Ksenia's logic, if Heta is a spy, then isn't Ksenia, too? What if that was just a thinly veiled confession?

I'm suddenly furious at being put in this position, that I let myself trust.

"I can go myself," I say, my voice hard. I soften it, try to relax my face. "I mean—I don't want . . . to make . . . inconvenient. I can see you there."

"Sounds good." She gives me a thin smile. "Hee-Young, I want to know you better," she says, before turning away on her heel.

I climb the stairs to the first floor—and almost collide with Ca-lee. Her hair and clothes are a mess, as if she spent the night roaming the halls.

Despite our near impact, she doesn't seem to notice me. As she passes, the thinnest corner of a smile tugs at her lips. It sends a shiver down my back.

I turn toward the dining room, my mouth sour from my thoughts. I don't know what Heta means: *get to know me better.* She hasn't shown any interest in me, save in asserting herself as the leader of this little group.

And Ksenia? I still want to be close to her, to know what makes her tick—but in the light of the day, I can't escape how strange her behavior was.

Let that go. Concentrate on getting out. I'm now sure my passport wasn't taken to fill out some forms. And if Ca-lee knows they're holding it to keep me here, then she's as guilty as Shepherd.

Entering the dining room, I'm hit with vertigo. The seats have all moved—Sarah and Sumi are still side by side, but now they're at the very end of the table, then Heta, then Ksenia—though there's a space between Ksenia and Heta, one clearly meant for me.

I take it. The facilitator brings out a tray, but my attention is pinned to Ksenia's face. At first, it seems like the bruises from last night are gone, but then I notice the matte texture of her skin, the makeup over the bumps on her forehead and cheeks.

I look down at my plate. The fare is simpler than usual—toast and different kinds of cereal, sliced fruits, a thin white substance I assume is yogurt. My greedy hands are halfway to my plate before I remember the shaft behind the painting. Somewhere in my brain, an old lightbulb stutters on.

I could get up into the shaft and investigate the door Ksenia found—*Hee-Young's door*—

if I was thinner.

My stomach rebels, but I fold my hands in my lap.

"It's the yogurt, isn't it?" Heta's expression is stiff, like one of those egg-based concoctions in a bakery window—like I could push my finger through her cheek and watch as her skin buckled and slid apart. "Before I came here, I'd never eaten thin yogurt like this. It's delicious, though." A pause. "I've noticed you don't eat meat—milk, too?"

I nod carefully. I'm not ashamed of this choice—I was, at first. After a lifetime of deprivation, turning down any meal seemed like a sin.

"Why is that?"

I don't know how to answer in English. A hundred meals flash before my eyes: watery soups stretched by chunks of a hot dog my mother pilfered from the stand. Half-finished gas station gimbap dug out of trash cans, hoping the tuna-mayonnaise filling hadn't gone bad. A glistening bun stolen from Paris Baguette—*no thank you, I'm just looking*—my heart beating rapidly as I edged my way out, the anticipated taste of sweet red-bean filling vying for dominance in my mouth with my fear. If caught, that one bun could've ended my entire life.

And the instant noodles. Always the noodles.

"Life is painful," I finally manage. "I want to *choose*. I don't want . . ." I trail off, because I don't know how to finish.

"To make more pain," Ksenia finishes for me. "*I* think that's very admirable."

She's right, but she's wrong, too. Pain is a part of it—but the *choice* is a bigger one.

Heta shoots her a glare. Once again, I'm embroiled in a conversation with layers I don't understand, and the not knowing what's safe, what isn't—it makes my breath come hard. I imagine fleeing from the room, from the building, out into this wild terrain that looks both utterly alien and vaguely familiar.

"Ad-mi-ra-ble," I say, feeling the shape of the word in my empty mouth. I can be *admirable*. For Hee-Young, and only for Hee-Young, I can be hungry again—because whatever she hid up in that shaft, it could be the key to saving myself.

I look up just long enough to catch Ksenia's expression, her furrowed brow and pink cheeks—I'm sure it's rage, but then she turns away, and I no longer know what I saw.

"How did you sleep?" asks Heta, speaking directly to me.

Seconds after we're out the door and on our way to the studio, the skies open up. The girls sprint for the greenhouse, but I hang back, desperate for a moment alone.

Cold, fat drops slap into my skin. They pour so rapidly down my forehead, I have to shield my vision with one hand to avoid being blinded. Even then, I can only see a few feet in front of me. I angle off in the wrong direction and almost miss the studio, before correcting course at the last second.

Inside the repurposed greenhouse, it's steaming, the moist heat trapped by the glass roof. The rain beats down angrily: hollow, percussive taps that blend into a threatening hiss.

"I'll get you a towel," says Heta.

"Thank you," I say, but her back is already toward me, her pace brisk. I don't know if she heard me. Even her steps are soundless, their taps swallowed up by the rain.

"This sound could swallow anything." Ksenia's voice, reading my thoughts.

My blood goes cold. I spin, panicked, my hair flying out, water whipping away from me as if I were just a scruffy dog. But Ksenia's not behind me—in fact, she's not inside the studio at all.

Then I see, distorted by the waves pouring down the glass studio wall: a lone figure, deliberately trudging across the lawn. I can't make out her face, but I know it's her.

My studio is different. Someone's neatly lined up a series of objects on the workbench: folded newspapers, a block of gray clay, a bowl of water, and a cup of tools that would be at home in a dentist's office. I pick up one that looks like a scalpel and imagine standing over a body, the blade parting white flesh into red oceans.

Someone taps the glass door behind me. I feel guilty, as if my thoughts were visible to everyone, but I don't put the scalpel down.

Ksenia doesn't wait for permission to enter. "You ran away from me." Her accent is so thick on the word *away* that it takes me a moment to parse it. Her expertly applied makeup is running, revealing a series of moles that peek through the remnants of her concealer like mountains through a mist. They range from flat to protrusions as large as a pea, making me again surprised that I ever could've missed them in the first place.

I wonder what would happen if I squeezed one. If it would crumble between my fingers like a bug's dried-up shell.

"I didn't run away. I need . . . practice." I'm hyper-aware of my pronunciation, the way every syllable is so labored and painful. There are only half-walls in here. Everyone can catch each word I say, even over the rain.

"OK." Ksenia turns away, leaving the long, wet trail of a slug in her wake.

Maybe I'm going about this all wrong. If Ksenia's a viper, it might be best to hold her close. And do I really trust Heta more? She's already shown herself to be the kind of person who's happy with talking trash about *everyone*. And if she's really in love with Shepherd—

"Wait."

Ksenia glances over her shoulder like a starlet. I walk toward her, get close enough to smell the rain on her. "The first morning. Breakfast. You were . . . late."

She narrows her eyes. "And you want to know why."

I swallow, but I nod.

"I was meeting with Shepherd."

My stomach feels like I've just stabbed it with the little scalpel-tool. Heta was telling the truth. "Why?"

"I've been here too long. I thought . . . that if I did him a favor, he'd let me leave."

My heart hammers. "And?"

She shrugs. "He gave me to Pepperdine instead." She turns away and points to the clay. "It's paper clay. Easier to work with. I thought you might like that." Moisture is dripping off her white sleeve, soaking the floor.

I jump at Heta's voice behind me. "What's going on in here?" She says it playfully, with a smile, but there's no ease in her body.

I suddenly realize I'm pressing the scalpel-tool's length against the back of my wrist, as if hiding it.

"Nothing," Ksenia says coolly. "We were talking about technique."

"Well, I think it's time to get to work on our own projects, don't you? Ca-lee or Shepherd will be by soon. They're not going to like us just socializing."

Ksenia turns and nudges her way past Heta, who waits a moment before following her out. As the door swings shut, I slip the scalpel-tool into my bra, adjusting the capped blade up and away from my body.

I chance a glance at the door when I'm done. Though the frosted glass distorts our view, I can make out Heta in her studio. Her body's turned toward her workbench, but I get the feeling she's been watching me this whole time.

FORTY
Callie

From the moment Shepherd takes me, he doesn't stop. I marvel at his desire, even as the pleasure turns to pain—but it's such exquisite pain, so needed. I welcome it as thoroughly as that which came before.

I came here at the break of dawn. Hours later, when the bell-tone for breakfast goes off and all the house's automatic lights flip on, we haven't left the sitting room's leather chairs. Finally, though, he's done. He kisses me on the forehead and rolls over.

A sudden cramp squeezes my insides. I feel like all the toxins that infected our marriage have been sweated out to hang thick on our skin. I want to ask him to shower with me, to dress with me—for us to bury this last chapter of our lives for good.

But now that the throes of passion are over, my gaze is pulled back toward the bedroom, this place where other women have tread. Is it possible to rehabilitate it—change the bed and the curtains, repaint—or should we claim a different room?

He draws his finger down my neck, making me shiver, until it disappears into the dead spot on my chest. For a moment, I imagine I can feel the warmth of his hand even in that void. "I noticed you're not wearing your key," he says softly. "Did you lose it?"

I swallow and shake my head. "I just—I got tired of everyone knowing how I felt, all the time."

"I see." It's only two words, but I can tell from the inflection that he's disappointed, and I resolve to put it back on once I'm in my room. It's really such a small thing—

His phone buzzes on the coffee table. He grabs it and starts rapidly typing a text message. Before I can work up the nerve to ask about it, he turns back toward me. "I have to attend to something. Can you let yourself out?"

I feel like a balloon, all the air hissing away. But I nod and gather my clothes, put them on.

"Oh, and Calleigh—"

I pause, my heart suddenly pounding.

"That was Garin. The Aviary display tonight, he wants Hee-Young in it."

"Hee-Young," I say bitterly.

"Yes." He looks up at me and smiles, and I can't help it—it tugs at my heart. I feel like a teenager again. "Wear something nice for me tonight, won't you?"

And once again, I am mended.

I run down to my bedroom. I need to shower and change and check on Lisa—

Lisa. Despite the giddiness in my heart, there's a cold, pragmatic part of me that isn't ready to let her know about this. It's best to proceed slowly where children are involved, and although I'm sure we're doing the right thing, both for her and ourselves, after everything I've done, I can't run the risk of hurting her more than I already have.

I solemnly promise to put her first. And then I strip off my clothes, start the shower, and sit on the edge of the tub. The room fills with tepid warmth, the hiss of steam—but my mind is slowly filling with last night, uncertainties leaching into the spaces the departing glow of our union left behind.

Is it possible that Shep's right—that someone drugged me?

He admitted to Ksenia—but have there been others?

Does he know I went into his bedroom?

I suddenly feel dizzy. I have to scoot to the bathroom wall and lean against it for support.

Nobody's perfect, I plead with myself. *We've both made mistakes. Can't we be gracious? Can't we be forgiven? We could make this entire marriage anew.*

But the dizziness gets worse. Black wings fold in from the corners of my vision, covering me like a blanket, and I hear a soft voice from a forgotten memory: *Mommy?*

Lisa, dear, I'm coming, I think, and I sink underneath the dark.

I wake up. For a moment, I forget where I am, why I'm here—but the water's running, and I can smell my body odor.

That's right. I was going to shower.

Runnels have collected on the tile, but there's no steam. When

I reach out and touch the stream, it's frigid, so I flip the diverter. I wet a washcloth under the tub spout, wring it out, and bathe myself the best I can.

There's nothing to do for my hair but stick it in the water. The cold's so bracing, it floods me from the inside out—and once I'm done, my head thumps, angry at the temperature change.

Clean enough. I towel off and step into fresh underwear, throw on the key. I'm less enthused about the morning than I was—*when was that?*—but before I can think on it, my stomach growls. I realize I'm impossibly, ravenously hungry, even over my exhaustion and the headache. I can smell food in the air: finger sandwiches, small tapas-like dishes of pickles and bean salad, miniature bowls of arugula and watercress with a sharp citrus vinaigrette. It's an odd choice for breakfast, but I can make out every single scent.

Except that's not breakfast. That's the food they served the night of the dinner—the night I crashed the car and nearly killed my daughter.

The walls vibrate softly, as if they had better manners than to completely disrupt my grief. I sit down, shut my eyes, and take a deep, shuddering breath. The scents ebb, little by little—flashes of mint and cucumber, the metallic taste of the ice cubes—but they do, and after a moment, the sensations pass.

It's OK. I'm just exhausted. And as soon as I have that thought, my mood lifts, as if the room's suddenly been cleared of a fog. I stand up and put on my skirt, a fresh bra. I'm slow now, my arms heavy—and I'm tired, so tired; it's like when I was twenty and spent an entire night at a snowy bonfire keg party in the kind of clothes that are only worn to be seen. I'd been so depleted afterwards that I'd slept for two days. I'm worn out by joy and—

There's a blank where the next thought should be. For a moment, I panic—and then there's a flash, Shepherd's lips on mine, and wonder fills me up like an overflowing cup.

That's right, I think. *My husband loves me again*. Somehow, I'd forgotten.

I collapse forward, weeping. Above me, the ceiling sags, bowing in toward me as if I'd been the button fastening it up. I feel a hot spike of rage toward Shep and his stupid biometric pendant and his stupid funhouse of an art project, but then the raw feeling washes back over me again.

It takes me a long time to get it all out, but when I do, underneath is fresh and green. I dry off my bathroom mirror with anticipation—I can't wait to do something special with my hair to catch his eye—

There are red marks on my right shoulder, like two perforated half-moons. I stare until it comes together: the clear impression of teeth.

I don't remember being bitten—but that's impossible. I think back, starting with that flash of a kiss, trying to work my way forward, but everything is like overworked wet paint until . . . until something I can only hear and not see. An impression of Shep's voice: *Make sure Hee-Young is in the Aviary display. Garin wants to see her there.*

Panic fills my breast. The ceiling moves again, this time lifting up and away, as if being nudged by a helium-filled balloon. It pulses silently, once, twice, the movement small and yet somehow frenetic.

I *know* I was up in his room. I was up there, and we . . . we must've had sex. I have his bite mark on my shoulder. I am sore in all the places that matter. There's no way—

I pull down my new panties. They're still clean.

I search the room, but I can't find my old ones. I can't find *any* of my clothes from last night. *The facilitators came while I was in the shower, that's all. They took the laundry*. I don't know if I believe it.

I go back to the mirror, study myself again. The bite mark closest to my face is slightly smaller—as it would be if I had bitten myself. I reach up and dig my finger into the mark, *hard*. Even if my eyes lie, the pain in my flesh can tell the truth—

There are bruises on my forearm. Five ovoid bruises: four on one side, one on the other. I try again to remember when he would've held me this way, but it's still that overworked blob of paint—not quite a blank space, but so vague as to be meaningless.

My memory, betraying me again. Which means that Shepherd was wrong.

It wasn't drugs that night. It was *me*. And I'm not getting better. I'm getting worse.

My legs give out. I hit the floor and land awkwardly on my side. I curl into a ball, so tightly my knees touch my chest, and then I start to weep.

FORTY-ONE
Callie

Ring the bell, and the mouth will water. The stimulus elicits a response.

When children in school learn about Pavlov and his dogs, there's a lot the teachers leave out.

They don't mention his nasty personality, his deep-seated, public antisemitism, the way he terrorized his staff. They omit the earlier experiments that won him his Nobel prize—like his system of "sham feeding" in which he cut out a dog's esophagus to ensure its stomach stayed empty no matter how much it ate, until it died leaking and starving. They never bring up the way he funded his laboratory, the "gastric juice factory" where dogs with holes in their guts were harnessed to a wooden beam and tilted to face a large bowl of meat, so that the secretions of their endless hunger could be sold as a treatment for indigestion.

My stomach doesn't care about my fear and grief. With each bell-tone—studio time, lunch, more studio time—it clenches violently, making me sway on my feet, but I can't rip my gaze away from the mirror, the bruise on my shoulder.

I've checked a hundred times, leaning over and pressing my teeth into my flesh. If I strain so hard my jaw burns, I can just barely reach—but I *can*, and that millimeter of a difference is enough to break me inside. I'm sure, now, that I *could* have done this. Could've bitten and bruised myself.

My ex-husband could be in his room above, no idea of the turmoil in my mind.

The kiss was real, though. And as soon as I think that, I realize my memory of it has a soft, fluid quality, like petroleum jelly over a lens. It could be part of a dream, a too-fervent fantasy.

My mouth is still watering. Am I hungry? Or have I just spent so long in this house that it's become a part of me, like the glass cannulae Pavlov implanted in those dogs' jaws, turning their pain and need into something quantifiable?

I can't leave this room again. Can't face Shep. If I turn toward him, and what I see is not recognition, but instead pity—or worse, apathy—it'll kill me. I know it will, and if it doesn't, I'll kill myself.

And yet, I have no choice. I have to go out there, see his face, and find out if that kiss was real. If I was really up there; if we lay together as husband and wife.

Warmth suffuses me at that image, like lying full-length on summer grass—but then the breeze turns cold. No matter what, I can't let him know that I've started to lose time again, not when I just told him I'm starting to get better. He'll think I'm a liar, or crazy.

I have to act like I remember—which means I need to get to the studio, right now, because the only detail I have of last night is that voice telling me that Garin wants Hee-Young in the Aviary display. I need to relay those instructions.

I put on my least favorite of the costumes, the one that Shep loves the most, and then I close my eyes and breathe until it feels like I'm outside my body.

I will just drift out to the studio, I think, and then I do.

I know Shep isn't here from the easy stance of the few facilitators I encounter as I pass through the halls. When he's around, they all tighten up: chests thrust out, chins raised until they probably can't see the floor. But me? I'm just window-dressing.

My guess is he's taken the patrons golfing, although sometimes he takes them into the city, to his private box at the Pittsburgh Opera or a show at Carnegie Music Hall. And despite how *provincial* the Dirty 'Burgh must seem to these people, compared to what they're used to—Paris, New York, LA, London, Berlin—they seem to enjoy what Shep sometimes calls *playing Americana*.

The worst of them go so far as to affect a *Piks-burgh* accent for the duration of their three-day stay, throwing out numerous *yinz*s and *jagoff*s and demanding their clothing *needs washed* when Shep takes them *dahn-tahn* for the *Stillers* game. And although there are still a few old-timers that still speak fluent

Pittsburghese, the truth is that the City of Bridges has changed since the 1980s and the implosion of the steel industry. Now, the biggest employers in this thriving metropolis are world-class universities, cutting-edge medical centers, the federal government, and technology companies, like Uber, Carnegie Robotics, and Google.

At least none of this current batch are like that. Jones, Carlson, and Smallet all seem nice enough, and Garin is . . . Garin. If it wasn't for Pepperdine—

(No, you can't think about him right now, you have to act normal)

—I might've actually enjoyed myself at dinner.

They'll all be back tonight, along with Shep, who never misses the display. He says it's for the patrons, but I've always wondered if that's only a partial truth. Either way, it'll be my first opportunity to suss out what happened last night.

And even though I'm afraid, I'm also excited. What if that kiss was real, and I can pull this off? Then maybe, something beautiful could unfold between us. Something delicate and worthy of protection.

It's not until I'm halfway to the greenhouse that I remember I forgot to check on Lisa. The guilt that hits me is sharp—

And then, as if by a miracle, I see her in the garden to my right, next to one of the facilitators. She's stalking a butterfly, her hands cupped out in front, her tongue curled over her top lip in deep concentration.

I wait as she pounces, but she misses, and her prey flutters away. It's cute enough that I have to laugh.

Her head snaps up, and then she smiles big and runs for me with outstretched arms. Joy surges in my chest. *Yes, my darling. If I can pull this off, we'll be a real family again soon.* "I'm going to the greenhouse," I say into her hair. "Do you want to come?"

She pulls away and nods before taking my hand. We walk, swinging our arms together, as if we're about to go picnicking. I catch the facilitator's disapproving expression as we pass—*why are they always so stern?*—but then he's behind us, and it's as if he never existed at all.

We pause by the greenhouse door. "Remember, Lisa. We can't touch anything. Just looking with our *eyes*, right?"

She nods exuberantly. Her joy is infectious, and I can't help smiling as I hold the door open and she scampers in.

I start with Heta. Today, she's painting a man from behind. His coat and hair swirl together into a dark fog. "Very nice," I comment, before pointing at some shading in the background. "But you need to be more judicious with your use of black. It's too eye-catching."

She scowls at me, but my attention is diverted by a rattle from behind us. I spin around. "Lisa!"

She's got a cup in her hand, one filled with small paintbrushes. She guiltily releases it and steps back.

"I'm sorry about that," I say to Heta. Her eyebrows are up, judging me, making my headache spike worse—in fact, my whole body aches, as if I'm coming down with a flu, or a fever.

I hate her, I suddenly realize. Maybe it's Ksenia that slept with my husband—Ksenia, in whose direction I've been carefully *not* looking since I stepped in this room—but it's Heta I hate the most. She's so open about how much she doesn't respect me, so obvious about how badly she wants to control this little group.

I feel the urge to punish her. And I know the perfect way to do it. "You know, Heta, you haven't seemed very focused lately. Maybe you've gotten too used to being in the display."

This is one of the few ways I haven't been entirely truthful with the girls. Although I usually tell them who's going to be featured in the Aviary that week, Shep's the one that decides.

But she doesn't know that, and she stiffens like a frozen deer. I relish the change. Maybe I haven't been myself these last few years, but I was here before her, before all of them, and I—and my *husband*—will be here long after they leave.

"I think I'll put Hee-Young in there this week. But who should she replace? Last time, there was you, Ksenia, and Sumi. I'll have to think about it—"

Anger snaps over her face, a hatred I can't fathom. "This is because of Garin, isn't it?"

My stomach twists. Yes, Shep and Garin haven't gotten along lately—but Heta's response feels odd, even if I can't quite put my finger on why. Maybe if my head wasn't pounding so hard. Maybe if there wasn't a missing spot in my memory that itches to be tongued, like the gummy vacancy of a lost tooth.

I don't want petulant Heta to run to Shepherd and complain. "I think I'll have Hee-Young replace Sumi," I say calmly.

Her expression is still tight, but she nods. "OK," she says softly. "I understand. Thank you."

It's clear from her response that she's layered hidden meanings onto this interaction between us. I just wish I knew what they were.

All at once, I lose my nerve. I feel hot and thirsty, and I need to lie down. "I'll see you at dinner. Why don't you let the other girls know about the Aviary selections for this week?"

And then I leave before she can see the sudden chill that's passed over my face.

FORTY-TWO
Hee-Jin

In the hours since Ksenia's revelation—that she was late to my first breakfast because she was meeting with Shepherd for permission to leave—all the questions I should've asked expand in my mind. Things like: What was the favor you were offering? Sex is the obvious choice—but does that make sense? Could it even really hold value, here in this place, where it's so easily bought and sold, and where Shepherd holds so much power?

Is pairing you with Pepperdine a punishment? If so, for what?

But Heta's been hovering since she interrupted us earlier, watching me through the glass. When the bell-tone sounds for lunch, she walks me to the dining room and sticks to my side like a burr. There isn't a moment where I can speak to Ksenia alone, and she won't explain anything in front of Heta, who she so hates.

Finally, during studio time after lunch, I look up and don't see Heta. I tense, ready to dash out into the hallway, to pour my questions down Ksenia's throat—but then Heta moves back into view . . . with Ca-lee.

I hold my breath, caught in the memory of Hee-Young's malevolent glow as she floated into the room, only to be replaced by Ca-lee's wild hair and snapping eyes.

The rain starts up again, and Ca-lee exits the room. She glances up, making my chest squeeze, and I drop my gaze and jam both my hands into the clay, destroying the muddled fox I've spent the last few hours approximating.

But she doesn't come. I sneak up to the door, and the still-empty hallway expands through the glass. It's only when I poke my head out that I spy a moving smudge: Ca-lee, obscured by the rain pouring over the frosted glass of the front door, the colors of her dress blurring together like a paint smear.

"Wait here," Heta says behind me.

She knocks on all the studio doors, and one by one, the girls arrive. They hold their doors open, reluctant to fully leave their work. In that moment, they remind me of prostitutes—not on street corners or in cramped basements marked with twin barber poles, but the ones in the movies in places like Amsterdam, advertising in fancy window displays.

"Ca-lee stopped by to announce the Aviary spots. It's going to be me, Ksenia—" my stomach clenches as Heta glances at me—"and Hee-Young."

Sarah doesn't look at me, but it's clear from Sumi's glare that I've taken a prize from her. I don't know how to tell her that it's one I don't want.

Heta nods at me. "Go get dressed for dinner, but don't spend too long. You'll be taking it off soon enough."

She turns away. The girls break like waves, but I'm frozen to the spot. Ksenia said that I had time—likely months—before I had to sleep with one of the patrons.

I guess she was wrong.

FORTY-THREE

Hee-Jin

As I make my way to my room, I try to convince myself that I've misunderstood Heta's words. That Garin couldn't possibly want to sleep with me, now that he knows I'm not the real Hee-Young—but do I know that to be true? After all, he chose Hee-Young to sponsor at one point. Perhaps he just liked the look of her—or maybe he just wants to punish me. *And that's assuming it's even Garin, at all*, I think, suddenly remembering Jones and her constant questions.

I didn't have time to find my passport or map out an escape. Maybe, if I went to Shepherd right this moment and asked to leave instead of appear in the Aviary and whatever comes after, he might say yes and send me back. But in the back of my mind, I can hear my mother's voice, saying, *the table is hot, the table is hot*, and I know that I'm lying to myself.

If it *is* Garin waiting for me, skipping straight to this sought-after step means he must've laid down a ton of money. Either that, or I'm some kind of dowry, a gift that buries the hatchet with Shepherd, the daughter of a god-king lost in a game of transformations.

Which means the only way out of this is through.

This morning, I shed the black kimono like a snakeskin before tossing it down, but it's missing when I get back to my room.

This must be the work of the facilitators. I have a vague recognition of Ca-lee telling me they'd launder things left on the floor. Still, even though the black kimono probably *needed* to be washed after the night I spent in it, its absence means I have no choice but to pick one of the others: deep purple, bright red, or the sunset.

I put on the purple one. I wash my face and hands in the sink and start attempting to fix my hair, but the feeling that this room has been violated won't go away.

I open the painting-door and peer into the shaft. The paper

imugi is still there, the yeouiju floating in the juvenile dragon's mouth, the storybook and the folded square of paper I found in Hee-Young's passport underneath. Next to them are the broken lock, one of the flashlights (*where's the other one?*), the small bag of hair, and the scalpel-tool.

I close the painting-door and check the wardrobe, where I stowed everything that didn't need to be kept secret. I find the beetle dress, iridescent and sheath-like, as well as Hee-Young's folded clothes and the pop-up paper owl.

But Hee-Young's favorite costume ring, tin with a green stone, is missing.

My pulse speeds up as I shake out her clothes. After searching the wardrobe, I get down on my hands and knees on the chance it's fallen to the floor, but I don't see it.

Who would steal something so *cheap* looking? Or did I lose one of the only truly good memories I had of my sister?

"Hee-Young? What are you doing?"

I close my eyes, but I know already the voice that has ripped its way into my thoughts. Heta walked me to my door. For all I know, she's been waiting outside of it. "I . . . dropped . . . a thing."

"Right," she says dubiously. "I came to bring you to dinner. It's good to arrive early on Aviary nights." And then her tone softens, more empathy than I could've ever guessed blending into her whisper. "Don't worry. The patrons will all be gone by sometime tomorrow. They usually don't stay long."

I stand, taking a moment to regard her, but her kindness has faded behind a fake smile. She comes close, giving me a sniff. "I think we'd better get you in the shower first," she says, and I have no choice but to submit.

The next minutes are like a stage production, and Heta's nominated herself to play my big sister. She lets me bathe myself, but from the moment I emerge from the bathroom, wrapped in a towel, she is on me again like a louse.

Finally, when she's doing my hair, I can't take it anymore. I grab the comb from her and pull away. "Is it Garin?"

"Is who?"

"The patron. For me. Is it Garin?"

Her eyebrows pull together. "Of course it—"

"But he *knows*," I say, punctuating my words with a slap of the comb on the bed. "I am not Hee-Young."

She clears her throat. "I thought it was his idea. To pretend? That's what you said."

After his outburst at dinner, I didn't know anyone still believed that. I shrug.

"Right," she says, clearing her throat. "Then I don't know—and to be honest, I'm jealous. Some of us have to *earn* our spots in the Aviary." The comment is so outlandishly ghoulish—who could possibly *want* this?—that I'm shocked into silence.

By the time we make it to the hallway outside the dining room, I have a splitting headache, and despite the horror of what could happen in the next few hours, part of my mind is on that missing tin ring, and it's so strange, I wonder if I am finally losing my grip on reality.

When we push open the door, I discover that once again, we're the last to arrive—save Garin. I stare at the empty chair as we sit down, unsure how to interpret this sign. Perhaps he's still getting ready.

And although I'm dressed, *I'm* not ready, though my mother's memories have done their best to prepare me. When she drank heavily, she'd tell us of her work: how important it was to use your hands to save your mouth, to make sure the client was never between you and the exit—and about how some men were as nervous as they'd be on any real date: showering, wearing nice clothes, doing their hair. A few even brought small presents or flowers.

Whoever it is, hopefully I'll be able to steer them away from the things I most don't want to do.

The table is hot.

Dinner starts shortly after we arrive. Like last night, Jones bombards me with questions from the moment the meal arrives. *How do you like the food? Is it what you're used to? Did you grow up eating food like this?*

I do my best to foist her off, but my mind is fractured: watching Heta, who seems intent on avoiding Smallet's attention. Ksenia, who doesn't look at me or Pepperdine while resolutely demolishing the food on her plate.

Shepherd, who stares at me more than once before finally gesturing at my patron's empty seat. "Garin conveys his disappointment at missing dinner," he says with a smile. "There's a minor scandal involving the senator, so he's going to be in his room for the next few hours taking calls, but he'll try to make it down for the display."

Confused looks circulate among the girls. The relief I felt suddenly evaporates—this reprieve is only temporary. As for the patrons, they don't seem to care.

At Shepherd's wave, a facilitator comes out with a tray, this time with only three glasses. He gives one to Heta, then Ksenia, then me.

It's one of those drinks that looks like a sunset, bands of color made of fluids with different densities carefully layered on top of each other, though all of the bands are shades of red or pink—except the top layer, which is milky and pearlescent. When I lift the glass to my nose, I catch grapes in the sun, though there's something strongly botanical behind it.

I don't want to drink it, but Ksenia gives me a wink and downs her glass. I can tell from the way the entire table watches me I'm expected to partake.

I drink it down.

After a few minutes, a soft, floaty feeling takes over my body. The colors around me appear brighter, and the churning in my stomach calms. The next glass they bring tastes fresher, the flavors popping over my tongue with the bubbles. I can feel my heart beating in the middle of my chest, suffusing my blood with a soft euphoria.

Ksenia said they drug us for everything. *If Shepherd and Ca-lee will let me have some of this whenever I have to sleep with someone—well, maybe it won't be so bad.* I sense horror, but it's in some distant part of my brain, cut off from the rest.

"It's time to get ready," Ksenia says into my ear. My skin tingles with her words, gold light shooting up and down my neck. She stands and bends her elbow, an invitation. From the smile blazing across her face, the pink drink is affecting her, too.

I take her arm, and she leads me out of the dining room. Heta is already waiting in the hallway—I didn't even notice her leave. "Let's do this in her room."

Ksenia leads me down the hallway, down the stairs. I feel like I did on the plane—like I'm floating above my body, watching the scene below, and for the first time in days (weeks? years?) I feel a whisper of excitement mix in with the sludge of my horror. Something new is happening, something I don't understand.

Ksenia sits me down on the bed. "I can get her started," she says, pursing her lips as she turns my chin back and forth like a sunglass carousel. "Unless you want me to grab her costume? I'll need the key."

Heta's eyebrows furrow briefly. "No, I'll get it." She lingers before leaving, as if she doesn't trust us alone.

As soon as she's out of the door, Ksenia turns my face towards hers and kisses me. My skin sings with waves of color that undulate, flame-like, from each place we touch.

"It's magnificent, isn't it?" In the quiet of my room, her magnified whisper pulses with its own music. "I never get to share this with anyone—not like this. It's almost worth how tomorrow will feel."

I kiss her again. The room spins, almost too fast, as if I was back on that platform, whirling around in the center of a swamp—but I haven't been able to get her alone all day, and I need answers.

I pull away, aching like a three-day-old bruise. I want so badly to kiss her again. To find her earlobe, her cupid's bow. The soft, beating pulse under the apex of her jaw. "You told me you . . . offered Shepherd a favor. What was it?"

She blinks and shakes her head as if warding off a fly.

"What about the . . . hiss last night? You were . . . afraid of the noise?"

"I don't know what you're talking about."

Something dark twists roots in my heart. I can remember it distinctly: the soft sibilance in the background, the sudden terror in her eyes. "You were afraid. Of what?"

Her lips roll up like fat grubs. "Hee-Young, we're not allowed in each other's rooms after the final *echo-stick-cue*. We could've been punished."

My pulse quickens. "But you weren't in your room. Ca-lee must know—"

"I told her I was in the bathroom. She asked why I didn't answer when she called out, and I said I fell asleep on the toilet. She left me alone after that."

It should be enough. My body *wants* it to be enough—the pink and white drink is pushing through my arteries, making my neurons light up with well-being. I have to fight viciously to hold onto my suspicions. "When was this?" I've been on top of Ksenia the entire day, even with Heta watching me like a hawk.

"Right before dinner. You were late." She frowns and pulls backward, just a few inches, but I know further attempts to kiss her won't be welcome.

I wonder if she can hear my heart breaking.

The door swings open again. Heta barges in, hauling three huge black plastic bags in her wake. I step back before I realize what I'm doing. In that moment, I see the room the way Heta must: my face and Ksenia's, inches apart—and then my retreat, as if to say, *no, that was nothing.*

It's clear from Heta's squint that the rule against being in each other's rooms after dark extends to other types of intimacy. I wonder how Sarah and Sumi manage.

"Here." She plunges her hand into one of the bags and pulls out a hairy white bundle. "Put this on," she says, pushing it against my chest.

I unfold it and find a pair of tights. I've never seen anything like them: every square centimeter is covered in white fake fur. I pull them on, and the room's instantly twenty degrees warmer.

Next, she hands me a knee-length dress with puffy sleeves. It's covered in uneven vertical stripes of gray and white sequins. On the back are two massive white projections shaped like half-hearts. It takes me a moment to realize they're wings.

"Now, turn around." She doesn't wait for me to comply, but instead grabs me by the shoulders and spins me. I can feel every small adjustment of her fingers. I wish they were Ksenia's.

We are birds, all of us, because of course we are.

Ksenia is a peacock, her jewel-green dress covered with coin-sized scales that spin to catch the light when she moves. Her asymmetrical train pools at one side like a chiffon oyster shell, and above her brow sits a golden tiara topped with glass beads painted like eyes.

I don't know what kind of bird Heta is, but her bright-red satin dress falls to her ankles. Over it, she wears a short jacket of a brilliant cerulean blue and a black and white speckled train, shot through with a line of red feathers every two inches. Instead of a crown, the cowls of a large yellow and black striped hood drape invitingly around her shoulders.

She looks uncomfortable as I take her in. "It's some kind of Indian pheasant," she says, shifting inside of the hood's voluminous folds. "Supposed to be very lucky and, um, wise. And shy, if you can believe it."

My costume befuddles me. Heta and Ksenia work together to lower a great wire cage around my form and secure me into an inner harness of straps. I watch as they let the straps out a few notches—once, and then again.

It's heavy, although not overly. I eye the doorway. "I'm not sure . . . I will pass."

"You will," says Ksenia, smiling. She easily crushes one side of the cage in with her hand. When she removes it, the cage springs back into place. "You'll just have to be careful."

Once the harness is tightened to Heta's satisfaction, they lower the dress, stretching it over the cage like a tent over its poles. Heta kneels and pulls more out of the garbage bag: a long robe, covered with white and black feathers, and a rough-hewn wooden mask. At first, I panic at the idea it might be another tal—but when I see the curving beak, the flat face, the giant, round sockets for the eyes, filled with some kind of amber glass, I realize what I'm supposed to be.

"Why . . ." I don't remember the word for owl. "Why this bird?"

"Ah! Hee-Young—I mean, other Hee-Young—picked it. It's the only other costume that's been recently cleaned. Isn't it nice?"

I nod. It does feel nice, although I know that's just the influence of the pink drink. I can see it working on them, making them flit around like two gleeful hummingbirds, easing the tensions between us—the way boats stop straining against their ropes once the water rises.

I should be horrified that Hee-Young picked this echo of the paper owl in the wardrobe. Was it to spite our mother? Or did she just identify with an unhappy, lost soul, hunting in the darkness? Why didn't she choose a costume like Heta's or Ksenia's, something vibrant and elegant?

On second thought, I like this costume's shape, like a dumpling. It would've protected me from perverts like the man on the bus—though it can't protect me tonight.

"Hurry up," says Heta, breaking into my reverie. "We're going to be late." She steers me toward the door as Ksenia fits the wooden mask to my face. The glass lenses cast my whole world in amber.

They fasten it behind my head and drag me out the door.

FORTY-FOUR

Hee-Jin

The wooden mask is tight against my face, letting no light enter from the sides. I have no peripheral vision, and the amber glass distorts the world enough that every step should feel treacherous, but with the joy of the pink and white drink in me, these shifts in perspective strike me as playful. As Heta and Ksenia guide me down the hallway, I can't stop myself from reaching out for the walls to test if their outlandish curves are only in my eyes.

At the end of the hallway, we run into Ca-lee, and I'm suddenly a child again, in the moments after my mother came home late: pretending to be asleep, my eyes screwed tightly shut. Trying to avoid her notice.

We pass by her, and the mood lifts again. We circle up three floors on the staircase and cut toward the room with all the gears and the curvaceous engines, the vine-shaped platform dancing underneath as if we're on a ship. The door is already open for us.

We pass through the engine room and cross to the very back, toward the ladder that looks like a fire escape. Heta maneuvers the ladder into place below the oval opening Ca-lee pointed out, and Ksenia sprints up, pulling me behind her giant peacock's train and drowning me in a school of flashing eyes. I can't get close enough, not with this lumpy cage body rudely shoving me away.

She breaks my grip and disappears through the hole. A moment later, her hand snakes down, reaching for me. I'm winded, nearly drenched in sweat—but there's an odd vibration deep inside my body, pulling me forward like an undertow. I grab her hand and squash myself through the hole in the ceiling, crawl through what feels like an interminable tunnel. "We're going through the roof," whispers Ksenia, but it's not until we emerge, gasping, into the giant white room at the top, that I realize what the Aviary really is: we've found our way into the house's giant glass heart.

As I take in my surroundings, I instantly forget the burning in my lungs. This—*this*—is a whole new world—an oddly shaped room just a bit wider than my bedroom, all the walls curving to the right. The floor, ceiling, and walls are made of a frosted white glass, like a lightbulb.

The room is packed with bright green objects: a kitchen chair, an easel, three or four potting containers, a small dresser, a coffee table, a shelf with a fake flower. All of them are rotated so that they're on their sides, as if a great wind has blown through this room and knocked everything flat.

Between them are a number of straight, clear poles that run from floor to ceiling, as if the room was a subway car and we'd need to grab them to keep our balance. It looks like every object is fastened to one of these poles, either glued directly, or by lengths of green chain.

A moment later, Heta comes through behind me, and a jubilant feeling zips between the three of us like static. She looks particularly radiant, like a woman just proposed to by the love of her life.

She catches me watching and turns away to adjust her hair. "We have to hurry now. It won't be safe for us if we're not in position." The glee in her voice belies her words, and by now, my body is floating, riding waves of sensation from the pink drink. It feels so wonderful that I'm almost resentful when Ksenia takes my hand and guides me forward.

As we near the back of the room, it becomes easier to understand the shape of this place—a narrow, continuous tunnel that curves round to the right to fill up the sculpted heart on the top of the building, just like the interior of a nautilus shell. I avoid the trailing arc of her tail as we circle around the spiral, dodging the poles reaching from floor to ceiling, the odd pieces of furniture all laid upon their sides. Every so often, rows of lights run across the floor or up the walls. At certain spots, the poles are replaced by long, vertical boards of the same clear plastic about a foot wide, though these also go from floor to ceiling. In addition to the objects, several areas have art supplies: giant canvases, paints and brushes, little vials of water.

It takes me a moment to notice that the objects are changing color, from green, to a light purple, to orange—and then we reach a dead end, one that must lie at the very center of this place.

Here, everything is bright white, just like the frosted paint behind the glass walls.

I like this area the least, though it has the most interesting objects: a white wicker chair, a white piano, the black keys instead some kind of mother of pearl, a white kitchen chair, a white potted tree, no doubt fake, shaped like one of those fancy topiaries. There's even a small white birdcage chained to one of the poles.

I reach out and touch one of the iridescent keys. Although the piano is turned sideways, it makes a gentle chime. Ksenia beckons at the chair. "Sit down."

The joy of the moment recedes like a wave from the shore. The chair lies flat on its side—does she mean for me to perch on one of the legs? "I don't know—"

"Lie down on the floor. Then sit. You have to be sideways, just like the chair." She glances behind her, as if there's anything to see but the curving white wall. "And you have to hurry. Heta wasn't kidding—it *will* be dangerous if we're not ready."

I have no idea what she means, but the word *dangerous* sends a galvanizing shiver down my spine. I creep forward and stretch out on my side. The kiss of the white glass floor on my skin makes me feel alive.

Ksenia quickly bends to snake a belt under my costume and fasten it over my lap. "The chair's safe," she says, smiling. "So, sit back and enjoy the show."

Before I can respond, she takes off, back the way we came. After a minute, I start to get nervous. My head clears a bit more. "Ksenia?"

"I'm fine." Her faint call bounces around the various walls of the room. "Just stay in the chair!"

And then, everything happens. Not all at once, but my mind is slow, and as soon as I start to grasp one thing, the next has already started. A terrific groaning and clanking emanates from beneath me, a heavy *click-click-click* that reminds me of the rattling noise ascending drawbridges make in movies.

A moment later, the room vibrates, and then it moves. Everything that's not fastened down slides to my right as it tilts. I can feel my head being raised off the ground by the change in my center of gravity—ten degrees, then twenty, my body stabilizing as my weight shifts more fully into the chair, as the floor gains a steeper and steeper angle, chains singing as attached flowers and birdcages and windcatchers reach their end and suspend in the air—and still, it doesn't stop, not until the room has shifted ninety degrees. I'm sitting upright, but my head is swimming from vertigo, and suddenly glad Ksenia strapped me in.

All around me is the tinkling of glass and bells, the rattle of chains. I look down at a drop of about a story and feel queasy; it's enough to break a bone or damage my brain.

Humming fills the air, then static. The room explodes into light as a thousand bulbs blink on. Around me, the walls, ceiling, and floor all turn clear, and I can see down to the house below. We're right over the roof. I wonder what kind of apparatus could have possibly rotated the entire heart sculpture ninety degrees.

Only slightly distorted from the multiple layers of glass, the patrons are sprawled in the gardens below us in what look like white wicker chairs, white-suited facilitators zipping between them with trays of drinks. Garin is still missing, but for a moment, my gaze connects with Shepherd's. Electricity passes down my spine, though it's attenuated by the pink drink's warm glow.

A movement close below me catches my eye. It's Ksenia, though she's not in a chair, but sitting on some kind of swing. She pushes her legs back and forth, and the swing starts to move.

It makes me a bit sick, seeing her like that. I want to call out, but my voice is stuck somewhere in my chest.

From somewhere above me, Heta giggles faintly. "Look up, Hee-Young!"

Just like before, the pink drink in me responds to the infectious energy of her laugh. I look up to find the source of the joy winding into my body, and there is Heta, sitting on a round board, and she, too, is swinging, though it's in a circle.

"What's happening?"

Another series of groans—and suddenly, everything is much quieter, and the room starts to lurch again, this time rotating. Heta arcs overhead, like a slow comet, as Ksenia rises from below me, but I don't move, even as everything moves around me.

The heart's spinning like a wheel, I realize. Like the big red-and-white Ferris wheel in Daegu—but instead of riding around in little cars, we're all spinning on the *inside*, in kitchen chairs and stools and swings.

"How does it feel?" Ksenia calls from below—no, above me,

because she's already come a half-revolution. Upside down, I watch as she sets like the sun. She's tossed her great train behind her, and as she swings back and forth, she maneuvers in the air, throwing her arms overhead and leaning back across the seat. I feel afraid for her, until I remember that she, too, must have a harness hidden under that dress. We're all safe, chained to the seats and the poles and who knows what else.

Ksenia laughs, then Heta. The bubbles of their glee fill the entire glass structure, ringing against the walls, through my body. All at once, I understand the world—that their laughter is real and genuine. That it has a color, one as perfect as the wind roaring down the mountains. "We're the *art*!" Ksenia calls.

Music suddenly winds its way through the room. Upright again, I startle, almost falling off my chair—but no, I'm safe, *I'm safe*, and although it's too loud for me to talk to Ksenia and Heta anymore, I can't help but laugh, because the air really is filled with birdsong. The calls of thousands and thousands of birds, squawks and tweets and whistles and chirps, and all against the soft waterfall of a harp. As the notes pluck and glide, I'm filled with such ecstatic joy—of course Hee-Young came here, of course she wanted this, and how lucky I am, that this is me, that this is *my life*.

Tears spring to my eyes. My heart's beating so hard my chest hurts, as if any moment now, it will break in half and let out everything I've ever felt, the pain and the joy and the misery and the relief—

I see Heta again, and the whole world falls away. She's spinning in circles, making her dress glint and sparkle, her revolutions as quick as a figure skater's. Her toe is pointed down, pressing on a small pane of clear plastic I can just barely see. Over and over, she spins around her anchoring foot.

In the next second, her position changes and she can no longer reach the pane—but she leans backward, hard, the platform beneath her wobbling as she reaches with her arms, her legs crossed over each other.

My heart lunges up into my throat. I'm sure she's going to fall off—but then she curls with the core strength of a gymnast and reaches up to grab the rope. As she passes below me, out of my view, my last glimpse shows her covered in sweat, her chest and shoulders heaving with the effort, but she looks so beautiful that it's hard to breathe, as if she were the awe-inspiring curve of a comet across an ancient sky, and still she's glistening, green and yellow sparkles all over her legs, her arms, her hand—

For a moment I glimpse something important, something that moves too fast for me to be sure. But then Hee-Young's voice whispers in my ear, reciting the poem I found in her room:

My effervescent, astrological queen / I give you my secrets / as you shine / dark and light / two sides of a moon / Can something so inhuman / still have a heart?

My stomach drops and my sweating limbs go cold. Knowledge floods deep into my bones, poison that sprays directly into my liver.

I wait another revolution, two. Heta spins too fast for me to make sure of what I saw—but then, on the third revolution, she pauses for a moment, and I can clearly see a cheap tin ring with a green stone, identical to the one that went missing from my room.

I'm suddenly certain that Hee-Young's poem is about Heta. *But that's crazy, right?*

The pink drink wraps soft fingers around my limbs, begging me to come away with it, but I fight it. I look for Heta again, trying to convince myself the new suspicion blossoming in my chest doesn't make any sense. Maybe she stole the ring from my room—but Hee-Young and Heta, an item?

I have no evidence save the poem and the sudden churning in my guts—but the more I roll the possibility around in my mind, the more certain I feel.

Maybe it's because Hee-Young was my sister. It doesn't matter that we were estranged, that I could never understand the person she became before she died. Childhood taught me how she *loved*: alternating waves of adoration and reservation, being torn between total annihilation and fear. I feel myself moving in that direction every time I look at Ksenia.

Something about the cadence of her poem, the image impressed upon me as Heta rotated round and round—connecting them was like the singularity of an eclipse, an event that becomes a shorthand of experience between two people for the rest of their lives.

Practically speaking, if Heta and Hee-Young *were* involved, it would've been complicated. And in her poem, Hee-Young had called Heta *inhuman*. Not *supernatural*, or *transcendent*, or *godlike*.

Inhuman.

What might an *inhuman* creature do, in a place like this?

FORTY-FIVE
Hee-Jin

From the moment I wake, I feel terribly sick: a ringing head, a whirling stomach—and the entire second half of the night is blank. I have no idea when I left the glass heart or shed my missing costume, much less how I wriggled into one of the nightgowns from the armoire.

I close my eyes and lift the skirt, check with my fingers. I don't *think* I had sex last night. Did I just get lucky, earn a temporary reprieve, somehow?

I stumble to the bathroom for water and freeze at the sight of myself in the mirror. There are bumps all over my face and arms—small, reddened mounds with irregular borders. A reaction to my costume? Or is it the effect of the pink drug? And bright-red marks dot the tops of my temples, the bridge of my nose: pressure burns from the mask.

The worst one is above my right nostril. As I reach to touch it, my sleeve falls to my elbow, revealing a soft pattern of bruises around my forearm.

I examine them closely. They could be from the costume's wings—but they also look like fingerprints, so much like the marks on Hee-Young's body that I yank the sleeve back down to my wrist, hiding them from view. I shower quickly, taking care not to look at myself, and return to the wardrobe for a clean sweatsuit.

The hair on the back of my neck stands on end. The right side—the one that I stashed Hee-Young's clothes in—is closed. I don't think I did that, though there's enough missing from last night that I can't be sure.

Still.

I open it again and pull out the beetle dress, Hee-Young's things. I shake out the sandwich tee shirt with its blocky triangles—*I'll always be half without you*—but my pulse is accelerating, because I know what's missing: Hee-Young's paper owl.

I toss everything onto the floor and dig through the piles. I open up the other side, tear the kimono off their hangers and shake them out—I could've moved the owl during the part of the night I don't remember, though I can't figure out why I'd do that. I check the bathroom, under the bed.

Tears sting my eyes as I bolt to the painting, but whoever's been taking things from my room didn't discover this hiding place. My scalpel, the children's book, the padlock, the file, they're all still there. The bag of hair and the imugi have migrated to the shaft's back wall, no doubt because of the HVAC system. I spin the ball in the imugi's mouth before pinning it under the file. It won't get away again.

The bell-tone for breakfast rings. I shove everything back and shut the painting-door. A headache presses on my left eye on the way to the dining room, and by the time I sit down at the table—*last, why am I always the last to arrive?*—frustration has stretched through me like a vine. I'm sick of the way this place keeps shifting under my feet. Sick of being surrounded by people that drip-feed me information while plotting against me. Sick of the way things appear and disappear—

And then a flash of last night surfaces from the depths, part of the evening I *do* remember: Heta spinning like a planet, the green stone of the tin ring winking on her finger. Almost every one of the others has probably snuck into my room at some point, but I at least *know* Heta took the ring—

My certainty dissolves. Yes, I *saw* it, but I also heard Hee-Young reciting a poem in my ear. Bubbles filled the air, and sparkles cascaded all over Heta's body. This could've been just another hallucination.

My head throbs harder. I flinch away from the scraping of spoons, the shuffles of the facilitators, as an idea wriggles in my mind.

I need proof. And if Heta took the ring, the little folded owl—they're likely still in her room.

When the bell-tone rings for studio time, we line up like soldiers and tread down the hallway, though both of my partners from last night drag behind. I can't help but notice how bad they look in the foyer's reflected lights: the skin of Heta's face is so puffy it hangs from her cheekbones, and she's tried—and failed—to cover the circles around her eyes. Ksenia looks marginally more focused, though a ring of bruises circles her wrist, a bracelet made of shadows. And her skin has gotten worse, the bumps more pronounced.

They're not so different from the bumps on my face and arms. I wonder if, given time, they would grow into long spines—if it's the pink drink that caused such a horrendous transformation in my sister.

We pass through the door that leads out the house's right wing, the sky threatening rain.

If Heta *is* the subject of the poem . . . Hee-Young's affection might have been mutual. It'd make sense for Heta to steal trivial things of sentimental value, like a paper owl.

"Hee-Young?"

I stopped walking a few paces after the door—have been standing long enough for Ksenia and Heta to pass me. "I forgot . . . something . . . I need for my art. I will come back."

"You *really* shouldn't. If one of them comes while you're gone—"

"It's OK, Heta."

"I should come with you—"

"I'll be right back. I promise." I turn so she can't see my face and dart back to the house. My pulse quickens as I cross the foyer and slide down the stairs. I glance behind me, but for once, I don't see any of the facilitators.

Pushing in Heta's door reveals a museum: the bed made, every cabinet door shut, every drawer pushed in, like nobody's been living here. Even the triptych paintings on the wall, which depict the same vase from three different angles, are shinier, the color deeper. I know before dragging my finger across one that it'll come away dust-free.

I can feel the seeping of cool air from the ventilation slits in the sides of the bottom painting. The padlock tucked up behind its lower edge is intact and has been taped against the back to hide it. Unless she has the key, she hasn't opened the door.

I feel odd going through her cabinets, so I start by checking under the bed and in the bathroom, where the white soap dispenser sits sadly on the rim of the tub. Two towels hang on the back of the door, but there's nothing else.

It unnerves me how clean Heta's room is, reminds me I don't know her at all. The way she holds herself, the inflections in her voice—I'd assumed she came from wealth. Everyone thinks rich people are clean because their homes are neat, but from my experience, they're slobs. They throw things wherever they want, sure it will get absorbed in the gaping chasm of their giant homes—until someone like me cleans up while staying out of sight.

But in small spaces, everything has to be perfectly put away just to make room for your body. And the poor have to keep their belongings light, because although tonight they might have their own place, tomorrow it'll be a friend's floor, under a bridge, or in the sauna.

But this room is more than clean. It's . . . strict. Regimented. It reminds me of a place I couldn't afford in Yeongdeungpo, in a dormitory for students that ran a lucrative side business housing undocumented immigrants. Three times the market rate got you a single room with a lofted bed, a desk built underneath. It was so cramped that if you pulled the chair out from the desk, you couldn't open the door without ramming into it. Everything had to be in the *exact* right place, creating a tension that made it hard to ever relax.

This room is like that, but different. I don't understand, not until I go back and check the soap dispenser. It's the way it's aligned—*exactly* in the middle of the tub rim, turned until its square front is parallel with the tub wall, the head of the dispenser at ninety degrees.

A compulsion. I need to be incredibly careful, because unless everything is exactly the way I left it, Heta's going to notice.

And I might have already messed up. I can't remember if the bathroom door was open or closed. *Closed*, I think—tentatively, until I dig my heels in. *The table is hot, and the door was closed.*

I shut it behind me and check the right side of the armoire, looking for a hair, a string, some tape—anything that'll let Heta know if someone trespassed here, but there's nothing. I open the door.

The armoire is full of clothes I never would've imagined for Heta. Frilly white skirts, pressed white blouses with shell buttons and sparkling cuffs, gray slacks with perfect creases—it feels like the wealth of a fairytale, the stilted and misremembered depictions of a heyday. Heta would look absolutely macabre wearing all this. Behind the outfits are more white sweatsuits and the odd pastoral costumes.

I shut the cabinet and open the next. This one's more interesting. A leather trunk with rivets dominates the floor, as if Heta traveled here by steamboat. Centered above is—the word briefly escapes me—a *hatbox*, and on top of that is a smaller wooden box with flowers painted on each side. It's covered in a black lacquer, the style meant to imitate Japanese art: a Victorian jewelry box, maybe. The glossy finish is starting to yellow in places, but the brass hinges, though pitted, are polished to a sheen.

It makes me uncomfortable, this constant desire of the west to create poor facsimiles of Asian art. But having seen Heta's clothes, her neat room . . . something tells me she's unimaginative in her hiding places.

I hold my breath and nudge open the box. The inside is red velvet—a color of power, although I doubt she knows that. There's no jewelry inside, just some keepsake photographs and pieces of paper—including one that's been artfully folded into a small bird with a long tail. A pheasant, maybe.

Relieved and disappointed that it's not my owl, I slip it into my pocket.

The door opens behind me. I spin, but it's not Heta.

Ca-lee steps in as I try to put the jewelry box back into the armoire, but my hands are shaking, and it tumbles to the floor with a loud crack, its contents spraying around it. The photos have all landed face-up: an old woman, a smiling man in front of a waterfall, a captured painting of an elaborate candleholder, the kind Jewish people use.

Before I can scoop them up, Ca-lee grabs me so tightly, it feels like my hand will pop off.

"How *dare* you." Her voice is low and threatening, and there's an abnormal glossiness in her eyes. "They told me what you were doing, but I didn't believe it. Do you have *any* idea how much trouble you're in? Stealing from one of our participants—I should call the police!"

"Not stealing!" I cry, trying to explain. "Just looking! Just—"

She yanks my hand hard, throwing me off balance. "I don't want to *hear* it."

When people are this angry, they're like dogs; say anything to challenge them, and they'll bite. I let her drag me forward, out of Heta's room. We interrupt a facilitator in the hallway, and my face burns—I don't care what the staff think, but I'm sure word will spread like smallpox. What if one of them decides to violate the rules against talking to us and lets Heta or Ksenia know what I've done?

My stomach churns. I pull backwards, but Ca-lee is horribly strong. She shoves me straight into my room. The door closes itself, sealing us in that terrible silence. Before I can try to string together enough words to plead my case, she turns away from me, toward the door.

"Not now, Lisa," she says, speaking to nobody. "You shouldn't see this. Go on."

It hits me like a car. Her behavior had felt strange, but this is too much: Ca-lee is talking to someone that *isn't there.*

She turns back, and then she freezes, despite her rage. There's a soft trembling underneath her frame, like when a cat is about to take a bird, the little jumps and twitches of the muscles visible under the skin.

I should be afraid. I *am* afraid. But I also can't look at her without seeing my mother, desperately trying to convince us the table is hot. My mother, who was always looking over her shoulder for police, for immigration, for the man that trafficked her from North Korea to China.

I know what Ca-lee must see on my face: recognition of her paranoia—and pity.

She shrinks, smaller and smaller, folding into herself as if hollow. Neither of us speaks, and although I can't hear her heartbeat over my own, I know from her expression that it's breaking in her chest.

"You see her, don't you?" She says it so softly, her anger forgotten.

Should I give her the truth? Would the distraction be enough to get her off my back? For a moment, I imagine her leaving the claustrophobic confines of this house, this place where she clearly isn't happy, and finding a new, better life. Like my mother should have.

I choose my words carefully. I can't afford some errant

mistranslation, some awkward pause to derail my meaning. "No one there. In the door."

She looks behind herself again. Looks at me. She nods—just once, slowly—and then she spins on her heel and turns away. In that moment, all the tension evaporates. I even feel some tenderness for this poor woman that invented her own child. I send the feeling out behind her, like the smoke of a burned prayer on the wind.

The door shuts, returning me into the room's stillness. And then I hear a distinctive, heavy *kak*, and dread tickles in my throat.

That was nothing, I think, walking toward the door. *No locks here. The table is hot.*

I push on the door, but it doesn't open, not when I shove it hard with both hands, not when I throw my shoulder against it over and over, the hermetic seal preventing it from rattling in its frame.

When I've exhausted myself, I slump down against it, no choice but to wait.

FORTY-SIX
Callie

After I lock the door, I drop the pendant back into my collar, letting it bump against the numb void of space in front of my breastbone. It's as if I've shoved the key into another universe.

My feet move, one step, and then another, turning me away from the door. It's all so calm. Watching me, you wouldn't know I'm screaming inside, that my body isn't my own.

I don't know how it happened or how I'll explain to Shep. I was flustered by my tardiness to the studio, and now I've made choices I can't defend. This usage of my key is only for rare emergencies, like if an unruly resident breaks due to the stress and needs to be contained until the doctor can arrive.

I could tell him the truth, that I caught Hee-Young trying to steal from Heta—

It flashes in my mind: Heta's little jewelry box hitting the ground, all the pictures spilling out. In that moment, the tableau was oddly familiar. Maybe it's the contents of the pictures, the old men and women that remind me so much of Shep's own family photos, the painting I'm sure I've seen somewhere before—

Or maybe it's because it wasn't so long ago that I threw *my* pewter box against the wall and shattered the heart-shaped bulb, as if I was trying to free a spirit trapped within—

No, don't think about that.

I climb the stairs. The walls pull toward me as I approach, return to their original positions as I pass, guiding me forward as if by peristalsis. As I reach the door to my room and pull out my proximity key, I realize what I'm planning, how much it's really like being swallowed.

It's what I deserve, isn't it?

But I'm afraid. If I lock myself in, only Shep can get me out. And every time I close my eyes, the moment plays in my head:

Lisa, standing in front of Hee-Young's door, the bounce of her blonde curls as she shook her head petulantly, making the small pink bows I tied flop from side to side—

And then she dematerialized as if she'd never been there at all. Just like the nights I can't remember, the life I once had, the numb void at the front of my chest.

I back away from the door without locking it. I can't get trapped here, with that image of her disappearing, but there's a pressure mounting inside of me, building until I can hear my bones cracking—

And then the pain starts.

It's everything the loss of a daughter *should* be; all the years I should've grieved coming home to roost. The agony knocks me sideways, leaves me breathless and doubled over. I clamp my hand over my mouth as a wail splits me, one I didn't decide to make and can't seem to stop. Holes open in the walls, craters whose borders drip down like Dali's melting clocks, mouths like mine, though their wails are silent.

Lisa's dead. I killed her in the car, all those years ago.

And as terrible as that is, it's the next thought that drives me into the ground. *And Shep just let me pretend.*

Five years. Lisa's *seven* now—that's five years of marking her birthdays in front of staff that watched me babble to myself, five years of taking her on outings to the grocery store, chastising and bargaining with the empty air above the car seat. Five years of discussions about private tutors, the school I never visited. Five years of artists making their way into my home and out, watching me and my fictional daughter.

Did I know all along this was happening, and just refuse to see?

How fucking crazy am I? Is there a way to find out? Is *any* part of the last several years—the girls, the performances, the exquisitely painful night I spent with Shep—is any of that real?

For a moment, I imagine going to the studio, finding some clay, and taking a mold of my teeth. I envision biting down, and my mouth floods with the wet-earth taste, like mushrooms and cast iron. I fill the holes with glue, hold the cast up to my shoulder. Find out if it's a match, if the marks on my skin are from my own teeth, or Shep's.

I shudder. I thought I knew my husband, what he was capable of.

How wrong I was.

When my tears finally stop, a memory floats to the top: Shep, installing the doorbells for all the bedrooms. He asked if I wanted anything special for mine. I didn't understand until he explained that because it was just an electronic file being piped through a speaker, it could sound like anything I wanted.

If he'd caught me on any other day that week, at any other hour that day, I would've picked something serious and unobtrusive: classical music, or maybe just a muted ring. But it had been sunny, and I was both drunk enough for the pain to ease and not so drunk that my barriers against the pain had fallen. In a rare moment of levity, I picked a song from my youth, from when I was living with Cassie, the song I'd used for her ringtone. Back then, I always smiled every time I heard it.

Which is how, in this moment of terrible grief, the bouncy plucked-guitar refrain of Led Zeppelin's "D'yer Mak'er" permeates the room. It's the most horrific thing I've ever heard.

"*Oooh, oh, oh, oh, oooh, oooh—*"

I don't bother to get up and answer the door. If it's someone important, they'll come in. If it's not, they'll leave. Either way, this noise will stop.

"*You don't have to go—*"

The music fades. Whoever it is, they've stopped ringing the bell. A moment later, the door swings open, and there is Shep, his eyes hot as if with a fever.

I can't look at him. My insides feel like those chunks of pewter I once held in that ladle, melting as I try to sort through who's more at fault: the man that lied to me for five years, or me, who killed our daughter? And though I have no right to it, anger is in my mouth, bitter and thick, turning my words to venom.

Safest, then, to keep it shut, and let the vibrations of the ceiling above tell him what he needs to know.

"I brought you some wine," he says, and there's the dull, ringing thud of a bottle being dropped on my cabinet. "I thought you could use some for your nerves."

He's right, but I won't give him the satisfaction—despite how parched my throat suddenly feels, the anxious clawing in my chest. I know his opinion of my drinking. It doesn't help that he's right.

"Calleigh." It's a soft utterance—no, an *intoning*, like of a spell. He glances up, and the ceiling suddenly settles. "We have to talk about this. That poor girl's really rattled. I almost checked her in somewhere."

Ice settles over my skin. How many times have I imagined being confined to the mental hospital? I know in my heart of hearts that whatever Hee-Young was stealing from Heta doesn't merit being locked into a soundproofed room.

Finally, I find my voice. "How did you find out?" And then, quieter, "What's going to happen to her?"

He crosses the room, sits on the edge of my bed, and leans back onto his elbow, his legs spread, unaware or uncaring of how much his pose looks like a porn photo, someone inviting the gaze of the camera. I wonder if that's what I'd have to do—if the only way I could ever train myself to spread out with such a practiced casualness is money.

Jesus fuck, I really am crazy.

He doesn't answer the first question. "Dr. Pepperdine hadn't left yet and was kind enough to evaluate her. He thinks she'll be OK." He rubs his eyes; if he noticed the sudden shudder the walls gave at the word *Pepperdine*, he shows no sign. "Honestly, Calleigh, I'm not sure *what* to do. I think she'd like to stay with the program—it's a big deal for her, for all the girls—but she's afraid of you."

I let out a breath. "It's OK. I can leave. I was planning to, anyways."

He shakes his head. "I don't feel right about that, not now. There's obviously something wrong with you. Maybe Pepperdine—"

"*No*," I snap, as the walls shudder again.

His cheeks puff like a squirrel's as he exhales. "Fine. That's your choice. Listen, this is going to sound awful . . . but I was thinking that for now, maybe you could stay in your room. I can have your meals brought to you. Just until Pepperdine can get her in a good place. To be honest, I don't exactly know *what* happened, but—"

A crunch inside, like the snapping of a bone. "She told me

about Lisa. About how she's not really here. And then I had a breakdown."

Shep sags, his body curling as the muscles around his spine give up supporting his frame. "Oh, Calleigh. This isn't how I wanted you to find out."

The ceiling bows up and down, huge swells like a sail billowing. "*How could you keep that from me?*" I'm on my feet. It's like earlier, my body stirring of its own volition, except that now, its movements are as violent and erratic as my feelings inside. "*Five years*, Shep, that you let me talk to my dead daughter? How *sick* can you be?"

Shep doesn't answer. He's always had a talent for battening down hatches.

And despite my rage, there's suddenly nothing left inside of me, and I collapse onto the floor like a tower of blocks. "Five years."

"I *wanted* to tell you," he says softly. "But when you first got back from the hospital, Pepperdine thought you were too delicate, that it would hurt you in ways that couldn't be fixed. I'd already lost so much. I couldn't lose you, too."

A wound reopens in my chest. I take shallow breaths.

"And then, you know, the more time that went by, the harder it was. I saw you getting better and better, the life slowly returning to you. I just couldn't deal with being the one to break you all over again." His voice quivers: a perfect, movie-quality vibration. "And to be honest . . . I thought you knew she wasn't there, and you were just—not playing a game, exactly, but enacting a ritual that made it easier to go on. And if what you needed was a bit of pretend, I wanted to give that to you. I didn't know it was real for you."

He's crying. I'm disgusted, but the emotion quickly gives way. His expression's earnest, but his wet eyes still have that fever-hot quality.

"OK," I say, monotone. "I understand."

In the long silence that follows, he fidgets like Lisa—

(Stop.)

I don't even know how to think about her. Not the real girl that died, but the representation I've carried around this whole time. Is *that* Lisa, the Lisa I've known the longest—is she a *she*, or an *it*? Can I really compare Shep's fidgeting to a girl that's never existed for anybody but me?

Dizzy, I lean back against the wall.

"Let me pour you a glass of wine."

I try to tell him I don't want it, but I do. I want it so badly. I want to not be here. I want to not be *myself*.

He opens the bottle, the cork popping with a soft *pung*. He trickles red wine into the glass and hands it to me.

He's only brought one glass. "Do you want some?" I extend it toward him.

His gaze flicks to me, and then the glass again. "It's OK," he says, the corner of his mouth twisting. "I'm not thirsty."

What he means to say is: *I know you're a drunk and you'll resent me taking any. I know that already, your heart is beating anxiously at the idea that this wine is not all for you.*

I bring the glass to my lips and take a sip. A drink in the Petite is always good, always an odd mix of flavors I can't place my finger on—the grape and herbal notes of the pink and white drink before the Aviary, the sour undercurrent of the green cocktail used in the welcoming ceremony. This wine tastes different from those—like hibiscus, both sweet and tannin-bitter.

He sets the bottle down and slips his hand in mine. "What do you think?"

Another sip. "About what?"

"Do you think you can stay? Meet with Pepperdine—just a little, Calleigh, just talking. It's just, I've had this terrible secret eating away at my heart for so long, and it's finally been lifted off me. I can't believe you'd leave me now. And besides—this place doesn't work without you." He looks up at the ceiling, as if underlining his point.

Someone else can wear the stupid key! We're supposed to be having a screaming fight about this. I take a deep gulp. *It doesn't matter that you were trying to protect me. This trust can't ever be restored.*

But instead of saying anything, I take another gulp, and another, and before long, the soft buzz of the wine starts under my skin. The fibers of my muscles finally settle into place as the world becomes the way it always should've been. "I'll think about it."

He brings my free hand to his lips and kisses it, and my shoulder twinges, some memory held in the body alone. "It's more than I deserve."

For the first time, I remember the bruise. Remember waking up this morning, nothing but a smeared, fuzzy kiss left in my mind. "Shep?"

"Yes?" He watches me expectantly, but I sense a nervousness underneath his gaze. He's waiting to see if I say something crazy. If I ask him about last night, and he figures out there's a hole in my memory—it won't just be *talk* with Pepperdine. It'll be his treatments, again.

"Thank you," I say softly, and I take another long gulp of the wine.

PART V

The Room

When the stars threw down their spears
And water'd heaven with their tears:
Did he smile his work to see?
Did he who made the Lamb make thee?
'The Tyger', William Blake

FORTY-SEVEN
Hee-Jin

In the first hours after I was shut in, I screamed myself hoarse, my voice deafening in the small confines of this room. As the day wore on, the ring in my ears faded, but the muffling of the sounds, as if I was underwater—that hasn't improved.

At some point, I was exhausted enough to sleep, though I don't know for how long—just brief snatches of unconsciousness, each terrified wake like being plunged into cold water—but when I return to the land of the living, I can tell from the way my hunger has progressed that I've been locked in this room a day, if not more.

I wonder how many others this has happened to; if they did this to Hee-Young. If so, any signs of struggle have been erased. There are no scratch marks in the paint, no dents in the wood.

All at once, it feels like the walls are closing in. I hug myself, as if the cage of my arms could protect me from being crushed—

Something crinkles in the pocket of my robes. I reach in and pull out the paper pheasant from Heta's room. I don't even remember stashing it, but now its gentle lines are all smashed, its beak bent back. One of its wings is torn, the tip flopping down like a damaged flower stem to reveal a sliver of its paper insides—and what looks like pencil marks.

My mouth goes dry. What about the imugi in the shaft, the missing paper owl? Is it possible that Hee-Young meant for these to be more than just art pieces?

It hurts, unfolding the pheasant, unmaking something Hee-Young made. I wince as I open the wing, the tear growing despite my best efforts—but I was right. Unfolded, the crinkled paper square is about six inches on each side. The handwriting is spidery and curling. It takes me a moment before I recognize an *a* and realize it's English—cursive, I think. I never learned cursive, but by squinting and tracing my finger along the shapes, I laboriously make my way through the words.

Owl,

I'm sorry I haven't come to see you. I imagine you think it's because of what you told me Friday night, but that's wrong.

They're keeping a close eye on us. Lately, every time I venture out into the hallway, there's at least one of them watching me—and I know it's the same for you.

It's cowardly to tell you my feelings in a letter, but neither one of us can risk being caught, so here they are: I miss you. I love you. I love you so much that I will get on my hands and knees and beg you not to do this. It's too dangerous. Can't you see that?

Can't you just wait? Can't you be patient? This is difficult, but what comes after, being out there with each other—isn't it worth it? Isn't it enough?

I'm begging you. Stay here, with me, and I'm sure we can take care of it. We can take care of everything.

I can help you, Hee-Young.

Your Pheasant

The room swims. I bend forward and center my head between my knees.

Take care of it? It almost sounds like Hee-Young was pregnant. Is that why she lost favor with Garin—or why she fled back to South Korea, leaving her potential future behind? But that doesn't make sense. Hee-Young would've had no problem aborting, but maybe that wasn't an option. Maybe Garin wouldn't let her.

Maybe it was the opposite. Maybe *she* wanted the baby, and Garin didn't. A baby would mean she could have tried for citizenship—the baby would have been a citizen, right? Either because of being born here, or because of its father? And America wouldn't separate a baby and her mother.

Except that's exactly what China wanted to do with our mother. Send her back to North Korea, without us. And this government isn't so different, if its recent troubles are any indicator. Hee-Young would've known that.

A baby.

An odd, crawling calm fills me—like lifting a cup on the rim of the sink and finding a ring of mildew underneath. The image of her with a baby: rocking it, cooing at it, singing to it about mountain bunnies while making shadow puppets with her hands—it permeates the space inside my body, coldly pressing against my seams.

I don't know what she could've seen in that life. I try to step into the fantasy, replacing her with myself. Imagine holding a small, mewling thing, completely dependent on me for every need. Babies always put the light of love back into our mother in a way nothing else did.

I don't feel anything, at first. Then comes that cool trickle again, anxiety simmering underneath. Unlike Hee-Young, I've got a cruel streak in me—from my mother, from my father, I don't know. I could never love anything the way I love myself, and I know exactly what kind of mother I'd be.

Love is what you sacrifice for another. Maybe not word for word what Ksenia said, but close enough.

It feels like an hour goes by before I can make myself open the imugi and unfold its claws, its beautiful tail, my dread growing with each inch of unmarked paper gained. When I'm finished, I have nothing but a flat sheet of paper and a painted blue marble. My attempts to reassemble the dragon are hopeless and end with me folding the paper into a square and slipping it under the file in the shaft.

I hold the marble up to my face. I drag it slowly across my bottom lip, as if it can find a trace of Hee-Young when my fingers and eyes can't.

Something about its form tugs at my memory—it resembles the small stones in the white bowl on the dinner table, the ones I watched Ksenia eat. I picture myself putting it between my lips and trying to swallow—but with it here, between my fingers, I realize how big it is. I imagine choking on it, its paint dissolving into toxic chemicals in my stomach, its bulk catching in a kink in my small intestine and binding me up until I rot apart from the inside out.

Finally, though, I put it in my pocket and go back to the pheasant letter.

I don't find any more clues, not even a date. It could've been written shortly after she got here . . . or not long before she left.

Which would mean that her entire journey home—boarding the plane to Seoul, finding the drugs and doing them, dragging herself to my door—she could've been pregnant the whole time. Even now, there could be a fetus, decaying inside her corpse.

Nausea hits me like a train.

I sprint for the toilet, but I'm too late. I turn at the last second and manage to vomit into the bathtub. I can't stomach cleaning it, so I just turn on the water and rinse off my face and mouth, and then I leave it running, hoping the onslaught will do something for the mess.

My heart hammers, making me dizzy. Somehow, floating in that heady state, it's like achieving enlightenment—like the divine reaches down and moves the track of my thoughts to point at something I knew but previously refused to look at clearly: this whole place is fucking crazy. If Hee-Young was pregnant, Grandpa Garin was the father. Ca-lee and Shepherd must've known and interfered, even as Heta wrote her little love notes. And all the while, they were surrounded by white-suited facilitators, silent messengers of the underworld relegated to cooking and cleaning, while a great glass menagerie of teenage girls in bird costumes spun overhead.

Absolutely fucking crazy.

Laughter breaks over me like rain. The sound's loud enough to hurt my ears, but I don't stop, because I can't.

FORTY-EIGHT
Hee-Jin

At some point, I realized the bell-tones no longer ring in my room—that when Ca-lee locked me in here, she took away my only way of telling time, besides my stomach. I cannot decide which is worse—my hunger, my confinement, the loss of my hearing, the loss of my voice—but long after the fear ebbs into a dull anxiety that clings to me like a greasy filth, something new comes, something worse than everything before.

It starts while I'm trying to tear away the seal that lines the space between the door and its frame. The rubber's deep in the crack, and I can't get hold of it. I grab one of the hangers out of the wardrobe and try to wedge it into the crack, and it snaps—

Something races across the corner of my vision, a ghostly green image like an after-effect illusion from a children's magazine. I know from the way it moves that it can't be real. That sinuous, floating undulation, like an eel or some kind of jellyfish—I've seen it in too many movies and cartoons.

Imugi. The lithe body of a limbless dragon, spooling through the air.

It's gone now, but I understand what's happening. There's too much white and not enough sound. Add that to my fear, my anger, and whatever drugs might be left in my system . . .

My studies of history—British agents during the Troubles, the CIA, the MSS, the American prison system—have taught me what happens next. Sensory deprivation is easier, more palatable, and harder to prove than breaking the body, but it's no less damaging. It's come on slowly, because my eyes aren't covered, because *I'm* still making sounds—but it's not enough.

I'm hallucinating.

I've been in here at least a day. Maybe more—it's hard to tell, because the lights no longer go out—but either way, I'm unspooling quickly. I need to do something before I completely lose it. I pull everything out of the closet, all the kimono and my and Hee-Young's clothes, and spread them around the room like a fabric menagerie.

The relief is immediate. In a drawer, I find our mother's beetle dress, still folded; I repeatedly drape it over my face, absorbing the slight breeze, the crinkling sound of the stiff fabric, the musty smell of the cabinet. When I'm done, I stash it carefully in the painting shaft. I don't want it to disappear.

I stare at the paintings. I rub my hands together close to my ears, listening to the *rasp-rasp-rasp* of my skin. Once, I slap myself in the chest, hard enough that the thump reverberates into the core of me. *I am here,* I think. *I am here.*

Despite my terror, I somehow fall asleep again. I have odd dreams of jangma—rainy season—that few weeks from mid-June to the beginning of July when people hole up in restaurants sizzling with crisp fried pancakes and small cups of makgeolli.

The hiss of the cold-water pancake batter hitting the oil is supposed to mimic the sheets of torrential rain outside. I can hear it in my dreams—can smell the char of frying onions and gimchi, the sweet-sour notes of the fermented rice wine. As children, Hee-Young and I stared longingly into windows, but we never went inside.

I wake up. It feels like a few hours later, but I'm not sure. When I open my eyes, the imugi floats around my head, no longer content to appear in flashes at the corners of my vision.

Before long, it's joined by Hee-Young's paper menagerie: a pheasant and an owl, a pair of monkeys she made for a show, a fox with nine tails she left tucked in a bookstore's copy of her favorite novel. The animals roar and bark and growl—and then the fox swirls its tails and lands in front of me, its body growing as it descends.

I scuttle backwards, but my heart pounds, my guts filling with horror as legends of the monster fill my brain. Gumiho can take the form of beautiful young women, which allows them to seduce young men and eat their preferred foods: human livers and hearts.

My mother believed in them just as they were in the tales, but Hee-Young thought they were metaphorical: powerful, sexual, violent representations of women at a time when they were subjugated and policed.

A chair appears in the middle of the room. The fox takes it, stretching its legs out like a human might, its tails spilling over the back. It bares its teeth before speaking. "Why did you do it, Hee-Jin? Take Hee-Young's passport and her plane ticket?" Its Korean is tinged by a regional accent, the brisk fall of Busan dialect.

My limbs feel like I'm underwater, sluggish and floating at the same time. *It's not real,* I think, but I know that's not true.

It's not real. The table is hot. It's not real.

The fox bares its teeth again. "Maybe she meant for you to have it? She was dying anyways. Crawled right to your door. Is that what you thought?"

I close my eyes. *The table is hot.*

"Tell me about your mother," says the fox. The sluggishness in my limbs suddenly swells across my body, until I lose the strength to sit up and fall backwards. Everything goes dark.

And then, I'm again dreaming about rain. This time, I'm lying on the beach. The water sounds warm, and the sand smells like oranges.

When I wake up, the floor is still covered in sand, and a wave rolls in from the wall and breaks in front of my feet. At the edges of the room, though, are a series of objects: a kite, a hibiscus flower, a small stuffed bird.

I crawl forward and dip my hands in the spray. The ocean dissipates, but the objects remain: kite, flower, bird. I could touch them, see if they disappear like the ocean did, but I don't. I'm too afraid they won't.

I'm losing it. I'm alarmed to hear more than a little longing in that thought—a desire for a day where I don't have to hold on, an end to whatever is happening in this room.

The process of destroying my self, it's happening so much faster than I would have guessed. My isolated life didn't inoculate me against the torture of being alone.

FORTY-NINE
Hee-Jin

I dream about facilitators. Now, though, they really are Jeoseung Saja, their outfits white and not black, just like my mother said they would be. The reapers approach and touch my arms, my wrists, my hands. Each time, pain flares, sharp as a thorn.

They filter out of the room. There's a soft burst of—not sound, but the opposite, like the echo of the space expanding. When the door shuts again, a large white owl adorned in silver chains stands in the doorway. It speaks to me in English, a familiar voice I can't place.

Hullo, Hee-Young, it says. *Seems like you're in a huh-yuuuuuuge pickle.* And then it laughs and flaps its wings, and I recognize it after all. *Pepperdine*, I think, and a giant cowboy hat appears on its head. Just like in Hee-Young's stupid fairytales, the names of monsters have power.

The owl approaches until it looms over me, the hat dancing like a boat in the waves. *Sorry about this*, it says, and then its beak stretches longer and longer until it is a proboscis, uncurling down toward my face.

I scream and thrash, but my body is sluggish, and the army of Saja has reappeared to hold me down. Fire flares in my nose as the beak enters. It advances, through my sinuses, down my throat, burning me in its wake. I feel my stomach swell with something cold. I think of Hee-Young in my apartment, her body filled to bursting by the gases of her own decomposition—but instead of the stench of rot, there's the faintest taste of grapes in my mouth. Grapes, and something botanical, something pink and pearlescent white.

And then, I'm not afraid anymore. Instead, I'm being buoyed up by warm, gentle waves, and somehow, that's so much worse.

When I wake up, there are bruises on my arms, so fresh they're still red. Fat ones that circle my wrists like bracelets. Oblong ones on my forearm, like fingertips. I strip naked and bring myself to the mirror, trying to see if there's a pattern, if they were something I did to myself, or something that was done to me—but my reflection stops me short.

There are protrusions all over my face: angry, ruddy bumps like pimples, the size and shape of pencil erasers. They stipple my jawline, the bridge of my nose, my cheeks. I finger one gingerly; it's hard to the touch, and yet, it gives the tiniest bit under my finger. I press harder, hard enough to make me gasp—whatever these things are, they're part of me, sensitive as the rest of my flesh.

It feels like several days go by. The little stubs spread to my shoulders and my back, growing until they're almost as long as my thumbnail—and when I measure them, I notice my thumbnail has not only gone cloudy, but it has thickened, as if infected with fungus. Soon, the disease spreads to all my nails. An ache starts in my fingers, though it spreads to my hands, my arms. Before long, every movement is painful, as if all my joints have been dipped in acid.

Over and over, the owl returns to bore its beak into my nose. The fox visits me to ask its questions, its silky voice prodding into parts of my life I would never tell a stranger. I try to hold out against its interrogations, but whenever the beak has filled me with grapes and herbs, I can't help but let things slip.

I tell it about the way my mother hummed when the sun was out and she thought nobody could hear her. The hopes she hid in the beetle dress: that the day would come when she was liberated, and all of us warm and full-bellied and safe. The way she sometimes sat next to me when she thought I was asleep and tucked the hair behind my ear, a tenderness she needed to express, but that I couldn't see, not when it might make me weak.

I tell it about her death, the forest peeping around us, her smile as the Saja came for her. I tell it about my vision of her hiding in the closet, her fear of the Russian bastard.

I tell it about Hee-Young tricking me at Crystal Island, about her friends dumping her overdosed body on my doorstep, about our shrieks of joy as we ran through the apple trees. In these moments, trapped in a small room with the fox and its questions, it's as if my onggi pot has a grief of its own. Despite the light mood brought on by the drugs, tears pool in my eyes and spill down my cheeks. More than once, I wonder if I will drown in my tears, disappear in them like Shim Cheong beneath the waves.

Between visits, I stow the scalpel-tool in my bra and wait—but during visits, I can't even lift my head off the floor. My body always goes slack long before either the owl or the fox appears, as if they've worked some binding spell over me, sapping my will to live—though sometimes, I hear a hiss beforehand, the same as when Ksenia was in the shaft.

I lose all sense of time. In those moments where I feel the least sluggish, the most lucid, I know it has passed—days, if not more, by the length of the spines on my face and the progress of the bruise on the back of my hand. It transitions in spurts, never changing when I'm watching it, flashing through different shades of purple and then green every time I look away.

When it fades completely, I feel unmoored. After some contemplation, I pinch the skin of my thigh and twist hard enough to ensure it will bruise again. *Two weeks for the old ones to fade,* I think. *Maybe more, maybe less. When this one disappears, it will be a month.*

I have water from the bathroom, but no food—yet the insatiable hunger that always fills me is gone. Maybe this is some undiscovered power of survival, waiting latent in my genes for a moment like this—but I doubt it. I've been hungry before.

Hungry or not, I need to get out of here. It seems impossible, though. I've scratched enough paint from all four of the walls *and* the door to know that underneath the white is metal, thick enough to break the tip off the scalpel-tool's blade, and there isn't any angle for me to apply the file.

My only hope is the shaft. Over and over, I jam myself in, but my gains are by inches. I'm not sure if I'll make it up to the door Ksenia saw before I starve to death.

FIFTY
Callie

I count the bells to track time, follow the cycles of light and dark. On the second day after Shep asks me to stay in my room, I'm lying in my bed when someone arrives, someone that doesn't do me the courtesy of ringing the little doorbell to make his presence known. Instead, Pepperdine just lets himself in, moving with the brisk efficiency of any healthcare worker.

He wears his profession strangely—as if he were the flesh-puppet of a Lovecraftian creature, unaware of how uncanny its behavior reads.

The door shuts behind him. "Shep told me to come see you—"

I cut to the chase. "How is Hee-Young?"

Too late, I realize that he probably can't talk about one of his other patients—especially the girl I confined like a kidnappee—but he smiles and tilts a palm up as if checking for rain. "She's fine. But I'd like to focus on you."

She's fine. That's something. Maybe I haven't damaged her for life.

"May I sit?"

I don't want him to, but being contrarian could be taken as a sign that what happened with Hee-Young was not just an isolated outburst, but instead the first step of a full-scale slide back into the dark. Before long, Pepperdine will be here daily, administering his treatments.

And would that be so bad? The thought comes unbidden, but it's mine, in my voice. *After all, if you're losing time again—*

I cut it off by speaking. "Please sit."

After a moment, he settles in next to me on the bed. "Looks like Shep's got a man stationed outside." He jerks his thumb at the door.

"It's in case I need anything," I say, careful to not let my resentment bubble through.

"Still, it's got to feel *confining*."

For just a moment, I get a flash of *something* from him—empathy, humanity—and it makes me sick.

He rubs his fingertips against his chin. Thankfully, this movement is more artifice than genuine, and I go back to hating him. "Why don't we start with something easy? How have the last few days been?"

I shrug. "It's hard, realizing—" my voice breaks—"what I did. But I've been trying to face it. To look at it clearly and truthfully." I hope he understands both the things I've said and the things I haven't—that for two days, I've sat here in this room and repeated it to myself over and over: *Lisa isn't real, Lisa was never there, Lisa is dead, Lisa is dead*, until I felt my own words echoing around me like a shimmering wall of harmonics. "I'm *ready* for that. To face the truth."

He nods sagely. It's so ridiculous, I only barely manage to stop myself from laughing. "I'm glad to hear you say that, Calleigh. Shep told me you might be open to treatment again?" The ceiling shudders, but he doesn't seem to notice. "I'd like to try something new."

"You mean a new medication?" *Something other than the tranquilizers and mood stabilizers that sapped all my energy and made me sleep around the clock?* A soft hope rises in my chest.

He nods. "Yes, among other things. You have to understand . . ." He furrows his brow, but this time, I don't feel like laughing. "When we initially started working together, you had just suffered a devastating loss." He shakes his head. "After what happened to Lisa, I determined you were extremely high risk for a full break with reality, or even suicide. Treating you was damage control, like trying to plug the holes in a dike. My first—and only—priority was keeping you alive, and that work alone was difficult."

A knot squeezes in my chest. I've spent hundreds of hours hatefully turning Pepperdine around in my head and never once imagined he'd really been thinking about my welfare. Even now, I can't quite believe it—but the fact that I don't completely *disbelieve* it is earth-shaking.

"So, I took extreme measures—stronger medications than I'm normally comfortable with, but we felt like chemical restraint was necessary at the time."

I nod carefully. "And now?"

His pained expression shocks me. "And now we can do the real work. Instead of just trying to keep you safe, we can work on making you *better*. The truth is I never stopped treating you, Calleigh. Shepherd's been operating under my instruction for years—giving you space, keeping your life free of stress, letting you explore your changed world at your own pace. He told me that until this little setback, you were improving." He furrows his brow. "And that's what this was, wasn't it? Just a setback?"

I swallow hard, but then I nod. "My memory's been coming back."

"I thought that would happen, once you were ready."

His smile is warm and lovely. I blossom in it despite my distaste for him. "Then why didn't you tell me?"

"Because I didn't know for sure. And if you thought you *should* improve and then didn't—that could be psychologically devastating. You didn't need that kind of pressure."

"So, what happens now?"

He opens his arms as if to embrace me. "Like I said. We start the *work*. We'll do daily visits. Talk therapy, journal entries. Guided exercises, meditation, role-play. I'd like to try a few very mild medications, smaller doses—just to steady you temporarily while we sift through what's been unburied. I think you'll feel much better after a few weeks—"

His pocket buzzes. The object he extracts reminds me how much cell phones have changed: less boxy and fewer buttons, but more screen. "Ah, I need to cut our visit short, but I'll be back soon. How about it—are you ready to work together?"

"Yes." I'm surprised to find the eagerness in my voice isn't all fake.

"Excellent. Have a good one, Calleigh."

He leaves without looking back. Once the room is empty, I take long, shaking breaths. It feels like I'm floating. Of all the things I foresaw after shutting Hee-Young in Heta's room, it was never this: validation. Empathy.

A path to getting better.

That night, as I'm drifting off to sleep, the flash hits me, deeper and more vivid than the memories that came before.

I'm on my back, the night sky framed by grasping trees.

It's the same view from when I was pouring the tea: after the accident, me being carried out by men that must be EMTs.

"You're sure she won't remember anything?"

"No, we were careful. Just get her in the car."

Electricity zings through my nerves. *Careful*? Careful about *what*?

The snap of a twig. *"It's a shame about the girl."*

And then it's gone.

I blink as the dark room swims back into view. It makes sense that they'd feel sad about Lisa—she was dead at the scene—but the odd wording, *get her in the car*, it throws me. Is *car* just slang for ambulance, like *bus* or *wagon* or *rig*?

It's a shame about the girl.

I'd clearly felt hands under both my shoulders and my hips. Two men, then, carrying me in tandem. On TV, rescue crews always use some kind of transport device—a gurney, a backboard—after an accident to protect the spine.

That's a real thing, right?

I glance around the room, but it's too dark to see anything. Still, the view gives me what I need, unsticking the gear in the back of my mind.

Is it possible this memory isn't what it seems? *Should I tell Pepperdine about this at our session, so we can figure out what's real?*

But then I remember the satanic panic, and I'm no longer sure. And those fabrications were by people who hadn't lost huge chunks of their life after a head injury. People that weren't being *evaluated*—because despite Pepperdine's uplifting talk, he's going to be watching me carefully, making sure I really *am* making progress.

I can't tell anybody about this. Not yet.

I take a deep breath and let the idea go, and then I roll over and go to sleep.

FIFTY-ONE
Hee-Jin

"*Good morning.*" Hee-Young's voice.

I bolt awake. I'm not in bed, because I nodded off in the middle of a bath I made with a big glob of the lavender-scented soap. I needed the heat, the rumble of the tub filling, the sensation of current trickling over my limbs.

The water's chilled, but I still enjoy it. How brisk does it need to be to cause hypothermia? Is an escape from this place currently concocting itself inside my organs?

But then I hear something shift on my left, by the door, and I slowly turn my head.

It's Hee-Young: pale-skinned, linen-suited, and floating an inch above the ground, her legs swept behind her like the dragging train of a wedding dress. At my gasp, she rolls her eyes and shakes her head, making the spines on her face waggle. "*Stop being so dramatic. Also, you look like shit. And, shibal, you've been getting the doses, right? Then how are you still so fat?*"

She's not there, I know she's not. But I've been alone long enough for the bruise on my thigh to turn green. Something's happening inside of me, some process of liquefaction, leaving behind an ever-growing hole.

"Hee-Young." My voice sounds strange, like it's been made tinny by a bad connection. "I missed you."

She snorts. "*Oh, really? Hee-Jin-ah, you stole my passport and my plane ticket.*"

I almost forgot, I think. *My real name.* I feel myself flower under it despite the diminutive added to the end, as if I was a child. "I'm so sorry, Hee-Young—"

"*Oh, shut up. You knew what this was.*" The way she says it, it's not entirely bad-natured. A cigarette appears between her lips. Hee-Young didn't smoke, not really, but as she leans back against the doorframe, a gray wisp trailing up and out of the bathroom,

I suddenly realize what I'm seeing, who she's become. Standing like that, she looks exactly like our mother, despite the spines and the bulging eyes and the gnarled curls of her fingers.

Mudang—shamans—often do rituals where they draw down goddesses or ghosts into their bodies. Can a ghost draw down another ghost? I have no idea.

"*After all—you were quick to forget about me and* these, *weren't you?*" she says, fingering the spines on her chin. "*You heard the* chollang-chollang *of coins on a string, and that was enough for you, eh?*" She exhales smoke. "*Listen, Hee-Jin-ah—I thought Garin was a viable plan, but it doesn't look like he's going to work out anymore. I don't know how I didn't see it in the first place—he's just not careful enough. I think it's time you got out of here. You're losing your grip.*"

I laugh, a short bark that makes my ribcage jerk, the water sloshing ever so slightly around me. The room's filling with the smell of her smoke, though it's not the metallic bitterness I associate with a cigarette, because she's no longer smoking one. It's turned into one of the traditional pipes in historical paintings: a thin barrel the length of her arm, a small, upturned bowl at the end. Back in the early Joseon era, even children smoked pipes like these.

"I can't get out, Hee-Young. The door's locked."

She shrugs. "*What are Christians always saying? Use the window, right?*" She passes through the bedroom wall, and her absence rakes at me like a sunburn. I pull myself out of the tub and go after her, dripping water that turns white and shines like a pearl as it hits the floor.

She's not in the room, though. Even my floating paper animals have deserted me. As devastating as that is, something in Hee-Young's words twists through my head, daring me to catch it.

I quickly dry off and get dressed, and then I wrap myself in the blanket to warm up while squatting on the floor. After a moment, her comment pops into my head—*how are you still so fat?*

Am I? I look down at my arms. I've definitely lost weight—and they look *longer*, as if the bones have stretched out somehow—but they're not nearly as skinny as I'd guess for someone that had not eaten for at least three weeks, if not longer. I'm not sure what that means, if I've entered some kind of survival mode, or if maybe my bruises have healed much faster than I estimated they would.

I put on a top and shorts from the clothes I brought with me, grab the flashlight magnet, and open the painting-door. The air that seeps out is brisk; the temperature inside the shaft never seems to match the room. It sometimes smells fresh and sometimes stale—which strengthens my theory that it must go somewhere.

I take a deep breath, get on my hands and knees, and push myself in. It's easier than I remember—so maybe more time really *has* passed than I thought.

The metal shaft isn't actually smooth. There are corners, flaps, rivets that stick out to catch my skin. Each time one snags on the nubs of my spines, I feel a sudden shock of pain, the red-hot cutting of pulling on a loose but anchored tooth. I proceed up the shaft little by little, my arms overhead to make myself as thin as possible. All the muscles in my body under the waist burn with my slow progress—but finally, *finally*, I make it all the way in without getting stuck.

Part of me thought I'd never accomplish it. I wonder if Hee-Young had something to do with this, before remembering *she's just a hallucination*, and then I shove that all down into my pot, squeeze the flashlight magnet, and discover what Ksenia saw.

The duct stretches above me, rising for perhaps another three feet overhead before bending ninety degrees, forming a ledge. After that, it must go horizontally toward the center of the house.

I wiggle my arms up. Standing on tiptoe, I can just reach the ledge with my fingertips, but that's enough to get a better view of the showerhead-like device I spotted the first time I jammed myself in here. It's lined up with the edge. From this angle, I can make out a long, thin pipe that flows out behind it to disappear in the horizontal stretch of the shaft.

I jump, once, twice, looking for Ksenia's ceiling door, the flashlight beam tracing up and down. On the third jump, I get enough air to illuminate a compact rectangular hatch, barely larger than a shoebox, in the ceiling of the shaft.

I'm not sure how Ksenia saw it. She's only a bit taller than me, and I'd have heard her jumping before Ca-lee busted in on us.

A shiver runs up my back.

"*Stay focused,*" whispers Hee-Young, her voice next to my ear. I know she's fake—there isn't enough room in this shaft for the two of us—but her breath is warm on my cheek.

Regardless, she's right. I can't let thoughts of Ca-lee derail me from the door.

The interior of the shaft is so tight, and there are no good handholds to aid my climb. After a moment, I reach up and grab the showerhead—I can *just* make it—and give it an experimental tug. It feels solid.

I position the flashlight's button between my back left molars and bite down to turn it on. I grab the showerhead again, take a deep breath through my nose, and pull hard while bending my knees as much as the space will allow. By jamming my feet against the sides of the shaft to keep myself from falling, I can lower the amount of force needed to pull myself up—but it's excruciating.

No, it's not. The table is hot, and this doesn't hurt.

I rise inch by inch, the little door coming closer. Before long, I'm a foot off the ground, then two. My hands ache from gripping the pipe, but I squeeze as hard as I can. Another foot, and then another.

When the showerhead jabs me in my throat, I bite to turn the light on, and the shaft's horizontal length comes into view. It runs straight back, farther than I can see, though my progress would be stopped by an impassible metal grate about three feet in.

On the ceiling above it is the door.

By now, my arms and legs are trembling. My heart thumps so quickly it feels like all the beats have fused into one, and my whole body is covered in sweat. I press on, though, until the ledge is level with my waist. I can't get the angle I need to go any farther—there isn't any more vertical shaft to push my legs against.

But my upper body is mostly free, which means I have more room to maneuver. I lean back, using my weight as a counterbalance to keep my feet pressed into the wall, taking a moment to catch my breath. If I can walk my feet up, I might be able to get enough leverage to slide them over the ledge—

The pipe groans, shifting under my hands.

If this pipe breaks, I won't be able to try again. And the door is so close. With another six inches, maybe another foot, I might be able to grab the little handle and get it open.

Quickly, I come up with a plan. I need to throw my body forward while pushing down hard on the ledge. Just like trying to clear a fence.

The pipe groans again, more urgently. "*Do it*," Hee-Young hisses in my ear.

I tense, then I spring and smash my hands down on the edge of the ledge. My upper body rises forward, out of the shaft, and for a single, glorious second, I think I've made it—

But it's not enough. I slide backwards. One of the spines on my cheek catches the side of the shaft and tears off in a brilliant shock of agony. I flail and manage to grab the handle of the door, which opens as I fall. I drop a foot before the door catches me, and then it swings me into the side of the shaft with a painful bang. I grab at the showerhead with my other hand, my fingers finally closing around the pipe.

But the hinges on the door give way, and it tears off the ceiling of the shaft. At the sudden jerk, the pipe with the showerhead rips away from the wall, and I plummet.

It's a short drop, but when I land, my ankle rolls, exploding with pain. I cry out as I fall sideways and lose the flashlight magnet, plunging me back into darkness. I don't see anything as my forehead smacks into the shaft, but I catch myself with my arms.

And then I stand there on one foot, trying not to cry and failing, the remnants of the door in one hand, the pipe in the other.

From somewhere high above me, Hee-Young laughs and falls silent.

FIFTY-TWO
Hee-Jin

In the quiet darkness, the pain grows, broadcasting in no uncertain terms that I've seriously injured my ankle—but in the same way this room distorts time, the shaft distorts the pain. Each time I breathe and the sound echoes inside of the shaft, I float farther from the body I entered it with.

"*What was that?*" asks Hee-Young.

I almost answer her, before realizing the question was in clear, unaccented English. And unlike the rest of my recent hallucinations, which are vivid and pressing, the voice was faint and distant.

The little door. When I ripped it off, it must have opened up some connection between my room and another.

"Hello!" I suck in a big breath that smells like mildew and scream at the top of my lungs. "Can you hear me? Is somebody there?"

There's a groaning noise, the scrape of metal on metal, and then I hear another voice, now louder and clearer. "Hello? Who is this?" It's Ksenia, I think.

Tears bristle at my eyes. I'm so overwhelmed, it's almost hard to answer. "It's Hee—"

Beside me, Hee-Young clears her throat. "Careful. You almost made a mistake."

She's right. I almost said *Hee-Jin*. A ghost calling my name a few times was enough to undo all my careful self-conditioning. "It's Hee-Young. Ksenia, you need to help me. I'm . . . stuck . . . in my room."

"What? Stuck how? Hee-Young, where have you *been*?"

"Ca-lee," I yell back. "She locked the door. She—" I suddenly remember why I got locked in here in the first place. Ksenia may have no love for Heta, but I don't want her finding out I was going through Heta's room—or why. "She is crazy. Please . . . get me out. I have no food. For weeks."

"Oh, god." There's a pause, long enough I start to panic, but then her voice echoes down. "Hang on, Hee-Young. I'll go get Shepherd. We'll get you out." And then comes the grating noise again. It must be another painting-door—these shafts must connect the ventilation system of all the rooms together. After seeing the shaft in my room, Ksenia must've opened hers—

Shit. I need to get out of this shaft. If someone opens the door, and they don't see me, they might leave. I could be trapped again.

I throw the broken door up onto the ledge and then squat on my good leg. I let myself sink toward the ground, kicking the file and the scalpel-tool out of the way. When I'm almost even with the hole, I use my hands to push my bad ankle out. Pain zings up toward my core, but I don't stop.

"*She's not going to help you*," says Hee-Young. Her voice has moved into the bedroom.

My heart quickens as I struggle through the little hole. What if Hee-Young's right? Ksenia must've noticed my absence. What if she was lying about getting Shepherd, or worse . . .

I've been imagining Hee-Young's voice. Why not Ksenia's, too?

I slide back into the bedroom and shut the painting-door, but my fear has taken root. It slides tendrils through my chest, my belly; it squeezes at my spine.

What if the door was never locked? What if none of this was real? What if I never heard those knocks in my apartment in the first place, and—

In that moment, the door opens. Shepherd stands there, wearing a charcoal-gray suit. Almost as soon as we make eye contact, his expression distorts, as if he's disgusted. "My god, your *face*."

I'm afraid to say anything. Afraid that my voice will disturb him into flickering away, the same way my hand made the ocean disappear. I'm suddenly more exhausted than I've ever been, so tired the room feels cold, and everything smells bitter and herbal.

I lean back against the wall and close my eyes. I hear someone crying. It takes me a moment to realize it's me.

"I'll get you a doctor," he says, and then he's gone again.

FIFTY-THREE
Hee-Jin

I flash forward through time. One moment, I'm exhaustedly staring at the door to my room, struggling to crawl forward on hands and knees—and then Shepherd reappears in the middle of the room, only now there's another man with him, a familiar one who also wears a suit, though this one is tweed.

Pepperdine, I think, as he spins toward me with a syringe.

I try to scream out, but he's faster than me, though he's no longer an owl. I feel the prick of it entering my flesh, like the Saja and their thorns, and then I'm sliding down a tunnel—but it's not like in the movies, that instant fade to black. Instead, I detach from my body and swim. I listen to their conversation—*start an IV. Think we should move her*—while a softly darkening curtain pushes at me from the sides.

When I wake up, I'm alone in a bedroom I don't recognize: heavy drapes, nice furnishings. Along one of the dark red walls is an odd assortment of curvy shelves grouped like a school of fish, though they're too shallow and crammed too closely together to be of any practical use.

I try to sit up and discover a clear plastic tube leading into a needle in my arm. A second later, my muscles give out, and I flop back against the sheets. Whatever Pepperdine dosed me with is still affecting me. When I try again, I don't even clear the mattress.

My alarm grows. The dullness fades from the edges of my mind, leaving a world sharper and brighter than I remember. I can tell from the volume of each rustle and breath that this room is soundproofed like mine. I stretch my arms to the side and explore the soft sheets. I push against the mattress, trying to lever my pelvis off, and manage to rock myself to my side.

My tongue brushes something gummy wedged against one of my back teeth. I flick it away, and it explodes into sweet juice that tastes like oranges. Some effect of the medication—or something I don't remember eating?

I shiver. Once I start, I can't stop. This room is as cold as a crosswalk on a windy winter day, no buildings to stop the air from blasting you with its chill.

My muscles are starting to feel less like lead. I throw my knees to the other side, trying to get more momentum in my roll—and discover that I'm not alone. Next to me, Hee-Young lies flat on her back, her arms crossed over her chest. "*Do I look like a mummy?*"

I've never seen a mummy in real life, but I nod.

She turns to face me and smiles. "*You don't have mites yet, at least. That's good.*" But then her already-enormous eyes widen, as if she hears something. "*He's coming. Be careful.*"

And then she's gone.

The hair on the back of my neck stands on end as the room gets even colder. I've felt this before, this deep, twisting brush of frigid malevolence. Felt it when Ksenia was hiding in that shaft, the moment before Ca-lee burst into my room.

My body hums with déjà vu. And then there's a click, and the door opens—but this time, a monster steps in, a slavering wolf standing on its back legs, with huge, glistening fangs.

In the split second it takes my eyes to focus, the fearsome creature changes, its curved claws turning pale and thickening into the arc of curled fingers bearing a tray, its fangs shortening into perfectly handsome teeth. Shepherd looks . . . guilty, like a dog that's just been whipped in the street.

"I'm so sorry." Each word is a sentence. "I had no idea—"

"How long?"

"Pardon?"

"How long. Was I in . . . the room?"

There's a pause, so brief I almost think I imagine it. "Just overnight. Ca-lee said you weren't feeling well, but when the facilitators told me you missed breakfast, I came to check on you, and the door was locked. I opened it and found you on the floor."

I don't hear the rest of what he says. It's not possible, is it? That I was only in there a single day? That all the hours I spent picturing the owl and the fox and the paper menagerie and the beach—the hours I spent cramming myself in the entrance to the shaft—that all of that happened in roughly the time it took for me to travel from Korea to here?

I look down at my hand, checking for the bruise. It's missing—but my wrists are thinner, so much thinner than they were before. My fingernails are like caramel lozenges, my arms dotted with dark spines. He's lying.

I can feel his gaze on me.

"When we found you, you were *dah-leer-ee-us*," he says softly. "Going on and on about a fox and an owl. Your fever was off the charts." He shakes his head. "We were so lucky Pepperdine was already here—he put two and two together, realized you had *men-in-ji-tus*—"

"What is . . .?"

"It's an infection in part of your brain. Honestly, I don't understand it well myself, but he said this happens a lot, in people that come from . . ." He averts his eyes for a moment. "It can be caused by bacteria. There's a vaccine for it, but if your country doesn't have good medical care?" He shrugs, looking uncomfortable. "It's spread to your skin, unfortunately. We're working on that."

Korea has some of the best medical care in the world. People routinely travel from other countries—including western countries, like the United States—to get procedures. And my mother believed in vaccines with the fervor that can only come from growing up without access to them and watching her friends and family die from preventable diseases. Although I don't know how, she'd managed to get us our shots—this, she told us more than once.

"I was . . . sick," I say, trying to buy time.

"Yes," he nods. "We weren't sure if it was viral or bacterial, so we treated you for both. We had to give you a lot of medicine for the pain, too."

I blink. "No . . . hospital?"

His face turns hard, then impassive—and finally, his expression falls, resigned. "You have to understand. We couldn't take you to a hospital, because . . ."

"Because I am . . . here illegally?"

He blinks, surprised. "Are you? I thought, with your passport—" He shakes his head. "Not you. But the other girls, some of them. We couldn't risk it."

"Because they are here for sex."

His face grows stony. "So you know. I was . . . hoping to shield you from that as long as I could."

"You lied."

He nods. "I did. I was desperate." He shrugs helplessly. "You have to understand. They all *agreed* to come here. They knew what they were in for. And rescuing all these women, it's expensive and complicated. If we did everything the legal way, many of them we wouldn't be able to save. Sumi, for example—I'd have never gotten her out of Dubai." He pauses, says it again, as if he's trying to convince himself. "They all agreed. You were the only one I couldn't tell."

I know something else isn't adding up, but my head is swimming, threatening sleep. Have I ever been this exhausted before?

"And how long? Was I in this room?"

"Four weeks."

I close my eyes. This doesn't match up with my memory. Everything feels like it happened *before* I was rescued by Shepherd, and—

Ksenia. I'd forgotten. "Did Ksenia . . . tell you? I am here?"

He shakes his head, his expression concerned. "Is she the one that locked you in?"

I swallow. "No. Ca-lee."

His face falls. He must've known who the real perpetrator was—didn't he just say that Ca-lee told him I wasn't feeling well? Is it possible that he was in denial, just hoping for another answer?

But if Shepherd's *not* lying, it means Ksenia never went to get help. Is she . . . in *league* with Ca-lee somehow?

The thought hurts almost as badly as my ankle, as the constant ache in my joints, but it shouldn't. I should've expected it. But despite everything, I didn't, and that's what hurts the most.

"But Hee-Young, we took good care of you, OK? We got you medicine, gave you food and kept you *hy-dray-ted*." He gestures at the bag connected to my arm. "Even had to *toob* feed you a bit, but you pulled through like a *champ*. You lost a little weight, but now that you're *loo-sid*, you'll gain it back. And I think you're well enough that we could go out to the garden and get some fresh air. If you want, I mean?"

I want to be outside more than I've ever wanted anything in my entire life. I nod.

"OK. Wait here."

He opens the door he originally entered from. I get a glimpse of a room that looks vaguely familiar, though I don't know where from. When he shuts the door behind him, I take a breath and glance nervously around the room, trying to anchor myself against the confinement by concentrating on the furnishings. A bed, a side table, a padded chair. They're simple, yet elegant and clearly expensive. Old wealth kind of things. Next to the bed is a small bowl filled with little painted balls the size of marbles, all different colors.

I've seen these somewhere before. I rack my brain. Then it comes to me: save the shade, they're exactly the same as the yeouiju that Hee-Young's paper imugi carried in its mouth. Did Hee-Young steal it from here—and if so, how and why?

I drop one into my pocket. A moment later, the door pops open.

Shepherd enters, pushing a wheelchair—one of the square, heavy looking ones, an odd thing to just have on hand. "I can get you as far as the stairs. I might need a facilitator to carry you after that, but we'll make it work."

He parks it by the bed at an angle, before flipping two small levers on the sides. "So it won't roll," he says, smiling. He pushes on the chair to demonstrate, and then he reaches out his hand. "Pepperdine splinted your ankle so you could bear a little weight on it, but you need to take it easy. Be careful."

I nod and take his hand. He pulls while I try to stand, and I come sliding forward on the bed. Once I'm on my feet—well, *foot*—I feel stronger.

I maneuver into the chair with a series of hobble-hops. He takes the handles and pushes me toward the door. We pass through what looks like a small sitting room—better furnished, with two leather recliner-type chairs and a small coffee table. Paintings and art pieces dot the walls, and there's a big bank of shelves on one side, their surfaces covered with antique-looking books and a number of small sculptures.

He pushes me out another door, and I suddenly recognize the landing from Ca-lee's tour. I was just in his room.

"Let me call a facilitator, and we'll get you down the stairs—"

"No!" I say it louder than I meant to, and take a breath before continuing. "Don't want . . . *facilitator.*" I have to slow down on that word, perhaps from the sedative still left in my system. "I want to try."

He beams. "Nothing can keep you down, yes? I'm glad to see it." And then he offers me his elbow. I don't want to touch him, but I want a facilitator less, so I grab it and take a deep breath, and then we heave me up into a standing position. With one hand on his elbow, and the other fastened tightly to the outer railing, I'm able to hop, little by little, down the stairs.

"Can you wait while I grab the chair?"

I nod, though I'm exhausted. My body is covered in sweat—that would've been difficult even when I had the use of both legs and hadn't been recently sick. Now, I feel like I've swum the Han River.

When he returns with the chair, I plop down gratefully.

On the way out the front door, I can't help but look up at him. His gaze is trained ahead, his expression miles away. I turn and give the stairs a last glance. *I needed so much help just to get down them*, I think, and the chill from earlier settles back into my bones.

FIFTY-FOUR
Hee-Jin

Shepherd struggles with pushing the chair in the grass, but he honors my request to proceed without a facilitator and soldiers forward, toward the outer ring of gardens.

The moment he opened the door and I saw outside, I realized I had been drugged. Or maybe my brain has been damaged in some way by my time in that room, leaving me with hallucinatory aftershocks that will stay with me long after its effects are gone. I can see a *new color*, something that glows not-quite purpley-blue with a soft, ethereal phosphorescence, and the natural objects around me—the leaves and the birds and even the spring flowers at my feet, mouths open as they beg for light and rain from the heavens—they're all either touched by this ghost shade or marked by bright, striking patterns they didn't have before. It's clear that months have gone by, that it's spring.

I should be relieved by the sight of the open horizon that stretches, endless, in front of me—but instead, a dull dread threads its way through my nerves. After all that time in a perfect, unchanging box, the riots of color and sound, the way the tree limbs overhead shake with each breeze—it all feels alien and strange.

I'm broken, I think, and then I laugh: a slow chuckle that burbles louder and louder. *It doesn't matter if I was really sick or if they were just drugging me, if I spent one day in there or four weeks, because I'm broken now, and it wasn't from sleeping rough or being mugged and assaulted or hiding from my mother's bogeyman or my sister's death. I was broken despite shelter and warmth and running water and heat, and now the table is just a table, and I'm going to die just like Hee-Young did.*

I laugh until I'm bent over and half-howling, until my face hurts from being stretched, my sides from heaving air.

Shepherd, perhaps understanding that I am crazy now and

require patience, is content to wait until I'm finished. When I can no longer make sound, he chooses a seat on a bench across from me, so that we are almost face to face. "This is all my fault."

I don't know how to answer him. He wasn't the one that locked me in. It wasn't his name I screamed as I banged and banged on the door. And yet, I believe him. He was lying about me being sick, about how long I spent in the room—maybe even about Ksenia never coming to find me. Look how he treated his wife, whom he must've known was unstable. Did he never tell her that her sightings of the child were imaginary? What could be the purpose of keeping the truth from her for so long?

"Hee-Young, *answer* me."

Though not loud, his interjection into my thoughts is jarring, like being caught by a seatbelt after a too-swift application of the brakes. One moment he's begging for contrition; the next, his voice falls an octave, and he's giving me commands.

"I don't know what to say."

"Just tell me—what are you thinking right now? What are you *feeling*?"

I feel like the ocean. I know I have emotions, embedded deep, and furious with the force of primordial currents—but they're so distant, where the light won't reach. Up here on the surface, everything is still.

But I don't move a muscle, and I don't say anything.

Something flickers over his face, but he relaxes on the bench. "Listen, Hee-Young. There's something you should know."

My stomach drops down, down, through my feet, through the earth. He rolls his bottom lip just far enough to flatten it under his top teeth, and then he tosses a piece of paper into my lap. It's folded in halves, so that the corners meet. I'm a fly caught in a spider's web, filled with a fear bone-deep and blood-true, but I open it.

In front of me is a picture of my face, eyes closed. Across the top of the flier, a headline in all caps: HAVE YOU SEEN THIS GIRL?

I drop the paper as if scalded. It lands sideways in my lap. I can barely focus my eyes enough to read the text:

Authorities are searching for one Hee-Young Song, last seen leaving Pittsburgh airport on March 30th. If you have information on her whereabouts, please call the missing-persons list at 412-555-0122.

Authorities. I flap the paper at him and try not to cry. "What is this? What is *this*?"

"I noticed them on my last trip to town. These fliers are everywhere—stapled up on telephone poles, taped in windows. I know we haven't talked much since . . ." He glances over his shoulder. "Since we came to our little arrangement. I was so happy to have my problem taken care of by you filling Hee-Young's spot, I didn't stop to think. But now, I wonder if that was a mistake. Who *are* you, and why are the police looking for you?"

My stomach cramps at that word: *police.*

His voice rises, commanding. "Did you *do* something to Hee-Young? Are you even really related?"

This situation has spun out of control so fast. "I did not do anything," I say slowly, making sure the words I select are the ones I need. "I found her. She died from drugs." *Your drugs. The same as you've been giving me.*

"*Drugs?*" He stands up and paces behind the bench. "Why didn't you take her to the hospital—"

"No." I shake my head urgently. "Hee-Young and I, we were not—we didn't have papers." A few minutes ago, I was angry at *him* for not taking me to the hospital. And I'm sure that he wouldn't have wanted her to go, not when there was even the slightest possibility her condition could one day be traced back to him.

He squints at me. "How did she get the passport in the first place?"

I shrug helplessly.

He folds forward on the bench, his face stern. "Hee-Young, or whatever your real name is—do you realize how serious this is? Forging a passport, taking someone's identity—and only now, you tell me that she's *dead*? No wonder the police are looking for you."

"OK." I make my voice very soft and quiet, as if I'm talking to an angry dog. "I will leave tonight, no trouble. Nobody will find out." *Nobody will find out about the girls, and the drugs, and what you did to Hee-Young. Isn't that what you want?*

He scoffs, his shoulders rising and falling like the bounce of a rubber ball. "Are you kidding? You can't just *leave*. There are probably *witnesses* to me picking you up at the airport. The girls have all seen you, the facilitators, the patrons. And when you're caught, they'll trace it back to me—*when*, not *if*, because there's no way some naïve slip of a foreign girl outruns the police. Do you have any idea how much you'd stick out in any town near here? You look like a *gay-sha* on death's doorstep—and that's without the limp and the IV bag." He rubs his forehead. "You can't leave, not until we figure this out. I have to protect myself, the other girls, my *wife*."

It's a long speech. I don't understand all of it, but with each piece I *do* comprehend, my dread grows. "You are saying—I cannot go."

He looks pained. "Not yet. Just let me get my lawyer in here. We can get a plan together—a story to explain who you are, how you got here. Make it look like a believable mix-up. We might be able to get you out of the country, into Canada or somewhere else where you can't be traced back to me."

He lifts his face. There's so much intensity to his gaze that I lean away from him, my ankle twinging with a warning as it grazes the ground.

"Promise me, OK? You need to stay put long enough for me to work out something with my lawyer. We can still figure this out if we work together."

There's no way I'm staying, not after what Ca-lee did to me. And I don't trust him. The second it's useful to throw me under the bus, that's exactly what he's going to do.

Besides, I've just realized—he claimed I'd been laid up sick and feverish for four weeks, but this sprain on my ankle feels fresh and raw.

"I promise. I won't leave," I say.

I can tell from his face he knows I'm lying.

FIFTY-FIVE
Hee-Jin

It feels like the conversation with Shepherd is ending, its energy spent, like a dying wind or a collapsing wave.

But then he looks at me, and his hard gaze makes me feel like I've been locked in my room again. I imagine jamming my thumb in his eye, leaping out of my chair, and sprinting for the safety of the woods.

Despite his age, he would easily catch me. Even grazing my heel against the wheelchair's footrest sends shocks of pain up my ankle.

He wheels me back across the grass with streams of one-way conversation, missives not meant to be returned. He tells me that I won't have to see Ca-lee, that she's going to be confined to her room or closely chaperoned by one of the facilitators to minimize the strain on both of us. That he'll call his lawyer right away to figure out my *legal troubles*, but that it may take a bit, as the man is traveling in Europe. That he's sure we can find a solution and *work this all out*.

It doesn't matter. I'm barely listening. I watch my surroundings carefully, cataloging hiding places, resting spots, angles of escape. I don't care that I don't have a vehicle or a good lay of the forest behind me—the second it's dark, I'm sneaking out.

I just have to take this step by step: navigate a way out of the fence, then some kind of shelter where I won't be found. There must be something in that abandoned village we passed on the way in.

We arrive back at the house and go through the same door we left from, the one at the end of the right wing. I notice the little alcove in the wall outside Ca-lee's room.

The phone is missing.

My stomach churns as he pushes me back toward the center staircase. "Where are we going?"

He clears his throat. "I'm taking you back to your room."

"Are you going to lock—"

"No," he says, shaking his head. "Of course not."

I don't know if this is worse or better than being in *his* bedroom, but one flight of stairs will be easier to navigate than two. That said, I don't want Shepherd or anyone else to touch me, but I need to save my strength if I'm going to climb up to the main floor later tonight. "Please call for facilitator," I say, the exhaustion only partially feigned.

He nods and disappears down the hall. A moment later, he returns with a white-suited man who easily hefts me over his shoulder and bears me down the stairs, Shepherd trailing behind with the chair. As we descend, I feel like Bari Gongju, the princess forced to journey to the underworld to retrieve a cure for her ailing parents. Every province has a different version of that myth, but my mother told us that in most of North Korea, Bari usually dies at the end.

It's not until we get to my room that Shepherd pops the chair back open and the facilitator sets me down. As they open the door, a soft plume of dread creeps up my neck, blossoming like dye in water.

And then I see Heta, sitting on the edge of my bed, and I understand why.

Is this revenge for me going through her room? If so, what thing of mine has she taken? I glance reflexively at the painting-door before making myself look away, but it was long enough to see that it was not *quite* flush against the wall. Did I forget to close it? Or has Heta already found my secret?

"Hello, Shepherd." Heta gives him a cautious smile, the look of a child hoping they've done right and fearing they've done wrong. "You asked for me to come down here?"

He pushes my chair the rest of the way into the room. "Yes. I'm sure you've heard what happened to Hee-Young."

Her eyes slide over my face, cataloguing the changes. "An illness. I wasn't trying to spy—"

"It's not your fault. Everyone knows the facilitators are gossips."

She nods and brushes a lock of hair behind her ear. In their previous interactions, she'd been different, more prickly. Now, there's an eagerness to the way she keeps her gaze carefully downturned. Maybe it's because there's nobody here to see her manifest open affection for him—nobody but me, who clearly doesn't matter.

"I think Hee-Young would enjoy some company for the next few days, especially as she's going to need some help—she's supposed to keep weight off her ankle. I want you to move into this room with her for a bit."

Move in here?

Heta's mouth falls open. "But—"

"Please." The word is perfectly neutral—neither a plea nor a command—and there's a long moment where her face twitches as she tries to filter through what he's really asking of her. "I don't want you to let her out of your sight. Day or night, I want you to make yourself available to her. I would consider it a personal favor."

My dreams of a bold escape as soon as the lights go out suddenly fade. No doubt Heta is meant to stay up and watch me, to make sure I can't flee.

Heta nods slowly. "I understand."

Heta takes Shepherd's command as gospel and is happy to play servant for me. As much as I hate it, she has her uses: over and over, I ask her to check that the door isn't locked, and she obliges without complaining, opening it a hand's breadth each time.

There are other signs, too, that this is not like my time in captivity: I have someone to talk to that isn't a hallucinated creature or my sister's ghost. Before long, I hear a sound I never thought I'd miss—one of the long bell-tones, reminding us of the schedule.

"It's for dinner," says Heta. "Are you up to eating?"

"Will we . . ." I don't know how to ask about the patrons, but she understands my worry and shakes her head. "No, it's only Wednesday. It's just us girls."

I nod, and she wheels me down to the dining room. Sumi and Sarah both smile at me as I enter, though the expressions are fake. They're clearly horrified by my appearance.

Ksenia and her plate are both missing. "Where is—"

"She left," answers Sumi, her lip curling into a scorn.

I glance around the room, trying to figure out what she means. Sarah looks away, uncomfortable, but she clears her throat and explains. "After you got sick, your patron, Garin . . . he came around a lot—'

"It was so weird at first," Sumi interjects. She squints, hard, as if that brings Garin into focus in front of her. "He had this wicked bump on his head, and his face was covered in little nubs. I think Ksenia gave him some kind of disease. Her skin was like that, too—" And then she takes in my face again, the spines jutting out of my skin, and she falls silent. I don't have to try hard to imagine what she must be thinking. "Well, anyways . . . Ksenia was definitely cozying up to him. They met a lot in secret."

Sarah gives me a sad look. You were . . . gone for weeks, yes? And maybe he . . . maybe he didn't want to wait anymore. He paid Shepherd the *necess*, the *necess*—" She closes her eyes. "The *needed* amount to take Ksenia away from here. To Spain, I think. Maybe it was Portugal. And then they just disappeared."

"I think they didn't want to be around Shepherd anymore," says Sumi, but her gaze is riveted to Heta. "It looked to me, sometimes, like he was *afraid* of him."

Questions rise up in my mind. Is that why Ksenia was trying to get close to me—visiting me in my room, asking me about my past, giving me little presents to butter me up? Was she doing some kind of . . . reconnaissance that would allow her to approach Garin? There had been hints, hadn't there, of some kind of past between them?

It has the weight of a true thing, but like everything else in this house, I don't have enough information to test it fully. And I'd heard Ksenia's voice from inside the shaft, heard her say she'd send help—and then help had arrived.

But Shepherd told me Ksenia hadn't mentioned me. And the night she went into the shaft, Ksenia had whispered about trying to make a bargain with Shepherd to leave.

What if Ksenia had approached Ca-lee with a similar offer? If Ca-lee had been looking for some excuse to get rid of me, my intrusion into Heta's room was perfectly timed. And what better way to keep me out of their hair than locking me in my room?

I finger one of the nodules on my cheek. "When? When did they leave?"

Glances circulate around the room. "Just a few days ago," Sumi says, and I have to close my eyes. Assuming Shepherd was lying about the timeline of my being locked away, that was after I was freed. *Of course.*

"Don't worry." At my silence, Heta gently pats my hand. "You'll have a new patron soon. You're too pretty not to." She says it with all sincerity, as if any patron would want a woman whose face is covered in spines. "And here—I have something for you." She waves at the back of the room.

A moment later, the door pops open, and a facilitator glides in, a large bowl held up in front like an offering. He sets it down in front of me.

It's filled with juk—rice and mushroom porridge. On top, someone has made an artful pile of toasted sesame seeds and strips of dark-green dried seaweed, drizzled all of it with golden sesame oil. I look at Heta, trying to understand.

"Oh. Hee-Young—the other Hee-Young—she asked for it, once, when she wasn't feeling well. She said it was good for illness? We thought you might like some after how sick you've been."

She glances at Sarah and Sumi, and the pair issue nervous smiles in return. All three of them carefully look me in the eyes, as if afraid to let their gaze wander over the sharpness of my spines.

I nod, but there's a painful lump in my throat. Juk *is* for sick people—easy to chew and digest—but it's also a symbol. A distillation of someone's care, especially for the patience it requires. When we were children, if we were sick, no matter how tired my mother was from working, she always found a way to make us some, even if it meant nodding off in front of the pot while the rice slowly broke down.

And after that terrible ordeal, it's *Heta* who's somehow brought me this bowl.

I give her a smile and stare at it, a glossy white cloud of porridge flecked with seeds and seaweed, and a soft dread unfolds in my gut. I told the fox in that room so many things, in the end. Was this memory of my mother one of them?

Then again, it's not like juk is some secret, special ritual. There are juk shops in every corner of Korea. The gesture of juk for the ill is featured in commercials, in songs, and on TV shows. *It's even on* Flower-Swallow, I think, my breath stopping in my throat.

Heta's voice breaks into my thoughts. "Is it not to your liking?

We can get you something else?"

"No, I'm sorry." I shake my head. "It looks good." And then I dig my spoon in, and under her watchful eye, I bring it to my mouth.

And it's delicious. I hate that it's delicious, hate it so much that tears leak out of my eyes, and I have to wipe them before I can continue.

Heta smiles, as if relieved, and turns to ask Sumi about their last session together in the studio.

FIFTY-SIX
Callie

There have been many times in my life where a month passed in the blink of an eye. Like my first weeks of undergrad, trying to take notes and finish homework and somehow navigate my way to classes through traffic and pelting rain, all while holding down two jobs and making desperate overtures toward a social life. Or the month that Cassie and I learned how to make hand-crafted cocktails on our own and spent six weeks entirely fucked up on liquor she'd stolen from various catering jobs. There was the entire *year* after Lisa was born, a year where, despite the help of Shepherd's army of laborers, I rarely slept more than a few hours a night.

As I stare into the bathroom mirror, drowning in the dark circles under my eyes, I have to admit that all of those pale in comparison to the last four weeks. Which seems impossible, given that all of the days have passed largely the same.

And yet, it's been the *best* month of my life. Isolating, in so many ways—part of Pepperdine's treatment had been to remove me from fears of judgment, the pressure of performing for the girls. At first, I resented being confined to my room—but after a few days, I had to admit I felt more relaxed than I had in years. Other than Pepperdine, the only other company I've had is the facilitator I see whenever I open the door to ask for food or drink or a magazine . . . and Shepherd. He is only allowed to visit once a week, at first, to prevent me being *emotionally unseated*—but every time I see his face, it feels like a reward, one I've worked hard to earn.

For the first time since the accident, I feel clean and light and pure.

Although I'm bored often, Pepperdine says that it's good. That we can only make progress during times of rest and boredom, because otherwise, all our energy is spent trying to survive.

And I am. Making progress, that is. All the worksheets and the talking about my mother and the breathing exercises, the books to read, the role-plays where I pretend to be a better partner, a better wife, a better mother—they're working, they really are. I know this because I asked Pepperdine when I thought I might be able to venture back out into the world outside my room.

Very soon, he'd said. *So soon.*

FIFTY-SEVEN
Hee-Jin

It's not until after the dinner is over and we return to my room that I realize the full shape of my confinement with Heta. There is only one bed, which means we'll have to sleep side by side.

For her part, she seems unconcerned by the proximity. After ascertaining I don't want any help getting undressed, she reads for a while, and then she slips under the covers, leaving me ample space. "Here you go," she says, patting the bed next to her. "Lights will be off any minute, I think. Anyways, this is kind of fun, isn't it? Like camping."

I nod and try to smile, but the muscles of my mouth have turned to rubber. I slide into my side of the bed under her watchful eye and wait until the lights go out.

Heta seems unconcerned about our proximity; I can think of nothing else. Lying on the mattress next to her in the dark, I can feel her every breath. It's different than with Ksenia—instead of that razor-sharp edge of tension, there's a careful wariness, like an aloof cat.

I wish I could tell what Heta's thinking, where her loyalties lie. All I know for sure is that she and Hee-Young had feelings for each other, and that at some point, she slipped into my room and stole Hee-Young's tin ring. No, that's not true—I also know that she fawns over Shepherd, even if I can't see why. Distasteful—but none are terrible offenses.

Still, Shepherd assigned her to watch over me. He wouldn't have done that if he thought she could be bought or convinced to let me go.

I've got to feel her out. Maybe she's been kept in the dark, too—and she'll slip and give me some information I need.

"I'm sorry." My words break the stillness. "I shouldn't have been in your room."

She turns, I think, to face me, the mattress groaning softly with her movement. "Then why were you?" she says, her voice carefully light. But it's that bully-voice again, that sweetness that disguises the threat of violence. "I couldn't figure that out, you know. I don't have anything in there except some old photographs." It's hard to tell when someone is being purposely nonchalant in a language that isn't your own, especially when you can't see them, but I think that maybe the photographs mean more to her than she is letting on.

What should I tell her? I decide to lie. "I was . . . curious. Other Hee-Young, she told me. That you were together."

I can tell she's gone stiff—there are no signs of movement from her side of the bed, not even the soft whisper of a breath. And then: "I'm surprised she told you. Hee-Young was . . . so secretive," she says softly. "Were you lovers, then?"

My shock that I was right—and that she admitted it—quickly turns to disgust. "No. We were . . . friends. From childhood."

"I see. What else did she tell you?"

Here it is, my chance to find out more—but it's going to be hard to lie convincingly when I don't have anything but the content of the note I found in the folded-up paper pheasant. "She said . . . she was going to have a baby." I wait, ears open, for a reaction.

Heta's gone back to being very, very still. "She said that, did she?" There's a snap of anger underneath her murmur, one warning me to be careful.

I clear my throat. "Hee-Young—she always tell me everything." I pause; my next lie will surely elicit punishment, one day. "She tell me that she loved—loves you."

My heart hammers, but if Heta's caught my mistake, she doesn't let on, though I can't see her face to confirm. "I cared for her. Very deeply. I was so sad to see her go." And she really does sound sad.

"You didn't want her to leave."

"No, not like she did. If she'd waited, or maybe gone about things differently, it would've been better."

"Different . . . how? Better?" I change tack, hoping to jar her into confessing something useful. "Did Hee-Young . . . when she was here, did she do drugs?" Ksenia had said no, but now that she's left with Garin, I can't trust what she told me.

"Drugs?" Heta laughs. "No more than the ones they give us." Her answer's the same as Ksenia's. "Sounds like you didn't know her as well as you thought."

Which matches what I'd suspected. Hee-Young's condition was something done to her, not something she did to herself. The next question bubbles out of my mouth as if it were made of helium. "Why do you like Shepherd? Cannot . . . trust?"

There's a pause, and then she sighs dreamily. "I was a present for him," she says, her voice drifting. "My father had trained me well, taught me how to pose and giggle, how to submit quietly. But he'd done something bad, something that had put him and my mother in a dangerous position and left him with a debt—I don't know what kind, but I know it wasn't money. We had all the money in the world." Another sigh. "When my father gave me to Shepherd, everything was wiped clean. That made me feel so *important*. My father always told me how grown up I was. I was always trying so hard to be grown up."

The sheets rustle, and I know from the way that her voice gets louder that she's turned to face me. "Shepherd is not a bad man. He has strong emotions that he sometimes struggles to control, but don't all men? And if you are good, and fortunate enough to be someone he prizes, he rewards you well."

My head is spinning, now, my eyelids drooping. She seems to know it, because she says, "Let me know if you need the bathroom or anything else. Otherwise, I'll see you in the morning."

I wait five minutes before I murmur her name. "Heta?"

She doesn't answer, but I can tell she's awake. I lay back against the pillow, resolving to wait for my opening to sneak out. But the adrenaline coursing through my body is no match for a month of hallucinations and near starvation. Before long, my eyes shut, and I'm sound asleep.

FIFTY-EIGHT

Hee-Jin

I wake, panicking at the view of my room's walls—but then I see Heta slumbering next to me. My panic ebbs, but it does not disappear: the door may be open, but I'm still locked in all the same.

To my surprise, she cracks an eye and smiles at me. "Hello, sleepyhead. Been waiting for you to wake up."

"Sorry. I was tired."

"Let's get dressed, shall we?" She stands to retrieve our clothes. Yesterday was Wednesday, which means today is Thursday, so it's white sweatsuits—but the patrons will arrive tomorrow, bringing greater security, more facilitators, more spying eyes. It's better to escape tonight—but where will I go? Was Shepherd's plan all along to make it impossible to slip unseen into the fabric of this country by turning me into a monster?

I plan as we wash our faces, as we brush our teeth, as she wheels me out to breakfast. I can tell she sees the spines on my face, the new ones growing on my neck—but she seems determined to ignore them. I wonder if Shepherd instructed her to pretend they weren't there.

The next few hours feel like the heavy pressure before a storm. I keep waiting for something to happen, feeling the throb of it in my head, the aching in my joints, but there's nothing definitive—just a fog of slights and not-quite threats, like Ksenia's absence, or the way Shepherd is at the side door of the right wing when the bell-tone for studio time rings, letting us in and out as if we were indecisive cats.

He's watching me. Reminding me he's here. Ca-lee is absent, as he said she'd be, though facilitators bustle down the halls with trays of wine and food. Each time we pass her door and the missing alcove phone, I have to fight to stop myself from trying to peer through the wall, as if I could catch a glimpse of the woman convalescing within.

By dinner, an entire day of fraught observation has left me both starving and exhausted—and if I'm going to make it far tonight, I'll need my energy. I wait while the facilitator sets down my platter, full of fish and potatoes and wine.

But I don't focus on the food. Instead, my attention keeps being pulled by the little white basket of stones in the middle of the table. I suddenly wonder how it would feel to insert one into my mouth—its iron-dust taste, the sensation of it scraping past my teeth, its pebbled texture on my tongue. Suddenly, my mouth is watering, and I want nothing more than to eat these rocks, one by one.

I turn and angrily stab my spoon into the fish. Is this, then, what compelled Ksenia to swallow those stones when she thought no one was looking? Could it be an effect of the sickness that Shepherd claims I have, my brain prodding me toward a mineral my body lacks?

Or is it from the drugs? Because Ksenia and Heta are right—we're being drugged, all the time, until there's no way to know if any experience we are having is really ours. Last night, I passed out minutes after Heta brought me back to the room. Was it just exhaustion?

Or maybe it was the rice porridge. That's what I would do, if I had a group of six women I wanted to keep quiet every night. I'd drug the food. Which means that despite my hunger, I can't eat tonight—and something tells me I need to keep my abstention a secret.

I cheek my dinner, stopping every so often to spit my food into my napkin. I pretend to drift, letting my head nod forward, acting as if I'm struggling to keep my eyes peeled. I wait for the right moment, which turns out to be an animated conversation during which Sarah and Sumi are playing hand games under the table.

I inch up to the edge of my seat. "Thank you," I say to Heta, and then I give her a theatrical yawn. "For taking such good care of me."

"Oh, you're welcome." She seems surprised but pleased. "I just—"

I pretend that I have nodded off and fall dramatically from my seat, grabbing the edge of the tablecloth while dropping my full napkin on the ground. The plates come sliding forward and tip over the edge of the table. Glasses empty, silverware clatters. Facilitators rush into the room; I can only hope one didn't see me spitting my food into my napkin.

"I'm so sorry." I wheeze and shake my head. "I don't know . . . I . . . so tired."

Heta pats my back. "Maybe we should get you back to your room."

Shouldn't she be more worried, asking for the doctor? Or is this proof there really were drugs in my food—and that she knew about it?

She beckons for the facilitators. One steps forward, knowing what she needs without asking. I hate it so much, his hands on my body, the warmth of his breath on my scalp.

As we descend the staircase, I do my best to go limp, like a sack of rice. I pretend to perk up a bit when they set me back in the chair.

"Thank you," she says, patting the facilitator on the back, but he of course doesn't answer.

She pushes me back to our room, trying to make idle conversation, but my mind's already on my next steps. Once they shut off the lights, I'll be stumbling around in the dark, trying not to wake her, unless I can get her away from the room while I grab what I need. "Heta . . . can you bring book from library?"

She's just stepped in, the door still closing behind her. "What?"

"The library. I would like book."

She snorts. "What book?"

"Any book." Too late, I realize that she might know about Hee-Young's storybook, might take my request as some kind of sign. But she rolls her eyes and leaves.

She'll only be gone for a minute. As quick as I can, I roll myself to the painting-door and retrieve my scalpel-tool, Hee-Young's marble, my flashlight magnet. I wrap my supplies in the beetle dress and shove the bundle under my pillow, where it'll be easy to grab. Everything else I leave in the shaft—the bundle is bulky as it is.

As soon as I finish tucking it in, she reappears with a small stack of books in her hands. "I couldn't find anything very fun.

There's some poetry, something about botany, a fantasy book, and a gothic novel that looks a hundred years old." She piles them next to my side of the bed. "All right," she says. "Let's get you changed."

"No . . . thank you," I say, my pulse hammering. I'll have better mobility in my sweatsuit. "Too cold."

She raises an eyebrow. For a moment, I think she'll press the issue—and if she does, I'll fold, because I can't have her getting suspicious—but then she shakes her head and moves to help me out of the chair. I hop slowly to the edge of the bed on one foot before sitting down.

For a moment, the room *is* cold, impossibly so. I lean back against the wall, grateful for the support. Anxiety rumbles through my guts like thunder. Maybe I wasn't drugged at dinner, but I'm already tired. Just getting into bed was taxing enough. I don't know how I'll manage an escape.

I try to remain seated, but my body aches. Heta steps into the bathroom to start her rituals—brushing her hair until it shines, polishing each tooth until it's perfect. A slob like me must be torture for her.

When I hear the doorknob turn, I slide down onto my back and close my eyes. If this is going to work, I have to pretend to be asleep.

But as the hours tick on, her doing nothing more interesting than reading, I realize there's no pretending.

FIFTY-NINE
Hee-Jin

"*Wake up, Hee-Jin.*"

The air smells vaguely of oranges and fresh mint. I open my eyes into the perfect darkness that fills our rooms at night, but there *is* something I can see: Hee-Young, standing at the foot of my bed. She's still wearing the linen summer suit, and on her finger is a ring I almost don't recognize, until I imagine myself tossing it up and over the back of the healthcare booth in the subway station: clear plastic, full of copper and gold and black fibers.

They look familiar. My mind almost makes the connection, but her urgent whisper breaks my train of thought. "Time to go." She turns her spined face away from me, once again the mirror of my own, and then she disappears.

For a moment, I can't move. When I saw her before, I was being tortured, alone, in a room where everything was always the same—conjuring Hee-Young was just my brain trying to cope.

Now she's back, and I don't know what that means.

But she was right about the time. Heta snores next to me, soft little croaks like the call of frogs. I can't pull the same stunt at the table tomorrow. It's act now, or face the patron dinner. And while Shepherd may be content to keep me under guard for the moment—how long before he decides he needs a more permanent solution to the problem?

Despite the fear stiffening my limbs, I slowly reach out until I feel the edge of the mattress. I grab it to anchor myself and roll, a centimeter at a time, my muscles shaking as they hold me at odd angles, my ears open and waiting for Heta's snores to stop. Halfway there, I have to put pressure on my ankle, which throbs with a warning, but I block it out the best I can.

Next comes pushing myself into a seated position. Heta must have removed my splint. Without it, I won't be able to walk at all. I find it on the side table and quietly strap it on, unlatching and closing the Velcro so slowly it's like I'm not moving at all, and then I slip my hand underneath my pillow to retrieve the bundle.

Finally, there's nothing left to do but stand—but it's pitch dark, and my ankle is only semi-functional. I don't want to alert Heta by shifting the bed, so I slowly slide my legs over the edge of the mattress and then lean forward until I feel the ground.

A frisson runs down my spine when my good foot touches—but then the bed creaks and Heta's snores stop. I freeze, halfway to a standing position, and try to come up with an excuse. *I needed to use the bathroom. I thought I heard a noise.*

She coughs lightly and rolls over. After a minute, she starts to snore again, though not as deeply as before.

I say a quick word of thanks to my mother, and then I carefully straighten the rest of the way until I'm standing and my weight is off the mattress. No change from Heta. Relieved, I limp forward with my arms held out until I find one of the walls. I use it to trace my way to the door, and then I push it open and slip out.

In the hallway, there's the thinnest trickle of brightness, reflected main-floor moonlight that has leaked down the staircase's aperture. And yet, as I lean against the wall and limp toward that small, dim pool marking the exit, trying my hardest not to make a sound, I can see the shape of the room so well that unease twists my stomach. I close my eyes and reach up, prod my lids with my fingertips. I can't be certain, but they feel bigger. Rounder.

But there's no time to think about this right now, so I resume limping forward. Every step lights up my ankle with fire, but I grit my teeth and start reciting to myself: *The table is hot. My ankle doesn't hurt. The table is hot.*

After a few minutes, the insistent pain seems to fade. "*Good job.*" Hee-Young appears down the hallway, in the middle of the small ring of light from the staircase. "I would've expected as much, given—" She makes a vee with her pointer and middle finger and points it at her own eyes, before blinking away again.

Sweat breaks out across my forehead, down my back. I stick close to the wall, careful not to push too hard and accidentally disturb one of the doors. When I make it to the staircase,

Hee-Young reappears, though she's now sitting on the bottom step. The clear resin of the ring on her finger sparkles so brightly in the light that I panic, before I remember that nobody else in the house can see the flashes.

"Move," I whisper, before realizing I can likely pass through her. Still, I'm not sure how I'll get up the stairs.

"*Like this.*" She leans backward and places her palms on the step above her, before using her arms to lift her body and scoot up one of the stairs, like a crab. "*This feels dangerous, though. Like it would be too easy to slip down.*"

I ignore her and grab onto the railing. But with stairs, I can't limp along like I did before—no matter what I do, at some point, I have to put all my weight on my bad leg. The sudden shock of pain sucks the breath from my lungs.

"*Or like this,*" she says, turning over. She climbs up on her hands and knees, her feet trailing off the step behind her. "*This is hard, too. Either way, you've got to be careful.*"

Hee-Young is right. If I don't follow her advice, I'll never get up these stairs—and any moment, a facilitator could see me and sound the alarm. I've got no choice.

I lower myself to the ground and roll over onto my hands and knees. One step, then the next. The pressure of the treads on my knees is meditation, sharpening the mind.

"*It's like when we were children.*" Now, her voice is at the top of the stairs.

For a moment, I think she means when we lived in that apartment with the roof access. We used to go up and down the stairs on all fours, pretending to be tigers or wolves—but then I remember when we were naughty, and our mother used to make us kneel on grains of uncooked rice. The longer we stayed in that position, the more they'd dig into our skin—and every time we shifted our weight, trying to relieve our agony, to find better balance, they'd light up our whole world with pain.

This, too, is agony, but I ignore it and follow Hee-Young up the stairs.

SIXTY
Hee-Jin

Once I'm finally on the main floor, there's more light to see by. I pull myself into a standing position and let out a long breath, thankful the torture is over. Remembering the loud groan of the front door when I first arrived, I decide on the side door off the right wing, which exits into the gardens.

I can almost taste my freedom.

Maybe my ankle has resigned itself to its lot, or maybe it's grateful for the rest it just received, but my progress is faster. My heart quickens as I get close—but when I'm six feet away, I catch a glimpse of something shiny hanging off the side of the door.

It's not until the cold metal of the massive padlock is under my hands, though, that I understand the truth. Maybe this is why I didn't instantly fall asleep tonight. Shepherd has secured the door with a hasp, so there was no need to drug me. If he padlocked this door, he no doubt secured the front door, as well.

Still, though, I need to check.

I turn and progress back toward the lobby. My ankle has started to throb again, but I push myself forward. Once I get close enough, I can make out the hanging form of another padlock, this one even bigger than the last.

I almost sink to the floor in the middle of the lobby, but then Hee-Young reappears to slip her hand in mine. I look down, surprised by its warmth. Even the spines that stick out from the back of her hand feel like they've been touched by the sun.

"*There's another door*," she whispers.

She's right. There's a door in the room Ca-lee called the *servant's kitchen*. Ca-lee pressed that token around her neck against it to open it on the day of my tour—which means that it's usually locked, too. But when Shepherd was picking doors to secure, he might not have thought it necessary to put a padlock on that one.

By now, even the limping and leaning on the wall has taken its toll, but I pick my way through the gloom, back down the tunnel hall that leads to the servant's kitchen in the left wing.

Just like I thought, there's no padlock on it—though when I try the knob, I can tell it's locked. I struggle with it for a minute before considering my options. I could try going out a window, though they're so far off the ground that it'll be almost impossible in my condition. And Ca-lee had mentioned that they don't open for safety, although I no longer believe that's the reason.

I could try escaping tomorrow, during the day, try to slip away from studio time or one of the meals, but I don't think Heta will let me out of her sight. Even when I go to the bathroom, she insists on standing right outside the door. In broad daylight, with all the facilitators around, there's no way I'll make it as far as the tree line. And by nightfall, the patrons will be here.

I need a key. *Now*. Like the one around Ca-lee's neck. Is there a chance she keeps it there, even when sleeping? If not, is it possible for me to find it in the dark without waking her?

Do I have any other choice?

I turn, looking for Hee-Young, but she's deserted me again. And I'm not sure, but the night outside looks just a bit brighter than when I first came up here.

In other words, I'm running out of time. I've got to get that key.

SIXTY-ONE
Hee-Jin

I double back down the hallway. It's not until I'm ten feet away from Ca-lee's room that the fear kicks in. This was the woman that caught me going through Heta's things and confined me for a month without telling anyone. I don't want to know what she'll do if she catches me tonight.

"*She's not so bad*," says Hee-Young, though it's clear from her tone that she's making fun of me. I ignore her and work on fishing the flashlight magnet out of the bag, before wrapping it tightly with the beetle dress. When I squeeze the button on the bottom, only the faintest glow leaks out.

I crack the door to listen. Ca-lee doesn't snore like Heta, and I can just make out the soft shuffling of her breath, like the rush of air through dead leaves. Little by little, I wedge the door open until it's wide enough to slide in.

Penetrating the warm, moist air is not unlike entering the studio, though the room assaults me with her scent: the miasma of unwashed sickness. I wonder if that's how I smelled when Shepherd opened the door to let me out, if he'd stepped in and been as revolted as I am now.

But I need to find the key.

I cup my hand around the flashlight's beam to stifle it and squeeze the button. Ca-lee is on the bed, and there's the glint of something shiny around her neck. I release the button and wait, breath held, to see if I've woken her.

I don't think so. Now comes the hard part.

I creep forward, sweeping my bad leg in front of me before taking a step to make sure I don't run into anything, but it's hard to tell how close I am. Even my improved vision can't compete with perfect darkness.

And then I get an idea, an impossible one so crazy that it makes me afraid I came up with it. But I need this pendant. *The table is hot*. "Hee-Young," I whisper as quietly as I can.

She pops into view in front of me, the white illumination of her body somehow doing nothing to dispel the dark. "*Yes, dear sister?*" she mocks.

"Go over there and hold onto her pendant so I can find it."

She giggles and skips forward on the tips of her toes like a ballerina. The noise makes me flinch, but I wait as she reaches down and cups something invisible in her palm. "*Got it.*"

I'm insane, I know it. Whatever happened to me when I was locked alone in that room, it's not reversible. But Hee-Young looks about the right distance away. I creep forward again, still checking with my bad foot as I limp across the room. I approach from the head of the bed until I'm two feet from where Hee-Young is standing. Then, I bend forward and reach out my hand, keeping it low and bringing it up slowly. My fingertips meet the mattress.

"*You can trust me, Hee-Jin.*"

I'm already terrified, but the cold in Hee-Young's voice sends electricity through my body. What if she's not just a hallucination? What if she really *is* a ghost, pinned to some object in this place by her outrage at her untimely death? If so, she could be unraveling, becoming more monstrous with every passing moment.

I walk my fingers up the mattress as softly as I can, toward Hee-Young's cupped hand. The fabric is familiar, the sheets the same as the ones in my room.

"*Not like that,*" Hee-Young hisses. "*You'll wake her, touching everything like a spider. You're the one that asked me to hold onto this pendant—now grab it.*"

Maybe Hee-Young isn't a ghost. Maybe she's some deep, lizard part of my brain, one that emerges when a person's terrified for their own survival, one that mapped this room in the momentary glow of the flashlight magnet.

Or maybe the lack of things for my eyes to hold on to have just brought the trauma of being locked in my room to the surface.

Hee-Young, sensing my next move, opens her hand and lays it down flat, palm up. There's nothing there, but I reach forward in the dark with fingers I can't see—and feel something under my fingertips, right in the space I imagine her palm should be: cold and hard, like metal.

I hold my breath and open my fingers slightly, wiggle them under the edges of the thick coin of the pendant-key. Leaving as much slack in the cord as I can, I pull it toward me. My heart hammers so hard I'm sure Ca-lee will hear it, even in sleep. If I leaned forward, in this moment, I could kiss her upside down, like an illustration from Hee-Young's fairytale book.

Before long, I've brought it up as high as I can. The base of the cord is still pinned under her head. If I could just figure out how to wiggle it out from under her—

And then the pressure suddenly releases as she turns over. Before I can check if I've got it in my hand, I overbalance backward and windmill my arms frantically, dislodging something from my pocket. It hits the bedframe with a *pink* before I lose my center of gravity and fall onto my ass with a *thump*.

Ca-lee stops breathing and sits up.

I hold my breath again. I can hear everything—the crackle of salivary glands activating in her mouth, the pop of her eardrums as they adjust to her being awake. If she gets out of bed, she'll step on me.

I ready myself to fight. If I throw her down, I might be able to stun her enough to make it out of the room and into a hiding place before the lights go on and people come running out into the hallway.

And I can feel the solid edge of the pendant in my fist, too hard-won to let go of.

"Shep?" She clears her throat. "Is that you?"

She sounds afraid. It's delicious—I don't care that she's ill. She deserves to be afraid. Deserves to be terrified every night of her life for what she did to me.

"Shep?"

Another long pause. Hee-Young appears again, lowers herself down from the ceiling to float over the bed even as Ca-lee whispers, her voice trembling, "Lisa?"

We're too close, Ca-lee and I—her with her imaginary child, me with my dead sister.

I concentrate hard on Ca-lee, willing her back to sleep. Ten minutes pass, then twenty. Finally, though, she starts to breathe deeply again, and I crawl across the carpet on my hands and knees before letting myself out of the room.

There is no word for my progress now but agony. Agony, because my ankle burns like molten metal, because I'm more tired than

I've ever been, because at any moment, a flashlight could click on or a door could open, and all of this would be for nothing.

I can't think about that right now. I just have to keep going: hand in front of hand, foot in front of foot.

Somehow, I make it down the hallway to the servant's kitchen, where Hee-Young is waiting by the door. "*I wouldn't go out that way*," she says.

A jolt of fear. I wish I knew—is this Hee-Young's ghost, my own insanity, or just some part of my brain trying to warn me? But I can't stay here. I hold the pendant up to the door and try the knob.

Still locked.

A sob escapes me, frustration compacted down inside until it vibrates with the tense quiver of a stretched rubber band. I must've done it wrong. I hold the pendant up again, and again, and again, and still the door doesn't open.

Hee-Young starts to taunt me, singing a children's song in my ear, though it takes me a moment to recognize the words she's translated into English: "*Three bears, living in a house. Daddy bear, mommy bear, and baby bear—*"

I try to ignore her. Ca-lee's a bit taller than me, I think. Was her arm stretched high?

"*Daddy bear is fat, fat, fat—*"

I push the pendant up as far as I can, and then I let my arm fall slowly, dragging the pendant down the door.

"*Mommy bear is thin, thin, thin—*"

A loud *kak* echoes inches from my head. I grab the knob and turn it—

"*Baby bear is so, so-o-o-o cute—*"

The door swings open, revealing the night.

SIXTY-TWO
Hee-Jin

I gently close the door behind me. I'm tensed for an alarm, for the sounds of running feet and men's shouts, but nothing disturbs the endless chorus of the crickets save the calls of a few night birds and the peep of frogs. Behind the reflective lines of the greenhouse, the gardens stretch in front of me. They're still marked with odd patterns that shine with moisture set ablaze by the full moon, though their beauty quickly dissolves into the dark, undulating twists of the tree line.

My salvation, my chance to hide. I shamble forward as fast as I can, but the terrain is too uneven for my ankle, even dampened by the adrenaline running through my veins. The air chills my damp sweatshirt, making me shiver despite the exertion, and when I glance back at the house, I'm shocked to see traces of the purpley-blue glow shimmering around it like mist, the same as I did the day Shepherd wheeled me into the garden.

Once I make it to the tree line, I realize how desperate this plan was. The trunks are sparse at first, but after ten feet, they become too tight to pass through, crowded with brambles and bushes and new-growing vines. The ground shifts without rhyme or reason, full of jagged valleys hidden by piles of dead leaves. Without a path, there's no way I'll make it far enough to avoid being caught.

I double back, hatching a new plan as I go. When I make it to the gardens' manicured lawns, I hug the side of the property, looping toward the road. Surely, someone will eventually drive by, someone I can stop and beg to take me anywhere else—because out here, in the night air, everything that's happened since I set foot inside this house suddenly snaps into startling focus: *Ksenia's odd fear of Ca-lee, the way she hid in the shaft and seemed to exit her body. The gaps in time that must be from drugs in my food. Being locked in my room for weeks, then having Heta as my prison guard. Finding clues about Hee-Young that suddenly disappear. The flyers Shepherd showed me, now distributed all over town—*

I stop dead. In the close-cropped picture, my eyes were closed. I'd assumed it was just an airport photo, taken at the wrong moment—but thinking on it now, didn't it look as if my hair was spread out around my shoulders? As if I'd been lying down?

Another violation while I wasn't awake to see it.

I fight off the urge to vomit and make it to the tunnel we went through on our way in. From the other side, the house had looked otherworldly, floating in a circle of light. Now, though, there's just a dim patch where the exit should be. Halfway down its length, I hear a rustling, like leaves. I stop and listen, but there's nothing but the ragged sounds of my own breath.

I spy the hill sloping down in front of me, the twisting road as it rapidly vanishes. The small patch of sky I catch through the tunnel, though, is already turning gray. Not long until dawn.

Behind me, something snaps like a branch, its echoes bouncing softly around the tunnel.

My heart stops. *Run*, I scream inside, but my body's paralyzed. I fight it, until little by little, I manage to turn my head—

A tall man stands in the moonlight, his body powerfully built. He's wearing an unbuttoned suit jacket, either light-gray or beige, I can't tell—but across its front is a giant, dark stain that glimmers wetly.

Blood, I think, still frozen. And then he takes a step forward, the shadows falling away from his face. *Garin.*

His gaze connects with mine. He raises his fist, only he's clutching something—a long, fat blade, like a kitchen knife.

Fear tears through me. I finally uproot myself and flee the rest of the way through the tunnel, pain firing up my ankle, my leg, as terror shrinks my vision into a pinhole—

Something collides with my back, and I tip over forward. I hit the ground, but before I can try to scramble up or even turn to see, Garin grabs the back of my head and slams my face against the earth, stunning me and filling my ears with the roar of a train. A cloth is shoved in my mouth, a fabric bag descends over my face. Garin zips what feels like a plastic tie around my wrists before roughly dragging me to my feet. He's trussed me up as neatly as a game animal, and all before I even managed to get another look at him.

I try to fight again, but then he punches me in the head, hard enough to make my ears ring.

Pressure against my spine guides me forward. Even blind, I know I'm being turned, brought back to the house.

PART VI

The End

Tyger Tyger burning bright,
In the forests of the night:
What immortal hand or eye,
Dare frame thy fearful symmetry?

'The Tyger', William Blake

SIXTY-THREE
Hee-Jin

I've been carried up and down the stairs so many times that, even with the bag over my head, I know I'm descending the center staircase. At the end of the journey, Garin sets me in a chair and zip ties my legs to it: first my good leg, then my bad, making me scream.

A long pause comes next. I pant around the cloth, my breath moist and stinking inside the bag. Finally, the cloth is slid away from my head, but my eyes are sluggish to adjust to the dim light. Seconds pass as a shadowy figure materializes. I blink until the lines coalesce into a form.

Not Garin. It's *Heta*, a pillowcase in her hand. They must be working together.

We're in one of the bedrooms. It's hers; I recognize it. Behind her, on the bed, a battery-powered camping lantern throws a ghostly blue-white glow around the room. She leans forward and pulls the cloth out of my mouth.

"Heta . . . listen—"

"Shut up," she snaps. She paces back and forth before sitting on the bed and removing a phone from her pocket that she unlocks with her finger. I'm so surprised that for a moment, I don't ask myself what she's using it for.

She types something out and sets it down next to her on the bed. "You're a very stupid girl, even worse than your sister. You know that? He wasn't going to touch you. Do you understand how lucky you are? If you'd been anybody else, you would've had to suffer the same as the rest of us, and even though it would've been worth it in the end—" For just a second, her eyes go glassy, but then she shakes it off, and her face twists with something low and mean. "But you didn't have to. All you had to do was keep your head down, and once he knew he could trust you, he would've given you everything you wanted. You would've had it made. Why couldn't you just do that? You're just like *her.* Just ruining things for everyone."

My heart races. I don't understand what's happening—what Heta means by *worse than your sister*, or how she even found out we were sisters, or if *he* is Garin or Shepherd or someone else entirely.

"He's going to be in a terrible mood, after this. And he doesn't deserve it—he's so *good*, really, in his own way. As long as you follow the rules and do what he wants, he's the most wonderful person." She blossoms as she says this, her face glowing in the reflected light of the phone, turning sweet with the exalted expression of the pious.

It's ghastly.

When a soft *ding* sounds, she grabs the phone anxiously, but it's just the bell-tone, announcing that it's time to wake up. A moment later, the room suffuses with the artificial dawn.

Hee-Young appears in the corner of my vision. "*She's kind of a bitch, isn't she?*"

I know there's no way she's real, but I can't help the growing dread that Heta's somehow going to sense Hee-Young's presence and punish me for it.

"*I heard her family is rich,*" my sister says as she circles around behind Heta. "*Well-connected in the art world. They've got a bunch of paintings they bought off Nazis after the holocaust and refuse to give them back, so you know they're a lost cause.*"

By now, she's behind Heta, peering down at her phone. "*Aigo,*" she utters, the exact same way our mother used to do when she caught us as children, our pockets stuffed with stolen melon candies from the convenience store in front of the dry-cleaner's. "*I think you want to know what this says, Hee-Jin. Should I read it to you?*"

I swallow, but she doesn't do anything but stare at me, waiting for a response. Just because she's my hallucination doesn't mean I'm in control. I give her the slightest of nods.

Hee-Young clears her throat. "*It's some kind of text app. She sent:* She tried to escape. *And then there's a response*: Then she's proved we can't trust her. You know what you have to do, Heta. Show me how much you care and how devoted you are, and you will be rewarded. *And then there's another message from her*: I don't know if I can do that."

She raises her eyebrows and turns her face away while covering her mouth—a cutesy, exaggerated gesture that belongs more in a cheesy commercial than here in this terrible room, though it's made grotesque by the spines across her face and her bulging eyes. "*Heta's either going to make love to you or kill you*," she says with a conspiratorial wink.

No, that can't be true. Despite everything, despite all Heta's strangeness—there's no way that she'd actually commit *murder*, is there? Hee-Young's words are just my worst fears being routed through my imagination.

The phone buzzes again. They both lean over at the same time to check the message, but only Hee-Young reads it out loud. "I know you can. I love you, Heta. Don't you love me?" She continues, narrating in a high-pitched, breathy voice as Heta types: "Of course. But I'm afraid."

The other person is quick to respond. "Why don't you come up, and we can talk it over?" Hee-Young turns away before wrapping her arms around her body. Her hands skim up and down her own sides as she pretends to make out noisily with someone.

A moment later, Heta stands and leaves the room.

"*Wonder where she's headed*," Hee-Young cackles.

SIXTY-FOUR

Hee-Jin

I know in my heart of hearts that Hee-Young isn't real. That whatever the messages on the phone said, they couldn't have involved Heta openly discussing my murder.

I know it, but I can't make myself believe it. Indecision and anguish battle inside of me like two cats circling in an alley, until I realize that *it doesn't matter.* After months of feeling weak—sad, suspicious, terrified—I am now just *furious.* I don't care why any of this is happening, what someone has or hasn't done, what they will or won't do. I just want the *fuck* out of this chair.

I reach down with my bound hands and grab the zip ties on my good ankle. I pull so hard my arms tremble and the plastic digs hard into the skin of my leg, but there's no way I'm getting it off like this.

As I lean to check the other ankle, something pokes me in the abdomen. I reach into my pocket and pull out the flashlight magnet. I must have remembered to stash it once I was outside. Which means—

I shove my bound hands into the pocket of my sweatpants. There's something there, a hard, thin object along the side. I wiggle my fingers, scooping the best I can, until it's between my palms. Still, I don't dare to let myself hope until I pull it out into the light.

It's the little scalpel-tool. And looped over the protective cap is a cord, Ca-lee's key dangling on the end.

"*Nice*," Hee-Young says appreciatively.

I block her out. I need to free my hands first. I shake the key off and remove the cap with my mouth before sliding the handle of the scalpel-tool between my back teeth, the way I did with the flashlight before exploring the shaft.

Careful. If I drop it, I might not be able to reach it on the floor.

I bring my hands up and frantically saw at the zip tie. Spit trails down the metal handle. It's too close to see well, and I lean forward too fast and stab myself in the meat of my palm.

The cry is reflexive—a quick gasp, the opening of my jaws—and the scalpel-tool falls and bounces off the carpet. It comes to a stop three feet to my left. I lean over as far as I can before the chair rocks underneath me, threatening to tip.

"*Oh*," says Hee-Young. "*Seems like you're out of luck*."

I almost snap at her to help me before remembering she's not there. I refocus on my hands. The zip tie is still intact, but I've managed to cut a deep groove halfway through it. I bring it to my teeth and bite one side, and then I pull my arms away from me as hard as I can.

The tie snaps off. My hands are free.

But I still need the scalpel-tool, which means this next part is going to hurt. If I throw my hands out as I hit the ground, I might be able to break my fall—hopefully without breaking my wrist.

I lean as far as I can. The chair rocks but doesn't fully tip. I throw my weight sideways like a child trying to jump-start a swing. On the fourth rock, I feel myself teeter on two legs—and then I'm up and over. There isn't time to react before my head smacks into the floor.

I feel nauseated, my ears ringing. But I reach out with my hand, extending as far as I can, and I just barely brush the handle with my fingertips. It's not quite close enough.

I reach out with both arms, grab onto the carpet, and take a deep breath—and then I pull. My fingertips scream, but the chair slides forward, just an inch.

I do it again, and again. Blood from the cut on my palm stains the carpet fibers, leaving bright red smears. I reach again, and this time, I get my fingers around the handle. I curl back up and start with my good leg first, saw and saw until I snap through the tie. I go for the other leg—

There's that sudden rush of sound, the change in air pressure, as the door swings open. I'm too close to the bed to see Heta, but I hear her come thudding around the outside of the room. I try to push myself up, but I'm still lashed to the chair.

When she breaks into my view, my blood goes cold. She's holding a hypodermic syringe filled with a milky-white liquid, and for a moment, I'm transported to finding Hee-Young's body, that spray of pearlescent vomit.

"You have to make everything hard," she says, her eyes narrowing.

She raises the syringe overhead and lunges at me, ready to stab it down. Too late, she sees me move. The scalpel-tool flashes as it glides up. I ram it into the side of her throat as hard as I can and then pull down with all my weight.

A mist of blood sprays across my face, coating my open mouth in copper. She drops the syringe and grabs at her throat with both hands, but she can't stop the blood that spurts in a wide arc across the room.

She crawls backward, away from me, making gurgling noises. After a few more seconds, the light fades from her eyes.

I pick up the scalpel, now slick with her blood, and finish cutting myself loose.

SIXTY-FIVE
Hee-Jin

Once my leg is free, I grab the edge of the bed for support and drag myself into a standing position before stumbling over to Heta's body. I don't look at her face or the gash cleaving her throat. I try not to think about her hands, so saturated that it looks like she dipped them in a paint bucket.

I swallow my bile and go through her pockets. In the left one, I find a pen and a wrapped hard candy. The right holds what I need: the phone.

I fiddle with the buttons, and the screen comes to life. *Swipe to unlock.*

And then: *Use your fingerprint or enter PIN to unlock.*

Fingerprint?

I flip the phone over. There's a small ring on the back, underneath the camera lenses. When I tilt the phone, a smudge catches the light in the middle of the ring.

I lean over Heta and grab one of her hands. Press her warm index finger into it, but when that doesn't work, I try the other index and both middle fingers without success.

"*Try her thumb*," Hee-Young says from over my shoulder.

I pick her hand back up and extract her right thumb. Underneath her flesh, the protruding knob of her knuckle feels like the pit of a cherry.

I push the pad of her thumb to the circle, and the phone unlocks. I glance nervously in Hee-Young's direction, but she's not there.

The screen now shows three icons: a small phone, a speech bubble with the word *Messaging* underneath, and a stylized illustration of face with a hand covering one eye, called *Wispr.*

I select the phone and punch in 911, the emergency number I know from so many American movies. I hold my breath, but the green phone icon at the top turns red, the words *Unable to connect* underneath in gray.

"*No signal underground*," Hee-Young says, now at my right. I glance over my shoulder. She's squatting next to Heta's body, her chin in her palm, as if puzzling over an ant hill.

I check the display at the top of the screen, and she's right: no bars, an *x* over the icon for the data connection, though the wi-fi icon blinks off and on, as if syncing.

The messages that Heta and her unseen partner—Garin?—were sending must have been over wi-fi. If there's no phone signal, I might be able to place a call that way—but I'll need time to go through the phone settings and figure out how to change them. The lights are on, which means that the tone for breakfast will sound any second, and everyone will emerge to walk up to the dining room. Already, the whole floor above me is crawling with facilitators.

Maybe I can use that. I can run out and throw myself at the mercy of the crowd, beg them to help me—

Except that *I'm* the one that killed her, and I can't prove that it was self-defense, that she was going to stab me with the syringe. I don't even know what's in it; it could just be something to knock me out and make me more pliant until a doctor or the police come to claim me. But that milky-white color, I've seen it before, floating at the top of a drink with colorful pink bands of alcohol, pouring out of Hee-Young's body—somehow, I know it's all the same.

I don't know what to do. Even if I could somehow get the staff or the other girls to listen to me, I have no way of knowing how devoted they are, where their alliances lie. After all, they all told me Garin left with Ksenia, and yet I saw him behind me in the tunnel. It's possible they lied to cover for him, to help him . . . what? Take over the house?

It seems ludicrous, and I can't understand what he'd want with me, why Shepherd wouldn't let me leave. Could it be so simple as not wanting the police to find out about the girls?

The realization hits me like a frigid wave from the East Sea. I'm a murderer. I have to get off this property, and fast. As soon as Heta and I don't show up for breakfast, someone will come to check—but there's no way I'll get far enough away to escape, not right now.

What if I hid somewhere, and just let them *assume* I escaped? I can sneak out later, when it's dark again, after the patrons have all dined and gone to bed. I don't even have to make it all the way out of the house—if I can just make it to the main floor, I can get a signal on Heta's phone and call the police. I don't have to tell them who I am, or what happened. I could report Heta's murder to create a distraction and then escape while everyone is being questioned.

It's a desperate, risky plan, but it's the best one I have. And I think I know a place that nobody—save maybe Ksenia—would think to look.

My stomach drops. Ksenia's been missing, but Garin's still here. If he *didn't* take her away, then it's possible something terrible has happened to her, same as Heta was about to do to me.

There's no more time to think. I creep to the door, hold my breath, and peek out. There's nobody in the hallway yet. I can still make it back to my room.

"*I think you're forgetting something*," Hee-Young says from behind me.

Against my better instincts, I turn back and flinch. She's sitting on Heta's chest.

"What is it?"

She shrugs and reaches down to stroke one of Heta's fingers. "*How, dear sister, are you going to unlock the phone?*"

Too late, I realize what she means, but she's right.

"*Get her lantern, too*," Hee-Young says, as I reach for the scalpel.

SIXTY-SIX
Hee-Jin

I sneak into my room just as the bell-tone rings for breakfast. I can't hear the others yet, but they'll soon be out there, chatting and waiting for me and Heta.

There isn't enough time to wash Heta's blood off my face, though I grab a rag and wet it, along with a towel, a sheet, and some of the hangers from the closet. All of this I shove into the shaft before pushing myself in. I'm so thin now that I glide in easily, as if this space was made for me.

Once I close the painting-door, I jam the towel against it, blocking the little slits of the vent. It isn't perfect and wouldn't hold up at night, but by day, nobody will notice the faint light from inside the shaft. I turn Heta's lantern on and stand up on my tiptoes to put it on the ledge formed by the bend of the shaft above me. The faint light that trickles down is enough to work with for my new bird eyes.

I'm hoping the meager supplies I managed to grab are enough to make some sort of grappling system. If I can find a way to hook through the vertical grate up there without making too much noise, I might be able to pull myself up onto the ledge.

From there, I can try crawling through the door in the ceiling I managed to get open before falling down and spraining my ankle. If it doesn't go anywhere, the ledge will still give me a welcome place to rest and hide until I leave to place the call. Even if they get a dog and figure out I went into the shaft, almost nobody is thin enough to follow me all the way up.

But first, I need a rope.

I can't see into my room, which means I have to work quietly. When Heta's body is found, this room's the first place they'll check, and I don't want to alert anyone to my presence.

At this painstaking pace, it takes me forever to split the sheet into thin strips with the scalpel and braid them into a rope. I tie one end to the middle of the file. If it doesn't work, I'll try to make a hook with the coat hangers, but the file is sturdier. I wrap the file itself in another strip of the sheet, trying to pad it for the inevitable *clunk*.

There's no way, though, to completely avoid noise during the next part. I've got to try to throw the file between two of the grate's bars without being able to see them—and then I've got to slowly pull it toward me while hoping it will rotate enough that it gets stuck behind the bars.

It sounds impossible, but I have no choice.

I coil my sheet-rope so that it will unfurl easily and hold the file like a giant dart. With my eyes closed, I stop and listen, trying to hear into the room, but I don't catch anything.

I throw the file. It sails forward, the rope quickly unfurling—and smashes into the grate at the end with a *koong!* Even wrapped in the piece of sheet, it's loud.

I wait until I'm sure nobody is coming. And then I slowly take in the rope, the file dully grinding across the metal of the shaft. I pull until I've coiled the rope twice, three times, and then my heart sinks. If there's this much slack, it didn't catch the sewer grate.

"*This is fun*," Hee-Young says, her head popping over the top of the ledge. "*Do it again.*"

And because I have no other choice, I obey.

It takes seven attempts before I catch the grate. Seven crushing pulls of the file across the shaft, seven recoilings and loosings, seven times I have to stop, breath held, heart hammering, and wonder if this *koong* is the one that makes them decide to check my room and the shaft.

But on the seventh try, I coil the rope only a single time before there's a hard stop. If it wasn't for the shaft holding me up, I'd fall to the ground and weep.

I curl the rope around my hands like a mountain climber and give it a tug—first gently, and then harder, letting it take more of my weight. It feels steady enough, though I know that at any moment, the file could turn through the bars of the grate and send me crashing back down the shaft.

I plant one foot on the side of the shaft and pull, ignoring the sudden flare of pain. Plant the other. I take step after step as if scaling a rock face, winding the rope around my hands as I go.

When my eyes peer out over the edge of the ledge, horror fills my guts. The file's rotated so that it's almost vertical, like a minute hand at five to the hour. Only the slimmest fraction of it actually presses up against the bars.

I should go back down. Maybe give the rope a shake and try again from the bottom. Cresting the ledge and getting my body across will be the hardest part, and it would be safer to make sure I'm well anchored.

But the file could break at any moment, and it took me seven tries to hook it through the grate. It might've just been a fluke that I can't repeat.

I grit my teeth and pull as the edges of my vision go dark with pain.

Panting and slick with sweat, I make it over just as the bell-tone for studio time rings.

My body trembles, begging me to rest, but I'm just a few feet from the ceiling hatch. It's too narrow in here for me to sit up, so I crawl on my hands and knees. Once I'm squarely underneath, I straighten as far as I can with Heta's lantern, peering up into its dark confines.

It's another shaft, running horizontally, though this one has a long pipe running through it—just like the one I ripped off when I fell. The new shaft extends about a foot to my left before abruptly bending ninety degrees, stretching above me far enough that there's no way I can make it up there. To my right, it runs straight, parallel to the shaft I'm already in.

My spine tingles. An escape route, maybe. I need to see where it goes—but I also have to be careful. If I make too much noise or pop into view at the wrong time, I'll get caught.

I grab the edges to pull myself in.

"*Don't leave any of this stuff down here,*" Hee-Young admonishes. "*You might need it.*"

She's right, but I don't acknowledge her. I push everything into the shaft, far enough that I should be able to figure out a way to maneuver past it. Before I pull myself up, I remove Heta's phone from my pocket, along with my new cylindrical bundle. I unwrap the thumb and check the screen for signal, but there's still nothing.

I stash both back in my pockets and make my way into the shaft.

SIXTY-SEVEN
Hee-Jin

Without knowing where this shaft goes, I can't keep the lantern on and risk light leaking out and betraying my presence. Instead, I pull out the flashlight magnet and wrap the end in strips of sheet to stifle the beam, and then I crawl forward in the dark, stopping every so often to make sure I'm not about to fall through a hole.

It's hard to measure distance this way, especially when the need for stealth makes my pace impossibly slow, but I drag myself through the cramped shaft on my elbows and knees for what feels like forever. Before long, shapes dance in my vision again, though these are so mundane that I mostly ignore them: bobbing motes of light that weave before me like dandelion seeds, colored strips like tiny schools of minnows. When I squeeze the flashlight, they vanish, as if disturbed by a predator, though they come back more quickly after each scare.

Finally, though, I reach a dead-end. My heart sinking, I shine the light to reveal another ninety-degree bend that goes straight up, too tall for me to follow.

Panicking, I look back the way I came. Right behind me, the pipe that lays along the belly of the shaft splits. One branch climbs up the shaft. The other terminates here in a showerhead like the one I ripped away from the wall of the shaft in my room.

I slowly move the light back and forth, trying to decide what to do. Something glints in the metal to the side of my head. I bring the light closer, but when I recognize it as another one of those vented doors, the same as the painting in my room, I shut it off. There's no telling who might be on the other side.

I bring my ear up to it, holding my breath to hear better. When nobody answers, I push at it gingerly, testing if it's locked. The right edge pops away from the frame an inch. I peek through the crack, but I can't see anything, so I hold my breath again and open it a little more.

Finally, I recognize the room. It's the psychomanteum, where they held the welcoming ritual and spun me on the platform.

I close the door and try to think.

Maybe the best option is just to try the phone now. I'm on the first floor. If I call the police and report Heta's murder, that might be enough commotion for me to escape while the others are being questioned.

I pull out the phone. I have to try three times to unlock it with Heta's thumb, which tells me that my time with this method is limited—her digit is already deforming—but there's still no signal.

OK, new plan. I'll figure out how to remove the security on it and make the call over wi-fi now, before I lose access to the phone completely.

I shove some strips of cloth into the vents in the painting-door so the phone's light won't shine through and back up in the shaft several feet. Then I push the gear icon to display the phone's settings.

A black box appears in the center of the screen, a single word in gray in the middle: *Restricted.*

My stomach drops. I push the icon for *Messages.*

Restricted.

I try every button, every possible combination of swipes and touches. The only things that open are the phone app and the *Wispr* app, though that just brings me to a black screen with two speech bubbles, blue on the left and yellow on the right. There's no text in the bubbles.

"*It must delete them after a certain amount of time passes.*" Hee-Young appears in the shaft in front of me, her eyes glowing in the dark.

Fear trickles down my back. According to the clock on the phone, I've been trying to break into it for five minutes, but there's no way to change the settings and make the call over wi-fi. I'll have to wait until nightfall and either try to sneak out or find somewhere with signal—

I hear something. A soft hiss, like the sibilant warning of a snake. I look over at Hee-Young, but she's just smiling innocently.

I turn my head and listen harder. It sounds like it's coming from the end of the shaft, near the door to the psychomanteum. A moment later, a fan kicks on, and the shaft fills with a strong breeze that smells intense and sweet, like oranges, but with something bitter and chemical underneath. Something . . . botanical.

Fear takes hold of me as I shine the flashlight at the end, and—*yes*—there's a thin cloud of mist dispersing from the showerhead, one that would be blown through the slats in the painting-door . . . if I hadn't stuffed them closed.

Some kind of gas. I hold my breath as long as I can, backing up slowly through the shaft, but I've already breathed in plenty. Before long, the world around me swims, and my body turns heavy.

I lay my head down on my arms, suddenly too exhausted to open my eyes.

"*Don't worry*," Hee-Young whispers in my ear. "*I've got you, sister.*"

SIXTY-EIGHT
Callie

I wake up with the first bell-tone, shivering despite my blanket and sheets. I feel like the woman in Fuseli's painting, *The Nightmare*—the version from 1790, her sleeping body draped so far over the edge of the bed that her hands and hair trail across the floor. As if I've spent an entire night with an incubus crouched on my chest.

Fuseli's demon represented his obsessive anguish after seeing the woman he loved marry another man. I don't know what that means for my demons—for the fact that despite a month of therapy—a month of *improvements*, goddamnit—Lisa has returned to disturb my sleep. Because although the lights are on, and I can see that I'm alone, I still felt her presence in this room. The shuffling steps she took around the exterior, the uneven gait of a monster. The pressure of her hands crawling up and down my mattress, encircling my neck, tugging at my hair.

I told myself I didn't believe it was happening, even as I closed my eyes and pretended to sleep. But why pretend, if you don't already believe? Even after it was over, I couldn't bring myself to stop.

I slide out of bed and kick something small and round, sending it clattering into the side of my armoire. A clay marble, covered in blue paint, its bright shade a beacon in a sea of white.

One of Shepherd's marbles. It wasn't there last night. I would've seen it when I went to bed.

I sink back against the mattress with the gradual fall of a pneumatic tube. First comes the relief—*It wasn't Lisa. Shepherd was in my room last night*—but that's quickly followed by a nauseating swirl of betrayed confusion. What reason did he have for creeping in here like a ghost? For playing with my hair, for—

A flash of realization. I pat my throat, looking for the hard body of the pendant key, but it's missing.

So that's why he came. And though I don't understand why he needed it—did Pepperdine tell him I'm not making enough progress?—it hurts me that he'd steal it like this. He could have just asked.

I turn back onto my side and cover myself with my sheet.

SIXTY-NINE
Callie

The terms of my therapy—and Shep—were clear. No matter what, until Pepperdine says I'm ready to leave my room, I'm to stay in it unless Shep summons me.

But the pendant keeps twisting in my mind, and even though I have no right to feel angry at what Shep did, I do. Maybe it's because I've been trying *so hard*. Every single day is full of exercises, of *working on myself*, and yet he couldn't do me the respectful gesture of just talking to me? Asking me for the pendant, giving me the chance to be a good person and give it up on my own?

Guilt wraps hot talons around my intestines. I don't really have a leg to stand on. What I did to Hee-Young is so much worse.

I need . . . I don't know what I need. I think about it all day, listening to the bells mark time, all the activities I once shared. Lunch. Dinner. I've been marking days on the calendar. I know it's Friday, that the patrons are here.

It's not until shortly before the lights will go out that I finally decide: I need to talk to Shep, and not just about the key. The therapy's working—but it's time for me to start leaving the room.

I crack the door, intent on telling the facilitator to take me to Shep, but there's nobody there.

It makes me a bit nervous, this change. Like that moment before the rain breaks, when the shift in atmospheric pressure makes the hair stand up on the back of your neck. Something is *happening*, now, and I don't know what it is.

I slide out. A moment later, the bell-tone rings, and the lights overhead fade. I almost turn around—but instead, I make my way for the central staircase and climb it, all the way up to Shepherd's room. I hold my breath and knock.

The door opens almost immediately—a vicious swing, so fast and hard that I leap back away from it.

And then I see Shep, really see him for the first time in so long. His eyes are frantic and glassy, his posture ramrod straight. He looks like a man possessed.

"My *wife*," he says, before grabbing me and pulling me close. My heart beats wildly—I don't know what's happening, why he's so energetic and jubilant. Before I have a chance to ask, he grabs my hair in his fist and pulls it, hard, snapping my face up to his. I cry out, but then his mouth is over mine.

My body reacts with confusion, eagerness, fear. He tastes bitter, like tea left to steep. There's something different about him, something dangerous and captivating all at once, and when he drags me in through the doorway, I don't fight it.

Inside, his hands roam over my body, making me moan. "Oh, Shep. What's come over you? Are you on something?"

He doesn't answer. Instead, he throws me over his shoulder and walks straight back toward his bedroom, only this time, I don't have to steal a key to enter. This time, he opens the door for me himself, tosses me onto the bed, and then he's upon me again, feral and starving, his hands bringing pleasure and pain in equal measure.

"Tonight," he growls as he pins me against the mattress, "I will have *everything* that's mine."

We fuck long after the point it hurts, but I don't ask him to stop. It feels like penance, like it is mine to be endured.

And then his hands encircle my neck, squeezing. Stars float in my vision. I panic and try to call out, but I can't force any sound past his grip. I claw desperately at his arms to no effect.

Something dings on the other side of the room, and he releases me at once. I double over, gasping and coughing, rubbing at my bruised neck. Inside of me is shuddering, wailing, but I don't let it out. *He didn't mean it. He's on drugs. He didn't know what he was doing.*

He's already turned away and climbed off the bed to retrieve something off the topmost of his half-hull shelves, an object tucked back against the wall where I couldn't have seen it from the ground. His back is to me, but I catch a glow over his shoulder. His phone, I think.

"Get out," he says gruffly.

My stomach sinks. "What?"

"Get out of my bedroom. Go to your room. Stay there until I call for you."

This—*this* is what breaks me, but his tone brokers no argument. I grab my nightgown and press it to my body before skulking across the floor like a criminal. He watches me as I open the door to the sitting room and step through.

Questions swirl through my mind, making it hard to think. Who was contacting him on the phone in the dead of night? What happened in that bed between us—would he really have killed me, then?

No, no, he didn't mean it. He couldn't have.

When I reach the outer door, I stop and close my eyes. And then I turn back, toward his bedroom, and tiptoe across the floor.

The room is soundproofed, of course. I crack the door and listen to his conversation.

"I'm so glad you're ready to talk," Shepherd says. I hear footsteps, and then a scraping noise—like sharpening a knife on concrete. The same noise I heard the night I came up to spy on him.

"I'm ready." A woman's reply, muffled. It's hard to hear, but—I think I catch an accent, a flipped *r* sound versus one in the throat. *Does he have the phone on speaker?* The scraping noise echoes again.

I wait and count the seconds, trying to figure out who that was. She sounded young—maybe one of the girls? A minute goes by where I hear nothing. He's either taken the phone off speaker or hung up.

And then I hear his footsteps again, and ice water pours down my spine. As quickly as I can, I sneak behind one of his easy chairs and curl up into a ball. When I hear the door opening, I close my eyes and wait for his rage to burst upon me, but he flies across the room and exits without a word.

After the door shuts behind him, I hear an ominous *click.*

I wait as long as I dare before trying the outer door, but I already know he's locked me in.

SEVENTY
Hee-Jin

The touch that wakes me is soft and deliberate, a slow stroke like a wing against my cheek. I open my eyes and see Hee-Young, her finger dragging across my skin as if writing in wet beach sand.

"*Good morning.*" Her wicked grin sends a shiver down my spine. Hallucination or ghost, Hee-Young's becoming a darker thing every time I see her.

I groan softly and try to move my limbs. They feel like lead. Whatever gas Shepherd has been dosing us with—and I don't think it was just one drug—it was likely designed to disperse over an entire room. Instead, I trapped it into the shaft with me, and now, it pushes through my veins like sludge.

I almost ask Hee-Young how late it is before remembering the phone and turning it on. This time, Heta's thumb takes six tries before I manage to roll it on the reader just right. Not a good sign, but I hopefully won't need it much longer.

It's just past one a.m. The timing is perfect.

I crawl along the shaft, push open the door to the psychomanteum, and wait. When I don't hear anything, I slide out and drop to the floor.

A blow cracks into the side of my face, launching me across the room. I crash into one of the benches and collapse in a heap.

A lamp clicks on, casting the psychomanteum in an eerie yellow glow that bounces off the benches, the chain hanging from the ceiling. "You made me wait," says Shepherd, his voice trembling. "I *hate* being made to wait."

In the mirrors all over the room, I see his reflection: Shepherd after Shepherd after Shepherd, all of them rearing back for a kick. I roll out of the way, fast as I can, and scramble painfully to my feet, my injured ankle screaming.

A moment later, he catches me by my hair, lighting my scalp

up with fire. In a single, easy thrust, he pummels me back into the ground before yanking on my hair again, readying himself to repeat the movement.

As my hand drifts toward my sweatpants pocket, he slams me into the ground. Again. Again.

I fish the scalpel out and stab it down into the back of his foot. His scream is deafening, made of all the sound this place has stolen, but he lets go.

My ears ring as I take off—crawling, then running. My ankle is agony, but I don't stop, not with him thudding unevenly after me. "Run all you want," he shouts, his voice booming behind me. "All the windows are sealed, the doors secured—yes, even your little door out of the servant's kitchen! You're going to pay, *Hee-Jin*."

My throat closes up. *He knows my name.*

I burst into the dark lobby, trying to think of a plan. If he's telling the truth, there's no escaping this house. My only choice is to hide and call for help with the phone.

I run for the staircase, but the way down is blocked by an ornate metal door I've never seen before—it looks like it's swung out of a hidden recess in the wall. I pull on it as hard as I can, but it doesn't move.

The only direction left is *up*. I climb the stairs as fast as I can. When I get to the engine room, I slam Ca-lee's pendant against the door.

The lock disengages. As I run through, I glance over my shoulder and spy Shepherd, grinning as he limps his way up the stairs.

SEVENTY-ONE
Callie

At first, I don't know what to do but stand at the door to Shepherd's apartment and try the handle again and again. Good luck I wasn't caught by Shep as he left; bad luck that he's locked me in here. But what will he do when he gets back, after he explicitly told me to go to my room?

My throat throbs. I can still feel his fingers around it, and my breath is coming out in an odd, ragged whistle.

Move, says a voice in my head.

I look down. I'm still naked, still clutching my nightgown. I slip my arms into the sleeves and pull it on.

The marble I found in my room falls out of my pocket and rolls across the floor before coming to a stop. I bend over and grab it, but part of the clay chips away in my hand to reveal something off-white in the marble's center: a small stone like an olive pit.

Cold sinks over my limbs. It looks like bone, but that can't be right.

I turn toward the shelves, looking for something heavy and flat. My gaze settles on the basket that holds the pewter jewelry box—the broken one I told all my secrets to, the box he's been using to stash the bedroom key.

I put the cracked clay marble down on the shelf and carefully hammer the box down once. When I lift it again, an angular white mass floats in the middle of a miniature pile of blue and brown rubble.

A tooth. A front tooth, by the looks of it. Some freak accident, surely. Or maybe it's symbolic, retrieved from a medical supply, a cadaver—it could even be one of Shepherd's teeth, a baby tooth retained by his mother and passed down, only to find a place in his art.

So many good explanations. None of them make it so that I can breathe again.

I need another marble.

My heart thumps as I cross the room. When I close my eyes, there's Shepherd's face again, the fierce yet glazed look in his eyes as my vision started to go dark. My hand shakes as I reach for the knob, but I manage to turn it and let myself into the bedroom.

I avoid looking at the bed. I go straight for the bowl of marbles on the nightstand and pull out another. This one is harder to crack, but I'm less careful, picking up the metal bowl and smashing it down hard.

Inside is another tooth, lighter and pointed at the end. A canine.

Another marble. Another marble. Two more teeth. One is so white it fairly sparkles. The other is darker and yellow-stained, as if by tobacco smoke, and there's a V-shaped chip in the front that—

Oh god. Eliana. How many times did I look at that dead tooth and wish she'd just let me yank it out of her head?

There has to be an explanation for this. Whatever Shepherd is, he's not a murderer. He's *not* a murderer.

I sweep everything into my pocket, trying not to flinch as the mess rattles together. I replace the bowl.

SEVENTY-TWO
Hee-Jin

As I bolt through the engine room, looking for a place to hide, there are a thousand things I should be thinking about. Things that, if I'm lucky, could keep me alive.

But all I can think about is my mother, how reluctant she was to tell us about the past. The only way to get it out of her was to ply her with soju until her defenses were down. Then, if we were lucky, we could ask her a single question.

We planned these questions in advance. They had to be phrased perfectly, so as not to cause offense or let on that our inquiries were anything but the idlest of curiosities. It was as if the idea that Hee-Young and I might want to know something about where we came from was indicative of weakness, offensive and not to be tolerated.

When you were a kid, did you have a stove like this one?

What was your favorite treat at lunar new year?

Did your father smoke?

We usually failed in our attempts to get information. When we didn't, she'd give us a partial answer, some flippant comment that hinted at the trauma underneath. Those nights, we'd lie awake on the floor on our thin yo mattresses and wonder at the woman sleeping beside us, how it was possible a person survived that much pain and didn't become a monster.

When I give up on everything else and climb the stairs to the Aviary, the rapid flutter of Hee-Young's imaginary steps behind me, that's what I'm thinking about: how monsters are made. If they ever can be unmade.

I run around the spiral of the Aviary, straight for the center, smashing into poles and props, tripping on chains. I don't have a plan, just the realization that if Shepherd's smart, he'll have to slow down. I could be hiding behind any chair or shelf or upturned swing, my little scalpel at the ready. I'm hoping the extra time the distance buys me will be enough to call for help on the phone. The fact that I stabbed him in the foot, and he kept going, tells me everything I need to know.

He intends to kill me.

When I make it to the center, I hide behind the piano and pull out the phone while listening for Shepherd's approach. But Heta's finger's not in my pocket. I must've dropped it somewhere, must've—

In the glow of the lock screen, the gray words asking for a PIN code or a fingerprint are under another message, one I don't remember: *All calls blocked.*

But that doesn't make sense. I would've seen this message before—in my room, in the shaft. There's no reason for this sudden change.

My blood goes cold as Hee-Young chuckles in my ear.

It's not possible, is it? You can hallucinate *adding* something to your vision—but can your brain also just take something away?

"*Hee-Jin,*" Hee-Young whispers urgently. I have to press my lips together to stop myself from replying to this girl that doesn't exist, from betraying my position to the real threat. "*The table is hot.*"

A moment later, something loops around my throat and lifts, cutting off my windpipe. I stab behind me with the scalpel and hit open air, and then something smashes into my side. My world lights up with pain as the scalpel rattles to the ground.

Shepherd's wrapped a chain around my neck. I hear the cartilage pop, but already, the edges of my vision are going dark.

Too quickly for his liking, perhaps, because he loosens it the tiniest bit, just enough for my feet to touch down, for me to get the shallowest gulp of air. In front of me, I see Hee-Young, pivoting around one of the acrylic poles. She dances while humming to herself. I can't make out the tune.

"I would've given you everything," he says. His voice is soft, his fury controlled. "Your mother was a bitch, but I was ready to forgive you both. After all, you were just toddlers. You wouldn't remember anything. Do you have *any* idea how many strings I had to pull to expedite the DNA testing and prove paternity? How *lucky* you are that I was willing to shoulder this kind of obligation? I made Hee-Young a *citizen.*"

My brain is shorting out. I'm too afraid, too entrenched in the darkness dancing around the corners of my vision to understand most of his words. My heartbeat thumps like a giant ritual drum, fast and angry, as if calling down the goddesses.

"I was going to make her the centerpiece of my collection, do you understand that? But she *betrayed* me. She decided to work with *Garin*. She was collecting little bits of evidence—as if anything she could ever do could hurt someone like me. And even then, I was *kind*. I let her go, let her fly back home so that she could feel how excruciating the withdrawal from the *e-licks-sir* is. I followed her there, all the way to your doorstep, waiting for her to break, but she never did.

"But then there *you* were, you greedy little bird. A second chance, I thought. I chartered a private flight back and set everything up—do you understand how expensive that is? The connections I had to pull on? The *investment* I made in you? I could've just taken you, you know. But I wanted you to come to me of your own accord. I thought, then, you could become my greatest work—but I should've realized that there's just too much of *me* in *you*."

And then he yanks the chain again, and this time, my feet leave the ground.

SEVENTY-THREE
Callie

Panic sets in. No matter how crazy I am, no matter how many times I check my pocket, expecting its contents to change, I keep finding Eliana's little dead tooth. I keep seeing Shep in the hours before, his voracious sexual appetite. I keep pressing my fingers into the bites that cover my shoulders and trying to reconcile that with the man I've always known, and none of it adds up.

I pour all the marbles on the floor and smash them to pieces. At least forty teeth, all different sizes and shades. I fall to my knees.

"*Over here, Mama.*"

Another chill goes down my spine. Lisa's voice—the way it was before she died, when she was only two, just learning to speak. When I turn, I see her—not as she was in my hallucinations, not a seven-year-old with long wheat hair, but instead a toddler with a set of high pigtails. She's standing in the back of the room, by the odd crack I found in the plaster the day I snuck in.

I have to clear my throat to speak to her. "I need a key," I say, shaking my head.

"*No, Mama. Not for this door. Not for any door in this house.*"

I have just a moment to register the change in her voice, the sophistication of her vocabulary and the sudden crispness of her pronunciation—but then there's a brief click, and a large panel pops open an inch, its hinges no longer quite so invisible. My stomach goes cold, but I hurry to the crack, lever my fingers underneath, and pull. It groans as it opens, a scraping like a knife on concrete, revealing a room my mind struggles to assemble together: a wall of gray-green monitors. A bay of plants under a light table. Shelves full of pills and little bottles and books. In the far-right corner is a flat table, the kind medical examiners use. A dead body lies stretched out on its surface—*Garin*, I realize, my hand flying to cover my mouth—

And squatting next to it is a woman, her face turned away, her arms shackled to the side, but I've seen her from behind enough times to identify her. "Ksenia?"

When she turns toward me, I have to take a step back, repulsed. Half of the skin on her face is covered in dark, porcupine-like quills in a shape that reminds me of the phantom of the opera's mask, and her eyes look so swollen, I can imagine them popping out of their sockets.

She spits at me—or tries to. The reason for her failure becomes evident when she speaks, the hard corners of her words all filed off by the destruction of her anatomy; half her teeth are missing. "I know you're working for him—or with him. Or maybe he works for you, you crazy bitch."

There are angry red marks like fingerprints around her neck. Spatters of what looks like blood weaving across the floor. I have to ask the question, even if I know the answer, because some part of me won't believe it until I hear it. "Ksenia . . . what happened? Who did this to you?"

She squints as if I've just made her an offer she's considering. "Do you really not know? Listen—there's a key. On the table, over there." She reaches her arms out, the movement stopped short by the shackles. Her pink polish has mostly peeled off, revealing nails that have turned uneven shades of dark brown, the color and glistening texture like the carapace of a cockroach.

I look at the table she's indicated. Garin's slashed-open body lies in the middle like a centerpiece. The rest of the table's surface is covered in stains ranging from red-orange to rust-brown to black, save some that are a milky white, like the sap of a rubber tree. Across one corner is a grisly assortment of dental tools and blades. And burrowed in the center, like a gum wrapper in a nest, is a key.

I bring it to Ksenia. Some part of me is aware that I should be screaming; that I am, in fact, having a mental breakdown. She holds out her hands and I unlock the cuffs. As soon as she's free, she backs up several paces.

"Ksenia. What happened to . . .?" I glance at the body on the table.

"Shepherd caught us. Alone in the garden—we'd been meeting

since Hee-Young disappeared. We were trying to figure out what happened to the other one, the first Hee-Young. We knew it was dangerous, but—" She stops and turns her head to the side, spits out a tooth. "Ever since the night that Shepherd attacked him—"

"Since what?"

"When Garin figured out Hee-Young wasn't Hee-Young. The night she was wearing that ridiculous wooden mask at dinner?"

I blink. It must've been before I ran into Garin at the door, when he was storming out.

"He went up to Shepherd's room to ask what the point of this was—why have someone pretend to be Hee-Young, when they both knew Shepherd had done something to Hee-Young in the first place? And Shepherd hit him in the back of the head when he wasn't looking, stunned him just long enough to give him some kind of drug. And then Garin woke up in his own bed two days later, with no memory of what had happened in the meantime."

My skin crawls. How many nights have I laid awake, trying to piece together all the time I've lost? Is it possible that *Shepherd* had been drugging me all this time?

"Do you remember Priyanka? Garin was determined to figure out what happened to her. And that meant he needed to know what happened to Hee-Young. The first, real Hee-Young. But then Shepherd caught us in the garden, and he had his *facilitators*—" she spits the word like a slur—"drag us both into Shepherd's terrible playroom. He stabbed Garin—I was so sure he was going to die. But then Garin managed to escape by bribing one of the facilitators." She indicates the bay of monitors with her chin. "I watched it. He ran into Hee-Young out there, and then the facilitators took them both down. They brought him back here, and . . ." She looks away. "Shepherd wanted to know where the new Hee-Young disappeared to."

"Oh," I said, clearing my throat. "I locked her in her room, but that was over a month ago, and he knows—"

She actually laughs, then, displaying the gaps in her teeth, a dark and light alternating pattern like piano keys. "I mean today, Callie. Or yesterday, maybe." Her expression gets hard again. "He gave me injection after injection, asking where Hee-Young was, and I didn't know, I didn't know."

Her face hardens. "Until I suddenly did. And I called him on that little phone he'd left, the one that could dial only him, and told myself it was worth it, saving myself."

I don't know what she means by injections, but her agony is written all over her body. I imagine him choking her, poking the spines into her flesh, tearing her teeth out, the roots inside snapping like ginger as he pried them free from her mouth. "Where is he?"

She moves as if to glance up at the bay of monitors, but her eyes stop short. "I don't know. I don't want to know. But the girls are all locked in their rooms right now. There's a mouse and keyboard, over there." She turns back toward me, regarding me fully with her swollen eyes, and I hold my breath when I realize there's a glint to them—orange, or maybe amber. "You need to leave before he comes back, or he'll kill you, too."

And then she's gliding out of the room. She disappears, leaving me wondering if she was even here at all.

After a few moments, I go over to the monitors and find the mouse she mentioned. I jiggle it and am rewarded with a cursor moving across the bottom-right screen. Unlike the others, it doesn't show a view of the house, but instead a gray display with pairs of rectangular buttons, digital switches arranged in columns under titled black headers: *Dispersal. Locks. Network.*

I mouse over to the buttons under *Locks.* The pairs of buttons in this column all read *Engaged* on the left and *Disengaged* on the right. *Engaged* is selected on all of them.

I click the mouse rapidly, unlocking everything that isn't a patron's room, including the front gate and the side door, as well as one labeled *Lower stairs.* A moment later, there's activity on the monitors—Sarah. She creeps out of her room, and then, after a moment, she goes back for Sumi. They run, disappearing from the cameras, but there's no sign of Hee-Young, or whatever her name might be.

I know I should leave now—but instead, I trail through this room, picking up bottles from the shelf and examining the labels, some machine-printed, others hand-written: *scopolamine, flunitrazepam, ketamine, Xyrem.* I pull the books off the shelf as if trying to divine their meaning: mechanical and service manuals for something called an *HVAC diffuser*, anatomy and botany texts, pharmaceutical guides.

On one of the shelves, I find a wooden box with golden curlicues on the side. It's full of passports, their covers all different colors: olive green, sienna brown, government blue. I grab one at random and open it, expecting Shepherd's face, but a girl I don't recognize stares back. I open another, and another, and another. The third girl isn't a stranger. Instead, she's one of the very first artists that had a residency here.

Horror twists in my guts as I swallow and pull the last two passports out of the box. The first is Eliana's.

I recognize the second from the bright protective cover alone. Hee-Young's. My lip quivers at the sight of her photo—the closeness we shared, and then the betrayal. But when I glance down at the rest of the information, a memory crashes through my mind, the day Shep and I signed our marriage certificate.

Alex Pastukhov? I thought your name was Shepherd.

It's a nickname, Calleigh. That's what Pastukhov means. Pastoral. Shepherd.

And there it is, in the blank under father's name: *Alex Pastukhov.*

I stumble back from the shelves, brace myself against a wall. It doesn't seem possible—Shep was Hee-Young's father? Was he truly sleeping with her, then? Or did he just admit to sleeping with the girls to keep his real secret from me?

My head is spinning. I shove the passports back in the box and throw them on the shelf, but a movement catches the corner of my eye. A white figure, floating forward across one of the green monitor screens. Its gait is awkward—dragging a leg behind, as if injured.

I hold my breath and move closer. The display is some kind of night vision. Flashes of white appear in the figure's open mouth as they turn their head from side to side, searching, their eyes glowing, and I get a sudden glimpse of their face.

It's Shepherd. And from the looks of the objects around him, he's in the Aviary.

I watch as he pounces, grabbing a large, squirming mass from behind the piano. And then he lifts it up, and only too late do I realize: it's one of the girls.

I turn away, bracing myself to run—even though I know I likely won't make it to them in time—but when I turn to the door, Lisa is standing in the doorway. "Honey, you have to move." I should feel crazy talking to her, especially when someone's life might depend on it—but I don't.

"*How did you get in here, Mama? Remember? No key?*"

I shake my head. "You opened the door," I say, but as soon as the words are out of my mouth, I know it's a lie. She didn't, because she can't. Because she died years ago. Because even her ghost wouldn't look like this—she looks like a child, not a toddler or a baby, but a seven-year-old *child*. "I don't understand." My voice is gruff, choked with emotion, though I can't feel anything; it's like the numbness in my chest has spread through my whole body—

And suddenly, I know. What the numbness is, how I opened the locked door, why the walls and ceiling on the first floor respond to me in such a fantastical way, a sophisticated way no motor could explain. It was never just the proximity key. It was *me*.

I reach my hand to my chest and press hard. My fingertips feel the skin giving under them, and still I press and press, until there's a sudden flare of pain as my fingers punch through, as easily as pushing into a rotten peach—and that's exactly what it feels like to my fingers, a rotten peach chilled by a refrigerator, as if my organs and breastbone and my pectoral muscles have all been forgotten so long they're disintegrating into mush—

And then my hand closes around something hard with sharp edges. I pull it out with a sucking pop to reveal a little glass anatomical model of a heart, cracked and terribly mended with a milky-white glue, now glittering in the green glow of the monitors. The missing topper from the jewelry box, the little bulb I blew, all those years ago.

I try to understand what this means. What Shepherd did to me—what he did to this *house*. But then I realize it doesn't matter, because I can *feel* the house, its connection to me. Can feel the way each girder and beam, each column, post, and stud, runs through the walls and floor, and like roads converging on a city port, they all run back to me.

What had Shep said? That he made this house in my image. That it was my art. That this place didn't work without me.

I search through the threads by feel, pulling on each one to figure out where it goes. And then I find the thread for the Aviary, and I give it a hard pull. A rumble starts above me, and I know the glass heart is rotating up onto its side. Another pull, and it's spinning, but I don't stop. I let the cylinder accelerate, more and more, and the rumble grows into a roar.

Almost there, I think, and I glance over to Lisa. She watches me, her face perfectly still, as if she knows what is about to happen and is only waiting for it. "I'm sorry, baby," I say, and then I crush the little glass heart in my hand. Over the groans of metal and the whines of the engine, three horrendous booms echo above me, as if a massive hammer is being flung against the machinery—but still, the cylinder spins faster. Two more huge booms echo.

There's the shriek of breaking glass and tearing metal—and I've heard this sound before, it's the same sound as when you've been drugged at a party and ram your car into a tree, only wrought earth-shatteringly large—

And suddenly everything is silent.

SEVENTY-FOUR

Hee-Jin

The Aviary springs to life around us. Shepherd's hold on the chain around my neck slips, and I fall sideways and slam into the rapidly tilting floor. Chains rattle as the Aviary's interior contents all drop to hang down, competing with the rumble and rattle of the engine. A moment later, the walls become transparent and the music and the lights turn on, casting a fun-house glow.

Shepherd rallies first, grabbing my injured ankle with his hand and dragging me toward him. I kick with my other foot as hard as I can, but we're both sliding down, the room rotating even as it tilts, and I don't land more than a glancing blow. I grab onto a pole and pull hard to keep from falling farther, but the room is spinning faster, the engine making an unholy, deep whine that sounds for all the world like screaming.

He pulls me toward him, hard, and I can't maintain my grip. I fly down past him before catching another pole. My leg is free, but the spinning is accelerating. For the first time, I feel the forces of its revolution pulling at me, trying to rip me away from my handhold. Something is happening, something terrible.

A burst of woman's laughter behind me drowns out the music, and out of the corner of my eye, I see Shepherd's head turn, as if tracking the sound.

Something white bangs down in front of me—the kitchen chair. I reach out for it and curl my arm in one of its chains, but Shepherd hasn't given up on me. He inches toward me, hand over hand, all the muscles of his body straining as he progresses. The skin on his face pulls back as the wheel spins ever faster, as if he was a dog sticking his head out of a car window.

And then, suddenly, the wheel stops, flinging us both sideways. I smash my face into the chair in an explosion of pain. Alternating waves of stars and darkness dance across my vision like an aurora, and I can barely make out the image of him jumping for me, his arms reaching out.

And then, a woman's form in a series of blurs: black hair, a face covered in spines. *Hee-Young*, I think, squinting desperately to see around the blood pooling in my eye. Her body is cloaked in something that shimmers metallic in the light—*the beetle dress? Or the aura of a ghost?*—and she leaps for him and wraps his neck with a length of the chain. Her fist beats against his chest with the fury only a ghost can know—*three knocks, two knocks*—

And then the world behind us echoes with a terrible, booming crack. I feel it deep inside of me, and I know it's the onggi pot, that never again will I be able to store my emotions in my mother's final gift.

The room fills with the scream of metal shearing apart. Around us, the glass heart suddenly descends.

We smash into the top of the house. The roof gives immediately as thousands of pounds of glass and metal slam down to overwhelm the beams, the supports. The house collapses like a bad cake, third floor into second into first, and the air around us fills with a terrible cloud of black dust.

I land on my back. One of my eyes is completely useless. When I close it, the forms I see out of the other are blurry, marred with dark spots and what looks like blood. I can barely make out the shape dangling three feet above me: Shepherd's legs, the rest of his body swinging from the chain. I can't tell what he's snagged on, but I know from the angle of his neck that he's dead.

And though I am sitting on top of a giant pile of broken glass and rubble, covered in cuts that bleed from a thousand places, I am somehow alive.

But then I look down and find what I somehow could not feel: my left arm is crushed under a giant piece of glass. Blood blooms around me in a massive pool, though it's what's floating on top that scares me most: a thin layer of white milky fluid. Somehow, I know it came from inside of me.

My heartbeats grow shallower, faster. I look around this terrible place, the last place I will ever see—and there, glowing in a dirty white sweatsuit and climbing across the rubble with the grace of a spider, is Ksenia, a backpack slung across one of her shoulders. I laugh when I realize her face is covered in spines.

When she reaches me, she pulls a shirt out of her bag. "Hang on. I'm going to get this off you, but first—" She tears into it, ripping at it with her hands and teeth, and as it cleaves, I imagine I catch a glimpse of the logo, a small sandwich cut in half.

She ties it around my arm, using a stick to wind it tighter. It hurts, but as if from far away.

It's hard to make words. "It was you. You fought Shepherd. You could've run." And even as I say it, I'm not sure. It *was* her, but it was Hee-Young, too, and I don't know what that means.

"But I didn't leave. That's what counts." She says it tentatively, as if she's not sure she believes it, as if she's trying it out. I remember what she said before: *Love is what you sacrifice for another.* "Now, come on. The police will be here soon." And then she grabs my remaining hand and pulls. It takes all of our strength to force my arm out from under the glass, but finally, I'm free.

With her help, I manage to stand, and we slowly begin the work of descending. "Where will we go?"

"Anywhere that's not here."

SEVENTY-FIVE
Callie

A single breath of being crushed under that gigantic beam, and the life that was once mine is snuffed out like a birthday candle.

That's what I think about, in those final moments. Candles. Lisa's second birthday. Shep had already given her a huge, tacky party, though not one he decided to grace with his presence—

(No, Mama, don't think about him. That's not what this time is for.)

I made her a cupcake. Nothing special, no ingredients with French names. Just sugar and butter and a little bit of vanilla. Shelf-stable buttercream icing out of a plastic jar. It was pink, so it must've been strawberry. I put two little candles on it, one pink, and one green, and then I lit it with an old Bic lighter and we blew it out.

One day, if you remembered it, I was going to tell you about *my* cupcake. The way my mama did that for me, when I was three or four, and how it was one of the only things I carried with me. How I wanted to give it to you. The way you looked when your cheeks grew big and you tried to *puff, puff, puff* it out. The way you giggled delightedly when I dabbed some of that pink frosting on the tip of your nose.

I'm sorry, Lisa, that I was too afraid and hurt to look at you, at your death. If I'd been stronger, if I'd had the courage to stay here, in this world, in this pain, and not retreat into a fairytale where you still lived, I would've seen all the pieces and realized they didn't fit. I would've gone to the police and demanded access to your body, would've had an autopsy and toxicology and the whole nine yards done and discovered the drugs in your system, the bruises hidden in places hard to find. It would've been too late to see the damage he'd done to your mind, but I'm your mother. I like to believe I would've known, that I would've figured out those half-remembered snatches of me being carried were not of my rescue.

He put your body in the car, and me with it, drugged to let me believe I'd killed you.

(Mama, I told you. It's not time for that now.)

A soft warmth, like the kind left in a teacup. Then, what is it time for?

(It's time to go.)

Yes it is, baby. Yes it is.

SEVENTY-SIX

Hee-Jin

As it turns out, Ksenia is an excellent escape partner. For example, although the house itself has collapsed, she knows the location of the garage, hidden behind a copse of trees, where all the patrons' cars are stored. "It's usually guarded, but I'm thinking the facilitators are all either busy or dead." She extracts a chunky rental car key from her pocket. "It's Garin's," she says, her voice grim.

She can also drive, as it turns out—maybe not perfectly, judging by the jerky stop-and-go of the car as we proceed down the hill, but I have no complaints. And given the fact that the vision in my remaining eye is getting worse by the second, it's not like I have another choice.

For a while, it's quiet in the car. There are some thin lights, the barest gleam of the trains that peels back the gloom, but she hasn't turned on the main headlights, and with my eye, it feels like the night could swallow us at any moment. Worse, I've started to feel fainter and fainter, as if the entire world is calling me from far, far away.

"Where . . . are we going?" I finally manage to stutter.

"I don't know. I grabbed what I could and ran. God, it's all gone to *shit*—" I hear her bang her hands against the steering wheel and take a deep breath. "But as my grandmother always says, nothing matters but *surviving*. Hey, keep your arm *up*." She hits the gas then, making the car jump, but she still doesn't turn on the lights.

I suddenly don't care if we crash. Still, I comply, raising the arm with the tourniquet higher. For some reason, it hurts less than it should. "You saved me."

A pause. Insects buzz in the empty space—or maybe that noise is just in my head. "I meant what I said before. Women like us, who have gone what we've gone through—we're not capable of loving anyone. Not really. But in the end, I decided I couldn't just abandon you."

I nod, because I understand. My mother loved me as much as she could, and that was a love that scarred even as it healed, that burned you whenever it bled.

My vision in my remaining eye is now so bad, I sense, rather than *see*, her turn toward me, then back to the road. "Why was he so interested in you, Hee-Young—"

"Hee-Jin," I say, and it feels like a sudden downpouring of rain to once again be myself. I collapse forward and start to cry.

"Arm *up*!" she barks. "We need to get you to a hospital. Fuck," she says again, and then she pulls onto a side road. "So, you didn't answer me. Why was Shepherd so interested in you?"

Maybe it's because of the dark that I suddenly feel ready to share my secrets, but I tell Ksenia about my mother, that Hee-Young was my sister, about using her passport to come here. About the things Shepherd said when he wrapped the chain around my neck.

And then it's her turn. She flicks the headlights on. "Your sister, Hee-Young—she was working with Garin."

"To take over."

"I don't think so. Shepherd and Garin used to be friends—went to the same high school, stayed in touch throughout. Garin was like all the rest of them, at first. Just a normal patron. But then, he fell in love with this girl, Priyanka. She never told us where she was from, but I think it was somewhere in Southeast Asia."

I hear her roll down the window, spit, and roll it back up. "Anyways—one day, Priyanka was dead. Shepherd said she committed suicide, but Garin never believed it. And sometime afterwards, Shepherd assigned him Hee-Young—I don't know the details of their arrangement, exactly, but I think she was helping Garin. Finding him some clues or something. But then Shepherd must've found out, because she suddenly left—and you're the one that told me how that turned out." A pause. "She thought she was being poisoned, you know. *Tha-lee-yum*. She was eating paint, blue paint, because she thought it would protect her—but it didn't."

I press my lips together, thinking of Hee-Young, the midnight indigo inside of her mouth. Even here, in the gisaeng house, she'd been brave. "Why not . . . just kill Garin?"

"I don't know. I think Shepherd thought he was untouchable. He *was* for a long time. So many famous and rich patrons—I think any of them would've killed someone to hang on to their lifestyle. And I think, too, that he liked control. He liked playing with people, liked making them doubt their realities."

I shiver. "And you were working with him, too? Garin?"

"Not until after you disappeared. They said you were sick, but I realized—we were dropping like flies. And then he came to me after one of the patron dinners and made me an offer—if I helped him get some evidence against Shepherd, something that would give him the proof he needed to shut this place down for good, he'd take me away from here." She shakes her head, bangs the steering wheel again. "That was stupid. I got greedy—but of course, Shepherd was always watching." I sense her move again, glancing back at me, I think.

"What kind of evidence?"

"Sorry?"

"What kind . . . did Hee-Young find?"

Ksenia shrugs. "I don't know. I think Garin said something about keeping a log, and something about hair. I don't know more than that."

I hear a rustle behind us. My already fast heartbeat speeds up as I turn—but it's Hee-Young sitting there, and despite the injury to my eyes, I can see her perfectly clearly. She points a finger at me, the clear plastic ring somehow glinting in the low light, making the black, copper, and gold filaments dance inside. Filaments the shades of human hair, like the bag I found in her workshop.

"I think . . . I know," I say, but I don't elaborate. Instead, I reach down with my good hand toward where she's pointing—my pocket. Inside, I feel a folded wad of paper. I pull it out. I have to hold it directly in front of my eye, and still, the blurry characters swim, but I recognize the odd note I found inside of her passport an eternity ago, the combinations of dates and random Hangeul letters.

"So, you were his daughter," Ksenia says, oblivious to Hee-Young's presence in the back of the car. "It explains why your English comprehension is so good: when babies are exposed to a language, it's much easier to learn later in life. Did you . . . did you live with him then? In Korea?"

"China," I say, but the world around me is going dark.

I fall asleep at some point. I wake up in front of a hospital. I don't want to go in, not when it's where all the bright lights and questions are—and when the men and women in white jackets come, even though I know they're not facilitators, I scream until one of them finally puts me under.

For once, there are no dreams, nothing but drifting along in the dark.

When I wake up, I'm blind. I can tell that I'm in a bed, that there's a bandage wrapped around my eyes. I shift and discover a body next to me—though it's not Hee-Young, this time.

"You're awake," Ksenia says softly. "I told them we were in a car accident."

"There's something wrong with my arm," I say, and then I remember the huge chunk of sculpted glass. But when I reach down to assess the damage, everything after my elbow is empty air.

"I'm sorry," she says. "They had to take it off. Something about the way it got crushed—they said the tourniquet made it worse, made more tissue die, but it also . . . it probably saved your life. You had torn blood vessels, and the increased pressure . . ." I hear her shift—shrugging, maybe.

I grope around the mattress until I find her, and then I hold her close. She smells wonderful, like a cold wind. "When can we leave?"

She stiffens under my fingers. At first, I think it means that we will *never* leave this place. That we're locked in here the way I was locked in my room—and some part of me thinks I'm in that room still, that I'll always be in that room.

But then I realize the more likely conclusion—that she isn't planning to leave with me. "You're going. Now."

And even though we're no longer in the soundproofed bedrooms, I hear her swallow. "I'm not injured like you—a broken finger, broken ribs, maybe a broken nose. Guess I'm not quite the beauty I was. *Petite Sea House.* I knew it was cruel. I thought, maybe, it was a joke about drowning. But it means *bird* in Russian. I should've known." She chuckles darkly, but it feels like there's honest mirth in it. "Hee-Young, *nu*, Hee-*Jin*—I can't stay here. The only thing wrong with me, now, is the *changes*."

It takes me a moment to understand. "You mean . . . the needles," I say, because I don't know the word for spines.

"Yes," she says. "The pinfeathers. The nails. The skin. The eyes—I think we can see *ul-tra-vai-let*, did you know that? I don't—I don't know if it can be reversed. I *think* . . ." Her shiver shakes the bed. "I can feel it in me, now. I think it's like a drug, a disease. I can't be here when the need hits me."

I don't fully understand the meaning of her words—but I don't need to. From her tone, I know she's leaving me here, alone and blind, and that nothing I can do can change her mind. I look for my onggi pot, ready to put this feeling in there, the same I've done with all the others, but there's no protection left inside of me.

"I slipped your passport and some money underneath your bed. There's some clothes, too—I found something, while we were leaving. Cleaned it up nice for you."

"Stay," I say, and I hate myself for it.

She is silent for a long moment, and then I feel the bed shift as she stands. "When you leave the hospital, there's a bus station across the street. A bus comes every fifteen minutes or so. Ride it until you get to a big station at the end, and then transfer to bus 265. It will take you out of the city, to a little place called *Pa-een Town-ship*. I'll wait for you there as long as I can."

And then she's gone.

SEVENTY-SEVEN
Hee-Jin

It takes three days for the withdrawal to begin, a soft and tender ache that grows more ferocious, until it shakes me with piercing fangs. There is no escaping from it, not even in sleep—because there *is* no sleep for me once it starts. It's as if a wick has been threaded through every part of me, like my muscles and skin and bones are *drip, drip, dripping* to the ground as its flame works its way down. Every nerve in my body screams to go back to that place, to its too-quiet rooms and milky-white fluid, and for the first time, I understand how strong my sister was—for she was much more transformed than I, and yet she didn't return to Shepherd and the relief he could provide, not even when her body fell apart, as if her previous experiences with addiction and withdrawal had fortified her against this hell.

After five days—or maybe seven—they let me take the bandages off my eyes. Not permanently, but just to try. They warn me against looking in the mirror, but I do it anyway, and the creature that stares back at me would haunt my nightmares if I could sleep. My bulging eyes are covered in crimson spots from broken vessels, and a strange callus stretches over my lips, spreading onto my cheeks and chin. The spines cover every inch of my face now, furring down my neck, across my abdomen, but instead of a shiny black, they look dull and gray.

I grab one on my chin and rip it out. The pain is earth-shaking; the spurt of blood is immediate. But when I crush it in my hand, pulverizing the casing into dust and revealing the feather tightly wrapped inside, I feel something other than agony for the first time since Ksenia left.

One by one, I pull them out. And when I finish, the need is still there, burning through me—but still, I close my eyes and stumble into something approaching sleep.

SEVENTY-EIGHT
Hee-Jin

Just as I once marked time with the progress of my bruises, the changes of my body become the clock. The bandages are removed from my eyes, and my vision starts to clear. The drains are pulled from my wounds, and the stump of my missing arm stops weeping as the skin fully shuts. I hear a nurse mention that I will be *dis-charj* soon, and I know that is my cue to leave.

I pull the small bundle out from under my mattress: money, my passport, a white sweatsuit, and the beetle dress, which Ksenia must have found for me in the rubble.

I decide to put the dress on. The zipper is hard to manage with one hand, but I get it eventually. I put the sweat-suit jacket on over that—it's ripped and stained, but the sleeve helps obscure my arm.

I slide out into the hallway, but there's nobody there. As far as I can tell, I'm not under arrest—which means those fliers Shepherd showed me were probably fakes. My luck holds all the way to the stairwell, and despite my worst fears, no alarms go off as I push through the door and wind down to the main floor.

I walk across the street. It's busy here, an actual city, with cars and lights. The kind of place that feels familiar, the kind of place where I might be able to blend into the background, although I think I'll get as far away from here as I can.

I wait, my breath held, for the bus. I transfer at the big station, ride the number 265 to the end.

When I arrive, she's waiting there for me, as if she knew I'd come.

EPILOGUE

Two women get off a plane. Maybe it's in Amsterdam, or Bolivia, or China. It doesn't matter. These details are interchangeable. The less you know, the better—at least, that's how they feel about it. And locations and identities are lies anyways: all they have to do is extract two of the passports from the box one of them found as they were crawling out of the rubble, and they will be someone else.

Not every passport is a safe one, of course. Less of them all the time. One by one, the teeth in the house have been identified, and news has traveled to this country or that, and a *girl missing* becomes *missing, presumed deceased.* Some are matched with hair samples extracted from a resin ring that was discovered in a subway station, of all places—behind a healthcare booth, after an anonymous letter to the Korean police. In the same envelope was a crumpled piece of paper and a note detailing that the enclosed Sino-Korean numbers were dates, the letters stand-ins for initials of powerful men and women who had visited the now-infamous sex-slavery house in Pennsylvania to avail themselves of its services.

As with most other crimes, the media has already started trying out narratives. Actors come out of the woodwork to paint Shepherd alone as the villain: convenient, as he is dead. A fairytale emerges, one in which Calleigh is both victim and savior—though this story of course has its many detractors, especially once the secret stash of photos is discovered in Shepherd's *kill room*, including a six-year-old photo of a man who'd died in an unsolved hit and run. Many are quick to link the suspicious circumstances to the equally suspicious death of Pastukhov's daughter, Lisa, who supposedly mistook pills for candy and passed away in her sleep—though there are also rumors that she died in a car crash, or that she was poisoned by her father. And they're happy to finger Calleigh—emotional, drunk Calleigh—though they can't seem to agree on a reason. Some are sure that she's evil; others claim she's being maligned, the same as always happens when a woman strays too close to a powerful man.

But the two women don't care. They get on planes with names that are not theirs to have, and they know that. They are only borrowing, just for now. Just until they figure out where they're going.

It's hard, because they don't trust each other, not completely, and not through any fault of their own. It's said that being close to a monster changes something deep inside of you, turns parts of you into the darkness you fear—but the women know better.

The truth is that monsters are just seemingly average people with a bit of privilege and power, that they will engage in depravities without a second thought. That at any step, any of the workers or patrons that came to that house could've spoken out against what was happening—and none did. Every single one delighted in the benefits they received and turned the other way.

And that's what the women earn, in exchange for all their pain. The truth, and maybe each other. It'll never be worth what they lost. It'll never hold back the nightmares—but there's nobody else they *can* trust. And they have places to go, and recovered money to spend—and more importantly, lives to live, and someone to hold at night, like a single candle against the dark.

Acknowledgments

I gave up the first several times I tried to write these acknowledgements. Five years had passed since this novel's initial drafts, and my world had changed so much.

Thank you to my family, and especially Justin, whose dedication to my writing inspires my own.

Thank you to my lovely agent, Amy Bishop-Wycisk. To my wonderful team at Severn House for giving this book a perfect home—and especially my editor, Rachel Slatter, for her patience, enthusiasm, and keen eye.

Thank you to Steve Westenra for your excellent editorial insights, to Dr. Eliot Mason for your knowledge of all things monstrous, and to Linda for our writing dates. This book would also not exist without the written works of the scholar Maria Tatar, the book *The Devil in the White City,* and the TV show *90 Day Fiancé*; do with that information what you will.

Finally, thank you to S.E. Fleenor (and the rest of the Cunt Club), who carried my love for this book when I couldn't.